聽外電新聞，貼近真實口語英文，
唯有真正外國人會說、會用的英語，才能聽出英文即戰力，
牛刀小試╳ 背景提示╳ 單字補給 ╳ 精準翻譯
簡單四步驟，英文聽力，聽這本絕對就夠了！

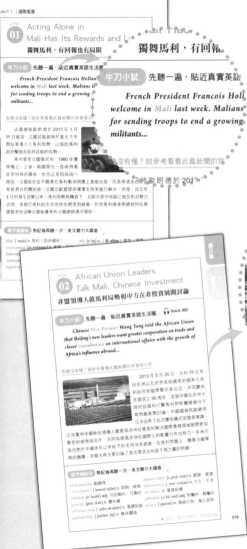

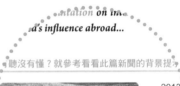

How to use 使用說明

Step.1

先聽一遍「牛刀小試」

全書共 9 大分類主題、95 篇出自
美國之聲的真實新聞英語，讓你
靠新聞英語走出世界，將聽力潛
力徹底開發，進化成為聽力即戰
力！

Step.2

再來看看「背景提示」

本書除了提供新聞英文文章作為
練習，更貼心撰寫新聞事件背後
相關小故事，啟發你對新聞事件
的好奇心，一聽再聽欲罷不能！

Step.3 接著學點「單字補給」

忙碌的你要在有限時間內學到有用的單字,就從新聞英語開始下手!每天都在說在用的單字,本書皆貼心補充,讓你邊聽邊學馬上會!

單字補給站 熟記後再聽一次,英文聽力大躍進

Mali [`malɪ] n. 馬利(西非國家)
insurgency [ɪn`sɚdʒənsɪ] n. 叛亂,起義
Islamist [`ɪzlæmɪst] n. 伊斯蘭教徒
intelligence [ɪn`tɛlədʒəns] n. 情報
logistics [lo`dʒɪstɪks] n. 後勤

ally [ə`laɪ] n.(複 allies)盟友,盟軍
combat [`kɑmbæt] n. 戰鬥
fatigue [fə`tig] n. 疲勞
deployment [dɪ`plɔɪmənt] n. 部署

▶ 原文、譯文與解析,請見 P.130

Step.4 最後看看「新聞原文」、「精準翻譯」和「關鍵解析」

在牛刀小試聽過一遍以後,你可能會覺得疑惑,聽不太懂,別擔心,本書 95 篇新聞英語皆附上新聞原文、超明白易懂的翻譯及關鍵重點解析,讓你從只聽懂一點點→大致都聽懂了→到完全聽懂!

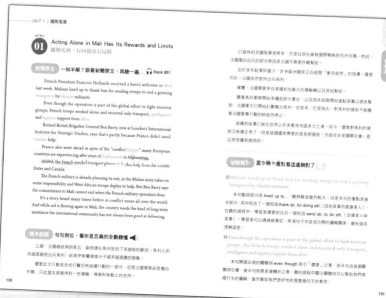

Content 目錄

Unit 1 國際風雲

Unit 2 生態環境

Unit 4 政治熱點

Unit 5 教育科技

Unit 6 財經商貿

Unit 7 社會百態

Unit 8 體育娛樂

Unit 9 文化博覽

Unit 1 國際風雲

聽力技巧 高手接招

圖式學習法

　　圖式理論（Schema）最早是由西方哲學家康德提出來的，後來逐漸被引入教育領域。所謂圖式，根據前人的歸納，是指圍繞某一個主題組織起來的知識的表徵和貯存方式。根據圖式理論，學習者在接觸新事物的時候，會調動、聯繫過去的背景知識和經歷，從而形成對新事物的認識。在聽力練習中，激活對某一主題的圖式，可以幫助學習者彌合聽力理解中的訊息差。學習者激活已有的圖式是前提，而在聽的過程中，學習者不斷把新輸入頭腦中的內容與自己已有的圖式進行對比。如果學習者根據已有的認識，對新材料的預測與實際聽到的內容相吻合，則所聽的內容更容易被理解；如果有所偏差，學習者就會進行調整和修正，而在此過程中，理解的訊息差更能激發聽者積極主動去聆聽新材料的興趣和好奇心，從而達到事半功倍的效果。

　　比如，針對本單元的「國際風雲」篇，學習者可以平時多關注國內外的重大外交、政治新聞，尤其是時事熱點事件，多積累背景知識。當聽到有關某個國家的報導時，學習者可以調動自己積累的背景知識，在聽材料的過程中積極進行預測。這樣堅持下去，學習者不僅能增強聽的興趣，也能提高聽力理解能力。

NEWS 01

Acting Alone in Mali Has Its Rewards and Limits

獨舞馬利，有回報也有局限

牛刀小試 先聽一遍，貼近真實英語生活圈 *Track 001*

French President Francois Hollande received a hero's welcome in Mali last week. Malians lined up to thank him for sending troops to end a growing insurgency by Islamist militants...

有聽沒有懂？就參考看看此篇新聞的背景提示吧

法國總統歐朗德於 2013 年 1 月 11 日確認，法國武裝部隊於當天下午開始軍事介入馬利局勢，以協助馬利政府擊退反政府武裝的攻勢。

馬利曾是法國殖民地，1960 年獲得獨立。之後，兩國間也一直保持著非常特殊的關係。但也正是因為這一原因，法國起初並不願意在馬利衝突問題上直接出面，而是希望由西非國家經濟共同體挑頭，法國及歐盟提供軍事支持來進行解決。但是，自去年 3 月份發生政變以來，馬利局勢急轉直下，北部大部分地區已被反對派勢力占領，首都巴馬科的安全很快也將受到威脅，於是馬利過渡期總統特拉奧雷緊急致函聯合國秘書長和法國總統請求援助。

單字補給站 熟記後再聽一次，英文聽力大躍進

Mali [`mɑlɪ] n. 馬利（西非國家）
insurgency [ɪn`sɝdʒənsɪ] n. 叛亂，起義
Islamist [`ɪzlæmɪst] n. 伊斯蘭教徒
intelligence [ɪn`tɛlədʒəns] n. 情報
logistics [lo`dʒɪstɪks] n. 後勤

ally [ə`laɪ] n.（複 allies）盟友，盟軍
combat [`kɑmbæt] n. 戰鬥
fatigue [fə`tig] n. 疲勞
deployment [dɪ`plɔɪmənt] n. 部署

▶ 原文、譯文與解析，請見 P.130

NEWS 02 African Union Leaders Talk Mali, Chinese Investment

非盟領導人就馬利局勢和中方在非投資展開討論

牛刀小試 先聽一遍，貼近真實英語生活圈 🎧 *Track 002*

Chinese Vice Premier Wang Yang told the African Union that Beijing's new leaders want greater cooperation on trade and closer consultation on international affairs with the growth of Africa's influence abroad...

有聽沒有懂？就參考看看此篇新聞的背景提示吧

2013 年 5 月 25 日，大約 75 位來自非洲以及世界其他國家的國家元首和政府首腦齊聚衣索比亞，共同慶祝非盟成立 50 周年，並就中國在非洲大陸的投資和打擊馬利伊斯蘭極端分子等問題展開討論。中國國務院副總理汪洋出席了此次慶祝儀式並發表演講。

汪洋重申中國新任領導人願意與非洲在貿易和解決國際事務領域展開更加緊密的磋商與合作，共同為提高非洲在國際上的影響力作出努力。非洲方面也對於中國多年以來給予的支持深表感謝。在馬利問題上，隨著法國軍隊的撤離，非盟主席主要討論了是否要派出地區干預力量的問題。

單字補給站 熟記後再聽一次，英文聽力大躍進

vice premier 副總理
consultation [ˌkɑnsəlˋteʃən] n. 諮詢，磋商
reliable [rɪˋlaɪəbl] adj. 可信賴的，可靠的
priority [praɪˋɔrətɪ] n. 優先權
infrastructure [ˋɪnfrəˌstrʌktʃɚ] n. 基礎設施
partnership [ˋpɑrtnɚˌʃɪp] n. 夥伴關係

appreciation [əˌpriʃɪˋeʃən] n. 感謝，感激
intervention [ˌɪntɚˋvɛnʃən] n. 介入，干涉
al-Qaida n. 蓋達組織
affiliated [əˋfɪlɪˌetɪd] adj. 附屬的，隸屬的
piracy [ˋpaɪrəsɪ] n. 海盜行為，海上劫掠

▶ 原文、譯文與解析，請見 P.132

NEWS 03 BRICS Bank Provides Opportunities for Africa

金磚銀行：非洲的發展機遇

牛刀小試 先聽一遍，貼近真實英語生活圈 🎧 *Track 003*

Chinese investment in Africa is soaring, reaching nearly $20 billion last year alone.

In China, hundreds of thousands of Africans have come to work...

有聽沒有懂？就參考看看此篇新聞的背景提示吧

2013 年金磚國家領袖第五次會晤在南非德班舉行，這也是金磚國家高峰會首次舉辦於非洲。相關人士預測，隨著南非在 2011 年正式成為金磚國家的成員，金磚國家未來在非洲國家和地區的投資和貿易將倍增，從而為非洲帶來巨大的發展機遇。

此次高峰會的主題是「金磚國家與非洲：致力於發展、整合和工業化的夥伴關係」。除了金磚國家領袖之外，非盟主席以及相關非洲國家領袖也出席了此次高峰會，共同就本次高峰會的主要議題「成立金磚國家開發銀行」展開討論。

單字補給站 熟記後再聽一次，英文聽力大躍進

soar [sor] v. 猛增
investment [ɪn`vɛstmənt] n. 投資
reach out to 接觸
BRICS abbr. 金磚國家，金磚五國（包括巴西、俄羅斯、印度、中國和南非）

founding [`faʊndɪŋ] n. 建立，創立
alternative [ɔl`tɝnətɪv] n. 可供選擇的事物
analyst [`ænlɪst] n. 分析家
beckon [`bɛkn] v. 很有吸引力

▶ 原文、譯文與解析，請見 P.134

^{NEWS}
04 Britain Could
Be on Path to EU Exit

英國可能已踏上退出歐盟之路

牛刀小試 先聽一遍，貼近真實英語生活圈 🎧 *Track 004*

Britain's economy relies on trade and financial services. The free flow of goods and services with the European continent has been a boon, but more and more Britons see the European Union as an unwelcome infringement on their sovereignty...

有聽沒有懂？就參考看看此篇新聞的背景提示吧

自歐債危機爆發以來，英國民眾和議會中的保守派人士擔心英國會被拖入債務危機的泥淖，要求退出歐盟的呼聲越來越高。在歐洲一體化過程中，英國與歐盟政策上的分歧也越來越嚴重，歐盟其他成員國民眾紛紛指責英國漠視及拖累歐盟經濟整合化和債務危機的解決。

迫於公眾輿論和保守黨內部的壓力，英國首相卡麥隆 2013 年 1 月 23 日在倫敦發表的演講中首次正式提出，如果保守黨能在 2015 年再次贏得大選，將與歐盟重新談判，並將於 2017 年前就英國在歐盟的去留問題舉行全民公投。

單字補給站 熟記後再聽一次，英文聽力大躍進

rely on 依賴
boon [bun] n. 恩惠，實惠
infringement [ɪnˋfrɪndʒmənt] n. 侵犯
sovereignty [ˋsɑvrɪntɪ] n. 主權
referendum [ˌrɛfəˋrɛndəm] n. 公投

preserve [prɪˋzɝv] v. 維持，保持
regulation [ˌrɛgjəˋleʃən] n. 規定，規則
endorse [ɪnˋdɔrs] v. 公開支持
divorce [dəˋvors] n. 離婚，分離
be fraught with 充滿

▶ 原文、譯文與解析，請見 P.136

NEWS 05
Cyber Threat:
Top Concern for NATO

網路威脅：北約的頭號隱憂

牛刀小試 先聽一遍，貼近真實英語生活圈 🎧 *Track 005*

Cyber attacks on corporations and governments are no longer unusual. Suspects and their computers are hauled away on a regular basis...

有聽沒有懂？就參考看看此篇新聞的背景提示吧

　　如今，人們在日常生活和工作中使用網路和電子郵件的頻率越來越高，各種網路安全和威脅問題也隨之湧現出來。全球著名會計師事務所安永（Ernst & Young）日前發布的第十五份全球資訊安全年度調查報告顯示，77% 的受訪企業表示它們在資訊安全方面所面臨的外部威脅正不斷增加。除了企業之外，各國軍事、政府部門，各大銀行及相關金融機構也成為了網路攻擊的「高危險群」。國家間的網路安全戰也已經開始，各國都不惜投入重金發展自己的網路安全部隊。即將離任的北約最高軍事長官詹姆斯‧斯塔夫里迪斯海軍上將也表達了自己對未來網路威脅的擔憂。

單字補給站 熟記後再聽一次，英文聽力大躍進

suspect [sə`spɛkt] n. 嫌疑人
haul [hɔl] v. 拖，拉
on a regular basis 定期地
cyber security 網路安全
successor [sək`sɛsɚ] n. 繼任者
capability [ˌkepə`bɪlətɪ] n. 能力，性能

nuisance [`njusns] n. 妨害行為
theft [θɛft] n. 盜竊
be accused of 被指責，被指控
grievance [`grivəns] n. 怨憤，不滿
counterattack [`kaʊntərəˌtæk] n. 反攻

▶ 原文、譯文與解析，請見 P.138

NEWS 06 Far-Reaching American Legacy in Iraq Debated

美國對伊拉克的深遠影響引發爭議

牛刀小試 先聽一遍，貼近真實英語生活圈 🎧 *Track 006*

Black smoke rises to the sky after a *suicide* ***bombing in Baghdad's Sadr City, one in a series of deadly attacks marking the 10th*** *anniversary* ***of the U.S.*** *invasion...*

有聽沒有懂？就參考看看此篇新聞的背景提示吧

伊拉克戰爭結束十年之後，有關美國給伊拉克帶來的影響的爭論仍在持續。儘管美國前總統布希鄭重地向世界宣告伊拉克作戰行動的成功，但一些人卻認為美國並沒有給伊拉克帶來所謂的民主和安全，反而讓伊拉克局勢變得更加動盪，頻繁的炸彈襲擊和其他暴力事件已使得越來越多伊拉克人選擇逃離家園。

在這種形勢下，一些前美國官員聲稱伊拉克仍需要美國人民的幫助，並號召美國重返伊拉克，幫助其實現國內的穩定局面。這樣的建議招來了不少指責，前美國國家安全顧問布里辛斯基就一針見血地指出，是美國一手造成了伊拉克如今的局面。

單字補給站 熟記後再聽一次，英文聽力大躍進

suicide [`suə͵saɪd] n. 自殺
anniversary [͵ænə`vɝ·sərɪ] n. 周年紀念
invasion [ɪn`veʒən] n. 侵略
blast [blæst] n. 爆炸
dash one's hopes 使某人的希望破滅

out of balance 失去平衡的
ambassador [æm`bæsədɚ] n. 大使
renewed [rɪ`njud] adj. 更新的
engagement [ɪn`gedʒmənt] n. 參與，介入
escalate [`ɛskə͵let] v. 升級

▶ 原文、譯文與解析，請見 P.140

NEWS 07 Missile Defense System Keeps Watch on Syria

北約部署導彈防禦系統監視敘利亞

牛刀小試 先聽一遍，貼近真實英語生活圈 🎧 *Track 007*

These U.S. soldiers are maintaining Patriot Missiles. Since January, the missiles have been stationed at a Turkish military base outside Gaziantep. The city is 50 kilometers from Syria, where an increasingly bloody civil war has killed at least 70,000 people...

有聽沒有懂？就參考看看此篇新聞的背景提示吧

敘利亞危機是敘利亞政府與反對派之間的長期紛爭。自 2011 年 3 月爆發以來，已經造成 10 多萬人死亡。反對派與政府軍之間的武裝衝突使大量平民無家可歸，大量難民紛紛湧向敘利亞周邊鄰國。

自危機爆發之初，美國就一直支持反對派軍隊將巴沙爾政權趕下臺。隨著衝突局勢的不斷加劇，土耳其、埃及等鄰國開始擔心戰火會燒到本國境內。北約在 2012 年底批准了土耳其的請求，決定在土耳其和敘利亞邊境地區部署「愛國者」導彈防禦系統，以防範可能來自敘利亞的導彈襲擊。

單字補給站 熟記後再聽一次，英文聽力大躍進

patriot [`petrɪət] n. 愛國者
missile [`mɪsl] n. 導彈
station [`steʃən] v. 駐紮，安置
military [`mɪləˌtɛrɪ] adj. 軍事的，軍用的
bloody [`blʌdɪ] adj. 血腥的
back [bæk] v. 支持

NATO abbr. 北大西洋公約組織，北約
(the North Atlantic Treaty Organization)
defensive [dɪ`fɛnsɪv] adj. 防禦的
nevertheless [ˌnɛvəðə`lɛs] adv. 雖然如此

▶ 原文、譯文與解析，請見 P.142

NEWS 08 U.S. Helping Africa Rise
美國希望幫助非洲崛起

President Barack Obama said of his recent visit to sub-Saharan *Africa that "the reason I came to Africa is because Africa is rising, and it is in the United States' interests — not simply in Africa's interests ...*

有聽沒有懂？就參考看看此篇新聞的背景提示吧

　　隨著非洲的不斷崛起，世界各國越來越重視與非洲國家的合作與交流。為了進一步加強 21 世紀美國在非洲的影響力，歐巴馬政府已於 2012 年 6 月份公布了對撒哈拉以南非洲的新戰略，將非洲定位為「建立在經濟增長、共同責任和相互尊重基礎上的合作夥伴」。在國務卿希拉蕊的非洲七國行之後，獲得連任的歐巴馬總統也於 2013 年 6 月底開啟了自己的撒哈拉以南非洲之行，旨在宣揚自己對非洲的重視，贏得更多非洲國家和人民的支持。同時，在對非新戰略的指導下，美國將會更加重視同非洲國家在經貿和能源領域的合作，以謀求實際的利益。

sub-Saharan [sʌb-sə`hɛrən] adj. 撒哈拉沙漠以南的
partnership [`pɑrtnɚˌʃɪp] n. 夥伴關係
potential [pə`tɛnʃəl] n. 潛力，可能性
dawn [dɔn] n. 黎明，開端
emerging [ɪ`mɝdʒɪŋ] adj. 新興的

triple [`trɪpl] v. 成三倍，增至三倍
foreign direct investment 外商直接投資
take root 紮根
paradigm [`pærəˌdaɪm] n. 範式，模式
Senegal [ˌsɛnɪ`gɔl] n. 塞內加爾（西非國家）

▶ 原文、譯文與解析，請見 P.144

NEWS 09

UN Team Faces Tough Task in Syrian Chemical Probe

敘利亞化學武器調查，聯合國小組面臨困境

牛刀小試 先聽一遍，貼近真實英語生活圈 🎧 *Track 009*

These were some of the survivors of what the Syrian government says was a chemical weapon attack by rebels on the northern town of Kahn al-Asal...

有聽沒有懂？就參考看看此篇新聞的背景提示吧

自敘利亞內部衝突爆發以來，其境內的化學武器問題便成為外界關注的焦點。2013 年 3 月，在敘利亞阿薩爾地區的一次炸彈襲擊中，敘利亞政府軍和反對派互相指責對方使用了化學武器。在這種情況下，聯合國接受了敘利亞的請求，開始對此事展開調查。然而，調查過程卻面臨重重阻力，一方面是如何獲准進入敘利亞，另一方面是如何保證調查取證能夠順利進行。

單字補給站 熟記後再聽一次，英文聽力大躍進

survivor [sə`vaɪvə] n. 倖存者
emit [ɪ`mɪt] v. 釋放
figure out 弄明白，搞清楚
U.N. Secretary-General 聯合國秘書長
unfettered [ʌn`fɛtəd] adj. 不受限制的
mandate [`mændet] n. 授權，委託

faction [`fækʃən] n. 派系
oust [aʊst] v. 逐出，驅逐
autocratic [ˌɔtə`krætɪk] adj. 獨裁的，專制的

▶ 原文、譯文與解析，請見 P.146

NEWS 10 US Troop Reduction to Test Afghans
美國減少駐軍考驗阿富汗安全部隊

牛刀小試 先聽一遍，貼近真實英語生活圈 🎧 *Track 010*

In his State of the Union address this week, President Obama put the drawdown of U.S. forces in Afghanistan into high gear ahead of next year's withdrawal deadline...

有聽沒有懂？就參考看看此篇新聞的背景提示吧

　　美國前國務卿季辛格曾說過，塔利班遊擊隊可以不輸則贏，而美國則是不贏則輸。在長達 10 年的阿富汗戰爭中，據美國國防部稱，美國已經花費了 3,232 億美元，2,200 名美軍士兵身亡。如今歐巴馬總統在國內輿論、慘淡的經濟形勢和大選在即三重壓力的促使下，已決定提前從阿富汗撤軍。

　　然而，如此大規模的撤軍對美軍在阿富汗取得的既得利益和阿富汗安全局勢來說必將是一個巨大的考驗。大部分阿富汗人認為，如果美軍完全撤離，阿富汗的安全局勢將會失控。對於由美國和盟軍訓練的阿富汗安全部隊而言，美國駐軍的減少也意味著他們面臨的將是一個更大的挑戰。

單字補給站 熟記後再聽一次，英文聽力大躍進

State of the Union address 國情咨文
drawdown [ˋdrɔ͵daʊn] n.（軍隊人員的）撤減，逐步減少
put...into high gear 使……加速，加快進行
withdrawal [wɪðˋdrɔəl] n. 撤退，撤出
announce [əˋnaʊns] v. 宣布

at the forefront 處於最前線
sufficient [səˋfɪʃənt] adj. 充足的，充分的
coalition [͵koəˋlɪʃən] n. 聯盟，聯合
insurgent [ɪnˋsɝdʒənt] n. 叛亂分子，反叛者
bilateral [baɪˋlætərəl] adj. 雙邊的

▶ 原文、譯文與解析，請見 P.148

NEWS 11

Venezuela-US Relations Unlikely to Change After Chavez

後查維茲時代委美關係不太可能發生改變

牛刀小試 先聽一遍，貼近真實英語生活圈 🎧 *Track 011*

The death of President Chavez is being mourned by his supporters, while many inside and outside Venezuela wonder what the future holds...

有聽沒有懂？就參考看看此篇新聞的背景提示吧

2013 年 3 月 5 日「反美鬥士」委內瑞拉總統查維茲去世之後，世界各國紛紛猜想未來委內瑞拉政局以及委美關係的走向。

查維茲一生都在反對美國在拉美地區的統治地位，試圖把美國趕出拉丁美洲，因此查維茲時代的委美關係

一直充滿了敵意。有分析人士稱，儘管「後查維茲時代」的兩國關係存在很大的不確定性，但是可以確定的一點是，這種一直以來的敵對關係不會迅速發生轉變。最終，查維茲指定的接班人馬杜羅贏得了大選，他隨即就以危害委內瑞拉安全為由將兩名美國外交官驅逐出境，進一步表明了自己對美國的態度。

單字補給站 熟記後再聽一次，英文聽力大躍進

mourn [morn] v. 哀悼
commanding [kə`mændɪŋ] adj. 權威的，威嚴的
charismatic [ˌkærɪz`mætɪk] adj. 魅力非凡的
dominance [`damənəns] n. 統治，控制
coup [ku] n. 政變

tacitly [`tæsɪtlɪ] adv. 心照不宣地，暗中
antagonize [æn`tægəˌnaɪz] v. 使對立，使敵對
convene [kən`vin] v. 召開（正式會議）
expulsion [ɪk`spʌlʃən] n. 驅逐，驅趕
counternarcotics [`kaʊntənəˌkatis] n. 禁毒

▶ 原文、譯文與解析，請見 P.150

NEWS 12

VP Biden: US Not Bluffing on Iranian Nuclear Weapons

副總統拜登：美國在伊朗核武問題上沒有虛張聲勢

牛刀小試 先聽一遍，貼近真實英語生活圈 🎧 *Track 012*

More than 12,000 pro-Israel activists are in Washington for the annual conference of the American Israel Public Affairs Committee — or AIPAC....

有聽沒有懂？就參考看看此篇新聞的背景提示吧

一直以來，美國和以色列的關係就極為特殊。在伊朗核問題、以巴衝突以及其他一些中東問題上，美國都站在以色列一邊。但是兩國就伊朗核問題的具體走向，以及該採取什麼措施來遏制伊朗卻存在很大的分歧。

最近召開的一次美國以色列公共事務委員會（AIPAC）年會就吸引了大批親以色列活動家參加，共同就本次會議的首要議題——伊朗核問題——展開討論。儘管歐巴馬總統一再宣稱美以兩國間的紐帶是「牢不可破的」，並極力表達阻止伊朗擁有核武器的決心，但以色列領袖卻認為伊朗是藉談判以繼續發展自己的核武器，一些猶太組織也指責 AIPAC 沒有充分代表其成員的利益。

單字補給站 熟記後再聽一次，英文聽力大躍進

activist [`æktəvɪst] n. 活動家，積極分子
top [tɑp] v. 居於……之首
period [`pɪrɪəd] n. 句號；到此為止
on the table （計劃等）提交討論的，考慮的

bluff [blʌf] v. 虛張聲勢恐嚇，吹牛
critical [`krɪtɪkl] adj. 批評的，批判的
delegate [`dɛləˌget] n. 代表
lobby [`lɑbɪ] v. 遊說

▶ 原文、譯文與解析，請見 P.152

NEWS

13

Washington Week: Focus on US-Asia Ties

華盛頓週：聚焦美亞關係

牛刀小試 先聽一遍，貼近真實英語生活圈 🎧 *Track 013*

South China Sea maritime disputes will likely figure prominently in Thursday's discussions between President Obama and President Truong Tan Sang...

有聽沒有懂？就參考看看此篇新聞的背景提示吧

隨著亞太地區軍事、經濟和戰略地位的不斷提升，美國開始把戰略重心轉移到亞太地區，以便從中獲取更多利益。本週，在越南戰爭結束四十年之後，美國總統歐巴馬首次在白宮會見了來訪的越南總統張晉創，雙方就有關南海爭端、氣候變化以及經濟合作等問題深入交換了意見。

與此同時，在美國國會內部，兩黨卻對「移民改革法案」爭執不下。儘管參議院之前已經通過了一項全面的改革法案，使得非法移民有了獲得美國公民身份的機會，但是眾議院中保守派人士卻對這一做法表示強烈反對。

單字補給站 熟記後再聽一次，英文聽力大躍進

maritime [`mærəˌtaɪm] adj. 海的，海事的
figure [`fɪgjɚ] v. 重要，搶眼
prominently [`prɑmənəntlɪ] adv. 顯著地
Secretary of State （美國）國務卿
ASEAN abbr. 東南亞國家聯盟，東盟
（Association of Southeast Asian Nations）
conduct [kən`dʌkt] n. 行為，舉動

Vietnamese [vɪˌɛtnəˋmiz] adj. & n. 越南人（的）
front [frʌnt] n. 形勢，範圍
overhaul [ˌovɚˋhɔl] n. 改造，全面修改
citizenship [`sɪtəznˌʃɪp] n. 公民身份
conservative [kən`sɝvətɪv] adj. 保守的，保守派的
debt ceiling 債務上限

▶ 原文、譯文與解析，請見 P.154

Weapons Flowing to Somali Militants
大量武器流向索馬利亞武裝份子

牛刀小試 先聽一遍，貼近真實英語生活圈 🎧 *Track 014*

The military offensive against the al-Shabab militia in Somalia has made major advances over the past year. However, al-Shabab has not been defeated. U.N. monitors reportedly say the group is receiving weapons from distribution networks with ties to Yemen and Iran...

有聽沒有懂？就參考看看此篇新聞的背景提示吧

　　索馬利亞「青年黨」是索馬利亞最大、最主要的反政府武裝組織。該組織控制著索馬利亞中南部大部分地區，一心想要推翻非盟和西方社會（尤其是美國）支持的索馬利亞政府，建立自己的伊斯蘭政權。長期以來，「青年黨」一直與蓋達組織保持密切聯繫，頻繁派遣成員到蓋達組織接受訓練，並且宣布效忠賓拉登。

　　近年來，「青年黨」不斷製造各類恐怖襲擊事件，其中包括挾持和殺害外國人質及襲擊聯合國駐索馬利亞機構，已經被國際社會定義為恐怖組織。

單字補給站 熟記後再聽一次，英文聽力大躍進

Somalia [sə`malɪə] n. 索馬利亞（東非國家）
advance [əd`væns] n. 進展
Yemen [`jɛmən] n. 葉門（西南亞國家）
battle [`bætl] v. 與……作戰
AU abbr. 非洲聯盟，非盟
（African Union）

improvised [`ɪmprəvaɪzd] adj. 簡易的，臨時製作的
embargo [ɪm`bɑrgo] n. 禁運
in effect 生效的
premature [ˌprimə`tʃʊr] adj. 為時過早的

▶ 原文、譯文與解析，請見 P.156

Unit 2 生態環境

聽力技巧 高手接招

閱讀促聽力

　　對於初、中級水平的英語學習者而言，大家可以自問這樣一個問題：如果閱讀中不認識的詞彙或看不懂的句子出現在聽力中，你能聽懂的機率是多少？排除那些可以通過語境大致推測出意思的情況，那麼剩下的便是無法通過反覆聽來解決的詞彙和句子。如果聽力文本中有大量的詞彙和句子都無法看懂，那麼聽懂便是難於上青天。而有此困擾的學習者，可以通過大量閱讀，擴大詞彙量，提高自己的閱讀理解能力，從而達到間接提高自己的聽力理解能力的效果。

　　那麼選擇什麼樣的閱讀教材較為適合呢？以本書第二單元「生態環境」篇為例，自學者可以根據每一則新聞的標題，在網絡上輸入關鍵詞，搜尋出中英文的文本來閱讀，讀的過程中注意總結中英文描述同一主題時常用的不同詞彙、習慣用語表達，句型和觀點。

　　學習者可以根據自己的時間，安排每天聽一則新聞，並閱讀與之相關的中英文新聞文本一篇。這樣堅持下去，你定會受益匪淺！

UN Chief Warns of Perils Ahead of Climate Change Conference

氣候變遷大會召開在即，聯合國秘書長警告危機

牛刀小試 先聽一遍，貼近真實英語生活圈 *Track 015*

The first decade of this century was the hottest on record, and the vast majority of scientists attribute the changes to greenhouse gases that trap heat in the lower atmosphere...

有聽沒有懂？就參考看看此篇新聞的背景提示吧

聯合國秘書長潘基文稱，氣候變遷給國際社會帶來的挑戰是有目共睹的，世界各國必須聯合起來，治理頻發的極端天氣事件，共同為緩解氣候變遷帶來的影響作出努力。2012 年年底，《京都議定書》設定的第一承諾期即將結束。11 月 26 日到 12 月 7 日，

來自近 200 個國家的氣候談判代表將齊聚卡達首都杜哈，出席新一屆聯合國氣候變遷大會，共同為包括確立第二承諾期在內的議題展開討論。美國儘管不是《京都議定書》的締約國，但也聲稱自己在溫室氣體減排方面取得了不小的進步。此外，一些工業化國家也希望，未來的減排方案應將所有主要經濟體包含在內。

單字補給站 熟記後再聽一次，英文聽力大躍進

attribute…to 把……歸因於
greenhouse [`grin͵haʊs] n. 溫室
trap [træp] v. 吸收，阻止……逃脫
fossil fuel 化石燃料
Kyoto Protocol 《京都議定書》

binding [`baɪndɪŋ] adj. 有法律約束力的
expire [ɪk`spaɪr] v. 期滿失效，到期終止
extension [ɪk`stɛnʃən] n. 延長，延期
curb [kɝb] v. 抑制，限制
at the expense of 在損害……的情況下

▶ 原文、譯文與解析，請見 P.160

NEWS 02 Asian Water Summit Focuses on Security, Disaster

亞太水資源峰會聚焦水安全與水災害

牛刀小試 先聽一遍，貼近真實英語生活圈 🎧 *Track 016*

There was no sign of a water shortage here in northern Thailand as delegates gathered for the Asia-Pacific Water Summit. But inside, there was talk about an impending crisis facing Asia...

有聽沒有懂？就參考看看此篇新聞的背景提示吧

隨著亞太地區人口規模不斷擴大和工業化水準不斷提高，各國對水資源的需求量也逐年增加。如今，在中國和印度這兩個亞太地區需水量最大的國家中，一些地區已經出現了嚴重的水資源短缺現象。而與此同時，由於治理不善，某些國家的暴雨和洪水災害依然相當嚴重。

在 2013 年 5 月 16 日到 20 日於泰國清邁召開的第二屆亞太水資源高峰會上，與會的 1500 多名代表針對「水安全和水災害挑戰：領導與承諾」這一主題展開深入討論，交流各自在應對水資源短缺和洪水災害方面的經驗和教訓，探討如何共同應對未來的水災害挑戰，確保亞太地區的水安全。

單字補給站 熟記後再聽一次，英文聽力人躍進

Thailand [ˈtaɪlənd] n. 泰國（東南亞國家）
impending [ɪmˈpɛndɪŋ] adj. 即將發生的
U.N. Habitat 聯合國人居署
reliable [rɪˈlaɪəbl] adj. 可靠的
hygiene [ˈhaɪdʒin] n. 衛生

cubic [ˈkjubɪk] adj. 立方的
claim [klem] v. 奪走，奪去（生命）
imperiled [ɪmˈpɛrɪld] adj. 陷入危險的

▶ 原文、譯文與解析，請見 P.162

NEWS 03 US Coast Guard Monitors Receding Mississippi River Levels

美國海岸警衛隊持續監測不斷下降的密西西比河水位

牛刀小試 先聽一遍，貼近真實英語生活圈 🎧 *Track 017*

Crew members on board the U.S. Coast Guard Cutter Gasconade are struggling to keep traffic flowing on the Mississippi River...

有聽沒有懂？就參考看看此篇新聞的背景提示吧

　　世界第四長河密西西比河是北美地區流程最長、水量最大、流域面積最廣的河流，也是世界上最繁忙的商業河道之一，扮演著貫通美國南北航運大動脈的角色。但如今，乾旱少雨的天氣卻使得美國這條最重要的內陸航道水位達到了歷史最低點，對航行

在河道上的船隻構成了極大威脅。作為一個負責水上安全的部門，美國海岸警衛隊正在密切監視密西西比河不斷下降的水位，盡力確保航道通暢和船隻的航運安全。與此同時，他們也祈禱老天能盡快降點兒雨雪，以緩解密西西比河流域的乾旱狀況。

單字補給站 熟記後再聽一次，英文聽力大躍進

on board 在（船、車或飛機）上
cutter [`kʌtɚ] n.（海岸警衛隊的）武裝快艇
beneath [bɪ`niθ] prep. 在……之下
buoy [bɔɪ] n. 浮標
navigation [͵nævə`geʃən] n. 航行，航海

recede [rɪ`sid] v. 消退，逐漸減少
barge [bɑrdʒ] n. 駁船
disruption [dɪs`rʌpʃən] n. 擾亂，中斷
precipitation [prɪ͵sɪpɪ`teʃən] n. 降雨，降水
plot [plɑt] v. 繪制，標示

▶ 原文、譯文與解析，請見 P.164

NEWS 04 Agriculture and Forestry: Key to Mitigating Climate Change

農林業：減緩氣候變遷的關鍵

牛刀小試 先聽一遍，貼近真實英語生活圈 🎧 *Track 018*

While historically both agriculture and forestry have kept a low profile at climate change talks, the 2012 climate convention in Doha saw some attention being paid to the important role forests play in landscaping, biodiversity and food security...

有聽沒有懂？就參考看看此篇新聞的背景提示吧

2012 年世界氣候變遷大會於 11 月 26 日至 12 月 7 日在卡達首都杜哈舉行，與會國就確立《京都議定書》第二承諾期和氣候變遷綠色基金等主要議題展開討論，並在各方的努力下最終取得了一定成果。此次氣候變遷大會雖然未就農業和林業在降低碳排放、緩解溫室效應等方面所發揮的重要作用作出任何決議，但值得開心的是，已有一些與會人士開始設想將農林業納入到未來氣候變化的談判，使人們充分理解這兩個領域對於保護生物多樣性和維護經濟、社會永續發展的重要意義。

單字補給站 熟記後再聽一次，英文聽力大躍進

forestry [`fɔrɪstrɪ] n. 林業
keep a low profile 不引人注意
landscaping [`lændskepɪŋ] n. 景觀美化
biodiversity [baɪodaɪ`vɝsətɪ] n. 生物多樣性
CIFOR abbr. 國際林業研究中心
（The Center for International Forestry Research）

conservation [ˌkɑnsɚ`veʃən] n. 保存，保護
optimistic [ˌɑptə`mɪstɪk] adj. 樂觀的
sustainable [sə`stenəbl] adj. 可持續的
monitor [`mɑnətɚ] v. 監測

▶ 原文、譯文與解析，請見 P.166

NEWS 05 Scientists Say Climate Change, Dams Threaten Mekong Livelihoods

科學家稱，氣候變化和 大壩建設會威脅湄公河流域民眾生計

牛刀小試 先聽一遍，貼近真實英語生活圈 🎧 Track 019

An estimated 60 million fishermen and farmers depend on the Mekong River for its rich nutrients and abundant fish...

有聽沒有懂？就參考看看此篇新聞的背景提示吧

湄公河流域豐富的物產和充足的漁業資源一直以來都是河流沿岸各個國家和地區賴以生存的天然寶藏。但近年來，不斷加劇的氣候變遷和暖化趨勢使得湄公河水位嚴重下降，河流沿岸的泰國、越南等國都曾出現嚴重的旱情。一些科學家警告，如果東南亞各國無法適應不斷變化的氣候，那麼氣候變化所帶來的極端天氣將會導致魚類和當地主要作物減產。此外，他們還提到湄公河流域的水壩建設有可能給東南亞各國人民賴以生存的漁業資源帶來威脅。

單字補給站 熟記後再聽一次，英文聽力大躍進

fishermen [ˋfɪʃɚmen] n. 漁民
nutrient [ˋnjutrɪənt] n. 營養物質，養料
abundant [əˋbʌndənt] adj. 豐富的
basin [ˋbesn] n. 流域，盆地
intensify [ɪnˋtɛnsəˏfaɪ] v. 加劇
species [ˋspiʃɪz] n. 物種
inland [ˋɪnlənd] adj. 內地的，內陸的

relocate [riˋloket] v. 遷移，搬遷
capacity [kəˋpæsətɪ] n. 能力，容量
hydropower [ˋhaɪdroˏpaʊɚ] n. 水電
compound [kamˋpaʊnd] v. 使加重，使惡化
controversially [ˏkɑntrəˋvɝˈʃəlɪ] adv. 備受爭議地

▶ 原文、譯文與解析，請見 P.168

Report: Widespread Trafficking of Great Apes

NEWS 06

報告：野生人猿的非法交易日趨普遍

牛刀小試 先聽一遍，貼近真實英語生活圈 🎧 *Track 020*

It's estimated at least 3,000 great apes are illegally seized and sold every year. For every ape that is captured alive, many others are slaughtered. A new report says law enforcement is undermanned and too poorly equipped to stop it...

有聽沒有懂？就參考看看此篇新聞的背景提示吧

據相關機構統計，全世界每年非法捕獲和販售的野生類人猿至少有 3,000 隻。這其中有的被富人買來當作寵物收養，有的則被關進了動物園的鐵籠中供遊客觀賞取樂。與獵殺大象獲取象牙不同的是，偷獵者往往需要的是活著的猿。他們常常為了從一個猿類族群中活捉到其中的一隻，殘忍地把剩餘的猿全部殺死。類人猿救生協會協調員克雷斯說，如今的猿類偷獵和販賣行為已經發展成組織犯罪需要世界各國聯合起來才能將其鏟除。

單字補給站 熟記後再聽一次，英文聽力大躍進

ape [ep] n. 類人猿
seize [siz] v. 抓住
capture [`kæptʃə] v. 捕獲
slaughter [`slɔtə] v. 屠殺
enforcement [ɪn`fɔrsmənt] n. 執行
undermanned [ˌʌndə`mænd] adj.
人手不足的
coordinator [ko`ɔrdnˌetə] n. 協調員

lucrative [`lukrətɪv] adj. 賺錢的
poacher [`potʃə] n. 偷獵者
trafficker [`træfikə] n. 走私者
crackdown [`krækˌdaʊn] v. 鎮壓，打擊
confiscate [`kɑnfisˌket] v. 沒收
sanctuary [`sæŋktʃʊˌɛrɪ] n. 禁獵區，保護區

▶ 原文、譯文與解析，請見 P.170

Poachers Kill Elephant Family in Kenya

NEWS 07

偷獵者在肯亞獵殺了一個大象家族

牛刀小試 先聽一遍，貼近真實英語生活圈 *Track 021*

A manhunt has been underway since the weekend in Kenya for a gang of poachers that killed a family of elephants. The Wildlife Service says 12 of the animals were slaughtered. Poaching is on the rise across Africa as demand grows in Asia for ivory and rhino horns...

有聽沒有懂？就參考看看此篇新聞的背景提示吧

近些年來，儘管世界各國加強打擊偷獵和非法售賣野生動物製品的行為，但是在高額利潤的誘惑和驅使下，仍有許多偷獵者不惜以身試法。最近一段時間，在象牙高昂的價格和不斷上漲的市場需求下，肯亞偷獵大象的行為變得愈發猖獗。2013年 1 月 9 號發生在肯亞的一起偷獵事件總共造成 12 頭大象死亡，是近年來發生在肯亞最為惡劣的野生動物偷獵事件。肯亞當局稱，隨著象牙貿易利潤逐步升高，越來越多人開始加入偷獵者的行列，當地野生動物保護組織也面臨越來越大的挑戰。

單字補給站 熟記後再聽一次，英文聽力大躍進

manhunt [`mæn͵hʌnt] n.（對逃犯的）追捕
Kenya [`kɛnjə] n. 肯亞（非洲東部國家）
ivory [`aɪvərɪ] n. 象牙
rhino horn 犀牛角
remote [rɪ`mot] adj. 遙遠的，偏遠的
infrastructure [`ɪnfrə͵strʌktʃɚ] n. 基礎，設施

legislation [͵lɛdʒɪs`leʃən] n. 法規，立法
hand down 正式宣布，正式宣判
penalty [`pɛnḷtɪ] n. 懲罰
misdemeanor [͵mɪsdɪ`minɚ] n. 輕罪

▶ 原文、譯文與解析，請見 P.172

Natural Disasters Displace 32 Million in 2012

2012 年，自然災害迫使 3,200 萬人流離失所

牛刀小試 先聽一遍，貼近真實英語生活圈 🎧 *Track 022*

A new report says more than 32 million people were forced to flee *their homes in 2012 due to natural disasters. Most of the* displacement *occurred in developing countries, but even rich nations, like the United States, were not* spared...

有聽沒有懂？就參考看看此篇新聞的背景提示吧

　　如今，在全球暖化的現象下，世界各地洪澇、乾旱等自然災害發生的頻率也越來越高。自然災害一方面給當地的農、工業發展帶來了巨額損失，另一方面也使得大量人口失去家園，成為環境難民。總部位於日內瓦的國際顯示製程前瞻技術研討會發布的一項最新報告就顯示，2012 年因自然災害而流離失所的人數是 2011 年的兩倍之多。儘管因自然災害而流離失所的情況絕大多數發生在亞洲和非洲的開發中國家，但是在自然災害的侵襲下，已開發國家也有大量人口被迫離開自己的家園。

單字補給站 熟記後再聽一次，英文聽力大躍進

flee [fli] v. 逃離
displacement [dɪs`plesmənt] n. 背井離鄉，流離失所
spare [spɛr] v. 放過，使逃脫
on the run 在奔逃中，在逃跑中
chief spokesperson 首席發言人

onset [`ɑn͵sɛt] n.（尤指不愉快事件的）開端，開始
hurricane [`hɝɪ͵ken] n. 颶風
triple [`trɪpl̩] adj. 三重的
tsunami [tsu`nɑmi] n. 海嘯

▶ 原文、譯文與解析，請見 P.174

NEWS 09 Minister: Zambia Losing Too Many Lions and Leopards
旅遊部長：尚比亞失去了太多獅子和花豹

牛刀小試 先聽一遍，貼近真實英語生活圈 🎧 *Track 023*

Zambia's tourism minister has announced a partial ban on the hunting of lions and leopards. She warns their numbers may be too low to allow safari hunting to continue for now...

有聽沒有懂？就參考看看此篇新聞的背景提示吧

　　長期以來，生活在廣袤非洲大陸上的珍稀野生動物一直在相對安寧的棲息環境中繁衍生息。然而近年來，非洲許多國家在利益的驅使下紛紛開放狩獵活動經營權，再加上非法偷獵行為日益猖獗，大象、獅子、豹等野生動物的數量正急劇下降，有些動物

甚至已經瀕臨滅絕的地步。如今，尚比亞正在作出改變，開始摒棄以往以犧牲野生動物為代價換取利益的政策，把保護野生動植物的工作放到重要位置，努力維護本國生態系統的平衡，為尚比亞人民長久的發展和利益著想。

單字補給站 熟記後再聽一次，英文聽力大躍進

partial [`pɑrʃəl] adj. 部分的
leopard [`lɛpəd] n. 豹
safari [sə`fɑrɪ] n.（在非洲的）遊獵
corruption [kə`rʌpʃən] n. 腐敗
compensation [ˌkɑmpən`seʃən] n. 補償

lease [lis] n. 租約
bid [bɪd] v. 投標
ranch [ræntʃ] n. 牧場，大農場
fence [fɛns] v. 圍住，隔開
cartel [kɑr`tɛl] n. 卡特爾，企業聯盟

▶ 原文、譯文與解析，請見 P.176

NEWS 10 Final Vote Nears on Conserving Sharks

保護鯊魚的最終投票將近

牛刀小試 先聽一遍，貼近真實英語生活圈 🎧 *Track 024*

Shark fin soup is a delicacy in Asia. But its popularity is helping to decimate shark populations. However, governments voted Monday (today) to protect five species of the predators. Preliminary approval came at a U.N. meeting on wildlife trade in Bangkok, Thailand...

有聽沒有懂？就參考看看此篇新聞的背景提示吧

　　很多人都知道魚翅是一種名貴的美食，但是卻很少有人了解獲得魚翅的過程非常殘忍。多年以來，環保人士不斷努力想辦法保護鯊魚，但是在高額利潤的驅使下，捕撈鯊魚的行為卻屢禁不止。要保護日益稀少的鯊魚資源，歸根究柢還是要從根源上著手，喚起人們對鯊魚的保護意識，就像著名野生動物保護大使姚明所呼籲的那樣：沒有買賣，就沒有殺害。最終，人們保護鯊魚的努力在 2013 年瀕危野生動植物國際貿易公約（CITES）大會上取得了重大突破，有 5 類鯊魚被列入了公約的保護範圍。

單字補給站 熟記後再聽一次，英文聽力大躍進

delicacy [ˋdɛləkəsɪ] n. 佳餚
popularity [ˌpɑpjəˋlærətɪ] n. 流行，受歡迎
decimate [ˋdɛsəˌmet] v. 嚴重毀滅，大批殺死
predator [ˋprɛdətɚ] n. 食肉動物，捕食者
preliminary [prɪˋlɪməˌnɛrɪ] adj. 初步的

conservationist [ˌkɑnsɚˋveʃənɪst] n. 自然資源保護者，生態環境保護者
endangered [ɪnˋdendʒɚd] adj. 瀕危的
prize [praɪz] v. 珍視
gill [gɪl] n. 鰓
appendix [əˋpɛndɪks] n. 附錄

▶ 原文、譯文與解析，請見 P.178

NEWS 11 Despite Pollution Worries, China Experiments with Carbon Trading

汙染困擾下的中國碳交易試驗仍在持續

牛刀小試 先聽一遍，貼近真實英語生活圈 🎧 *Track 025*

Beijing's smoggy days are literally off the charts, with small airborne particles that reduce visibility and threaten health.

It has been a persistent concern in recent years, but spiking pollution levels in January are sparking a public outcry...

有聽沒有懂？就參考看看此篇新聞的背景提示吧

在 2013 年 1 月份中，北京的霧霾天氣天數達到創紀錄的 25 天，街上的行人個個「全副武裝」，嚴防吸入有害氣體或顆粒物。儘管相關部門已經採取了一些應對措施，例如關閉重汙染企業，鼓勵市民乘坐公共交通工具

等，但居高不下的汙染水平仍然引起了公眾的巨大恐慌。在此情形下，中國政府開始試驗開放碳交易市場。除了在天津成立天津排放權交易所之外，還在其他多個城市展開碳交易試點，鼓勵更多企業運用綠色科技降低二氧化碳等溫室氣體的排放量，在發展經濟的同時，維護人們賴以生存的環境的健康。

單字補給站 熟記後再聽一次，英文聽力大躍進

smoggy [`smɑgɪ] adj. 煙霧彌漫的
literally [`lɪtərəlɪ] adv. 真正地，確實地
airborne [`ɛr͵bɔrn] adj. 空氣傳播的
visibility [͵vɪzə`bɪlətɪ] n. 能見度
persistent [pə`sɪstənt] adj. 持續不斷的

spike [spaɪk] v. 急劇升高
spark [spɑrk] v. 引發，觸發
outcry [`aʊt͵kraɪ] n. 強烈抗議，大聲疾呼
carbon dioxide 二氧化碳
windfall [`wɪnd͵fɔl] n. 意外之財，橫財

▶ 原文、譯文與解析，請見 P.180

Unit 3 衛生健康

聽後反思

　　對於各個程度的英語學習者而言，聽後的反思都是至關重要的。所謂聽後反思，具體是指學習者在聽完一段英文材料之後，對自己的聽力理解效果進行自我剖析和評估。它可以幫助學習者診斷和找出自己在聽力理解中的薄弱環節，比如注意力分散問題、短時記憶問題、語音辨識問題、詞彙掌握問題、句法結構理解問題、相關背景知識空白問題等。學習者進而可以根據自己的主要問題來調整自己的聽力學習策略和訓練重點，比如是著重進行集中注意力訓練，還是進行發音跟讀訓練、詞彙記憶訓練、長難句分析訓練等。最後學習者還可以制定針對性比較強的聽力學習計劃，變被動學習為主動學習，從而改進自己在聽力理解方面較為欠缺的地方，使自己的聽力程度得到實質性的提高。

　　具體的做法可以是：學習者利用本單元的聽力教材，邊聽邊記錄下自己聽力不懂的地方。聽完之後，對照聽力文本，找出導致聽力不懂的具體原因，然後有針對性地去訓練、改進。要做好每一次的聽力記錄。比如：如果是由於句法理解問題導致的，那麼學習者可以把該句子從聽力文本中挑選出來，進行細致的句法結構分析，必要時可到語法書中找到相應的知識點和習題進行練習，直到完全攻克這種句型為止。

NEWS 01
Findings Could Help Slash Child Malnutrition
減少兒童營養不良問題的新發現

牛刀小試 先聽一遍，貼近真實英語生活圈 🎧 *Track 026*

Child malnutrition is a global problem. It exists even in rich countries. It affects a large number of children in Asia, especially in south Asia...

有聽沒有懂？就參考看看此篇新聞的背景提示吧

　　充足的營養對於兒童的發育與成長至關重要，營養不良可能會造成智力發育不全，誘發多種疾病，長遠來看甚至還會威脅到一個國家的發展與穩定。聯合國兒童基金會相關專家稱，發展中國家有三分之一的兒童死亡與營養不良有關。在撒哈拉以南的非洲地區，營養不良問題甚至已經嚴重到危及兒童的生命安全。最新醫學研究結果顯示，從長遠看，增加對懷孕婦女和兒童的營養補充將是一項收益頗高的投資策略，因為營養攝入不足的兒童患病率更高，而治療所需費用相當高昂。

單字補給站 熟記後再聽一次，英文聽力大躍進

malnutrition [ˌmælnjuˋtrɪʃən] n. 營養不良
threaten [ˋθrɛtn̩] v. 威脅
UNICEF abbr. 聯合國兒童基金會
Ethiopia [ˌiθɪˋopɪə] n. 衣索比亞（非洲東北部國家）
acute [əˋkjut] adj. 急性的；劇烈的
stunting [stʌntɪŋ] n. 生長（或發育）受阻

folic acid 葉酸
calcium [ˋkælsɪəm] n. 鈣
supplement [ˋsʌpləmənt] n. 補充劑，補充物
zinc [zɪŋk] n. 鋅

▶ 原文、譯文與解析，請見 P.184

NEWS
02 Kerry Praises
Genetically Modified Crops
克里推崇基因改造作物

牛刀小試 先聽一遍，貼近真實英語生活圈 🎧 *Track 027*

U.S. Secretary of State John Kerry said Wednesday the United States supports the use of biotechnology to develop so-called "smart" crops that can withstand droughts and floods and require less fertilization.

有聽沒有懂？就參考看看此篇新聞的背景提示吧

　　基因改造作物是利用基因工程研究出的新型作物，與傳統作物相比具有產量高、抗病性強以及耐旱、耐洪等優勢，因而在世界上受到許多政府和科學家的推崇，開始在世界範圍內被廣泛種植。但與此同時，也有一些糧食安全組織和環保主義者擔心基因改造食品會給子孫後代的長期健康帶來不利影響，他們在全球各地舉行遊行示威，反對種植基因改造作物。而基因改造作物的支持者們稱，並沒有科學證據證明基因改造作物會帶來危害。

單字補給站 熟記後再聽一次，英文聽力大躍進

biotechnology [ˌbaɪəntɛkˈnɑlədʒɪ] n. 生物技術
withstand [wɪðˈstænd] v. 承受，經得起
drought [draʊt] n. 乾旱
fertilization [ˌfɝtḷəˈzeʃən] n. 施肥
virtuous [ˈvɝtʃʊəs] adj. 有德行的，良性的

alleviate [əˈlivɪˌet] v. 減輕，使……緩和
genetically modified food 基因改造食品
alter [ˈɔltə] v. 改變
thrive [θraɪv] v. 繁榮，茁壯成長
pest [pɛst] n. 害蟲
label [ˈlebḷ] v. 貼標籤

▶ 原文、譯文與解析，請見 P.186

NEWS
03

Tools to Fight Infectious Diseases Rely on Public Health Programs

戰勝傳染性疾病需仰賴公共衛生計畫

牛刀小試 先聽一遍，貼近真實英語生活圈 🎧 *Track 028*

A simple bite from a mosquito can end someone's life or change it forever. A sneeze, a handshake or even sharing of a desk can do the same thing. That's how H1N1 — or swine flu — spread around the world a few years ago...

有聽沒有懂？就參考看看此篇新聞的背景提示吧

　　縱觀整個歷史，傳染病為人類的生存和健康帶來了巨大威脅，僅愛滋病一項，自 1981 年發現以來就已經奪去了 2,500 萬人的生命。如今，在霍亂、黃熱病、肺結核、瘧疾等古老的傳染病仍在威脅人類健康的情況下，一些新型傳染性疾病又不斷湧現出來。

這其中有的是因為病毒或細菌發生了變異，對傳統治療藥物產生了抗藥性，有的則是之前從未見過的新傳染病。面對新的威脅，美國國立衛生研究院的安東尼·福西博士認為，人類應該加快研發預防新型傳染病的抗體，同時各國也要進一步加強公共衛生項目的建設。

單字補給站 熟記後再聽一次，英文聽力大躍進

mosquito [mǝs`kito] n. 蚊子
sneeze [sniz] n. 噴嚏
malaria [mǝ`lɛrıǝ] n. 瘧疾
tuberculosis [tjuˌbɝkjǝ`losıs] n. 肺結核
symposium [sım`pozıǝm] n. 專題研討會

persistent [pɚ`sıstǝnt] adj. 頑固的，持續的
mutate [`mjutet] v. 變異，突變
elapse [ı`læps] v. （時間）逝去，過去

▶ 原文、譯文與解析，請見 P.188

NEWS
04 World AIDS Day 2012: More Hopeful Than in Past

充滿更多希望的 2012 世界愛滋病日

牛刀小試 先聽一遍，貼近真實英語生活圈 🎧 *Track 029*

According to the United Nations, about 34 million people worldwide are living with HIV, and 2.5 million were infected *last year alone. In the United States, the Centers for Disease Control says there is an* alarming *rise in the spread of HIV among teenagers and young adults, with 1,000 new infections each month...*

有聽沒有懂？就參考看看此篇新聞的背景提示吧

世界愛滋病日由世界衛生組織於 1988 年 1 月首次提出，此後每年的 12 月 1 日，世界各國都會舉行各式各樣的活動，宣傳預防愛滋病的知識。2012 年，世界迎來了第 25 個愛滋病日，這次各國把重點放在了對愛滋病的投入和預防上。聯合國方面稱，僅去年一年世界各地感染愛滋病病毒的人數就達 250 萬。此外，美國疾病控制中心所掌握的數據也顯示，過去一年美國青少年感染愛滋病的人數呈現驚人的增加趨勢。不過，一些醫護人員也表示隨著愛滋病治療方法的不斷改進，以及投入的努力和預防意識的不斷增強，全世界的愛滋病總體情況正趨於好轉。

單字補給站 熟記後再聽一次，英文聽力大躍進

infect [ɪn`fɛkt] v. 感染
alarming [ə`lɑrmɪŋ] adj. 嚇人的，令人驚恐的
head [hɛd] v. 領導，主管
advance [əd`væns] n. 進步，進展

productive [prə`dʌktɪv] adj. 富有成效的
odds [ɑds] n. (pl.) 機會，可能性
routine [ru`tin] adj. 常規的，例行的
steep [stip] adj. 急劇的

▶ 原文、譯文與解析，請見 P.190

NEWS 05

World Health Day Raises Awareness of Deadliest Condition

世界衛生日：提高對高血壓致命性的意識

牛刀小試 先聽一遍，貼近真實英語生活圈 🎧 *Track 030*

It's evening at Dakar beach in Senegal, and the sands are packed with people exercising.

But a recent World Health Organization report indicates one out of eight Senegalese women aged over 20 are obese — and suffer from related diseases like high blood pressure...

有聽沒有懂？就參考看看此篇新聞的背景提示吧

　　高血壓是一種常見慢性病，嚴重的話會引發腦中風、心肌梗塞、心臟病等併發症，是危害人類健康的一大殺手。據世界衛生組織統計，全世界每三個成年人中就有一人患有高血壓，而且這一比例在貧窮的非洲國家甚至高達 40%。但令人擔憂的是，長期以  來人們對高血壓的認識卻嚴重不足，一些貧困地區的高血壓診斷仍面臨很多困難。

　　2013 年世界衛生日以高血壓為主題，旨在提高人們對高血壓的認識，更好地進行預防和診斷工作。一個由多名專家組成的團隊還專門研發出了一種太陽能血壓計幫助貧困地區的患者診斷和治療高血壓。

單字補給站 熟記後再聽一次，英文聽力大躍進

Senegal [ˌsɛnɪˈɡɔl] n. 塞內加爾（西非國家）
pack [pæk] v. 塞進，擠進
indicate [ˈɪndəˌket] v. 表明
obese [oˈbis] adj. 過度肥胖的
cardiovascular [ˌkɑrdɪoˈvæskjʊləˋ] adj. 心血管的

stroke [strok] n. 中風，腦卒中
access [ˈæksɛs] n. 使用權
diagnosis [ˌdaɪəgˈnosɪs] n. 診斷
obstetrics [əbˈstɛtrɪks] n. 產科學；助產術

▶ 原文、譯文與解析，請見 P.192

題目篇

詳解篇

Discovery Could Lead to New Drugs to Block Deadly Viruses

新發現促使新藥物研發，有望阻斷致命病毒複製

牛刀小試 先聽一遍，貼近真實英語生活圈 🎧 *Track 031*

Viruses are strange things. Though they are not alive, they have a basic genetic structure that allows them to be biologically active. But they don't have the built-in reproductive capacity of bacteria...

有聽沒有懂？就參考看看此篇新聞的背景提示吧

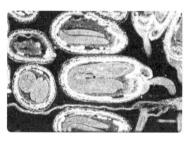

　　許多病毒的傳播和繁殖能力很強，在短時間內就能通過劫持宿主細胞，強迫其複製病毒，從而給人體帶來致命威脅。如今，美國的研究人員通過對上千種化合物進行篩選，發現了幾種能夠阻斷病毒複製的強效化合物。由這些化合物製成的藥物能夠阻斷包括高致命性的伊波拉病毒、馬爾堡病毒，以及引起狂犬病、腮腺炎和麻疹的病原體等許多病毒在人體細胞內的複製過程，從而達到預防和治療病毒性感染的目的。然而，這種化合物並不是萬能的，例如它對愛滋病病毒就起不到任何作用。

單字補給站 熟記後再聽一次，英文聽力大躍進

reproductive [ˌriprəˈdʌktɪv] adj. 繁殖的
virologist [vaɪˈrɑlədʒɪst] n. 病毒學家
hijack [ˈhaɪˌdʒæk] v. 劫持
machinery [məˈʃinərɪ] n. 系統，機制
screen [skrin] v. 篩查，甄選
molecule [ˈmɑləˌkjul] n. 分子

replication [ˌrɛpləˈkeʃən] n. 複製，冉造
pathogen [ˈpæθədʒən] n. 病原體
measles [ˈmizl̩z] n. 麻疹
mumps [mʌmps] n. 流行性腮腺炎
thwart [θwɔrt] v. 阻撓，阻礙
antibiotic [ˌæntɪbaɪˈɑtɪk] n. 抗生素

▶ 原文、譯文與解析，請見 P.194

051

NEWS 07 FAO Aims to Quickly Measure World Hunger

糧農組織致力於全球饑餓狀況的快速評估

牛刀小試 先聽一遍,貼近真實英語生活圈 🎧 *Track 032*

Measuring the scope of world hunger is a long and complicated process. Often officials and policymakers don't have the most up-to-date information. Now, the U.N. Food and Agriculture Organization, the FAO, hopes to change that with a new project called Voices of the Hungry....

有聽沒有懂?就參考看看此篇新聞的背景提示吧

鑒於當前的全球饑餓監測方法過程漫長,數據時效性差,聯合國糧農組織發起了一項名為「饑餓之聲」的新項目,旨在更加快速、更加準確地監測全球各地的饑餓狀況。糧農組織分析師稱,這一項目與傳統監測方法的最大不同之處在於新方法是從每個遭受饑餓威脅的個體那裡直接得到數據,而不是如以往那樣,只是間接地對一些數據和報告進行評估。此外,「饑餓之聲」項目還大大縮短了調查所需的時間。傳統調查方法通常需要花費幾年時間才能完成的工作,新方法在三個月內便可完成。

單字補給站 熟記後再聽一次,英文聽力大躍進

complicated [ˋkɑmpləˏketɪd] adj. 複雜的
up-to-date [ˋʌptəˋdet] adj. 最新的
evaluate [ɪˋvæljʊˏet] v. 評估
statistician [ˏstætəsˋtɪʃən] n. 統計師
precise [prɪˋsaɪs] adj. 精確的

severity [səˋvɛrətɪ] n. 嚴重性
annually [ˋænjʊəlɪ] adv. 每年地
collaboration [kəˏlæbəˋreʃən] n. 合作
subjective [səbˋdʒɛktɪv] adj. 主觀的
respondent [rɪˋspɑndənt] n. 調查對象

▶ 原文、譯文與解析,請見 P.196

NEWS 08 Horse Meat Scandal Spreads Across Europe

「馬肉風波」席捲歐洲

牛刀小試 先聽一遍，貼近真實英語生活圈 🎧 *Track 033*

The horse meat scandal started in Ireland and the United Kingdom in January, but has since spread all around the EU. DNA checks on beef have found that some products, including hamburgers, contained as much as 30 percent horse meat...

有聽沒有懂？就參考看看此篇新聞的背景提示吧

自 2013 年 1 月份以來，歐洲的「馬肉風波」持續發酵，已經從最初的英國和愛爾蘭蔓延到幾乎整個歐洲大陸。包括連鎖業巨頭沃爾瑪在內的多家大型超市捲入其中，引發了消費者莫大的反感和恐慌。瑞典、法國和德國等國相繼在對本國銷售的牛肉製品的 DNA 檢測中發現了馬肉成分，商店和學校紛紛將疑有馬肉成分的牛肉製品下架，超市也開始召回「假牛肉」。歐洲警察署開始介入調查，截至目前已在英格蘭和威爾斯逮捕了三名犯罪嫌疑人。一些食品安全專家表示，解決「馬肉風波」的關鍵還是加強對生產和運輸環節的監管。

單字補給站 熟記後再聽一次，英文聽力大躍進

scandal [ˋskændl] n. 醜聞
taint [tent] v. 汙染
widen [ˋwaɪdn] v. 擴大
lasagna [ləˋzɑnjə] n. 義大利千層麵
tortellini [ˌtɔrtəˋlinɪ] n. 義大利式餃子

bolognese sauce 番茄肉醬
fraud [frɔd] n. 欺詐
squeeze [skwiz] v. 擠壓，壓榨

▶ 原文、譯文與解析，請見 P.198

NEWS 09 Looking Better Helps Cancer Patients Feel Better

好看的容貌有助於癌症病人的恢複

牛刀小試 先聽一遍，貼近真實英語生活圈 🎧 *Track 034*

Millions of women who undergo chemotherapy around the world face the harsh reality of hair and weight loss and skin damage. But many are turning to "Look Good, Feel Better;" a program that teaches women simple beauty techniques so they can once again not only look better physically but also feel stronger emotionally...

有聽沒有懂？就參考看看此篇新聞的背景提示吧

研究顯示，許多癌症病人在接受化療的過程中不僅要面對病魔的侵襲，還要忍受治療所帶來的副作用的折磨。化療所造成的頭髮脫落和皮膚損傷常常會打擊癌症患者的自尊心，減弱他們戰勝病魔的決心和勇氣。但是個人護理產品協會在美國癌症協會

支持下所展開一項名為「容貌好，心情好」的項目卻能比較有效地改變癌症病人的這一狀況。該項目目前已經在 25 個國家展開，透過對癌症病人進行化妝培訓使很多人又重新燃起戰勝病魔的勇氣。

單字補給站 熟記後再聽一次，英文聽力大躍進

chemotherapy [ˌkɛmoˋθɛrəpɪ] n. 化療
harsh [hɑrʃ] adj. 嚴酷的，殘酷的
physically [ˋfɪzɪklɪ] adv. 身體上
emotionally [ɪˋmoʃənlɪ] adv. 情感上
makeup [ˋmek͵ʌp] n. 化妝品

bald [bɔld] adj. 禿（頭）的
flattering [ˋflætərɪŋ] adj. 奉承的；顯漂亮的
kit [kɪt] n. 成套工具，工具箱
cosmetics [kɑzˋmɛtɪks] n. 化妝品
visible [ˋvɪzəbl] adj. 看得見的，可見的

▶ 原文、譯文與解析，請見 P.200

NEWS 10 Parasites, Trauma: Causes of Epilepsy

寄生蟲、外傷：癲癇病的誘因

A new study says it's possible to substantially reduce the number of epilepsy cases in Africa. The neurological disorder, which is characterized by seizures, is much more common in poor countries and rural areas...

有聽沒有懂？就參考看看此篇新聞的背景提示吧

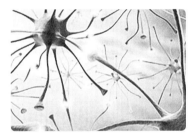

　　癲癇是一種由大腦神經元突發性放電所引起的慢性神經性疾病，患者常會出現抽搐、痙攣等癥狀。癲癇病的病因複雜多樣，包括遺傳因素、先天性腦部疾病、寄生蟲感染等，因此診斷和治療起來十分困難。與發達國家相比，這種疾病在貧困國家出現得更為頻繁，其中很大一部分原因是由於生活在這些落後地區的人們更容易感染寄生蟲病。一項最新研究結果顯示，透過展開寄生蟲控制行動能夠有效降低癲癇病的發病機率，盤尾絲蟲病的成功控制就是一個很好的例子。

單字補給站 熟記後再聽一次，英文聽力大躍進

substantially [səb`stænʃəlɪ] adv. 大幅地，實質性地
epilepsy [`ɛpəlɛpsɪ] n. 癲癇（癥）
neurological [͵njʊrə`lɑdʒɪkəl] adj. 神經病學的
seizure [`siʒɚ] n.（癲癇等的）突然發作
Uganda [ju`gændə] n. 烏干達（非洲東部國家）

Tanzania [͵tænzə`nɪə] n. 坦尚尼亞（非洲東部國家）
Ghana [`gɑnə] n. 迦納（非洲西部國家）
genetics [dʒə`nɛtɪks] n. 遺傳現象，遺傳特徵
parasite [`pærə͵saɪt] n. 寄生蟲
trauma [`trɔmə] n. 創傷，外傷
natal [`netl] adj. 出生時的

▶ 原文、譯文與解析，請見 P.202

NEWS 11 Report: Superfood for Babies
報告：嬰兒的超級食物

牛刀小試 先聽一遍，貼近真實英語生活圈 🎧 *Track 036*

A new report says more than 800,000 babies' lives could be saved every year, if all women began breastfeeding within the first hour of giving birth. Save the Children calls breastfeeding one of the best ways to prevent malnutrition, a major killer of children under age five...

有聽沒有懂？就參考看看此篇新聞的背景提示吧

　　在奶粉品質問題屢見不鮮的今天，越來越多的母親開始選擇給自己的孩子餵養母乳。就如相關專家指出，母乳餵養有助於促進新生兒身體和智力的健康發育，能有效預防和減少嬰幼兒營養不良狀況的發生，降低五歲以下兒童的死亡率。最近發布的一項報告甚至稱母乳是嬰兒的「超級食物」，並且特別強調了嬰兒出生後的幾個小時內母乳餵養的重要性。然而，除了母親自身的排斥外，

母乳餵養仍面臨許多障礙，許多母親迫於生活和工作的壓力，不得不早早就給孩子斷奶。

單字補給站 熟記後再聽一次，英文聽力大躍進

breastfeed [`brɛst‚fid] v. 母乳餵養
vital [`vaɪtl] adj. 關鍵的
colostrum [kə`lɑstrəm] n. 初乳
immunization [‚ɪmjənə`zeʃən] n. 免疫
Niger [`naɪdʒɚ] n. 尼日（非洲中西部國家）

obstacle [`ɑbstəkl] n. 障礙
minimum [`mɪnəməm] adj. 最少的
maternity leave 產假
mortality [mɔr`tælətɪ] n. 死亡率

▶ 原文、譯文與解析，請見 P.204

^{NEWS}
12
South African Traditional Healers Face Increased Competition
南非傳統治療師面臨日益激烈的競爭

牛刀小試 先聽一遍，貼近真實英語生活圈 🎧 *Track 037*

It is estimated that South Africa has about 200,000 traditional healers and more than 30 million people seek their counsel...

有聽沒有懂？就參考看看此篇新聞的背景提示吧

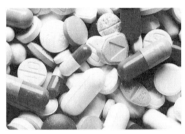

　　有著「巫醫」之稱的傳統治療師在南非文化中占據著舉足輕重的地位。在很多南非人眼裡，巫醫不僅能夠幫助他們治好身體和精神上的各種疾病，還能保護家畜，給他們帶來好運。正因如此，約翰尼斯堡法院甚至在 2012 年審理的一起訴訟案中，明確裁定工人們可以如請病假去看醫生般，請假去諮詢巫醫。然而，巫醫在現代社會面臨著諸多挑戰。許多現代人把巫醫視為不擇手段的巫師，損害了其在民眾中的形象。另一方面，來自西藥日趨激烈的競爭也使巫醫的生存狀況變得更加艱難。

單字補給站 熟記後再聽一次，英文聽力大躍進

healer [ˈhilɚ] n. 治療師
counsel [ˈkaʊnsl̩] n. 勸告，建議
fringe [frɪndʒ] adj. 邊緣的，非主流的
tarnish [ˈtɑrnɪʃ] v. 玷汙
allegedly [əˈlɛdʒɪdlɪ] adv. 據稱，據傳

potion [ˈpoʃən] n. 藥液，神水
sangoma [sʌŋ goʊmə] n. 巫醫
lobby [ˈlɑbɪ] v. 遊說
physiology [ˌfɪzɪˈɑlədʒɪ] n. 生理學

▶ 原文、譯文與解析，請見 P.206

Unit4 政治熱點

聽力技巧 高手接招

精聽和泛聽相結合

在聽力訓練中，既要練習準確無誤地聽出重要細節，如數字、時間、人名、地名、事實等，又要兼顧把握大意的訓練，這就要求學習者要有意識地把精聽與泛聽結合起來，交替練習。

學習者既可以對同一篇新聞先泛聽，再精聽；也可以把一篇新聞分成精聽、泛聽段落，某些部分精聽，其餘泛聽；還可以把精聽和泛聽分開來獨立練習，精聽某一篇或幾篇新聞，另幾篇則進行泛聽。在精聽時，學習者首先要熟悉聽力教材中的生詞，遇到有難度的句子可以反覆聽；而泛聽則著眼於全局，重點要求掌握大意，不必太過專注於細節。精聽的遍數不限，直到完全聽懂為止。泛聽的遍數則由教材難度和自己的英語程度來決定，但一般不要超過三遍，否則就失去了泛聽的意義。泛聽時，中間不宜停頓或打斷，要一氣呵成。精聽則可在句子之間或困難之處停下，重放重聽。

泛而不精，容易養成似是而非、不求甚解的習慣；反之，則容易見樹不見林，抓不住大意。總之，這兩種訓練哪一種也不應偏廢。

NEWS 01 "Fiscal Cliff" Deal Highlights Messy US Democracy in Action

「財政懸崖」決議凸顯美國民主制度的混亂

牛刀小試 先聽一遍，貼近真實英語生活圈 🎧 *Track 038*

Many visitors to the U.S. Capitol, like David Stark from Maryland, come to admire this monument to democracy but express frustration with the political polarization inside its halls...

有聽沒有懂？就參考看看此篇新聞的背景提示吧

美國是一個實行兩黨制的國家，兩黨制建立之初是為了相互制衡，避免出現一黨獨裁的局面，保護美國的民主制度。但是隨著時間的推移，這種相互制衡逐漸演變成一種惡性的矛盾與衝突。兩黨經常在一個問題上相互推諉，或大唱反調，一個問題通常

要在參、眾兩院經過多次辯論後才能得以解決。當下，這種黨派紛爭所造成的辦事效率低下就在「財政懸崖」問題的解決中顯露無遺。來自民主黨的美國總統歐巴馬就自己提出的預算法案與共和黨人爭執不下，越來越多的美國人開始對美國當前的這種民主制度產生懷疑。

單字補給站 熟記後再聽一次，英文聽力大躍進

monument [`mɑnjəmənt] n. 紀念碑
frustration [ˌfrʌs`treʃən] n. 挫折，失望
polarization [ˌpolərə`zeʃən] n. 兩極分化
avert [ə`vɝt] v. 避免，防止
deadline [`dɛd.laɪn] n. 最後期限

steep [stip] adj. 陡的，過高的
postpone [post`pon] v. 推遲，延期
deficit [`dɛfɪsɪt] n. 赤字，逆差

▶ 原文、譯文與解析，請見 P.210

NEWS 02 US "Patriotic Millionaires": "Tax Us More"

美國「愛國百萬富翁」呼籲：「向我們徵收更多的稅吧！」

牛刀小試 先聽一遍，貼近真實英語生活圈 🎧 *Track 039*

In Washington — a group calling themselves "Patriotic Millionaires," storming Capitol Hill with their message for the president and Congress: "tax us more, we can take it."...

有聽沒有懂？就參考看看此篇新聞的背景提示吧

美國「愛國百萬富翁」協會是由兩百名年收入超過 100 萬美元的富翁組成，這些人多數就職於金融或科技等高收入行業。

如今，兩黨正為避免美國墜下「財政懸崖」展開政策上的博弈。就在眾議院議長約翰·博納強烈反對總統歐巴馬對富人增稅的提案時，「愛國百萬富翁」協會卻逆風而行，選擇支持總統一邊，支持對占美國人口 2% 的最富有階層徵收更高的稅。在他們看來，中產階級在美國經濟中發揮著重要作用，如果他們在解決政府財政赤字的問題上承受過重的稅收負擔，那麼對國民經濟的發展將極為不利。

單字補給站 熟記後再聽一次，英文聽力大躍進

patriotic [ˌpetrɪˈɑtɪk] adj. 愛國的
storm [stɔrm] v. 激盪，突然襲擊
Capitol Hill （美國）國會山
tax [tæks] v. 向……徵稅
vow [vaʊ] v. 宣誓，鄭重宣告

budget [ˈbʌdʒɪt] n. 預算
looming [ˈlumɪŋ] adj. 隱約可見的，正在逼近的
take issue with 對……提出異議

▶ 原文、譯文與解析，請見 P.212

NEWS
03

US Presidential Election Has Global Implications

美國總統大選的全球性影響

牛刀小試 先聽一遍，貼近真實英語生活圈 🎧 *Track 040*

> *If the polls are right, the 2012 election will be decided by a few crucial votes in a handful of hotly contested states. But far from being just a domestic ballot — Bruce Stokes at the Pew research Center says the U.S. election will have global implications...*

有聽沒有懂？就參考看看此篇新聞的背景提示吧

　　美國作為世界第一經濟大國，其一舉一動都會牽動世界，其政策的調整可能會對世界的格局動向產生影響。

　　美國的總統大選歷來都是世界性的重要事件，2012 年的大選似乎更成了全球關注的焦點。究其原因，主要是因為現在全球正面臨著前所未有的金融危機，美國也不例外。當前的美國面臨經濟疲軟、失業率高漲和迫在眉睫的財政危機，因此也難怪全世界都在關注這場重頭戲。

單字補給站 熟記後再聽一次，英文聽力大躍進

crucial [`kruʃəl] adj. 關鍵的，決定性的
ballot [`bælət] n. 投票表決，選舉
implication [ˌɪmplɪ`keʃən] n. 影響，可能的後果
output [`aʊtpʊt] n. 產量，產出
refrain [rɪ`fren] n. 常說的一句話

sniffle [`snɪfl] v. 吸鼻子，流鼻涕
candidate [`kændədet] n. 候選人
overwhelmingly [ˌovɚ`hwɛlmɪŋlɪ] adv. 壓倒性地
geopolitical [ˌdʒiopə`lɪtɪkl] adj. 地緣政治的

▶ 原文、譯文與解析，請見 P.214

NEWS 04 US Public Split Over NSA Surveillance

美國民眾對國安局監聽事件反應不一

牛刀小試 先聽一遍，貼近真實英語生活圈 🎧 *Track 041*

The American public is split over whether the National Security Agency, or NSA, should continue phone and email surveillance to stop terrorists...

有聽沒有懂？就參考看看此篇新聞的背景提示吧

愛德華‧斯諾登曾是美國中央情報局技術分析員，美國國家安全局防務承包商博斯公司的雇員。在斯諾登揭露美國政府的「稜鏡」監控項目後，歷來爭吵不休的美國國會兩黨與白宮罕見地步調一致，同聲指責斯諾登為「叛國者」，要求政府迅速予以懲罰。

　　《華盛頓郵報》的最新民調卻顯示民眾對此事反應不一：有 56% 的受訪者支持美國國家安全局監聽民眾電話，41% 的人則認為此舉不可接受。報導稱，許多美國人認為「追蹤」恐怖威脅電話比他們不可侵犯的隱私重要得多。

單字補給站 熟記後再聽一次，英文聽力大躍進

split [splɪt] adj. 分裂的，分開的
surveillance [sɚˋveləns] n. 監視，監聽
anti-terrorism n. 反恐怖主義
civil liberties 公民自由（權）
pollster [ˋpolstɚ] n. 民意調查員

erode [ɪˋrod] v. 侵蝕
monitor [ˋmɑnɪtɚ] v. 監控
petition [pəˋtɪʃən] n. 請願書，訴狀

▶ 原文、譯文與解析，請見 P.216

NEWS 05 Italian Political Gridlock Threatens Euro

義大利陷入政治僵局威脅歐元區

牛刀小試 先聽一遍，貼近真實英語生活圈 🎧 *Track 042*

Italians surprised the world, and perhaps themselves — splitting their vote among disgraced *former Prime Minister Silvio Berlusconi, a center-left* coalition *and a protest movement led by a former comedian. The current prime minister, an economist praised by the international community, got only 10 percent of the vote...*

有聽沒有懂？就參考看看此篇新聞的背景提示吧

義大利議會選舉引起了全球關注，其初步結果已於當地時間 2013 年 2 月 26 日凌晨出爐。中左翼聯盟在眾議院中以些微優勢領先中右翼聯盟，但雙方在參議院均未獲得過半席位，組閣難度非比尋常。此次選舉結果意味著，若沒有一派政治力量能夠順利組閣，義大利恐將迎來新的大選。分析人士擔心，義大利目前的政治僵局也許會導致全球投資者對義大利還債能力及整個歐元區經濟的信心直線下滑，增加漸行消退的歐債危機捲土重來的風險。

單字補給站 熟記後再聽一次，英文聽力大躍進

disgraced [dɪsˋgrest] adj. 失去權力的，不受歡迎的
coalition [ˌkoəˋlɪʃən] n. 聯合，聯盟
virtually [ˋvɝtʃʊəlɪ] adv. 事實上，幾乎
extensive [ɪkˋstɛnsɪv] adj. 廣泛的，大量的

deadlock [ˋdɛdˌlɑk] v. 使陷入僵局
revive [rɪˋvaɪv] v. 復興，復甦
paralyze [ˋpærəˌlaɪz] v. 使癱瘓

▶ 原文、譯文與解析，請見 P.218

NEWS 06 John Kerry: First White, Male Secretary of State in 16 Years

約翰‧克里：美國 16 年來首位白人男性國務卿

牛刀小試 先聽一遍，貼近真實英語生活圈 🎧 *Track 043*

For the first time in almost a decade, members of the Senate Foreign Relations Committee were using the term, "mister," to address a prospective Secretary of State...

有聽沒有懂？就參考看看此篇新聞的背景提示吧

美國參議院於 2013 年 1 月 29 日舉行了投票表決，批准約翰‧凱瑞出任國務卿。凱瑞正式成為美國第 68 任國務卿。自 1997 年初克里斯托弗卸任美國國務卿起，奧爾布賴特、鮑威爾、賴斯及希拉蕊先後擔任美國國務卿，四人或是女性或是黑人。凱瑞是美國 16 年來第一位白人男性國務卿。出任國務卿後，凱瑞將成為歐巴馬第二任期首席外交政策顧問，也是代表美國站在國際舞臺上的首席外交官。他將負責管理美國在 180 多個國家設立的領事館和駐外機構，並負責監管美國的對外援助項目。

單字補給站 熟記後再聽一次，英文聽力大躍進

decade [ˋdɛked] n. 十年
prospective [prəˋspɛktɪv] adj. 未來的，預期的
buzz [bʌz] n. 興奮的説話聲
post [post] v. 在網絡上發（帖子）

satirically [səˋtɪrɪklɪ] adv. 諷刺地
diplomatic [ˌdɪpləˋmætɪk] adj. 外交的
confirmation hearing 審議聽證會
quality [ˋkwɑlətɪ] n. 優秀品質，才能
relegate [ˋrɛləˌget] v. 使……歸屬（於）

▶ 原文、譯文與解析，請見 P.220

NEWS 07
Kenyatta Follows Father to Win Kenya's Top Job
肯雅塔子承父業，當選肯亞總統

牛刀小試 先聽一遍，貼近真實英語生活圈 🎧 *Track 044*

After days of vote counting, Kenya's electoral commission announced Uhuru Kenyatta has been elected the country's fourth president...

有聽沒有懂？就參考看看此篇新聞的背景提示吧

2013 年 3 月，烏胡魯‧肯雅塔以 50.07% 的得票率擊敗得票率為 43.28% 的奧廷加，贏得肯亞總統選舉。4 月 9 日肯雅塔宣誓就職，正式出任新一屆國家總統，成為肯亞自 1963 年獨立以來的第四位總統。

　　肯雅塔是肯亞開國總統喬莫‧肯雅塔之子，曾擔任地方政府部長、政府副總理等職務。肯雅塔在就職儀式上說，他將「毫無偏袒地與所有肯亞人共同合作，服務所有肯亞人」。他還表示：「最重要的是，讓我們繼續為國家的和平祈禱。」

單字補給站 熟記後再聽一次，英文聽力大躍進

announce [ə`naʊns] v. 宣告，宣布
razor-thin adj. 極薄的，極微弱的
run-off n. 決賽，（競選的）決勝選舉
overshadow [ˌovə`ʃædo] v. 給……蒙上陰影

trial [`traɪəl] n. 審判，審訊
disputed [dɪ`spjut] adj. 有爭議的
complicate [`kɑmpləˌket] v. 使複雜化
meddle [`mɛdl] v. 干涉，干預

▶ 原文、譯文與解析，請見 P.222

NEWS
08

Obama Hopes Charm Offensive Will Lead to Grand Bargain

歐巴馬寄希望於魅力攻勢

牛刀小試 先聽一遍，貼近真實英語生活圈 🎧 *Track 045*

If you've come to Washington for a tour of the White House, you're out of luck. Because President Obama and Republicans in Congress could not agree on legislation to prevent automatic government spending cuts, White House tours are canceled for now, and many other government operations are on hold.....

有聽沒有懂？就參考看看此篇新聞的背景提示吧

2013 年 3 月 23 日，美國國會參議院以 50 票贊成、49 票反對的投票結果通過了 2014 財政年度預算法案，該法案計劃未來 10 年增加近萬億美元稅收。目前，該法案已被提交給眾議院投票表決，但預計眾議院通過的機率極低。

　　歐巴馬不斷主張削減開支與增加稅收並重。自本月初簽署了自動減支計劃之後，他便一改從前不愛同議員們打交道的做法，積極地接洽兩黨議員，更主動出擊去國會參加議員們的餐敘，被媒體形容為發動了一場「魅力攻勢」。報導稱，他將於下個月推出歐巴馬版本的 2014 財政年度預算案，屆時就是驗收其「魅力攻勢」成果的時候了。

單字補給站 熟記後再聽一次，英文聽力大躍進

legislation [ˌlɛdʒɪsˈleʃən] n. 立法
cancel [ˈkænsl] v. 取消
charm offensive 魅力攻勢
response [rɪˈspɑns] n. 響應，反應
cautiously [ˈkɔʃəslɪ] adv. 謹慎地，慎重地

adviser [ədˈvaɪzɚ] n. 顧問
slip [slɪp] v.（逐漸地）下滑，下跌
pessimistic [ˌpɛsəˈmɪstɪk] adj. 悲觀的

▶ 原文、譯文與解析，請見 P.224

題目篇
Unit 5 教育科技

聽力技巧 高手接招

擴充詞彙量

　　對於一般的英語學習者而言，詞彙量是聽力理解的一大瓶頸。詞彙是聽力理解的基礎之一，詞彙的掌握對提升聽力程度具有相當重要的意義。學習者應該全面、立體地掌握詞彙，包括單字的發音、詞性、意思、習慣搭配、用語知識、同義詞、反義詞等。另外，英語學習者還要積極促成將自己的閱讀詞彙轉化為聽力詞彙，在聽的過程中習得詞彙，並將習得的詞彙應用到理解新的聽力教材中去，形成詞彙和聽力共同提高的良性循環。

　　標準語速的 VOA 新聞是非常適合積累詞彙的素材，其語速大致在 130–160 詞 / 分鐘。學習者可以根據自己的程度，從自己比較熟悉的主題篇章入手，先快速瀏覽一下聽力文本。如果聽力文本中有超過 5% 的陌生詞彙，那麼學習者可以先對照每篇給出的關鍵詞彙註解提前熟悉陌生詞彙的發音和詞義，將詞彙的發音和詞義建立有效的對應後，再去聽新聞。對於陌生詞彙比較少的聽力文本教材，學習者可以直接進行聽力訓練。聽完之後，將詞義不太確定的詞彙在文本中標出來，並謄寫在筆記本上以備後續的記憶。

　　冰凍三尺，非一日之寒。相信這樣堅持積累下去，學習者定能收穫驚喜。

NEWS 01 BlackBerry Unveils Two New Smartphones

黑莓機發布兩款新智慧型手機

牛刀小試 先聽一遍，貼近真實英語生活圈 🎧 *Track 046*

Two brand new devices and perhaps a fresh start for a company that has seen its global market share plummet from 20 percent three years ago to just over three percent today...

有聽沒有懂？就參考看看此篇新聞的背景提示吧

　　以安全性和 QWERTY 全鍵盤設計而著稱的黑莓機曾經是美國總統、政府官員和華爾街高階主管們最青睞的手機品牌，但如今隨著智慧型手機市場競爭日趨激烈，黑莓機的市占率已經被以蘋果 iPhone 為首的各路對手擠壓得所剩無幾，公司的股價也跌去了

90%，製造商 RIM 公司不得不在全球各地大量裁員。2013 年，黑莓機 Z10 和 Q10 兩款新產品的誕生似乎宣告 RIM 公司欲捲土重來，與眾手機廠商展開最後一搏，重新奪回自己的市場。不過分析人士指出，這兩款產品能否助黑莓機實現翻身還有待市場檢驗。

單字補給站 熟記後再聽一次，英文聽力大躍進

plummet [`plʌmɪt] v. 垂直下降，驟跌
faded [`feɪdɪd] adj. 黯淡的，凋謝的
browser [`braʊzɚ] n. 瀏覽器
intuitive [ɪn`tjʊɪtɪv] adj. 憑直覺的
revamped [ri`væmpɪd] adj. 修訂的，改進過的

feature [fitʃɚ] v. 以……為特點
rival [`raɪvl] n. 競爭對手
trademark [`tred͵mɑrk] n. 商標，標記
anticipation [æn͵tɪsə`peʃən] n. 預期
credit [`krɛdɪt] v. 歸功於，授譽於

▶ 原文、譯文與解析，請見 P.228

NEWS 02

Giant Airship Could Move Huge Amounts of Cargo

能夠運載大量貨物的巨型飛艇

牛刀小試 先聽一遍，貼近真實英語生活圈 🎧 *Track 047*

The prototype unveiled in this immense World War II hangar near Los Angeles is just half the size of the final working model. But the prototype is massive, at 75-meters-long...

有聽沒有懂？就參考看看此篇新聞的背景提示吧

2013 年 3 月 6 日，在洛杉磯附近一個二戰時期的大型飛機庫中展出了一艘以氫氣為動力的軍民兩用巨型飛艇原型機。該飛艇由美國五角大樓和國家航空航天局共同出資 3,500 萬美元設計建造，雖然目前仍處於試驗階段，但是相關人士稱，如果試驗進展順利

且市場反應良好的話，那麼最終的工作模型在幾年之內即可完成，並且很快就可以生產出商用的飛艇。與傳統運輸工具相比，該飛艇不僅可以一次獨立運輸多達 60 公噸重的貨物，還可以穿越複雜的地理環境將貨物運往較偏僻的地區。

單字補給站 熟記後再聽一次，英文聽力大躍進

prototype [`protə͵taɪp] n. 原型，樣機
unveil [ʌn`vel] v.（向公眾）展示
hangar [`hæŋɚ] n. 飛機庫
massive [`mæsɪv] adj. 巨大的
craft [kræft] n. 飛船，飛行器
Pentagon [`pɛntə͵gɑn] n. 五角大樓（美國國防部總部）

metric ton 公噸
rigid [`rɪdʒɪd] adj. 堅硬的，堅挺的
aluminum [ə`lumɪnəm] n. 鋁
propeller [prə`pɛlɚ] n. 螺旋槳，推進器
helium [`hiliəm] n. 氦氣

▶ 原文、譯文與解析，請見 P.230

NEWS 03 Holiday Season Features Latest, Hottest Electronic Gadgets

節慶日：新款、熱門電子產品的銷售旺季

牛刀小試 先聽一遍，貼近真實英語生活圈 🎧 *Track 048*

When it comes to electronic devices, there are more choices today than ever before, which can be daunting for some consumers...

有聽沒有懂？就參考看看此篇新聞的背景提示吧

節慶假日是各大電子廠商大展身手的時機，也是為消費者們追逐最酷、最炫、最時髦的電子產品帶來選擇。一家專門關注電子產品流行趨勢的網站，CNET.com 的資深編輯就為我們列出了目前最熱門的幾款電子產品：Apple iPad Mini、Google Nexus 7 平

板電腦、擁有無線上網功能的智能相機和串流媒體盒，以及無線擴音器等。此外，日漸流行的網路購物在為消費者帶來便利和實惠的同時也為像百思買（Best Buy）這樣的實體零售商店帶來了衝擊，迫使其開始調整經營和銷售策略，以吸引更多的消費者。

單字補給站 熟記後再聽一次，英文聽力大躍進

electronic [ɪlɛk`trɑnɪk] adj. 電子的
daunting [`dɔntɪŋ] adj. 令人氣餒的
review [rɪ`vju] v. 評論
tablet computer 平板電腦
gadget [`gædʒɪt] n. 小裝置，小器具

upload [ʌp`lod] v. 上傳
Bluetooth n. 藍牙（一種無線傳輸技術）
laptop [`læptɑp] n. 筆記型電腦
retail [`ritel] adj. 零售的

▶ 原文、譯文與解析，請見 P.232

NEWS 04 iPhone Becomes Low Cost Microscope

iPhone：價格低廉的顯微鏡

牛刀小試 先聽一遍，貼近真實英語生活圈 🎧 Track 049

The Apple iPhone can be used for a lot of things—make calls, send pictures, video and text, and play games. But scientists say it also can be converted into a low-cost microscope that can detect worm infections in children...

有聽沒有懂？就參考看看此篇新聞的背景提示吧

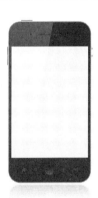

科學技術日新月異，手機領域也發生了翻天覆地的革命。智慧型手機的出現打破了消費者對手機的傳統認識。手機不再是一種僅能打電話、發簡訊的通訊工具，而是已經發展為一種可以和電腦匹敵的智能裝置。人們不僅可以通過手機實現傳統的通訊功能，還可以在小巧便攜的智慧型手機上享受購物、娛樂和辦公帶來的樂趣。此外，一些強大的應用軟體還可以使智慧型手機變身為像汽車導航一樣的實用工具。如今，多倫多綜合醫院的傳染病專家伊薩克・博高什醫生就成功將 iPhone 手機變身為價格低廉的顯微鏡，為貧困地區的疾病檢測和預防帶來了福音。

單字補給站 熟記後再聽一次，英文聽力大躍進

convert [kən`vɜˑt] v. 轉變
microscope [`maɪkrəˌskop] n. 顯微鏡
infection [ɪn`fɛkʃən] n. 感染，傳染病
diagnose [`daɪəgnoz] v. 診斷
readily [`rɛdɪlɪ] adv. 容易地

ingenuity [ˌɪndʒə`nuətɪ] n. 創造力，機靈
make-shift adj. 臨時湊合的，權宜的
parasitic [ˌpærə`sɪtɪk] adj. 寄生的
intestinal [ɪn`tɛstɪnl] adj. 腸道的

▶ 原文、譯文與解析，請見 P.234

NEWS 05 New Generation of Laptops Unveiled

新一代筆記型電腦亮相

牛刀小試 先聽一遍，貼近真實英語生活圈 🎧 *Track 050*

For over three decades Intel has been providing semi-conductor chips for computer hardware makers around the world. Intel's chips have been running many computers for years ...

有聽沒有懂？就參考看看此篇新聞的背景提示吧

　　如今，電腦正朝著更小巧、更輕便、運行速度更快的趨勢發展。自從平板電腦和其他移動裝置上市以來，桌上型和筆記型電腦的銷量均出現了下滑。但全球最大的半導體芯片廠商英特爾在 2013 年年初發布的一款名為「超極本 TM」的全新筆記型電腦卻再一次顛覆了人們對筆記型電腦的認識。這款筆記型電腦集個人電腦和平板功能於一身，體積更小，性能更強，而且在 Ivy Bridge 處理器技術的幫助下耗電量也更低。除此之外，與以往的超薄筆記型電腦和傳統的平板電腦相比，「超極本 TM」的價格優勢也極為明顯，很可能會在消費者中間引起搶購熱潮。

單字補給站 熟記後再聽一次，英文聽力大躍進

semi-conductor chip 半導體芯片
hardware [`hɑrd͵wɛr] n. 硬體
genre [`ʒɑnrə] n. 類型
convertible [kən`vɝtəbl̩] adj. 可轉換的，可折疊的

multiple [`mʌltəpl̩] adj. 多樣的
feature [`fitʃɚ] v. 以……為特徵
capability [͵kepə`bɪlətɪ] n. 性能
announcement [ə`naʊnsmənt] n. 公告，宣稱

▶ 原文、譯文與解析，請見 P.236

NEWS 06 Online Universities Offer Free Classes to Millions

網路大學為數百萬人提供免費課程

牛刀小試 先聽一遍，貼近真實英語生活圈 🎧 *Track 051*

This engineering class at Stanford University is also being recorded as an online course. The university is offering 30 to 40 free courses online, and more than 1.5 million students have enrolled...

有聽沒有懂？就參考看看此篇新聞的背景提示吧

免費網路公開課始於歐美國家，像劍橋、耶魯和哈佛這樣的世界名校把一些名師的授課或講座錄製下來，放到網上供全世界的求知者共享。如今，北大、清華和復旦等中國知名學府也紛紛開設了自己的網路公開課。自推出以來，這一新型課堂受到了各國學習者的追捧，比如一位史丹佛大學教授免費開設了一門有關人工智能的網路公開課，竟吸引了來自世界各地的 160,000 名學生踴躍報名註冊。當然，各校開設網路公開課也有自身的考慮，很多大學希望能透過這樣的課程吸引更多的學生前來就讀。

單字補給站 熟記後再聽一次，英文聽力大躍進

engineering [ˌɛndʒəˈnɪrɪŋ] n. 工程學
enroll [ɪnˈrol] v. 登記，註冊
provost [ˈprɑvəst] n. （美國一些大學的）教務長
entice [ɪnˈtaɪs] v. 誘惑，吸引

utilize [ˈjutḷˌaɪz] v. 利用
flaw [flɔ] n. 缺點，瑕疵
dropout [ˈdrɑpˌaʊt] n. 輟學
proponent [prəˈponənt] n. 支持者
evolving [ɪˈvɑlvɪŋ] adj. 演化的，進化的

▶ 原文、譯文與解析，請見 P.238

NEWS
07

Turkey Provides Schools for Syrian Refugee Children

土耳其為敘利亞難民子弟設立學校

牛刀小試 先聽一遍，貼近真實英語生活圈 🎧 *Track 052*

Gaziantep's school for Syrian refugees. These fourth graders are studying in their native Arabic though their coursework follows Turkey's curriculum. They also are learning the Turkish and English languages...

有聽沒有懂？就參考看看此篇新聞的背景提示吧

隨著敘利亞危機愈演愈烈，該國大量難民紛紛逃往伊拉克、土耳其、黎巴嫩等鄰國避難，為周邊國家帶來了巨大的經濟和社會壓力。據聯合國統計，截至 2013 年 2 月底，土耳其接納的敘利亞難民總數已經突破 20 萬。與其他國家相比，土耳其為難民提供

的條件也更好一些：難民們不僅可以在這裡享受免費的醫療和食宿，他們的孩子還可以接受免費教育。土耳其政府專門在設於敘利亞邊境的難民營中開辦學校，教孩子們學習基本的課程和一些語言課程。

單字補給站 熟記後再聽一次，英文聽力大躍進

Syrian [ˋsɪrɪən] adj. 敘利亞的
refugee [ˏrɛfjʊˋdʒi] n. 難民
Arabic [ˋærəbɪk] adj. 阿拉伯的
curriculum [kəˋrɪkjələm] n. 課程表
disturbing [dɪsˋtɝbɪŋ] adj. 令人不安的
trauma [ˋtrɔmə] n. 心理創傷

tension [ˋtɛnʃən] n. 緊張
humanitarian [hjuˏmænəˋtɛrɪən] adj.
人道主義的
dismiss [dɪsˋmɪs] v. 解散，讓……離開
engulf [ɪnˋgʌlf] v. 吞沒，席捲

▶ 原文、譯文與解析，請見 P.240

NEWS 08
TVs: Bigger, Better at Las Vegas CES
拉斯維加斯消費電子展上更大、更好的電視

牛刀小試 先聽一遍，貼近真實英語生活圈 🎧 *Track 053*

Technology enthusiasts gathered by the thousands for CES 2013. And what they got was eye-opening. Bigger TVs. 3-D TVs. TV screens that are curved...

有聽沒有懂？就參考看看此篇新聞的背景提示吧

國際消費類電子產品展會，簡稱國際消費電子展（CES），創始於 1967 年，於每年 1 月份在美國內華達州拉斯維加斯舉行，是全球規模最大的消費類科技產品展會之一。作為科技領域的頂級盛宴，展會每年都會吸引來自世界各地的眾多電子廠商、電子產品愛好者和媒體前往參觀。

2013 年國際消費電子展就吸引了數以千計的科技迷齊聚拉斯維加斯會議中心，共同體驗琳瑯滿目的電子產品帶來的享受。此次展會不僅展出了螢幕更大的 3D 電視和平板電腦，還展示了一些更加人性化的智慧型手機應用軟體。

單字補給站 熟記後再聽一次，英文聽力大躍進

enthusiast [ɪn`θjuzɪ͵æst] n. 愛好者，熱衷者
eye-opening adj. 大開眼界的
curve [kɝv] v. 使彎曲
tough [tʌf] adj. 堅固的
refrigerator [rɪ`frɪdʒə͵retə] n. 冰箱

discount [`dɪskaʊnt] n. 折扣
tempt [tɛmpt] v. 誘惑，吸引
addicted [ə`dɪktɪd] adj. 沉迷的
interconnected [͵ɪntə·kə`nɛktɪd] adj. 互聯的

▶ 原文、譯文與解析，請見 P.242

題目篇

Unit 6 財經商貿

數字聽力訓練

對於英語學習者而言，由於中英兩種語言裡數字表達方式和計量單位的差異，加上人的認知負荷程度、短時記憶能力的限制，聽力教材中的數字常會成為學習者在聽力解讀過程中的一個難點。尤其是初、中級的英語學習者，在將聽到的英文數字轉換為中文數字的過程中，常會出現偏差，不是聽錯了數字，就是理解或轉換過程中出現差錯。因此，有意識地進行英文數字聽力訓練是很有必要的。

首先，學習者必須弄清楚中英文數字不同的分段法。中文裡數字是以萬為單位，也就是每間隔四個數位分一段；而英文是以千為單位，也就是每間隔三個數位分一段。大家需要重點記住如下的數字表達：ten thousand（一萬），hundred thousand（十萬），million（百萬），hundred million（億），billion（十億），trillion（萬億）。學習者可以找一個學習夥伴，兩人交替進行一組數字的英漢和漢英快速反應練習。除此之外，學習者在聽力訓練中還需要注意英語和漢語裡計量單位的表達和換算，比如貨幣單位、重量單位、長度單位、時間單位等。

本書的「財經商貿」單元所選的素材就非常適合數字聽力訓練。比如本單元的第四則新聞 EU Confronts Youth Unemployment Crisis 中就出現了多個數字。學習者可以在聽音檔時，專門記錄其中出現的數字，包括數字的單位。

NEWS 01 Banks in Cyprus Remain Closed after Bailout

財務紓困之後，賽普勒斯多家銀行仍在歇業

牛刀小試 先聽一遍，貼近真實英語生活圈 🎧 *Track 054*

On March 15 banks in Cyprus closed their doors, and they haven't re-opened. The trickling cash flow has already taken its toll...

有聽沒有懂？就參考看看此篇新聞的背景提示吧

　　自 2009 年底歐債危機爆發以來，銀行業危機已經從希臘蔓延到越來越多的國家。繼希臘救助方案實施之後，歐元區島國賽普勒斯又與歐盟和國際貨幣基金組織達成了一項高達 130 億美元的救助計劃，以幫助該國挽救即將破產的銀行業。

　　但是與其他救助方案不同的是，賽普勒斯的救助計劃是由銀行股東、債權人和無保儲戶承擔，而不是由納稅人來買單。存款額超過 130,000 歐元的賬戶上 40% 的資金將轉為銀行股票。賽普勒斯第二大銀行也將關閉。有分析人士稱，賽普勒斯為了獲得這一救助所需付出的代價是相當沈重的。

單字補給站 熟記後再聽一次，英文聽力大躍進

Cyprus [`saɪprəs] n. 賽普勒斯（西亞島國）（歐盟成員國之一）
trickle [`trɪkl] v. 滴，淌，涓涓地流
take its toll 造成損失
lay off 解雇
shrink [ʃrɪŋk] v. 使收縮，壓縮

restructure [ri`strʌktʃɚ] v. 重組，重構
bailout [`bel͵aʊt] n. 緊急財政援助，紓困
foot the bill 付帳，埋單
depositor [dɪ`pɑzɪtɚ] n. 存款人
template [`tɛmplɪt] n. 樣板，範本
fiasco [fɪ`æsko] n. 慘敗

▶ 原文、譯文與解析，請見 P.246

NEWS
02 Despite Slow Start,
Starbucks Expands in India

星巴克在印度：起步緩慢擴張有序

牛刀小試 先聽一遍，貼近真實英語生活圈 🎧 *Track 055*

This Starbucks outlet in New Delhi's Connaught Place has been open for more than a month and still draws long lines and interest from young people like Vikram Maour, who until now had only seen the coffee chain on television...

有聽沒有懂？就參考看看此篇新聞的背景提示吧

　　如今，星巴克這家總部位於美國西雅圖的咖啡連鎖巨頭已經在全球 62 個國家和地區開設了 18,000 多家分店，其產品也受到各個國家中上層消費者的歡迎。然而，星巴克進軍印度——這一全球第二大茶葉生產和消費國——的努力卻充滿了坎坷。

　　最終，星巴克與印度塔塔集團旗下的塔塔全球飲料公司成立了塔塔星巴克，打開了印度市場的大門。星巴克一進入印度市場就受到了年輕人的熱烈歡迎，門市前不時會大排長龍。儘管擴張步伐並沒有預期的那麼快，但是星巴克仍然對印度巨大的市場潛力充滿信心。

單字補給站 熟記後再聽一次，英文聽力大躍進

outlet [`aʊt͵lɛt] n. 分店，專營店
chain [tʃen] n. 連鎖商店
joint venture 合資企業
beverage [`bɛvərɪdʒ] n. 飲料
giant [`dʒaɪənt] n. 巨人
economically [͵ikə`nɑmɪklɪ] adv. 經濟上

tremendous [trɪ`mɛndəs] adj. 巨人的，驚人的
espouse [ɪs`paʊz] v. 支持，擁護
deliberately [dɪ`lɪbərɪtlɪ] adv. 故意地，有意地
pay off （投資等）獲得回報

▶ 原文、譯文與解析，請見 P.248

NEWS 03 E-Commerce Challenges Traditional Stores

電子商務與傳統商店之爭

牛刀小試 先聽一遍，貼近真實英語生活圈 🎧 *Track 056*

> *Lynne Shaner used the Internet to buy everything she needed for her wedding and holiday gifts for her husband and step daughter.*
>
> *Other than food, 90 percent of her purchases are made on the computer in her Washington apartment...*

有聽沒有懂？就參考看看此篇新聞的背景提示吧

　　資訊爆炸時代的到來給人們的生活方式帶來了巨大改變，手機和網路在日常生活和工作中發揮的作用也越來越重要。如今，電子商務使得越來越多的人足不出戶就可以以更低的價格購買到自己心儀的商品，從而給消費者帶來了巨大的便利和實惠。調查

也顯示，美國網購的人數和網購的次數都在不斷攀升。

　　與電子商業相比，傳統商店有其優勢，也有其劣勢。在電子商務快速發展趨勢仍將持續的情況下，傳統商店面臨的緊迫任務是如何充分發揮自身優勢，以保住自己的市場份額。

單字補給站 熟記後再聽一次，英文聽力大躍進

step daughter 繼女，養女
purchase [`pɝtʃəs] n. 購買，購物
company [`kʌmpənı] n. 夥伴，同伴
merchant [`mɝtʃənt] n. 商人
e-commerce n. 電子商務

ship [ʃɪp] v. 運送，運輸
mortar [`mɔrtɚ] n. 灰泥，砂漿
please [pliz] v. 使高興，取悅

▶ 原文、譯文與解析，請見 P.250

NEWS

04 EU Confronts Youth Unemployment Crisis

歐盟正視青年失業危機

牛刀小試 先聽一遍，貼近真實英語生活圈 🎧 *Track 057*

In Spain and in Greece, unemployment among under-25 year-olds is running at over 50 percent...

有聽沒有懂？就參考看看此篇新聞的背景提示吧

歐債危機不斷惡化，為歐洲經濟帶來了重大影響。這場危機已不單是一場債務危機，不斷惡化的經濟形勢致使歐洲大量青年人失業，各國青年失業率屢創新高。在西班牙和希臘，25 歲以下青年人的失業率甚至突破 50%，越來越多的人開始把歐洲這一代青年人稱為「失落的一代」。如今，歐盟各國領袖已經達成了一項數百億美元的經濟刺激方案，以幫助解決青年失業問題，維持社會的穩定。與此同時，歐盟的成員數還在增加，繼克羅埃西亞成功加入歐盟之後，塞爾維亞也即將與歐盟展開入盟談判，拉脫維亞也將成為第 18 個使用歐元這一單一貨幣的國家。

單字補給站 熟記後再聽一次，英文聽力大躍進

Angolan [æŋˋɡolən] adj. 安哥拉的
consulate [ˋkɑnslɪt] n. 領事館
colony [ˋkɑlənɪ] n. 殖民地
concentrate on 集中精力於
SME abbr. 中小企業
（small to medium-sized enterprise）
credit [ˋkrɛdɪt] n. 信貸，貸款
commissioner [kəˋmɪʃənə] n. 委員

clinch [klɪntʃ] v. 確定，敲定（交易等）
Croatia [kroˋeʃɪə] n. 克羅埃西亞共和國
（歐洲東南部國家）
Serbia [ˋsɜˋbɪə] n. 塞爾維亞（歐洲東南部國家）
hail [hel] v. 為……歡呼
Latvia [ˋlætvɪə] n. 拉脫維亞（歐洲東北部國家）

▶ 原文、譯文與解析，請見 P.252

NEWS 05 EU Solar Panel Ruling Sparks Fears of Trade War with China

歐盟太陽能板裁決引發中歐貿易戰擔憂

牛刀小試 先聽一遍，貼近真實英語生活圈 🎧 *Track 058*

New estimates *show Chinese-made* solar panels *account for about 80 percent of the world's market share. But European* manufacturers *say that's because Chinese manufacturers are not playing fair...*

有聽沒有懂？就參考看看此篇新聞的背景提示吧

近來，中歐雙方有關太陽能板的爭端可謂甚囂塵上。一些歐洲製造商聲稱，中國高達 80% 的市場是靠無序地壓低價格得來的，他們要求歐盟對從中國進口的太陽能板徵收高額的反傾銷稅，以保護當地的生產製造商。歐盟方面稱將會在未來一段時間內對中國太陽能板徵收平均稅率為 47% 的懲罰性關稅。對此，中國方面迅速作出回應，聲稱將對從歐洲進口的葡萄酒展開反補貼調查。而在歐盟內部，有部分國家擔心歐盟此舉會引發與中國的貿易戰，令歐洲慘淡的經濟形式進一步雪上加霜。

單字補給站 熟記後再聽一次，英文聽力大躍進

estimate [`ɛstə‚met] n. 估計，估算
solar panel 太陽能板
manufacturer [‚mænjə`fæktʃərə] n. 製造商
impose [ɪm`poz] v. 徵（稅）
duty [`djutɪ] n. 關稅

resistance [rɪ`zɪstəns] n. 阻力，反對
phase in 逐步採用
tariff [`tærɪf] n. 關稅
subsidy [`sʌbsədɪ] n. 補貼，津貼

▶ 原文、譯文與解析，請見 P.254

NEWS 06 OECD Says Global Economy Rebounds, but Not in Europe

經合組織稱，全球經濟回升，但歐洲步伐滯後

牛刀小試 先聽一遍，貼近真實英語生活圈 🎧 *Track 059*

New government data shows the U.S. economy expanded at a faster clip last year than earlier estimates. And it's likely to perform better in 2013...

有聽沒有懂？就參考看看此篇新聞的背景提示吧

總部位於巴黎的經濟合作與發展組織（OECD）稱，在美國和日本的引領下，2013 年世界發達經濟體的增長前景將更加清晰，全球經濟呈現出逐步復甦的跡象。但是，在嚴重的債務危機和隨之採取的財政緊縮措施的拖累下，歐元區 17 國整體的經濟增長將仍處於落後局面。作為歐元區第二大經濟體的法國，甚至有可能在 2013 年出現零增長。此外，該組織對中國和其他新興經濟體的增長形勢仍持樂觀態度，甚至大膽預測中國經濟如果繼續保持如此快速的增長，最早可能會在 2016 年前後超過美國，成為全球第一大經濟體。

單字補給站 熟記後再聽一次，英文聽力大躍進

clip [klɪp] n.（非正式）（較快的）速度
OECD abbr. 經合組織（Organization for Economic Co-operation and Development）
post [post] v. 取得，達到
annualized [ˋænjʊəl] adj. 按年計算的
quarter [ˋkwɔrtə] n. 季度

release [rɪˋlis] v. 發布，公布
outlook [ˋaʊt͵lʊk] n. 展望，前景
imbalance [ɪmˋbæləns] n. 失衡，失調
optimistic [͵ɑptəˋmɪstɪk] adj. 樂觀的

▶ 原文、譯文與解析，請見 P.256

NEWS
07 Nigerian Gold Miners Seek the Right to Mine
奈及利亞黃金礦工尋求採礦權

牛刀小試 先聽一遍，貼近真實英語生活圈 *Track 060*

Gold mining in this part of northern Nigeria is not glamorous. But these men say it's more dignified than extreme poverty, which used to be the norm around here...

有聽沒有懂？就參考看看此篇新聞的背景提示吧

近年來，隨著金價的不斷上漲，非洲地區無證開採金礦的行為變得越來越普遍。奈及利亞北部金礦資源豐富的扎姆法拉州就是其中之一。當地人民為了擺脫窮困的局面，甚至不惜冒著鉛中毒的危險去開採金礦。

奈及利亞政府稱，當地人非法開採和加工金子的行為已經給環境造成了巨大汙染，截至目前已有數百名兒童和婦女因鉛中毒而死亡，因此政府相關部門已經在著手取締非法金礦，並制定了金礦開採的相關規定。但也有分析人士指出，政府的禁令並不能阻止當地人狂熱的開採行為，因為他們實在太貧窮了。

單字補給站 熟記後再聽一次，英文聽力大躍進

glamorous [ˋglæmərəs] adj.
迷人的，富有魅力的
dignified [ˋdɪgnəˌfaɪd] adj. 有尊嚴的
poverty [ˋpɑvɚtɪ] n. 貧窮
perch [pɝtʃ] v. 坐，棲息
laced with 摻有……的，點綴著……的

booming [ˋbumɪŋ] adj. 興旺的，繁榮的
couple [ˋkʌpl] v. 伴隨，結合
cripple [ˋkrɪpl] v. 嚴重損壞，使傷殘
aggravate [ˋægrəˌvet] v. 加重，使惡化

▶ 原文、譯文與解析，請見 P.258

Burger Makers Fight to Repeal Biofuel Law

漢堡製造商要求廢止生物燃料法

牛刀小試 先聽一遍，貼近真實英語生活圈 🎧 *Track 061*

When you drive up to Wendy's or other fast-food chains in the U.S., you are consuming corn in at least two ways.

The chicken or hamburger in your meal comes from an animal raised on corn...

有聽沒有懂？就參考看看此篇新聞的背景提示吧

如今，隨著國際油價的不斷上漲，再加上能源安全和經濟、環境可持續發展的要求，世界生物燃料發展迅猛。以美國、巴西和歐盟為主的一些國家和地區開始將發展生物燃料作為解決自身能源問題的一個重要途徑。中國在「十二五規劃」中也明確提出要開發利用生物質能等可再生能源。

然而，生物料的開發和生產在幫助解決能源問題的同時，也帶來了其他問題。許多美國快餐連鎖企業擔心生產生物燃料消耗了大量糧食作物，會推高食品價格，給食品企業的發展帶來不利影響，因而他們積極要求美國國會廢除發展生物燃料的能源政策。

單字補給站 熟記後再聽一次，英文聽力大躍進

hamburger [`hæmbɝ·gɚ] n. 漢堡
ethanol [`ɛθə·nol] n. 乙醇
otherwise [`ʌðɚ·waɪz] adv. 不同地，別樣地
gasoline [`gæsə·lin] n. 汽油
repeal [rɪ`pil] v. 廢除，撤銷
franchise [`fræn·tʃaɪz] n. 特許經營權，獲特許經營權的商店

mandate [`mændet] n. 命令，指令
waive [wev] v. 宣布取消
alternative [ɔl`tɝ·nətɪv] n. 可供選擇的事物，替代品
materialize [mə`tɪrɪəl·aɪz] v. 使物質化，實現

▶ 原文、譯文與解析，請見 P.260

NEWS 09 Fed Chief Warns of Economic Headwinds from Budget Stalemate

聯準會主席警告預算僵局將導致經濟下滑

牛刀小試 先聽一遍,貼近真實英語生活圈 🎧 *Track 062*

With no progress in Washington to avoid looming spending cuts, Federal Reserve Chairman Ben Bernanke warned lawmakers that inaction would sharply slow U.S. economic growth...

有聽沒有懂?就參考看看此篇新聞的背景提示吧

「財政懸崖」一詞由聯準會主席伯南克於 2012 年首次提出,用以形容在 2013 年 1 月 1 日這一「時間點」上,自動削減赤字機制的啟動,會使政府財政開支被迫突然減少,使支出曲線看上去狀如懸崖,故得名「財政懸崖」。如果美國政府墜入「財政懸崖」,美國經濟將會大受影響。

伯南克警告,如果國會兩黨不能撇開政見分歧和相互指責,盡快就削減財政赤字達成一項新的協議,隨後自動生效的高達 850 億美元的政府開支減少將會給本來就復甦緩慢的美國經濟帶來災難性的打擊。

單字補給站 熟記後再聽一次,英文聽力大躍進

looming [`lumɪŋ] adj. 隱約可見的,正在逼近的
Federal Reserve (美)聯邦準備理事會
stake [stek] n. 風險,利害關係
automatic [ˌɔtə`mætɪk] adj. 自動的
slash [slæʃ] v. 大幅削減,猛砍
security [sɪ`kjʊrətɪ] n. 安全

sequester [sɪ`kwɛstɚ] n.(美)自動減赤計劃
arbitrary [`ɑrbəˌtrɛrɪ] adj. 主觀的,獨斷的
grandstand [`grændˌstænd] v. 嘩眾取寵
discretion [dɪ`skrɛʃən] n. 酌情處理權,決斷權
squarely [`skwɛrlɪ] adv. 直接地

▶ 原文、譯文與解析,請見 P.262

IMF Lowers Its Global Economic Prospects

國際貨幣基金組織下調全球經濟增長預期

牛刀小試 先聽一遍，貼近真實英語生活圈 🎧 *Track 063*

> **The world's economy is not growing as fast as many had hoped. The IMF** *revised* **its global growth** *forecast* **in 2013 to just a little over 3 percent — down from earlier** *projections* **of 3.3 percent...**

有聽沒有懂？就參考看看此篇新聞的背景提示吧

在歐債危機、美債危機以及新興經濟體增速放緩的情況下，國際貨幣基金組織（IMF）在最新發布的全球經濟展望報告中下調了 2013 年全球經濟增長預期。其中，一直以來扮演世界經濟引擎的金磚國家經濟增速的放緩給全球經濟帶來了較大影響。美國方面，儘管經濟出現了復甦跡象，但受減赤計劃的影響，經濟增長動力仍然不夠強勁。此外，IMF 還稱如果世界主要經濟體能繼續實施有力政策刺激經濟增長，同時減少國內長期財政赤字，那麼世界經濟將有望在 2014 年好轉。

單字補給站 熟記後再聽一次，英文聽力大躍進

revise [rɪ`vaɪz] v. 修改，修正
forecast [`for͵kæst] n. 預測
projection [prə`dʒɛkʃən] n. 估計，預測
decline [dɪ`klaɪn] v. 下降，衰退
austerity [ɔ`stɛrətɪ] n. 緊縮

slump [slʌmp] n. 大幅卜降，衰退
vicious circle　惡性循環
repercussion [͵rɪpɚ`kʌʃən] n.
（不受歡迎的）後果，影響
steady [`stɛdɪ] adj. 穩定的

▶ 原文、譯文與解析，請見 P.264

089

NEWS 11

Robots Help US Manufacturers Compete with China

機器人助美國製造業與中國抗衡

牛刀小試 先聽一遍，貼近真實英語生活圈 🎧 *Track 064*

In what may be the beginning of a new trend in American manufacturing, Sunit Saxena recently moved his production operation from China to the United States...

有聽沒有懂？就參考看看此篇新聞的背景提示吧

如今，隨著中國勞動力成本的上升和人民幣升值的趨勢，中國製造業與美國相比優勢已不再那麼明顯，一些美國企業開始將加工基地由中國轉移回美國，從而給美國民眾創造了更多的就業機會。同時，隨著自動化技

術在生產過程中的應用和普及，越來越多機械性、重複性的工作開始由機器人代勞，提高了生產效率的同時，也進一步增強了產品在加工成本上的競爭優勢。面對這種趨勢，有人擔心自動化技術的廣泛應用會帶來大量失業問題，但多數美國製造業者則認為先進的技術會為工人們創造更多較高技術含量的工作機會。

單字補給站 熟記後再聽一次，英文聽力大躍進

manufacturing [͵mænjə`fæktʃərɪŋ] n. 製造業

operation [ɑpə`reʃən] n. 經營，活動

digital [`dɪdʒɪtl] adj. 數字的

productivity [͵prodʌk`tɪvətɪ] n. 生產能力

automation [͵ɔtə`meʃən] n. 自動化

identical [aɪ`dɛntɪkl] adj. 相同的

repetitive [rɪ`pɛtɪtɪv] adj. 重複性的

sensor [`sɛnsə-] n. 傳感器

dock [dɑk] n. 碼頭

▶ 原文、譯文與解析，請見 P.266

NEWS 12 Russia Re-Industrializes as Energy Boom Fades

能源熱消退後，俄羅斯開始再工業化進程

牛刀小試 先聽一遍，貼近真實英語生活圈 🎧 *Track 065*

*Post-Soviet Russia **is often seen as an industrial** rust **belt. But here, outside St. Petersburg, American car maker GM is investing to** triple **its production capacity.***

有聽沒有懂？就參考看看此篇新聞的背景提示吧

　　過去十年來，俄羅斯一直是世界上最大的能源出口國，石油和天然氣出口甚至占了其出口總額的 70%。但如今，隨著能源繁榮局面的逐步衰退以及油、氣出口收入的不斷下降，相關經濟學家稱俄羅斯正在開始再工業化進程。

　　而隨著這一進程的不斷推進，俄羅斯經濟在歐洲經濟總體呈現下滑的趨勢下卻出現了增長，這其中很大程度上是得益於國民消費熱情的上漲。俄羅斯總理梅德韋傑夫宣稱，要在 2018 年之前，將非能源出口占出口總收入的比重提高到 50%。

單字補給站 熟記後再聽一次，英文聽力大躍進

post-Soviet Russia 蘇聯解體後的俄羅斯
rust [rʌst] n. 鐵銹
triple [`trɪpl] v. 使成三倍
peak [pik] adj. 最高的
signal [`sɪgnl] v. 標誌
crowd out 排擠，擠出

diminish [də`mɪnɪʃ] v. 減少，降低
boom [bum] n. 繁榮，迅速發展
embark on 開啟，開始
the Kremlin 克里姆林宮（代指俄羅斯政府）

▶ 原文、譯文與解析，請見 P.268

NEWS 13
US Budget Impasse Could Affect Air Travel
美國預算僵局可能影響航空旅行

牛刀小試 先聽一遍，貼近真實英語生活圈 🎧 *Track 066*

Flying in and out of U.S. airports could become a challenge, with delays on the ground and in the air.

The disruptions could begin when automatic government spending cuts hit the nation's aviation sector in April...

有聽沒有懂？就參考看看此篇新聞的背景提示吧

在兩黨的相互指責聲中，美國政府高達 850 億美元的全面減支計劃開始自動生效。聯邦政府幾乎所有部門都將受到影響，自 2013 年 4 月 1 日開始，許多政府雇員被迫接受無薪休假政策。有分析人士稱，此舉將會給美國復甦緩慢的經濟當頭一棒。此外，預算削

減很可能會給美國的航空運輸和航天工業帶來不利影響。一些業內人士就聲稱投資減少會迫使美國航空業選擇裁員，從而進一步加劇航班延誤情況，長期下來會降低美國商業和投資機會的吸引力。此外，預算削減對於美國航空和國防工業的影響也不容小覷。

單字補給站 熟記後再聽一次，英文聽力大躍進

challenge [ˋtʃælɪndʒ] n. 挑戰
disruption [dɪsˋrʌpʃən] n. 中斷，混亂
aviation [͵evɪˋeʃən] n. 航空
clear [klɪr] v. 清（關），通（關）
checkpoint [ˋtʃɛk͵pɔɪnt] n. 關卡，檢查點

air traffic controller 空中交通指揮員
pilot [ˋpaɪlət] n. 飛行員
aerospace [ˋɛrə͵spes] n. 航空宇宙
compromise [ˋkɑmprə͵maɪz] v. 損害，連累

▶ 原文、譯文與解析，請見 P.270

NEWS 14
War in Syria Hurts Lebanese Tourism Sector

敘利亞戰爭影響黎巴嫩旅遊業

牛刀小試 先聽一遍，貼近真實英語生活圈 🎧 *Track 067*

The nickname of this Lebanese mountain town Aley is 'Arous el Masayif' — 'the bride of touristic places.' But the picturesque village outside Beirut that once attracted many Saudis and other Gulf nationals for its quaint atmosphere and cool evening breezes...

有聽沒有懂？就參考看看此篇新聞的背景提示吧

敘利亞內戰自 2011 年爆發以來，逐步顯現為周邊國家經濟帶來的影響。其中，黎巴嫩旅遊業就遭受重創。

黎巴嫩是一個嚴重依賴旅遊業的國家，旅遊收入占到了國民生產總值的 25%。憑藉著風光旖旎的海灘和眾多文明古跡，黎巴嫩每年都能吸引許多來自波斯灣國家的遊客。但如今，在安全局勢下降和大量敘利亞難民湧入的影響下，前往黎巴嫩的旅遊人數大幅下降，許多人出於安全考慮或其他政治原因選擇前往其他國家和地區。如今，敘利亞旅遊部已經制定了一些優惠政策來招攬來自波斯灣以外國家的遊客。

單字補給站 熟記後再聽一次，英文聽力大躍進

nickname [`nɪk͵nem] n. 綽號，暱稱
Lebanese [͵lɛbə`niz] adj. 黎巴嫩的
picturesque [͵pɪktʃə`rɛsk] adj. 風景如畫的
quaint [kwent] adj. 古色古香的，奇特的
breeze [briz] n. 微風
abandoned [ə`bændənd] adj. 廢棄的

stunning [`stʌnɪŋ] adj. 絕美的，迷人的
ruin [`rʊɪn] n. 廢墟，遺跡
lean on 依賴於
Jordanian [dʒɔr`denɪən] n. 約旦人
entice [ɪn`taɪs] v. 吸引，誘惑
diversify [daɪ`vɝsə͵faɪ] v. 使多樣化

▶ 原文、譯文與解析，請見 P.272

Unit 7 社會百態

聽力技巧 高手接招

長句理解

　　對於英語學習者而言，長句、難句的理解是聽力過程中的一大難點。歸結起來，長句、難句造成理解障礙的原因有：（1）中英文句法結構上存在語序差異，聽者常將母語思維帶入英語的理解中。（2）有些句子因為講話人語速快、停頓少而容易使聽者畏懼，致使其無法在短時間內準確處理句子所傳達的信息。（3）聽者缺乏必要的句法知識，不知道如何分析處理英文中的複合長句，聽力過程中往往顧此失彼。加強對長句、難句的分析訓練，能有效提高學習者的聽力理解程度。

　　學習者可以通過書面或口頭形式先反覆練習英文簡單句的五大核心結構：名詞＋謂語；主詞＋謂語＋受詞；主詞＋系動詞＋表語；主詞＋謂語＋間接受詞＋直接受詞；主詞＋謂語＋受詞＋受詞補語。其次，要注意熟悉和總結常見複合句的句法結構特徵：如主從複合句（子句包括形容詞子句、副詞子句、同位語子句、名詞子句、受詞子句等）和並列複合句。經過有意識的訓練，學習者再碰到長句和難句時，可以更迅速地理清句子的結構，抓住句子的主幹，更好地理解其意。

　　在聽本單元的每篇新聞時，學習者可以將其中自己感到理解比較吃力或者反應比較遲鈍的 1—3 個句子抄在聽力筆記本上，進行句法分析。

NEWS
01 Africa's First Ladies Promote Women's, Children's Health

非洲五國第一夫人聯合推廣婦女兒童健康

牛刀小試 先聽一遍,貼近真實英語生活圈 🎧 *Track 068*

The risk of death from childbirth is still very real for women in countries throughout Africa. Whether their children will reach adulthood is another worry...

有聽沒有懂?就參考看看此篇新聞的背景提示吧

　　如今,儘管世界各國改善婦女和兒童健康狀況的努力已經初見成效,但總體而言,距離實現聯合國千年發展目標還有很長的路要走。世界衛生組織總幹事陳馮富珍日前表示,在當前全球經濟普遍不景氣的背景下,她仍希望已開發國家能夠繼續擴大對發展中國家婦女和兒童健康事業的支持。

　　「非洲第一夫人健康高峰會」就是一個致力於改善非洲婦女和兒童醫療衛生狀況的會議。如今,這一高峰會的參與者已經不僅限於非洲國家的第一夫人,美國、英國以及其他國家的第一夫人和社會名流也開始積極參與其中,共同為改善婦女和兒童健康狀況出謀劃策。

單字補給站 熟記後再聽一次,英文聽力大躍進

childbirth [`tʃaɪld͵bɝθ] n. 分娩
adulthood [ə`dʌlthʊd] n. 成年(期)
Guinea [`gɪnɪ] n. 幾內亞(西非國家)
Mozambique [͵mozəm`bik] n. 莫三比克(非洲東南部國家)
Niger [`naɪdʒɚ] n. 尼日(非洲中西部國家)
Namibia [nə`mɪbɪə] n. 納米比亞(非洲南部國家)

voice [vɔɪs] v. 表達,吐露
maternal [mə`tɝnl] adj. 母親的,產婦的
sanitation [͵sænə`teʃən] n. 公共衛生,環境衛生
solidarity [͵sɑlə`dærətɪ] n. 團結一致
eliminate [ɪ`lɪmə͵net] v. 根除,消除

▶ 原文、譯文與解析,請見 P.276

NEWS 02 Around the World, 2012 Holiday Shopping is Subdued

2012 全球節日購物熱潮受抑

牛刀小試 先聽一遍，貼近真實英語生活圈 🎧 *Track 069*

At U.S. shopping centers, parking lots were full — as thousands of last-minute shoppers descended into crowded malls...

有聽沒有懂？就參考看看此篇新聞的背景提示吧

一般來講，節慶假日都是各大商場和商家大展身手的時機，各式各樣的促銷廣告充斥於每個角落，商場和店鋪前通常也都人頭攢動，熱鬧非凡。然而在全球多數商家眼中，2012年的生意卻不是那麼好做。相關預測顯示，與2011年相比，2012年歐美消費者的平均消費支出都下降了不少。受歐債危機、美債危機和隨之採取的財政緊縮措施影響，多數消費者的信心指數都有所下降。面對慘淡的經濟形勢，大多數人的消費選擇也更加審慎，從而導致了2012年假日消費的低迷局面。

單字補給站 熟記後再聽一次，英文聽力大躍進

parking lot 停車場
descend [dɪ`sɛnd] v. 突然來到
mask [mæsk] v. 掩蓋，掩飾
decoration [ˌdɛkə`reʃən] n. 裝飾
austerity [ɔ`stɛrətɪ] n. 緊縮

tempt [tɛmpt] v. 引誘，誘惑
brisk [brɪsk] adj. 活躍的，興隆的
recession [rɪ`sɛʃən] n. 衰退，經濟不景氣
bend [bɛnd] v. 讓步，屈服

▶ 原文、譯文與解析，請見 P.278

NEWS 03
Civil Rights Pioneer Rosa Parks Honored with Capitol Statue
民權先驅羅莎・帕克斯榮獲國會大廈雕像

牛刀小試 先聽一遍，貼近真實英語生活圈 Track 070

It's a lasting tribute to Rosa Parks — known as "the mother of the U.S. civil rights movement."...

有聽沒有懂？就參考看看此篇新聞的背景提示吧

　　羅莎・帕克斯是一位美國黑人民權運動主義者，後來被譽為「美國民權運動之母」。事情追溯到 1955 年，當時阿拉巴馬州的蒙哥馬利市在巴士、餐館其他公共場所實行種族隔離政策。身為黑人的帕克斯登上公車後，因拒絕給一名白人讓座，拒絕坐到巴士後面去而被捕。這一事件激起了黑人的強烈不滿，從而引發了震驚世界的「蒙哥馬利巴士抵制運動」。運動最終迫使美國最高法院廢除了公車上的種族隔離政策。

　　羅莎・帕克斯於 2005 年去世。美國政府為了紀念她為民權運動所做出的貢獻，在國會大廈的雕像廳首次為一名非裔女性塑造了一座全身雕像。

單字補給站 熟記後再聽一次，英文聽力大躍進

tribute [`trɪbjut] n. 悼念，致敬
dignitary [`dɪgnə͵tɛrɪ] n. 顯貴人物，權貴
unveil [ʌn`vel] v. 為……揭幕
sculpture [`skʌlptʃɚ] n. 雕像，雕塑作品
honor [`ɑnɚ] v. 向……表示敬意

segregated [`sɛgrɪ͵getɪd] adj.
（種族）隔離的
statue [`stætʃu] n. 雕塑，塑像
boycott [`bɔɪ͵kɑt] n. 聯合抵制
spawn [spɔn] v. 使大量出現

▶ 原文、譯文與解析，請見 P.280

NEWS
04 Families Still Rebuilding 5 Years After Massive China Quake

汶川大地震五年後家庭仍在重建

牛刀小試 先聽一遍，貼近真實英語生活圈 🎧 *Track 071*

Ma Tang was just 12 years old when the Wenchuan earthquake robbed him of his father. He is 17 now, his mother has remarried and his young step-sister keeps him busy...

有聽沒有懂？就參考看看此篇新聞的背景提示吧

2008 年 5 月 12 日，中國四川省南部的汶川縣發生芮氏規模 8.0 的特大地震，造成大量人員傷亡，眾多建築物倒塌，很多家庭不得不背井離鄉，永遠離開自己的家園。如今，「5·12」大地震——這場當今世界破壞性最強的自然災難之一——已經過去了五年時間，人們的創傷漸漸撫平，很多家庭的生活也重新走上了正軌。但是這並不意味著災後重建工作已經完成，許多深受地震影響的家庭如今仍在為過上和震前一樣安靜、祥和的生活而努力著。震後的新一代年輕人也在努力追尋自己的夢想。

單字補給站 熟記後再聽一次，英文聽力大躍進

rob [rɑb] v. 搶走，剝奪
tremendous [trɪ`mɛndəs] adj. 巨大的，驚人的
quake [kwek] n. 震動，地震
collapse [kə`læps] v. 倒塌

steel [stil] n. 鋼鐵
cement [sɪ`mɛnt] n. 水泥
elementary school 小學
keenly [`kinlɪ] adv. 敏銳地，深切地

▶ 原文、譯文與解析，請見 P.282

NEWS 05 Fiscal Cliff Could Have Greatest Impact on Poor, Unemployed

窮人和失業者可能成為財政懸崖的最大受害者

牛刀小試 先聽一遍,貼近真實英語生活圈 🎧 *Track 072*

> *At this Los Angeles center,* Catholic charities *provides food and other* assistance *to the poor, unemployed, and homeless.* Recipient, *John Wood says he doesn't know the details of the talks in Washington, but he says that an* eventual *agreement is important...*

有聽沒有懂?就參考看看此篇新聞的背景提示吧

　　2012 年 12 月 31 日晚上,美國眾議院沒有趕在截止日前就參議院提出的預算法案進行投票,而是選擇推遲投票日期。此舉讓美國民眾開始擔心:如果兩黨不能拋開政見分歧,盡快就預算法案達成一致,美國將會跌落「財政懸崖」,自動生效的減支和增稅計

劃將會給美國經濟帶來沈重打擊。相關分析人士稱,如果減支計劃也波及聯邦政府的救助計劃,那麼窮人和失業者將面臨巨大的打擊。但是也有部分美國民眾對此持樂觀態度,相信政府會竭盡全力盡快採取措施,將預算法案對民眾的不利影響降到最低。

單字補給站 熟記後再聽一次,英文聽力大躍進

Catholic charity 天主教慈善組織
assistance [ə`sɪstəns] n. 援助,幫助
recipient [rɪ`sɪpɪənt] n. 接受者,領受者
eventual [ɪ`vɛntʃʊəl] adj. 最後的,最終的
downturn [`daʊntɝn] n. (經濟等的)下行,回落

put aside 把……放到一邊
deadline [`dɛd͵laɪn] n. 最後期限
soften [`sɔfn] v. 緩和,減輕

▶ 原文、譯文與解析,請見 P.284

NEWS 06 Gay NBA Player Breaks Athletic Barrier

美職籃同性戀球員打破運動員心理障礙

牛刀小試 先聽一遍，貼近真實英語生活圈 🎧 *Track 073*

Jason Collins has spent 12 years in the NBA. But his playing career has never drawn as much public attention as his recent revelation. In an interview with ABC News...

有聽沒有懂？就參考看看此篇新聞的背景提示吧

「同性戀」在美國一直是個熱門話題，就算在四年一次的總統大選中也不例外。以自由著稱的美國人對待同性戀的態度可以說比許多國家都要開明，麻薩諸塞州、康乃狄克州等都準許同性戀者合法結婚。但是，多數同性戀者仍會受到很多非議和歧視。最近，美職籃華盛頓巫師隊中鋒賈森·科林斯就大膽「出櫃」，在一次採訪中公開承認自己是同性戀，成為北美職業體育聯賽中第一位公開承認自己是同性戀者的現役運動員。科林斯的這一舉動在美國引起了極大關注，包括歐巴馬總統在內的多數人都對他表示支持。

單字補給站 熟記後再聽一次，英文聽力大躍進

revelation [ˌrɛvl`eʃən] n.（秘密或真相的）揭露

sexual orientation 性取向

sexuality [ˌsɛkʃʊ`ælətɪ] n. 性偏好

convince [kən`vɪns] v. 說服

come out 出櫃，公開同性戀身份

outpouring [`aʊt͵porɪŋ] n.（源源不斷的）湧出，傾吐

defining [dɪ`faɪnɪŋ] adj. 起決定性作用的

locker room （尤指運動員的）更衣室

▶ 原文、譯文與解析，請見 P.286

NEWS 07 Nigerians Demand Return of Ancient Art
奈及利亞要求返還其古代藝術品

牛刀小試 先聽一遍，貼近真實英語生活圈 🎧 *Track 074*

What was once the ancient Kingdom of Benin is now the heart of the** Nigerian **art world, with statues** adorning **the streets and an art museum in the Benin City town square...

有聽沒有懂？就參考看看此篇新聞的背景提示吧

如今，隨著世界各國文物古蹟保護意識不斷增強，越來越多曾經遭受過侵略的國家開始要求以前的殖民國返還屬於自己的藝術品，奈及利亞就是其中之一。

位於奈及利亞西南部森林地帶的貝寧王國始建於公元 14 世紀，歷史上曾以製作精美的牙雕、木刻以及銅像而聞名於世。後來貝寧王國被英國殖民者占領，1879 年被併入英屬奈及利亞，大量的珍貴藝術品也隨之流往海外。然而，想要追回那些屬於自己的藝術品並不是那麼容易，奈及利亞許多文物專家就表示，除了民間團體的努力之外，文物追回工作還需要來自政府和相關國際組織的更多支持。

單字補給站 熟記後再聽一次，英文聽力大躍進

Nigerian [naɪ`dʒɪrɪən] adj. 奈及利亞的
adorn [ə`dɔrn] v. 裝飾
colonial [kə`lonjəl] n. 殖民者
curator [kjʊ`retɚ] n. 館長
punitive [`pjunɪtɪv] adj. 懲罰性的
expedition [ˌɛkspɪ`dɪʃən] n. 遠征

retaliation [rɪˌtælɪ`eʃən] n. 報複，報仇
aggression [ə`grɛʃən] n. 侵略，進攻
sack [sæk] v. 洗劫，劫掠
depose [dɪ`poz] v. 廢黜，罷免
repatriate [ri`petrɪˌet] v. 遣返，返還

▶ 原文、譯文與解析，請見 P.288

NEWS 08
Obama Calls for Action on Gun Violence
歐巴馬呼籲採取行動遏制槍支暴力

先聽一遍，貼近真實英語生活圈 🎧 *Track 075*

Gunfire erupted on December 14 at Sandy Hook Elementary School, where a heavily armed young man shot and killed 20 children and several school administrators. The entire nation recoiled in grief and horror...

有聽沒有懂？就參考看看此篇新聞的背景提示吧

2012 年 12 月 14 日美國桑迪胡克小學槍擊案發生之後，美國總統歐巴馬在每周例行電視談話中說：「政府正採取一系列措施，強化購槍背景調查和管理，幫助有意願的學校雇用更多安保人員，要求相關部門研究減少槍支暴力的最佳途徑。」

2013 年 1 月 16 日，歐巴馬就遏制槍支暴力發布對策，包括 23 項行政命令和交由國會討論的槍枝管制提案。但國會共和黨人對提案表示反對，認為這會侵害美國憲法第二修正案賦予民眾的持槍權。1 月 19 日，歐巴馬再次呼籲國會為遏制槍支暴力採取行動，並且重申他無意挑戰憲法第二修正案賦予民眾持有武器的權利。

單字補給站 熟記後再聽一次，英文聽力大躍進

erupt [ɪ`rʌpt] v. 突然發生
recoil [rɪ`kɔɪl] v. 畏縮，蜷縮
grief [grif] n. 悲痛
mourn [morn] v. 哀悼，悼念
spectrum [`spɛktrəm] n. 範圍，系列
advocate [`ædvəkɪt] n. 提倡者，擁護者

lethal [`liθəl] adj. 致命的
assault [ə`sɔlt] n. 武力攻擊
ammunition clip 彈夾
stun [stʌn] v. 使震驚
outrage [`aʊt,redʒ] n. 義憤，憤慨

▶ 原文、譯文與解析，請見 P.290

NEWS 09 Report: Up to Half of World Food Production is Wasted

報告稱，全世界多達半數的糧食遭浪費

牛刀小試 先聽一遍，貼近真實英語生活圈 🎧 Track 076

Every year the world produces around four billion tons of food. And between a third and half of it goes to waste, according to the report from the British Institution of Mechanical Engineers...

有聽沒有懂？就參考看看此篇新聞的背景提示吧

　　近年來，乾旱、洪水等極端氣候事件發生的頻率越來越高，包括美國和東南亞在內的主要糧食出口國家和地區都出現了糧食減產現象。越來越多的人開始擔心在全球人口持續增長的情況下，糧食減產會使世界各國，尤其是非洲國家的饑餓狀況更加嚴重。但是英國機械工程師學會新發布的一項報告卻顯示，全世界每年浪費掉的糧食竟占了糧食年產量的一半，其中糧食收穫、運輸、儲存和銷售環節的浪費量大得驚人。為了滿足不斷上漲的人口的糧食需要，世界各國必須開始行動減少糧食浪費行為的發生。

單字補給站 熟記後再聽一次，英文聽力大躍進

harvest [`hɑrvɪst] v. 收割，收穫
peak [pik] v. 達到高峰
efficient [ɪ`fɪʃənt] adj. 高效的，有效率的
wastage [`westɪdʒ] n. 浪費，損耗
sell-by date 保質期，最遲銷售日期
highlight [`haɪ͵laɪt] v. 強調，突出

▶ 原文、譯文與解析，請見 P.292

NEWS 10 Supporters of Gay Marriage Await US Court Rulings

美國同性婚姻支持者等待最高法院裁決

牛刀小試 先聽一遍，貼近真實英語生活圈 🎧 *Track 077*

Supporters of same-sex marriage rallied this week in Los Angeles and other American cities, urging the Supreme Court to overturn California's 2008 gay marriage ban, called Proposition 8, and the Defense of Marriage Act...

有聽沒有懂？就參考看看此篇新聞的背景提示吧

加利福尼亞州最高法院於 2008 年 5 月作出正式裁決，允許同性婚姻。隨後，反對者立即提出「8 號提案」，要求修改加州憲法，明確規定婚姻是一男一女的合法結合。同年 11 月份，「8 號提案」在加州公投中以 52% 的支持率獲得通過。從那之後，同性戀支持者就一直在試圖推翻「8 號提案」，最終將官司打到華盛頓最高法院，要求給予同性戀者合法的婚姻地位和權利。如今，數百名同性戀支持者聚集在最高法院門外，等待著法官的最終裁決。他們多數人都很樂觀，認為加利福尼亞州會給予同性戀者同等的婚姻權利。

單字補給站 熟記後再聽一次，英文聽力人人躍進

rally [`rælɪ] v. 聚集，集合
the Supreme Court 最高法院
overturn [ˌovə`tɝn] v. 推翻
proposition [ˌprɑpə`zɪʃən] n. 提案，議案
federal law 聯邦法律

gay [ge] adj. （尤指男）同性戀的
heterosexual [ˌhɛtərə`sɛkʃʊəl] adj. 異性戀的
favorable [`fevərəbl] adj. 肯定的，有利的

▶ 原文、譯文與解析，請見 P.294

NEWS 11 Abused Chinese Women Push for Domestic Violence Law

遭遇家暴的中國女性將推動相關法律的制定

牛刀小試 先聽一遍，貼近真實英語生活圈 🎧 *Track 078*

This woman, Kim Lee put a face on the otherwise anonymous stories of domestic violence in China, when she posted photos of her bruises online...

有聽沒有懂？就參考看看此篇新聞的背景提示吧

　　目前，家庭暴力已成為一個全球性社會問題，這一問題在中國也由來已久。據婦女權益保護組織估計，每四名中國女性中就有一名曾遭受過配偶肉體上的虐待，而且這一數字實際上可能會更高。因為中國目前尚無針對家庭暴力的專門立法，相關部門在處理此類事件時也面臨很多困難。

　　最近，中國著名英語教育家、瘋狂英語創始人李陽就因為對美籍妻子李金的家暴行為被輿論推到了浪尖上。李金在微博裡公布的一組照片顯示，李陽的家暴確實已經達到「瘋狂」的地步。不過從另一方面來說，此次公眾人物家暴事件也進一步推動了中國反家庭暴力的立法進程。

單字補給站 熟記後再聽一次，英文聽力大躍進

anonymous [ə`nɑnəməs] adj. 無名的，匿名的
bruise [bruz] n. 瘀傷，青腫
chronic [`krɑnɪk] adj. 慢性的，長期的
celebrity [sɪ`lɛbrətɪ] n. 名人，名流
abuse [ə`bjus] v. 虐待

spouse [spaʊz] n. 配偶
episode [`ɛpə͵sod] n. 插曲，片段
divorce [də`vors] n. 離婚
landmark [`lænd͵mɑrk] n. 里程碑
draft [dræft] n. 草稿，草案

▶ 原文、譯文與解析，請見 P.296

US Adds 171K Jobs; Unemployment Rate Rises to 7.9%

美國增加 171,000 個職缺，失業率反升至 7.9%

牛刀小試 先聽一遍，貼近真實英語生活圈 🎧 Track 079

The last major economic report before Americans head to the polls shows hiring accelerated in October. That's welcome news for more than 12 million unemployed Americans...

有聽沒有懂？就參考看看此篇新聞的背景提示吧

2012 年美國總統大選在即，共和黨候選人米特·羅姆尼試圖用當前美國居高不下的失業率來打擊競爭對手，以贏得更多選民的支持。數據方面，儘管 10 月份美國各大公司雇用的員工人數大幅上漲，增加 171,000 人，勞工部統計的新增工作職缺數量也比上兩個月份增加不少，但是失業率卻仍逆勢上漲了 0.1 個百分點，達到 7.9%，與歐巴馬總統上任之初承諾的低於 5.2% 的目標相去甚遠。很顯然，在當前疲軟的經濟形勢下，歐巴馬總統想要獲得連任面臨的困難相當大，因為自二戰以來，還沒有一位總統在失業率高於 7.4% 的情況下獲得過連任。

單字補給站 熟記後再聽一次，英文聽力大躍進

accelerate [æk`sɛləˌret] v. 加速，增長
private sector 私營部門，私營行業
revision [rɪ`vɪʒən] n. 修改，修正
inch [ɪntʃ] v. 緩慢移動
heal [hil] v. 恢復，康復
downturn [`daʊntˌɜ-n] n. 回落，下行

sway [swe] v. 使搖擺，使改變觀點
lingering [`lɪŋgərɪŋ] adj. 徘徊不前的，逗留不去的
paycheck [`peˌtʃɛk] n. 薪水
bounce [baʊns] n. 反彈

▶ 原文、譯文與解析，請見 P.298

題目篇

Unit 8 體育娛樂

聽力技巧 高手接招

做筆記

俗話說，好記性不如爛筆頭。在聽力練習中，適當地做筆記有助於學習者更好地理解和記憶聽力教材。做筆記不僅可以記下稍縱即逝的訊息，彌補短暫記憶的不足，還能增強聽者對聽力教材的加工處理能力。

那麼學習者在聽的過程中什麼時候開始做筆記以及怎麼做筆記才能使筆記更好地幫助聽力理解呢？

學習者可以在聽到一個自己可以分析處理的信息單元時開始記錄。記錄的內容是關鍵詞以及容易遺忘的訊息（比如數字、組織機構、名稱等）。除此之外，聽者應該在筆記上記錄下不同訊息單元間的邏輯關系（因果、轉折、並列、遞進等）。做筆記時，可以根據個人喜好和習慣，使用英文或者中文或者兩種語言混搭使用。最好能分段做筆記，每聽完一個大的訊息後，另起一行進行記錄。一開始嘗試做聽力筆記時，如果覺得比較困難，可以先看著聽力教材文本來規劃自己的筆記，之後再聽音檔來做筆記，隨後複述一遍，以確保真正理解了所聽到的內容。反覆練習做筆記的過程中，學習者可以形成一套具有個人風格的、系統的筆記符號。

本書每一個單元的新聞都是非常適合練習做筆記的素材。學習者可以根據個人喜好，從自己比較感興趣的某個主題單元，比如「體育娛樂」篇開始進行練習。

NEWS 01 Gay Documentary Makes Inroads in Turkey

同性戀紀錄片成功進入土耳其

牛刀小試 先聽一遍，貼近真實英語生活圈 🎧 *Track 080*

The Gala Night in Istanbul of the documentary My Child drew a packed audience. The film tells the story of Listag, a parent's support group of lesbian, gay, bisexual and transgender children, or LGBT...

有聽沒有懂？就參考看看此篇新聞的背景提示吧

　　儘管同性戀在土耳其是合法的，但在保守思想占主導的伊斯蘭社會裡，同性戀者仍面臨很多非議，仇視性犯罪時有發生，而且犯罪者往往是和他們比較親近的家人和朋友。最近，詹·詹丹導演拍攝的一部同性戀紀錄片《我的孩子》卻向人們講述了一個完全不同的故事。影片記錄了一個為男同性戀、女同性戀、雙性戀和變性兒童的父母提供支持的組織的故事，講述了它幫助家長接受孩子的性取向以及挑戰社會偏見的整個過程。該紀錄片一經上映就在土耳其引起強烈反響，受到了媒體的廣泛關注。不僅如此，這部紀錄片還走出國門，在鄰國亞美尼亞和巴勒斯坦上映。

單字補給站 熟記後再聽一次，英文聽力大躍進

gala [`gelə] n. 歡慶，歡聚
documentary [ˌdɑkjə`mɛntərɪ] n. 紀錄片
bisexual [`baɪ`sɛkʃʊəl] n. 雙性戀者
transgender adj. 跨性別的，變性的
come to terms with 與……達成妥協，接受

prejudice [`prɛdʒədɪs] n. 偏見
accustomed [ə`kʌstəmd] adj. 習慣的
screening [`skrinɪŋ] n. 放映
Armenia [ɑr`minɪə] n. 亞美尼亞（歐洲東南部國家）

▶ 原文、譯文與解析，請見 P.302

NEWS
02
Hollywood Celebrates Holidays with Great Films

好萊塢用精彩影片歡慶節日的到來

牛刀小試 先聽一遍，貼近真實英語生活圈 🎧 *Track 081*

Joe Wright's Anna Karenina, based on the Tolstoy novel, is a quintessential holiday production. It offers rich costumes, and enchanting music, and stellar actors...

有聽沒有懂？就參考看看此篇新聞的背景提示吧

聖誕節假期通常是好萊塢大片的黃金檔期，以至於每逢假日來臨之時，許多觀眾們期盼已久的影片會陸續上映，這麼做一方面是要贏得更多的票房收入，另一方面也是在為奧斯卡獎項展開角逐。2012 年的聖誕節假期，好萊塢就為影迷們準備了一場別開生面的盛宴，既有極富古典色彩的《安娜·卡列尼娜》和音樂劇《悲慘世界》，也有充滿魔幻和傳奇色彩的《哈比人》。此外，著名奧斯卡獲獎導演李安也再次為觀眾帶來自己的最新力作《少年 PI 的奇幻漂流》。

單字補給站 熟記後再聽一次，英文聽力大躍進

quintessential [ˌkwɪntɪˋsɛnʃəl] adj. 典型的
enchanting [ɪnˋtʃæntɪŋ] adj.
迷人的，令人陶醉的
stellar [ˋstɛlɚ] adj. 一流的，明星雲集的
aristocracy [ˌærəsˋtɑkrəsɪ] n. 貴族
stage [stedʒ] v.（在舞臺上）展現
lavish [ˋlævɪʃ] adj. 奢華的，豐富的

claustrophobic [ˌklɔstrəˋfobɪk] adj.
（地方）引發幽閉恐怖的，（人）患幽閉恐怖癥的
upbeat [ˋʌpˌbit] adj. 樂觀向上的
suspension [səˋspɛnʃən] n. 暫停，中止
cinematography [ˌsɪnəməˋtɑgrəfɪ] n.
電影製片術
prequel [ˋprikwl] n.（故事或影片的）前篇，前傳

▶ 原文、譯文與解析，請見 P.304

NEWS 03

N. Korean Film Screened at S. Korean Festival

北韓電影於南韓電影節上映

牛刀小試 先聽一遍，貼近真實英語生活圈 🎧 *Track 082*

The Busan International Film Festival is Asia's largest and features movies from across the continent and beyond. This year that included a film from North Korea...

有聽沒有懂？就參考看看此篇新聞的背景提示吧

　　韓國釜山國際電影節於每年 10 月份在港口城市釜山舉行。它如今不僅已發展成為亞洲最重要的電影節之一，而且在國際上的影響力也越來越大。每年 10 月份，這場亞洲頂級電影盛會都會吸引來自亞洲以及世界其他地區的眾多電影人和影迷朋友前往參加或

參觀，不僅推動了韓國電影的發展，也為整個亞洲電影的進步做出了突出貢獻。2012 年韓國釜山國際電影節就吸引了來自 70 多個國家的 300 多部影片在此展映，其中的一部浪漫喜劇《飛吧，金同志！》更是有史以來首次登上韓國大螢幕的北韓電影，在韓國影迷中引起強烈反響。

單字補給站 熟記後再聽一次，英文聽力大躍進

feature [ˈfitʃɚ] v. 以……為特色（或特點）
circus [ˈsɝkəs] n. 馬戲團
acrobat [ˈækrəbæt] n. 雜技演員
trapeze [træˈpiz] n. 高空鞦韆，吊架
ideology [ˌaɪdɪˈɑlədʒɪ] n. 意識形態

screenplay [ˈskrinˌple] n. 編劇，劇本
annual [ˈænjʊəl] adj. 年度的，一年一次的
peninsula [pəˈnɪnsələ] n. 半島

▶ 原文、譯文與解析，請見 P.306

NEWS 04 Russia's Winter Olympics to Break Spending Records

索契冬季奧運會將破冬季奧運會開支記錄

牛刀小試 先聽一遍，貼近真實英語生活圈 🎧 *Track 083*

It is the largest construction site in Europe: 100,000 men and 500 companies are working around the clock.

They are building hotels, skating rinks and ski jumps for next year's Winter Olympics in Sochi, on Russia's Black Sea coast...

有聽沒有懂？就參考看看此篇新聞的背景提示吧

俄羅斯當地時間 2007 年 7 月 4 日下午，在瓜地馬拉舉行的國際奧委會第 119 次全會上，俄羅斯索契以 4 票些微優勢擊敗韓國平昌贏得了 2014 年冬季奧運會的舉辦權，這也是俄羅斯有史以來第一次承辦冬季奧運會。如今，索契冬季奧運會的籌備工作正在全力地進行著，工人們甚至 24 小時開工，一刻不停，力爭趕在 2013 年年底完成各項設施的建設並交付組委會。但是，索契冬季奧運會高額的開支自一開始就在俄羅斯民眾中間引發了巨大爭議，這場史上最貴的奧運會預計將花費 500 多億美元，幾乎是上屆溫哥華冬季奧運會的 6 倍，甚至也遠遠超過了北京奧運會 400 億美元的支出。

單字補給站 熟記後再聽一次，英文聽力大躍進

construction [kən`strʌkʃən] n. 建築，建造
work around the clock 夜以繼日地工作
skating rink 滑冰場
deadline [`dɛd͵laɪn] n. 最後期限
firework [`faɪr͵wɝk] n. 煙火
countdown [`kaʊnt͵daʊn] n. 倒數計時

undor way 正在進行中
hoopla [`huplɑ] n. 喧鬧，嬉鬧
host [host] v. 主辦

▶ 原文、譯文與解析，請見 P.308

NEWS

05

Taylor Swift's "Red" Among 2012's Best Sellers

泰勒絲的專輯《紅》名列 2012 最暢銷專輯

牛刀小試 先聽一遍，貼近真實英語生活圈 🎧 Track 084

Taylor Swift is used to breaking sales records and she continues that trend with her new *album Red. The album sold more than 1.2 million copies in its first week of release...*

有聽沒有懂？就參考看看此篇新聞的背景提示吧

泰勒絲，美國著名鄉村音樂女歌手、演員，曾多次奪得葛萊美大獎，是美國當紅新生代歌手的代表人物之一。自出道以來，長相甜美的泰勒絲憑藉自己清新的氣質和優美的歌聲在全球範圍內贏得了眾多粉絲的支持，不僅長期霸占著暢銷單曲的前幾名，專輯銷量也是屢創新高。最為人津津樂道的是，泰勒絲不但能唱，更展現了相當成熟的創作才華，她在音樂上的才能毋庸置疑。在 2012 年 10 月發布的專輯《紅》中，泰勒更是大膽嘗試，不斷突破自己，專輯發布僅一週就取得了銷量超過 120 萬張的傲人戰績。

單字補給站 熟記後再聽一次，英文聽力大躍進

album [`ælbəm] n. 相簿；集郵簿；專輯
release [rɪ`lis] n. 發布，發行
consecutive [kən`sɛkjʊtɪv] adj. 連貫的，不間斷的
pop-rock n. 流行搖滾樂

previous [`priviəs] adj. 早先的，之前的
mature [mə`tjʊr] adj. 成熟的
session [`sɛʃən] n. （進行某活動的）一段時間
loyal [`lɔɪəl] adj. 忠誠的，忠實的

▶ 原文、譯文與解析，請見 P.310

NEWS 06 China-Hollywood Connection Changes Movie Business

中國與好萊塢聯合，改變電影產業

牛刀小試 先聽一遍，貼近真實英語生活圈 🎧 Track 085

The upcoming Iron Man 3 was partly filmed in China, and its script was subject to scrutiny by Chinese officials. And Chinese sensibilities influence the disaster epic 2012, says Stanley Rosen at the University of Southern California...

有聽沒有懂？就參考看看此篇新聞的背景提示吧

如今，中國已經成為了繼北美之後的全球第二大電影市場，電影業的票房收入正以每年 30% 的速度增長。在如此大好的形勢下，好萊塢自然不會錯過中國這一巨大市場。越來越多的好萊塢電影開始加入中國元素，有些電影公司甚至選擇不遠萬里到中國拍攝取景。最近，好萊塢著名導演李安的一部《少年 PI 的奇幻漂流》就在中國獲得了近億美元的票房成績。同時，中國也在持續擴大其在全球娛樂領域的投資。大連萬達集團就成功收購了美國第二大影院 AMC，因此我們能合理相信，中方和好萊塢在未來將會進一步加深合作，實現互利共贏。

單字補給站 熟記後再聽一次，英文聽力大躍進

upcoming [`ʌp͵kʌmɪŋ] adj. 即將推出的，即將來臨的
scrutiny [`skrutnɪ] n. 審查，審核
sensibility [͵sɛnsə`bɪlətɪ] n. （敏感的）情感，感情
reference [`rɛfərəns] n. 提到，談及

receipt [rɪ`sit] n. 收入
purchase [`pɝtʃəs] v. 購買
conglomerate [kən`glɑmərɪt] n. 企業集團

▶ 原文、譯文與解析，請見 P.312

115

題目篇

Unit 9 文化博覽

語篇分析

語篇分析也是學習者可用以提高聽力理解程度的方法之一。語篇分析主要是從聽力教材語言的整體性和連貫性出發，關註聽力文本中的邏輯銜接（如指代、替代）與連貫，對句子之間、段落之間的邏輯關係等進行梳理和分析。對聽力教材進行語篇分析，能幫助學習者在聽力理解中有意識地採取自上而下的聽力模式來處理訊息，從宏觀層面把握整篇教材的意思，而非斷章取義，孤立地理解詞句，導致出現「只見樹木，不見森林」的結果。在使用本書時，學習者完全可以透過對不同題材的新聞文本進行語篇分析來掌握這項技能。

新聞題材的聽力教材有自己的獨特之處，它的語言組織遵循一定的模式。學習者要關注新聞的六要素：時間（when）、地點（where）、人物（who）、事件的起因（why）、經過（how）和結果（what）。除此之外，比如就語篇的銜接手段而言，學習者要注意分析文本中的替代、指代現象，包括同一詞語的重複、同義詞或者近義詞的使用、代詞的指代等。

學習者可以每周選取本書中的一篇新聞，對文本進行分析。在此過程中，學習者便會熟悉新聞報道的語篇建構，在聽到新的語篇時，能快速地適應文章的結構，有效地進行聽中預測，更好地實現對內容的理解。

NEWS 01 Christmas Celebrations Underway Around the World
世界各地歡慶聖誕節

牛刀小試 先聽一遍，貼近真實英語生活圈 🎧 *Track 086*

It is an annual tradition in Thailand — elephants dressed as Santa Claus on parade*, handing out toys to school children.*

Halfway across the world in Mexico, Santa takes a human form, going for a swim with the fishes, delighting children at a zoo in Guadalajara...

有聽沒有懂？就參考看看此篇新聞的背景提示吧

　　一年一度的聖誕節對於世界各地的基督徒來說是一個重大的節日。在這一天，他們會放下手中的工作，以各種方式慶祝耶穌基督的降生。聖誕節期間孩子們往往是最快樂的，不僅商家推出裝扮各異的聖誕老人會為他們奉上各式各樣的禮物，大人們也會為他們準備各種節日禮物。當然，聖誕前夕也是各大商場展開促銷大戰的時節，人們會趁此機會購置過節所需要的物品。2012 年聖誕節來臨之際，世界各地的人們正以自己的方式慶祝著節日的到來，即便在戰火紛飛的敘利亞，也能聽到唱詩班的祈禱聲迴盪在空中。

單字補給站 熟記後再聽一次，英文聽力大躍進

parade [pə`red] n. 遊行，巡遊
appearance [ə`pırəns] n. 出現，露面
lug [lʌg] v. 用力拖拉
dampen [`dæmpən] v. 減退……的熱情
power outage 停電，斷電

Mass [mæs] n. 彌撒（天主教的宗教儀式）
war-ravaged adj. 被戰爭毀壞的
choir [kwaɪr] n. 唱詩班
pray [pre] v. 祈禱，祈求

▶ 原文、譯文與解析，請見 P.316

NEWS 02 Despite Paralysis, Hawking's Mind Soars

癱瘓的身體，活躍的大腦—霍金

牛刀小試 先聽一遍，貼近真實英語生活圈 🎧 *Track 087*

Hawking, born in Oxford, England in 1942, studied at both Oxford and Cambridge Universities. He became a math professor at Cambridge and held that post for more than 30 years. In 2009, he left to head the Cambridge University Center for Theoretical Physics...

有聽沒有懂？就參考看看此篇新聞的背景提示吧

史蒂芬・霍金被譽為繼愛因斯坦之後當世最偉大的理論物理學家之一。其代表作品《時間簡史》自 1998 年出版以來，就一直是全球最暢銷的科普讀物之一。

霍金因患有肌萎縮側索硬化症，全身癱瘓，長期被禁錮在輪椅上。他頑強地與病魔抗爭。坐在輪椅上的霍金仍然繼續著自己對宇宙的探索和研究，並且取得了豐碩的成果，提出了著名的黑洞輻射和霍金輻射理論。失去說話能力之後，他不斷透過電子合成器向世人傳遞自己對於宇宙和太空的理解。

單字補給站 熟記後再聽一次，英文聽力大躍進

theoretical physics 理論物理學
equation [ɪˈkweʃən] n. 方程式
encompass [ɪnˈkʌmpəs] v. 包含，包括
motion [ˈmoʃən] n. 移動
subatomic [ˌsʌbəˈtɑmɪk] adj. 次原子的
paralyze [ˈpærəˌlaɪz] v. 使癱瘓

incurable [ɪnˈkjʊrəbl] adj. 無法治癒的
degenerative [dɪˈdʒɛnəˌretɪv] adj.
（疾病）不斷惡化的，退行性的
synthesizer [ˈsɪnθəˌsaɪzɚ] n. 合成器

▶ 原文、譯文與解析，請見 P.318

Interfaith Worshipers Celebrate Sea, Surf

不同宗教信仰者共同表達對大海和衝浪的熱愛

牛刀小試 先聽一遍，貼近真實英語生活圈 *Track 088*

Each morning at Huntington Beach, which calls itself Surf City, the surfers are out early to catch the waves.

It is a passion and a lifestyle, says a veteran surfer, who invented a modified surfboard called the boogie board...

有聽沒有懂？就參考看看此篇新聞的背景提示吧

以其海灘而聞名的杭亭頓海灘市距離洛杉磯大概有一小時的車程，一直以來都享有「衝浪之都」的美譽。每天早上都有大批衝浪愛好者趕來追逐浪花，感受衝浪帶給他們的刺激和享受。一流的衝浪環境再加上美麗的海灘風光，自然就使得杭亭頓海灘成為了世界各大頂級衝浪賽事的舉辦勝地，這其中就包括一年一度的美國衝浪公開賽。如今，許多信仰不同宗教的衝浪愛好者每年都會聚集到這裡的海灘上朝拜祈禱，並享受大海和衝浪帶給他們的快樂。

單字補給站 熟記後再聽一次，英文聽力大躍進

surfer [`sɝ·fɚ] n. 衝浪者
passion [`pæʃən] n. 激情，熱情
veteran [`vɛtərən] adj. 經驗豐富的
surfboard [`sɝˌf·bord] n. 衝浪板
interfaith [`ɪntɚ`feθ] adj. 不同宗教信仰者的
blessing [`blɛsɪŋ] n. 祝福，賜福
Islamic [ɪs`læmɪk] adj. 伊斯蘭教的，穆斯林的

synagogue [`sɪnəgɔg] n. 猶太教堂，猶太教徒的聚會
horn [hɔrn] n.（牛、羊等的）角
immigrant [`ɪməgrənt] n. 移民
Tonga [`tɑŋgə] n. 東加（太平洋島國）
preside over 主持（會議、儀式等）
avid [`ævɪd] adj. 熱衷的，熱情的

▶ 原文、譯文與解析，請見 P.320

NEWS 04 Seattle, "City of Clocks" Keeps on Ticking

西雅圖─鐘錶之城

牛刀小試 先聽一遍，貼近真實英語生活圈 🎧 *Track 089*

> *If you've been to Seattle, Washington — or even just heard about it — you'd probably guess that its nickname is something like "The Space Needle City."* ...

有聽沒有懂？就參考看看此篇新聞的背景提示吧

西雅圖坐落於太平洋沿岸，是美國西北部地區最大的城市，微軟、波音和星巴克總部所在地，有「雨城」、「綠寶石城」、「飛機城」和「阿拉斯加門戶」之稱。1993 年湯姆·漢克斯主演的電影《西雅圖夜未眠》讓世人對這座城市的魅力有了更加深刻的了解。為 1962 年世界博覽會所建的「太空針塔」已經成為西雅圖的地標性建築。但是這座城市還有一個不那麼為人熟知的稱號——「鐘錶之城」，如今在西雅圖各大主要街區，人們仍能夠看到那些反映了這座城市歷史的「街鐘」的身影。

單字補給站 熟記後再聽一次，英文聽力大躍進

nickname [`nɪk͵nem] n. 綽號，暱稱
observation deck 觀景臺
landmark [`lænd͵mɑrk] n. 地標
drizzly [`drɪzlɪ] adj. 下毛毛雨的
testimonial [͵tɛstə`monɪəl] n. 證明
jewelry [`dʒuəlrɪ] n. 珠寶

faint [fent] adj. 微弱的，模糊的
resist [rɪ`zɪst] v. 抵抗，抵制
restore [rɪ`stor] v. 修復
timepiece [`taɪm͵pis] n. 計時器，鐘錶

▶ 原文、譯文與解析，請見 P.322

Afghan Youth Orchestra Prepares to Play US Venues

阿富汗青年管弦樂團赴美演出

牛刀小試 先聽一遍，貼近真實英語生活圈 🎧 *Track 090*

The Afghanistan Youth Orchestra performed for the Afghan community in Alexandria, Virginia. The venue was intimate, the audience small...

有聽沒有懂？就參考看看此篇新聞的背景提示吧

　　在戰火紛飛的阿富汗，大街上無家可歸的孤兒和流浪兒童隨處可見。塔利班控制的地區除了禁止八歲以上的女孩接受教育以外，還禁止人們從事任何與音樂有關的活動。

　　但是，自 2010 年創立以來，阿富汗青年管弦樂團就頑強地堅持活躍在世界各地的音樂舞臺上，力圖用音樂來改變人們對阿富汗的認識，讓世界更加了解阿富汗。如今，在美國駐喀布爾大使館的資助下，該樂團正加緊排練，爭取在美國甘迺迪藝術中心和紐約卡內基音樂廳分別為觀眾奉獻一場精彩的演出，讓美國觀眾了解一個不一樣的阿富汗。

單字補給站 熟記後再聽一次，英文聽力大躍進

orchestra [`ɔrkɪstrə] n. 管弦樂隊
venue [`vɛnju] n. （演出）地點，場地
intimate [`ɪntəmɪt] adj. 宜人的，舒適的
embassy [`ɛmbəsɪ] n. 大使館
ban [bæn] v. 禁止

ensemble [ɑn`sɑmbl] n. 樂團，劇團
rehearse [rɪ`hɝs] v. 預演，排練
debut [dɪ`bju] n. 首次登場

▶ 原文、譯文與解析，請見 P.324

NEWS
06 Chinese Pursue Volunteer Opportunities in Africa

中國人爭取擔任援非志工

牛刀小試 先聽一遍，貼近真實英語生活圈 🎧 *Track 091*

At a recent training session in Beijing, doctors, information technology specialists, business professionals and others prepare for a one- to two-year stint in Africa with international development charity VSO, Voluntary Services Overseas...

有聽沒有懂？就參考看看此篇新聞的背景提示吧

中國主席習近平上任之初的首次出訪就選擇了俄羅斯、坦尚尼亞、南非和剛果共和國，並於 2013 年 3 月 27 日出席了在南非德爾班舉行的金磚國家領袖第五次會議，這足以顯示出中國對中非的重視程度。同時，中國數十年來一直堅持向非洲派遣醫療、技術等方面的援外專家和青年志工，提供志工服務。然而，一些國家的媒體關注焦點卻是中國在非洲地區急劇增長的投資所引發的爭論。如今，越來越多的中國人開始以個人名義自願投身非洲事業，盡自己所能為非洲人民提供幫助，以實際行動來擊破來自外界的質疑。

單字補給站 熟記後再聽一次，英文聽力大躍進

session [`sɛʃən] n. 一堂課，一期（訓練）
specialist [`spɛʃəlɪst] n. 專家
professional [prə`fɛʃənl] n. 專業人員
stint [stɪnt] n. （工作）期限
continent [`kɑntənənt] n. 大陸

inclined [ɪn`klaɪnd] adj. 傾向於……的
represent [ˌrɛprɪ`zɛnt] v. 代表
highlight [`haɪ,laɪt] v. 強調，突出

▶ 原文、譯文與解析，請見 P.326

NEWS 07 First Lady's New Hairstyle Creates Buzz

就職典禮上，第一夫人的新髮型引起轟動

牛刀小試 先聽一遍，貼近真實英語生活圈 🎧 *Track 092*

When President Barack Obama took the official oath of office Sunday, the gray in his hair was noticeable. But it was First Lady, Michelle Obama's hair creating all the buzz — with her new haircut featuring "bangs."...

有聽沒有懂？就參考看看此篇新聞的背景提示吧

儘管在公眾場合美國總統歐巴馬一直是民眾和媒體矚目的焦點，但是在他身邊，身材高挑、外形時尚亮麗的第一夫人蜜雪兒‧歐巴馬有時更搶風頭，對於這一點歐巴馬也頗為自豪。

蜜雪兒在美國歷史上創造了兩項紀錄，她是第一位非洲裔第一夫人，

也是個子最高的第一夫人。憑藉對時尚獨到的見解和優雅的舉止，這位第一夫人已多次登上美國時尚雜誌的封面。在歐巴馬與共和黨候選人羅姆尼競戰激戰期間，蜜雪兒的魅力也為歐巴馬加分不少。2013 年 1 月 22 日在歐巴馬總統就職典禮上，蜜雪兒的新髮型更成為萬眾矚目的焦點。

單字補給站 熟記後再聽一次，英文聽力大躍進

oath [oθ] n. 宣誓，誓言
noticeable [`notɪsəbl̩] adj. 顯而易見的
buzz [bʌz] n. 興奮的談話聲，轟動
bang [bæŋ] n. 瀏海
shoulder-skimming adj. 齊肩的

high profile 引人注目的
timing [`taɪmɪŋ] n. 時機
spotlight [`spɑt͵laɪt] n. 聚光燈，公眾關注的焦點
cardigan [`kɑrdɪgən] n. 開襟毛衫

▶ 原文、譯文與解析，請見 P.328

NEWS 08 German Theater Company Helps Minorities Tell Their Stories

德國劇院幫助弱勢族群講述自己的故事

牛刀小試 先聽一遍，貼近真實英語生活圈 🎧 *Track 093*

> *It's not every day that you see Turkish-German school kids filming in the German parliament. These kids are interviewing the head of Germany's Roma community as part of a new program at a theater company in Berlin called Ballhaus Naunynstrasse...*

有聽沒有懂？就參考看看此篇新聞的背景提示吧

英國、德國、法國等歐洲國家對弱勢族群入境、移民、內部融合等議題持不同態度。德國在允許移民和弱勢族群進入勞動力市場的同時限制他們的權利和公民身份。像土耳其人、黑人這樣的弱勢族群很多時候還是會受到歧視和侮辱。如今，德國民眾正在就提高社會對非白人群體的包容度展開討論，呼籲媒體更加關注和報導弱勢族群的生活，使他們得到更多的社會認可。最近，德國的一家劇院就用錄影機把生活在德國的土耳其人和黑人的生活記錄下來，讓他們在螢幕上講述自己的故事。

單字補給站 熟記後再聽一次，英文聽力大躍進

Roma n. (pl.) 羅姆人（吉卜賽人自稱）
mentor [`mɛntə] n. 導師，教練
minority [maɪ`nɔrətɪ] n. 少數民族
racism [`resɪzəm] n. 種族主義，種族歧視

journalist [`dʒɜnəlɪst] n. 記者，新聞工作者
diversity [daɪ`vɜsətɪ] n. 多樣性，多樣化
hopefully [`hopfəlɪ] adv. 有希望地

▶ 原文、譯文與解析，請見 P.330

UN Spearheads Drive to Protect Journalists After Deadly 2012

致命 2012 年過後：
聯合國帶頭展開記者保護行動

牛刀小試 先聽一遍，貼近真實英語生活圈 🎧 *Track 094*

> *When shells fall on the Syrian city of Homs in February 2012, a building used by foreign media takes a direct hit — killing renowned Sunday Times correspondent Marie Colvin, along with French journalist Remi Ochlik...*

有聽沒有懂？就參考看看此篇新聞的背景提示吧

　　在資訊爆炸的今天，人們可以通過各種媒介即時地了解某一事件的進展。在這其中，記者發揮了十分重要的作用，他們通常衝往炮火紛飛的最前線，為世界人民帶來最新、最即時的報導。然而，2012 年對於媒體工作者來說卻是一個災難之年，聯合國稱總共有超

過 100 名記者被殺害，有的甚至被恐怖份子殘忍地被砍頭。最近在維也納召開的一次會議上，聯合國發起了一項行動計劃，旨在保護記者人身安全，打擊針對記者的犯罪行為。會議號召世界各國動員，保護記者安全，捍衛媒體自由。

單字補給站 熟記後再聽一次，英文聽力大躍進

renowned [rɪ`naʊnd] adj. 著名的
correspondent [ˌkɔrɪ`spɑndənt] n. 記者，通訊員
photographer [fə`tɑgrəfɚ] n. 攝影師
incident [`ɪnsədnt] n.（暴力）事件
profile [`profaɪl] n. 引人注目的時刻
fatal [`fetl] adj. 致命的

impunity [ɪm`pjunətɪ] n. 免受懲罰，豁免
symposium [sɪm`pozɪəm] n. 討論會，座談會
kidnap [`kɪdnæp] v. 綁架
unidentified [ˌʌnaɪ`dɛntɪˌfaɪd] adj. 身份不明的

▶ 原文、譯文與解析，請見 P.332

NEWS 10 Protesters Block Dismantling Part of Berlin Wall

拆毀柏林圍牆遺跡引發抗議

牛刀小試 先聽一遍,貼近真實英語生活圈 🎧 *Track 095*

The Berlin Wall was once of the starkest reminders of the Cold War. It was put up by communist East Germany in 1961, to stop its citizens from fleeing to West Berlin. But today, the wall that once snaked around the whole German capital is almost entirely gone...

有聽沒有懂?就參考看看此篇新聞的背景提示吧

2013 年 1 月 22 日,有關開發商要拆毀剩餘的柏林圍牆修建豪華公寓的消息在德國引起軒然大波,德國民眾和其他國家的遊客紛紛指責這一做法是在泯滅歷史。

始建於 1961 年 8 月 13 日的柏林圍牆是美蘇冷戰時期的產物。二戰後的德國和柏林被美、蘇、英、法分成了四個區,蘇聯在自己的占領區建立了德意志民主共和國(也稱東德),英、美、法占領區則成立德意志聯邦共和國(也稱西德)。後來東德為了阻止大批技術人才和勞動人口流往西德而修建起了柏林圍牆。1989 年,隨著東歐劇變的發生,柏林圍牆的大部分於 11 月 9 日後被推倒,1990 年德國完成了統一。

單字補給站 熟記後再聽一次,英文聽力大躍進

stark [stɑrk] adj. 明顯的,赤裸裸的
flee [fli] v. 逃跑,逃離
gallery [`gælərɪ] n. 畫廊
mural [`mjʊrəl] n. 壁畫
stir [stɝ] n. 騷動, 騷亂

arrest [ə`rɛst] v. 逮捕
decline [dɪ`klaɪn] v. 謝絕,拒絕
reconstruct [‚rɪkən`strʌkt] v. 重建
property [`prɑpətɪ] n. 地產,房產
vow [vaʊ] v. 發誓,鄭重宣告

▶ 原文、譯文與解析,請見 P.334

Note

英文聽力

聽這本就夠了

題目詳解

題目詳解篇

Unit 1 國際風雲

Acting Alone in Mali Has Its Rewards and Limits
獨舞馬利，有回報也有局限

新聞原文 一知半解？跟著新聞原文，再聽一遍 🎧 *Track 001*

French President Francois Hollande received a hero's welcome in Mali last week. Malians lined up to thank him for sending troops to end a growing insurgency by Islamist militants.

Even though the operation is part of the global effort to fight terrorist groups, French troops worked alone and received only transport, intelligence and logistics support from allies.

Retired British Brigadier General Ben Barry, now at London's International Institute for Strategic Studies, says that's partly because France didn't need combat help.

France also went ahead in spite of the "conflict fatigue" many European countries are experiencing after years of deployment in Afghanistan.

Indeed, the French needed transport planes and other help from the United States and Canada.

The French military is already planning its exit, as the Malian army takes on some responsibility and West African troops deploy to help. But Ben Barry says the commitment to Mali cannot end when the French military operation does.

It's a story heard many times before in conflict zones all over the world. And while aid is flowing again in Mali, the country needs the kind of long-term assistance the international community has not always been good at delivering.

精準翻譯 句句到位，看你是否真的全數聽懂 🔊

上週，法國總統弗朗索瓦‧歐朗德在馬利受到了英雄般的歡迎。馬利人民夾道感謝他出兵馬利，結束伊斯蘭激進分子越來越猖獗的叛亂。

儘管此次行動是全球打擊恐怖組織行動的一部分，但是法國軍隊卻是獨自作戰，只從盟友那裡得到一些運輸、情報和後勤上的支持。

　　已退休的英國陸軍准將本‧巴里目前在倫敦國際戰略研究所任職。他說，法國獨自出兵的部分原因是法國不需要作戰幫助。

　　由於多年駐軍阿富汗，許多歐洲國家正在經歷「衝突疲勞」的困擾，儘管如此，法國依然堅持出兵馬利。

　　確實，法國需要來自美國和加拿大的運輸機以及其他幫助。

　　隨著馬利軍隊開始承擔起部分責任，以及西非部隊開始進駐部署以提供幫助，法國軍方已開始計劃撤出馬利。但是本‧巴里指出，對馬利的援助不能隨著法國軍事行動的終結而停止。

　　這樣的故事已經在世界上許多衝突地區多次上演。如今，儘管對馬利的援助又恢複正常了，但是這個國家需要的是長期援助，而這並非是國際社會一直以來很擅長提供的。

- -

關鍵解析 英文聽力重點看這邊就對了

❶ Malians lined up to thank him for sending troops to end a growing insurgency by Islamist militants.

　　本句動詞部分是 lined up to...，聽辨難度雖然較大，但是本句的重點是後半部分，其中包含了一個短語 thank sb. for doing sth.（因為某事而感謝某人）。在聽的過程中，學習者還要抓住另一個短語 send sb. to do sth.（派遣某人做某事）。學習者可以通過做筆記，弄清句子中各成分間的邏輯關係，避免造成理解誤差。

❷ Even though the operation is part of the global effort to fight terrorist groups, the French troops worked alone and received only transport, intelligence and logistics support from allies.

　　本句開頭出現的關聯詞 even though 表示「儘管」之意，前半句由這個關聯詞引導，後半句則要表達轉折之意。聽的過程中關注關聯詞可以幫助我們理順行文的邏輯，進而幫助我們更好地把握整個句子的意思。

NEWS 02　African Union Leaders Talk Mali, Chinese Investment
非盟領袖就馬利局勢和中方在非投資展開討論

新聞原文　一知半解？跟著新聞原文，再聽一遍　🎧 *Track 002*

Chinese Vice Premier Wang Yang told the African Union that Beijing's new leaders want greater cooperation on trade and closer consultation on international affairs with the growth of Africa's influence abroad.

Ethiopian Prime Minister and African Union Chairman Hailemariam Desalegn says China is a reliable partner for Africa.

"It is encouraging to note that some of our friends and partners have given priority to infrastructure development in Africa in terms of their strategy partnership with our continent. In this regard I wish to take this opportunity to express my deepest appreciation to China for investing billions in this sector to assist us in our development endeavors."

On Mali, African leaders discussed a regional intervention force against al-Qaida affiliated terrorists in the north as French troops there withdraw. French President Francois Hollande,

"I consider that it is up to Africans themselves to ensure the security of Africa. But France is ready to work with Africans to give African armies the means to respond to all aggressions."

President Hollande says terrorism, trafficking and piracy in Africa are global issues that must be fought together.

精準翻譯　句句到位，看你是否真的全數聽懂 🔊

中國國務院副總理汪洋告訴非盟領袖，隨著非洲在國際上的影響力不斷增強，中國新任領袖很願意與非洲在貿易領域展開更緊密的合作，同時進一步加深雙方在國際事務上的聯繫。

非盟輪值主席、衣索比亞總理海爾馬里亞姆・德薩萊尼表示，中國是非洲值得信賴的合作夥伴。他說：「振奮人心的是，我們注意到我們的一些朋友

和夥伴在發展與非洲大陸的戰略夥伴關係時，優先考慮了非洲的基礎設施建設。在這方面，中國已經為我們的發展提供了數十億美元的援助，我想藉此機會向中國表達我們最誠摯的感謝。」

在馬利問題上，隨著法國軍隊的撤離，非盟領袖討論了是否要派出一支地區干預勢力，來打擊馬利北部隸屬蓋達組織的恐怖份子。

法國總統歐朗德說：「我認為，非洲的安全應該由非洲人民來保衛，而法國願意與非洲人民合作，為非洲軍隊提供所需的武器和裝備，來應對所有的挑釁。」

歐朗德表示，非洲的恐怖主義、走私和海盜行為是全球性問題，需要世界各國聯合起來共同打擊。

關鍵解析 英文聽力重點看這邊就對了

❶ It is encouraging to note that some of our friends and partners have given priority to infrastructure development in Africa in terms of their strategy partnership with our continent.

本句句首的 it 是形式主語，真正的主語是 to note that...，也就是說「注意到……令人歡欣鼓舞」。give priority to 意為「重視，優先進行」。in terms of 表示「就……而言，在……方面」。

❷ In this regard I wish to take this opportunity to express my deepest appreciation to China for investing billions in this sector to assist us in our development endeavors.

take this opportunity to do sth. 表示「借此機會做某事」。常用搭配 express one's deepest appreciation to sb. for doing sth. 意為「就……向某人表達最誠摯的感謝」。句末的 endeavor 作為名詞，是「努力」的意思，相當於 effort。

＊英語新聞廣播中有時會出現前後時態不對應的情況，特別是涉及間接引述時，時態可能會出現非連續性現象，但這並不影響語義表達的連貫性。學習者在此可不必細究語法，而把重點放在對新聞內容的理解上。

03 BRICS Bank Provides Opportunities for Africa
金磚銀行：非洲的發展機遇

新聞原文　一知半解？跟著新聞原文，再聽一遍　🎧 *Track 003*

Chinese investment in Africa is soaring, reaching nearly $20 billion last year alone.

In China, hundreds of thousands of Africans have come to work.

With the expanding trade and investment ties, says political scientist Tang Xiaoyang, it makes sense for China's new leader to reach out to developing countries.

Tang says reaching out to Africa not only helps developing countries, it also helps China and the other members of the BRICS grouping — Russia, India, Brazil and South Africa.

During their meetings in South Africa, BRICS leaders are expected to move forward with the founding of their own development bank. The bank will fund infrastructure development in places such as Africa and give BRICS nations a support network.

The bank is also a means of creating an alternative to development aid from the West.

Although efforts to raise funding for the bank have been slow, analysts note individual BRICS members have already been extending loans and development aid to Africa for years and opportunity continues to beckon.

精準翻譯　句句到位，看你是否真的全數聽懂 🔊

中國在非洲的投資正大幅增長，僅去年一年投資總額就將近 200 億美元。

與此同時，數十萬非洲人也來到中國尋找工作機會。

政治學者唐曉陽稱，隨著中非貿易的擴大和投資關係不斷加深，中國新任領袖人加強與發展中國家的接觸與溝通也再自然不過了。

唐曉陽認為，加深與非洲的關係不僅會幫助這些發展中國家，同時也會使中國和其他金磚國家——俄羅斯、印度、巴西和南非——受益。

金磚國家領袖在南非會晤期間，預計將會繼續推動成立開發銀行。該銀行將為非洲等地的基礎建設提供資金支援，並為金磚五國提供支援平臺。

此外，該銀行也為非洲獲得除了來自西方發展援助的新選擇。

儘管為該銀行籌集資金的努力進展緩慢，但是分析人士注意到，一些金磚國家成員國已經連續多年向非洲提供貸款和發展援助，未來的發展也持續被看好。

關鍵解析　英文聽力重點看這邊就對了

❶ Chinese investment in Africa is soaring, reaching nearly $20 billion last year alone.

　　本句中動詞 soar 表示「猛增，高漲」的意思，突顯了中國對非投資增長之迅速。表示「增長」之意的詞還有 increase, climb, rise, skyrocket 等。後半句用現在分詞 reaching 引導出投資增長迅速的具體表現。用分詞作伴隨狀語時，如果該動詞與其邏輯主語是主動關係，就用現在分詞；如果兩者是被動關係，就用過去分詞。

❷ Although efforts to raise funding for the bank have been slow, analysts note individual BRICS members have already been extending loans and development aid to Africa for years and opportunity continues to beckon.

　　本句開頭出現的關聯詞 although 表示「儘管」的意思，我們可以推測後半句要表達轉折之意。聽的過程中要注意提高對關聯詞的敏感度。句中使用了 have been doing sth. 這個現在完成進行時結構，體現了動作一直持續到現在，強調對現在造成的影響。

Britain Could Be on Path to EU Exit
英國可能已踏上退出歐盟之路

新聞原文　一知半解？跟著新聞原文，再聽一遍　🎧 Track 004

Britain's economy relies on trade and financial services. The free flow of goods and services with the European continent has been a boon, but more and more Britons see the European Union as an unwelcome infringement on their sovereignty.

That has pushed Prime Minister Cameron to promise a re-negotiation of Britain's ties to the EU and then a referendum within five years, if he is re-elected in the middle of the process.

Mr. Cameron said he wants to preserve the single market but avoid some of its regulations, an approach Stephen Tindale, at the Center for European Reform, says won't work.

That would seem to be bad for business but, on Thursday, 56 British business leaders endorse the prime minister's plan, including the heads of the London Stock Exchange and one of the country's major banks.

Prime Minister Cameron and his supporters don't want a divorce, just a better relationship. But the plan to negotiate with the 26 other EU members and then hold a referendum is fraught with uncertainty, and, experts say, could lead Britain where Mr. Cameron says he doesn't want it to go — out of the European Union.

精準翻譯　句句到位，看你是否真的全數聽懂 🔊

英國經濟依賴貿易和金融服務業。長期以來，英國與歐洲大陸之間商品和服務的自由流通給英國帶來了巨大實惠，但如今，越來越多的英國人將歐盟視為其主權的侵犯者。

這一不滿情緒促使首相卡麥隆承諾就英國與歐盟的關係重新展開談判，並

且如果他能連任的話，將在五年內舉行全民公投，決定英國在歐盟的去留問題。

卡麥隆表示，他希望在規避歐盟一些規定的前提下，保持單一市場。然而，歐洲改革中心的分析師史蒂芬·廷德爾卻認為這一方法根本行不通。

這一決策似乎會給商業帶來不利影響，但在本週四，56 名英國商界領袖卻聯名支持首相的計劃，這其中包括倫敦證交所和英國一家主要銀行的負責人。

首相卡麥隆和他的支持者們並不想與歐盟「分道揚鑣」，只是想與其建立一種更有利的關係。但是，與歐盟其他 26 個成員國的談判以及之後全民公投的計劃充滿著不確定性，而且有專家稱，此舉可能導致英國面臨卡麥隆首相所不想看到的結果——退出歐盟。

- -

關鍵解析 英文聽力重點看這邊就對了

❶ The free flow of goods and services with the European continent has been a boon, but more and more Britons see the European Union as an unwelcome infringement on their sovereignty.

本句較長，當聽到表示轉折關係的關聯詞 but 時，我們可以預測後面的內容有語意上的轉折。後半句中動詞詞組 see...as... 表示「將……看作……」。infringement on sth. 表示「對……的侵犯」的意思。unwelcome 表達了「越來越多的英國人」對歐盟的態度。

❷ Mr. Cameron said he wants to preserve the single market but avoid some of its regulations, an approach Stephen Tindale, at the Center for European Reform, says won't work.

本句的難點在於後面 an approach 這一同位語的部分。此處的 an approach 指的就是首相卡麥隆想要選擇的道路——保留單一市場但是規避一些規定。an approach 後面是一個關係子句，也就是說，Stephen says the approach won't work（這一方法史蒂芬認為行不通）。聽的過程中，理清各分句或成分的關係是理解整句話的關鍵。

Cyber Threat: Top Concern for NATO
網路威脅：北約的頭號隱憂

新聞原文 一知半解？跟著新聞原文，再聽一遍 🎧 *Track 005*

Cyber attacks on corporations and governments are no longer unusual. Suspects and their computers are hauled away on a regular basis.

That's why Admiral Stavridis sees cyber security as the top challenge for his successor. "Society is so dependent on all these cyber capabilities, and yet our level of preparation is very low, particularly as an alliance."

It's also relatively easy. Anyone with decent computer skills can do it.

Cyber attacks can range from nuisance attacks to strikes at computers that control banks or air traffic. There have been thefts of government intelligence and corporate secrets. And cyber attacks can have physical consequences, like disabling power plants. Last week, U.S. officials said a cyber attack helped a gang steal $45 million from cash machines around the world.

Many countries are developing offensive cyber weapons, and some, including Israel and the United States have been accused of using them.

But an individual with a grievance might not care whether his or her country suffers a counterattack, adding another dangerous dimension to the issue Admiral Stavridis already has at the top of his list.

精準翻譯 句句到位，看你是否真的全數聽懂 🔊

如今，對企業和政府的網路攻擊早已不再是什麼稀罕事。犯罪嫌疑人和他們的電腦定期就會被警察帶走。

這也是海軍上將斯塔夫里迪斯為什麼認為網路安全是他的繼任者面臨的首要挑戰。他說：「我們的社會如此依賴這些網路，然而我們的防備水準卻非常低，尤其是以一個同盟而言。」

另外，實施網路攻擊相對比較容易，任何電腦水平不差的人都可以做到。

網路攻擊的範圍甚廣，從妨害攻擊到控制銀行或空中交通的電腦皆有可能。目前已經發生過竊取政府情報和企業機密的網路攻擊事件。此外，網路攻擊也有可能帶來有形的破壞，比如讓發電廠陷入癱瘓。上週，美國官員稱，一個團體通過網路攻擊從全世界的自動提款機中盜取了 4,500 萬美元。

如今，許多國家正在開發自己的攻擊性網路武器，其中一些國家，包括以色列、美國等已經被指責使用這些武器。

但是，一個心懷怨憤的人也許並不會關心其國家是否遭到反擊，這讓斯塔夫里迪斯上將擔心的首要問題又增加了一層危險。

關鍵解析 英文聽力重點看這邊就對了

❶ Cyber attacks on corporations and governments are no longer unusual.

本句中 cyber attacks 是關鍵詞，如果學習者在聽的過程中對關鍵詞不太熟悉，那麼可以通過下文來猜測其意思。接下來的句子中緊接著出現了 computer，可以猜測出 cyber 跟電腦或者網路有關。cyber- 實際上也是一個字首，表示「計算機的，網路的」。多掌握一些字根字首，也可以幫助聽者減少聽力障礙。另外，句子中 no longer unusual 表示「不再不尋常」，雙重否定表達肯定的意思，即「司空見慣」的意思。

❷ But an individual with a grievance might not care whether his or her country suffers a counterattack, adding another dangerous dimension to the issue Admiral Stavridis already has at the top of his list.

本句現在分詞 adding 作伴隨副詞，進一步說明主句中「心懷怨憤的公民不關心國家是否遭受到反擊」的結果。at the top of the list 表示「在清單當中位於最前面、最優先的位置」。

NEWS 06 Far-Reaching American Legacy in Iraq Debated
美國對伊拉克的深遠影響引發爭議

新聞原文　一知半解？跟著新聞原文，再聽一遍　 Track 006

Black smoke rises to the sky after a suicide bombing in Baghdad's Sadr City, one in a series of deadly attacks marking the 10th anniversary of the U.S. invasion.

At the scene of another blast, frustration. Some former U.S. officials see the violence as something bigger — a symbol of U.S. hopes for Iraq being dashed.

"I think we've gotten out of balance now, and we need to try and bring it back." Former U.S. Ambassador Ryan Crocker still sees Iraq as a crucial ally, especially as Iran has been using Washington's seeming absence after its troop withdrawal as a chance to extend its influence over the region.

Iraq's former ambassador to the U.S., Samir Sumaida'ie, says with renewed U.S. engagement and support, Iraq could do even more.

But some, like former U.S. National Security Advisor Zbigniew Brzezinski, warn against such false hopes.

Brzezinski argues that U.S. involvement in Iraq helped cause much of the regional instability that has allowed problems to escalate elsewhere in the region.

With America's attention now focused on Syria and Iran, Iraqis are left to pick up the pieces of the violence and uncertainty that continues to influence their day-to-day lives.

精準翻譯　句句到位，看你是否真的全數聽懂 🔊

巴格達東部的薩達爾市行政區發生一起自殺性爆炸襲擊，一股黑煙升騰而起。這一事件只是在美國入侵伊拉克十周年之際發生的一系列致命襲擊事件中的一起。

另一起爆炸現場，也令人感到挫折。一些前美國官員把這樣的暴力事件看得更嚴重——它意味著美國對伊拉克抱有的希望破滅。

　　美國前任駐伊大使瑞安‧克羅克稱：「我認為我們現在已處於失衡狀態，我們需要努力找回平衡。」他仍然把伊拉克看作一個重要盟友，尤其是在當前情況下——美國撤兵伊拉克後似乎留下了空白，伊朗正利用這個機會擴大自己對於這一地區的影響力。

　　前伊拉克駐美大使薩米爾‧蘇邁達伊稱，如果有了美國的重新介入和支持，伊拉克或許可以更有作為。

　　但是也有一些人，比如前美國國家安全顧問茲比格紐‧布熱津斯基，對這樣的錯誤希望發出了警告。

　　布熱津斯基認為，美國介入伊拉克事務加劇了這一地區的動盪局面，並且使得一些問題在該地區的其他地方進一步加劇。

　　現在，美國將注意力放在了敘利亞和伊朗，剩下伊拉克人來收拾那些零散暴力和繼續影響其日常生活的不確定性殘局。

- -

關鍵解析　**英文聽力重點看這邊就對了**

❶ Former U.S. Ambassador Ryan Crocker still sees Iraq as a crucial ally, especially as Iran has been using Washington's seeming absence after its troop withdrawal as a chance to extend its influence over the region.

　　本句中有三個 as，第一個 as 出現在固定搭配 see...as... 中，意為「視……為……」。第二個，especially as... 中 as 是連詞，引出條件或原因，可譯為「隨著」。第三個 as 所在的搭配為 use...as...，意為「把……用作」。

❷ With America's attention now focused on Syria and Iran, Iraqis are left to pick up the pieces of the violence and uncertainty that continues to influence their day-to-day lives.

　　本句開頭是 with 引出的一個伴隨結構，本句主語為 Iraqis（伊拉克人），be left to do sth. 是一個被動結構。被動語態在聽力過程中一直是個難點，本句動作的實施者其實是美國，即 America leaves Iraqis to...。句末 that 引導的是一個關係子句，修飾 uncertainty。

NEWS 07 Missile Defense System Keeps Watch on Syria
北約部署導彈防禦系統監視敘利亞

新聞原文 一知半解？跟著新聞原文，再聽一遍 🎧 *Track 007*

These U.S. soldiers are maintaining Patriot Missiles. Since January, the missiles have been stationed at a Turkish military base outside Gaziantep. The city is 50 kilometers from Syria, where an increasingly bloody civil war has killed at least 70,000 people.

Syrian government forces appear to be mostly firing at rebels, who are backed by Turkey. But Syrian fire has landed several times in Turkey, in one instance killing five people.

Turkey's government asked NATO for the missiles.

The two U.S. missile batteries are staffed by 575 soldiers. Each battery includes six launchers carrying a total of 48 missiles. Germany and the Netherlands have each sent two similar batteries to Turkey.

NATO says the missiles are for defensive purposes only. So far none has been fired. Battery Commander Captain Leslie Dembeck says nevertheless, the team still must keep up its skills.

The soldiers don't know how long their deployment will last. Syria's rebels have been pushing for a multi-national no-fly zone in Syria, but without it, the missile batteries are the first-line border defense.

精準翻譯 句句到位，看你是否真的全數聽懂

這些美國士兵正在維護愛國者導彈發射系統。自 1 月份以來，這些導彈就被部署在加濟安泰普市外的一個土耳其軍事基地。而在距這座城市僅 50 公里遠的敘利亞，一場愈發血腥的內戰已經導致至少 70,000 人喪生。

敘利亞政府軍似乎主要是在向土耳其支持下的反對派武裝開火。但是，敘

利亞的戰火已數次波及土耳其，其中一次造成了五人死亡。

　　因此，土耳其政府請求北約為其提供導彈防禦支持。

　　部署在這裡的兩套美國導彈發射裝置共配備了 575 名士兵，每套發射裝置有 6 個發射器，共攜帶 48 枚導彈。德國和荷蘭也各將兩套類似的導彈發射裝置運至了土耳其。

　　北約方面稱，該導彈只是用於防禦目的。目前為止尚未發射過。但導彈系統指揮官萊斯利·登貝克上尉說，雖然如此，相關人員仍然必須熟練掌握其技能。

　　這些士兵不知道他們要在這裡駐紮多長時間。敘利亞反對派武裝一直在推動於敘利亞上空設立一個跨國禁飛區。但是沒有設立之前，該導彈發射系統仍然是第一道邊境防禦屏障。

關鍵解析　英文聽力重點看這邊就對了

❶ The city is 50 kilometers from Syria, where an increasingly bloody civil war has killed at least 70,000 people.

　　本句中 where 引導的是關係子句，修飾的是 Syria。子句修飾的先行詞是地點，所以關係副詞使用 where, 相當於 in which。從句中所用的 has killed 是現在完成時態，表示過去的動作對現在造成的影響。

❷ Syria's rebels have been pushing for a multi-national no-fly zone in Syria, but without it, the missile batteries are the first-line border defense.

　　首先，本句中 have been pushing 是現在完成進行時態，強調的是過去的動作一直延續到現在，而且還要繼續進行下去。這一句的意思是「敘利亞的反對派武裝一直在推動建立一個跨國禁飛區」。在第二個分句中，without it 表示一種狀況或條件，這裡的 it 指代的是上文提到的 multi-national no-fly zone。聽的過程中，聽者要注意前後的文意關係，尤其是要弄清楚代詞的指代對象。另外，missile battery 是一個軍事專業名詞，指「導彈發射裝置」。

NEWS 08 · U.S. Helping Africa Rise
美國希望幫助非洲崛起

新聞原文　一知半解？跟著新聞原文，再聽一遍　🎧 Track 008

President Barack Obama said of his recent visit to sub-Saharan Africa that "the reason I came to Africa is because Africa is rising, and it is in the United States' interests — not simply in Africa's interests — that the United States doesn't miss the opportunity to deepen and broaden the partnerships and potentials here."

Today, at the dawn of the 21st century, Africa is one of the most important emerging regions in the world, and one of the fastest growing. Trade has tripled over the past decade, and foreign direct investment in the continent approaches $80 billion a year. Since 1989, 20 new democracies have taken root across the region.

"We historically have been an enormous provider of development aid to Africa — food, medicine. But what I want us to do is to have a shifting paradigm where we start focusing on trade, development, partnerships, where we see ourselves as benefiting and not simply giving in the relationship with Africa," said President Obama during the first part of his visit in Senegal.

"This is going to be a continent that is on the move. It is young. It is vibrant and full of energy," he said.

精準翻譯　句句到位，看你是否真的全數聽懂 🔊

美國總統巴拉克‧歐巴馬在談到他最近的撒哈拉以南非洲之行時說道：「我之所以來到非洲是因為非洲正在崛起，美國應不失時機地加深和擴大和非洲的夥伴關係，尋求合作的各種可能性，這不僅符合非洲人民的利益，而且也符合美國人民的利益。」

在 21 世紀的今天，非洲是世界上最重要的新興地區也是發展最快的地區

之一。過去十年時間裡，非洲的貿易額已經是原來的三倍，外商在非洲大陸的直接投資每年接近 800 億美元。自 1989 年以來，已經有 20 個新的民主國家在這一地區紮根成長。

在此次非洲之行的第一站塞內加爾，總統歐巴馬這樣說道：「長期以來，我們為非洲提供了大量發展援助，比如食品和藥品。但是現在，我希望我們能轉變以往的合作模式，開始把注意力放在貿易、發展和夥伴關係上。在發展同非洲的關係中，我們不再只是給予，而是也能從中受益。」

「這將是一個不停發展、年輕、充滿生機和活力的大陸。」他說道。

關鍵解析 英文聽力重點看這邊就對了

❶ President Barack Obama said of his recent visit to sub-Saharan Africa that "the reason I came to Africa is because Africa is rising, and it is in the United States' interests — not simply in Africa's interests — that the United States doesn't miss the opportunity to deepen and broaden the partnerships and potentials here."

本句的主句是 Obama said that...。that 引導的是一個比較複雜的受詞子句，聽者需要了解這個子句傳遞的關鍵訊息。該從句中包含了一個強調句式：it is...that...。當需要強調句中的主語、受詞、補語等部分時，我們常採用「It is + 被強調部分 + that / who」這種句型。後半句中動詞 deepen 和 broaden 與後面的兩個並列名詞 partnerships 和 potentials 構成搭配，可譯為「加深和擴大夥伴關係，尋求合作的各種可能性」。

❷ Trade has tripled over the past decade, and foreign direct investment in the continent approaches $80 billion a year.

本句中 triple 表示「成三倍，增至三倍」。其他表示倍數的詞還有 double（成兩倍），quadruple（成四倍）等。foreign direct investment (FDI) 表示「外商直接投資」，這類經濟術語需要學習者平時多歸納總結。句中的 approach 用作動詞，意為「（在數額、水平或質量上）接近……」。

09 UN Team Faces Tough Task in Syrian Chemical Probe
敘利亞化學武器調查，聯合國小組面臨困境

新聞原文　一知半解？跟著新聞原文，再聽一遍　Track 009

These were some of the survivors of what the Syrian government says was a chemical weapon attack by rebels on the northern town of Kahn al-Asal.

Many of the people who rushed to a hospital in nearby Aleppo had breathing difficulties but no obvious external wounds. Syrian authorities said a rocket hit the town and emitted a gas that killed about 20 people. Syrian rebels said government forces fired it.

At Syria's request, the United Nations is preparing to send a team to the area to determine whether chemical weapons actually were used for the first time in Syria's two-year conflict.

Leading the team will be Swedish scientist Ake Sellstrom, who says it will be difficult to figure out what happened in the midst of a civil war.

Diplomats say U.N. Secretary-General Ban Ki-moon wants the investigators to start work next week and have "unfettered" access to the scene of the attack.

But, Syria first will have to approve their composition and mandate.

Syria's rebel factions have denied using any chemical weapons in their battle to oust autocratic President Bashar al-Assad.

The Syrian government has never confirmed that it possesses chemical weapons. But aides to Mr. Assad have suggested that any chemical weapons they may have would be used against foreign aggressors, not Syrians.

精準翻譯　句句到位，看你是否真的全數聽懂

這些倖存者來自敘利亞政府聲稱反對派武裝份子使用化學武器襲擊的北部小鎮卡恩阿薩爾。

很多感覺呼吸困難的人湧入了阿勒頗附近的一家醫院，但是他們身上並無明顯的外傷。敘利亞當局說，一枚火箭彈襲擊了這個小鎮，並且釋放出一種氣體，

導致大約 20 人死亡。但是，敘利亞反對派卻辯稱是政府軍發射了這枚火箭彈。

在敘利亞的要求下，聯合國正準備派遣一個小組到這一地區展開調查，以確定自敘利亞衝突發生兩年以來，是否真的第一次使用了化學武器。

一位名叫奧克‧塞爾斯特羅姆的瑞典科學家將領導這個小組。他認為，想要在一場內戰進行過程中弄明白到底發生了什麼是非常困難的。

敘利亞外交官稱，聯合國秘書長潘基文希望調查人員下週開始工作，並且希望他們能夠不受限制地出入襲擊發生現場。

當然，這首先需要敘利亞認可這個調查小組並給予授權。

一方面，敘利亞各反對派已經否認為將巴沙爾‧阿薩德總統趕下臺而使用過任何化學武器。

另一方面，敘利亞政府也從未證實過其擁有化學武器。但是阿薩德總統的助手曾經表示，他們即使擁有什麼化學武器，也只會用來對付外國侵略者，而不會針對敘利亞人。

關鍵解析 英文聽力重點看這邊就對了

❶ These were some of the survivors of what the Syrian government says was a chemical weapon attack by rebels on the northern town of Kahn al-Asal.

本句結構比較複雜，其主句為 These were some of the survivors of ... a chemical weapon attack...。句意理解的難點是 survivors of 後面的部分。what the Syrian government says was a chemical weapon attack，意為「敘利亞政府所稱的一次化學武器襲擊」。an attack by sb. on sth. 表示「某人對某地發動的襲擊」。

❷ Leading the team will be Swedish scientist Ake Sellstrom, who says it will be difficult to figure out what happened in the midst of a civil war.

本句可以理解為一個倒裝句，主語為 Swedish scientist Ake Sellstrom，後面 who 引導的關係子句對其作修飾說明，引出更多的信息。從句中 figure out 表示「搞明白，弄清楚」，in the midst of 表示「在……當中」。

US Troop Reduction to Test Afghans
美國減少駐軍考驗阿富汗安全部隊

新聞原文 一知半解？跟著新聞原文，再聽一遍 🎧 Track 010

In his State of the Union address this week, President Obama put the drawdown of U.S. forces in Afghanistan into high gear ahead of next year's withdrawal deadline.

"This spring our forces will move into a support role while Afghan security forces take the lead. Tonight I can announce that, over the next year, another 34,000 American troops will come home from Afghanistan…"

This year's fighting season begins shortly, and it will be the first time that Afghan national security forces — trained and assisted by the United States and its allies — will be at the forefront.

The troop reduction will be gradual, allowing a sufficient number of U.S. soldiers to be on hand to provide that support.

Most of the coalition forces are to be out of Afghanistan by the end of next year. And what happens in the country beyond that analysts say is a big question.

The U.S. has yet to announce how many troops it may leave beyond 2014 to advise and assist the Afghans as they continue the fight against insurgents. That will be decided in a bilateral security agreement that the U.S. and the Afghan government are negotiating.

精準翻譯 句句到位，看你是否真的全數聽懂 🔊

在本周的國情咨文演講中，歐巴馬總統宣布加快美軍士兵撤離阿富汗的步伐，提前於明年的撤兵截止日期前完成這次撤軍。

「今年春天，我們的部隊將轉變為支持角色，而阿富汗安全部隊將成為主導力量。今晚我可以向你們宣布，在接下來的一年時間裡，將會再有 34,000 名美

國士兵從阿富汗回家……」

今年的戰鬥季即將開始，由美國和其盟國訓練和協助的阿富汗國家安全部隊將會首次前往最前線。

當然，撤軍將會逐步進行，以確保阿富汗仍有足夠的美軍能提供相應的支持。

到明年年底，大多數盟軍士兵都將撤離阿富汗。分析人士稱，沒有了盟軍的阿富汗未來是個大問題。

美國尚未公布 2014 年之後將會在阿富汗保留多少駐軍來為當地人繼續打擊叛亂分子提供建議和幫助。這一決定將會在美阿正在協商的一項雙邊安全協議中作出。

關鍵解析 英文聽力重點看這邊就對了

❶ In his State of the Union address this week, President Obama put the drawdown of U.S. forces in Afghanistan into high gear ahead of next year's withdrawal deadline.

本句中 State of the Union address 指「美國的國情咨文」，是美國總統向國會發表的年度報告，主要闡述美國每年面臨的國內外情況，以及政府將要採取的政策措施。多了解政治背景常識，有助於聽者理解新聞的內容。drawdown 是個比較難的詞，你可能不熟悉其意，那麼可以根據下文的 withdrawal 推測出該詞的意思與撤軍有關。put...into high gear 是一個固定的搭配，原意為「換高速擋」，這裡表示「加快（美軍的撤出）」。

❷ This year's fighting season begins shortly, and it will be the first time that Afghan national security forces — trained and assisted by the United States and its allies — will be at the forefront.

本句中破折號之間的插入部分作定語，修飾 Afghan national security forces。其中的動詞與前面被修飾的名詞之間是被動關係，所以用過去分詞 trained and assisted，意為「受到……訓練和幫助的」。

NEWS 11

Venezuela-US Relations Unlikely to Change After Chavez
後查維茲時代委美關係不太可能發生改變

新聞原文 一知半解？跟著新聞原文，再聽一遍 *Track 011*

The death of President Chavez is being mourned by his supporters, while many inside and outside Venezuela wonder what the future holds.

A commanding and charismatic figure in life, Mr. Chavez played an outsized role on the world stage — largely by challenging the United States and what he saw as Washington's economic and political dominance of Latin America.

He repeatedly accused the United States of undermining his socialist revolution. A failed coup attempt in 2002 tacitly supported by the Bush administration further antagonized the Venezuelan leader and his supporters.

This antagonism is unlikely to change soon.

At a meeting convened the day Chavez died, Vice President Nicolas Maduro accused Washington of plotting to undermine Venezuela and announced the expulsion of two American diplomats.

Despite this, Venezuela is a major supplier of petroleum to the United States — and even provides free heating oil to poor Americans through a non-profit group.

American University professor Philip Brenner says this shows that relations between the two countries would be better if Washington recognizes certain realities.

Meanwhile, Maduro's accusations have been rejected by U.S. officials who have limited their comments to possible areas of cooperation such as counternarcotics and energy in the post-Chavez era.

精準翻譯 句句到位，看你是否真的全數聽懂

在支持者們對查維茲總統的去世表示哀悼之際，委內瑞拉國內外的許多人都在猜想未來會發生什麼。

查維茲一生是個威風凜凜、魅力非凡的人物，也是世界舞臺上的一大人物——他敢於挑戰美國，反對美國政府對拉美經濟和政治的控制。

他屢次指責美國破壞了他的社會主義革命。2002 年，一場布希政府暗中支持的政變企圖宣告失敗，這進一步加深了這位委內瑞拉領導人和他的支持者們對美國的敵意。

而這種敵意不太可能迅速發生改變。

在查維茲去世當天召開的一次會議上，副總統尼古拉斯·馬杜羅指責美國企圖暗中顛覆委內瑞拉，並且宣布將兩名美國外交官驅逐出境。

儘管如此，委內瑞拉仍是美國主要的石油供應商之一，它甚至還通過一個非營利組織免費向美國窮人提供取暖用油。

美國大學教授菲利普·布倫納稱，此舉表明，如果華盛頓政府能夠承認某些事實，那麼兩國間的關係可能會變得更好。

與此同時，美國官員對馬杜羅的那些指責予以否認，他們僅在發言中提到了後查維茲時代委美兩國可能會展開合作的領域，比如禁毒和能源領域。

- -

關鍵解析 **英文聽力重點看這邊就對了**

❶ A commanding and charismatic figure in life, Chavez played an outsized role on the world stage — largely by challenging the United States and what he saw as Washington's economic and political dominance of Latin America.

本句中 a commanding and charismatic figure 和 Chavez 是同位語關係。破折號後面 by 引出的內容表示方式，具體說明查維茲是如何在世界舞臺上扮演這一厲害的角色。challenge 這個動詞後面跟有兩個並列受詞成分，一是「美國」，二是「在他看來的美國在拉美的支配地位」。

❷ At a meeting convened the day Chavez died, Vice President Nicolas Maduro accused Washington of plotting to undermine Venezuela and announced the expulsion of two American diplomats.

convene a meeting 表示「召集一次會議」，句中 meeting 後面省略了 which was。關係子句 Chavez died 修飾的是 the day。片語 accuse sb. of... 表示「指責某人做某事」，of 是介詞，因此後面緊跟的動詞 plot 用的是現在分詞形式，相當於名詞。

VP Biden: US Not Bluffing on Iranian Nuclear Weapons
副總統拜登：美國在伊朗核武問題上沒有虛張聲勢

新聞原文 一知半解？跟著新聞原文，再聽一遍 *Track 012*

More than 12,000 pro-Israel activists are in Washington for the annual conference of the American Israel Public Affairs Committee — or AIPAC.

Concern about Iran's nuclear program is topping the agenda.

Vice President Joe Biden told the group that when it comes to Iran's nuclear ambitions, the U.S. position is clear. "It is to prevent Iran from acquiring a nuclear weapon. Period, period, end of discussion, period. Prevent, not contain, prevent."

Israel has threatened military strikes if Iran moves to develop atomic weapons. Tehran maintains its program is for peaceful purposes.

Biden says a military option is on the table if diplomacy doesn't work. "Well, big nations can't bluff and presidents of the United States cannot and do not bluff, and President Barack Obama is not bluffing. He is not bluffing."

Western nations are negotiating with Iran, but Israeli leaders warn that Tehran is using the talks to continue building its nuclear program.

AIPAC strongly backs the Israeli government both on Iran and the conflict with the Palestinians. But some Jewish groups are critical of that support.

On Tuesday, the final day of the AIPAC conference, thousands of delegates will head to Capitol Hill to lobby members of the U.S. Congress.

精準翻譯 句句到位，看你是否真的全數聽懂

12,000 多名親以色列活動人士來到華盛頓參加美國以色列公共事務委員會（AIPAC）年會。

對伊朗核計劃的擔憂成為此次大會的首要議題。

談到伊朗的核武野心，副總統喬・拜登告訴與會人員，美國的立場很明確。

他說：「那就是要阻止伊朗取得核武器。完畢，到此為止，沒有討論的餘地，就此終止。阻止，不是遏制，而是阻止。」

伊朗如果進一步發展核武器，以色列威脅將對其實施軍事打擊。而德黑蘭方面卻堅持宣稱其核計劃是用於和平目的。

拜登表示，如果外交途徑無效，將考慮通過軍事手段解決。他說：「大國無需虛張聲勢，美國總統不能也不會只是虛張聲勢，現任總統巴拉克·歐巴馬不是在虛張聲勢，他沒有在虛張聲勢。」

西方國家正在與伊朗進行談判，但是以色列領導人卻警告說德黑蘭是在藉談判之機繼續發展其核武計劃。

AIPAC 在伊朗核問題以及以巴衝突問題上都堅定支持以色列政府。但一些猶太組織對這樣的支持力度並不滿意。

週二是 AIPAC 會議的最後一天，數千名與會代表將前往國會山去遊說美國國會議員。

- -

關鍵解析　英文聽力重點看這邊就對了

❶ More than 12,000 pro-Israel activists are in Washington for the annual conference of the American Israel Public Affairs Committee — or AIPAC.

本句中 pro- 表示「擁護，支持」的意思，是個字首。學習者平時要注意多學習和了解類似字根或字首的意思，這樣在聽的過程中，可以更準確地猜測出相應詞語的意思。另外，專門的會議或者國際組織名稱，像這裡的 AIPAC 一般在第一次出現時會用全稱，後面再出現時多使用其縮寫，學習者要注意辨識其縮寫的讀法。

❷ Vice President Joe Biden told the group that when it comes to Iran's nuclear ambitions, the U.S. position is clear.

vice president 是「副總統」的意思。表示副職的英語常用詞還有 deputy。二者的選擇取決於約定俗成的語言習慣，比如 vice minister, deputy director 等。而當表示職稱副職的時候，一般用 associate, 如 associate professor 等。

Washington Week: Focus on US-Asia Ties
華盛頓週：聚焦美亞關係

  Track 013

South China Sea maritime disputes will likely figure prominently in Thursday's discussions between President Obama and President Truong Tan Sang. Secretary of State John Kerry pledged America's continued engagement at an ASEAN summit earlier this month. "We have a strong interest in the manner in which the disputes of the South China Sea are addressed and in the conduct of the parties."

The White House says Presidents Obama and Sang will also discuss human-rights concerns, climate change, and economic ties. The meeting will be closely watched by America's Vietnamese immigrant community.

On the domestic front, work continues in the House of Representatives on an overhaul of U.S. immigration laws. The Senate passed a comprehensive reform bill weeks ago that would dramatically boost border security while providing a path to citizenship for millions of undocumented immigrants. The citizenship provision faces strong opposition from many conservative lawmakers in the Republican-controlled House.

House Speaker John Boehner has said he hopes the chamber will deal with immigration before Congress turns its attention to once again raising the U.S. debt ceiling. The federal government is expected to reach its borrowing limit around October.

精準翻譯　句句到位，看你是否真的全數聽懂 🔊

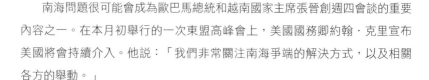

南海問題很可能會成為歐巴馬總統和越南國家主席張晉創週四會談的重要內容之一。在本月初舉行的一次東盟高峰會上，美國國務卿約翰・克里宣布美國將會持續介入。他說：「我們非常關注南海爭端的解決方式，以及相關各方的舉動。」

　　白宮方面稱，歐巴馬總統和張晉創主席還會就人權問題、氣候變化和經濟合作展開討論。美國的越南移民團體也將會密切關注此次會談。

　　在美國國內，眾議院仍盡全力修改移民法。參議院在數週前已經通過了一項全面改革法案，在大大提升邊境地區安全的同時，也為數以百萬的非法移民獲得美國公民身份提供了一條途徑。但是，法案中有關公民身份提供的條款遭到了共和黨控制的眾議院中許多保守派議員的強烈反對。

　　眾議院議長約翰‧博納表示，他希望在國會在將注意力轉向提高美國債務上限之前，眾議院能夠解決移民法改革問題。聯邦政府預計將在 10 月份前後達到債務上限。

- -

關鍵解析 英文聽力重點看這邊就對了

❶ South China Sea maritime disputes will likely figure prominently in Thursday's discussions between President Obama and President Truong Tan Sang.

　　本句中 figure 用作動詞，意為「重要，顯著」，並非學習者比較熟悉的表示「數字，人物」之意的名詞。因此，即使聽到熟悉的詞彙時，也要注意結合文意來判斷其具體意思。**President Obama** 和 **President Truong Tan Sang** 分別指美國總統歐巴馬和越南國家主席張晉創。這裡要注意國家領導人英文名字的正確發音。

❷ The Senate passed a comprehensive reform bill weeks ago that would dramatically boost border security while providing a path to citizenship for millions of undocumented immigrants.

　　本句中 that 引導關係子句，修飾的是 a comprehensive reform bill。while 表示「同時」，後面 providing 之所以用現在分詞形式，是因為它與前面的邏輯主語 reform bill（改革法案）是主動關係。millions of 表示約數，意為「數以百萬的」，注意英文中 trillion（萬億），billion（十億），million（百萬），thousand（千），hundred（百）前面如果是具體的數字，這些詞應該用單數形式。

NEWS 14 Weapons Flowing to Somali Militants
大量武器流向索馬利亞武裝份子

新聞原文 　一知半解？跟著新聞原文，再聽一遍 　🎧 Track 014

The military offensive against the al-Shabab militia in Somalia has made major advances over the past year. However, al-Shabab has not been defeated. U.N. monitors reportedly say the group is receiving weapons from distribution networks with ties to Yemen and Iran.

Reuters quotes sources who say U.N. monitors report weapons are entering Somalia through Puntland and Somaliland in the north. From there they are transported south where al-Shabab is battling AU, Somali and Kenyan forces.

The news agency says the weapons include IEDs, or improvised explosive devices and machine guns and that the weapons were made in Iran and North Korea.

Among those weighing what the U.N. monitors are reported to have said is Jonah Leff, of the Small Arms Survey, an independent research project.

The United States is lobbying for an end to the U.N. arms embargo on Somalia. It's been in effect since 1992. Some other countries are opposed to lifting it or want to see it gradually lifted.

Jeff Leff of the Small Arms Survey says lifting it would be premature.

The United Nations Security Council is expected to address the situation in Somalia over the next several weeks.

精準翻譯 　句句到位，看你是否真的全數聽懂 🔊

過去一年，打擊索馬利亞「青年黨」的軍事行動取得了重大進展，但是「青年黨」仍然沒有被徹底打敗。聯合國觀察員多次報告稱，這一組織正通過與葉門和伊朗有關的分銷網路，獲得武器。

路透社援引消息人士的說法稱，聯合國觀察員報告稱武器正通過北部的邦特蘭和索馬里蘭進入索馬利亞，而後被轉運到索馬利亞南部地區，供正在與

非盟、索馬里和肯尼亞軍隊交戰的「青年黨」使用。

　　路透社還稱，這些武器中包括簡易爆炸裝置和機關槍，它們是在伊朗和北韓境內製造的。

　　喬納·萊夫是「小型武器調查」這一獨立調查項目的成員，參與了對聯合國觀察人員所報告情況的評估。

　　美國方面正在為結束聯合國對索馬利亞自 1992 年開始生效的武器禁運四處遊説。但是，其他一些國家卻反對解除禁運或者希望聯合國逐步解除禁運。

　　「小型武器調查」項目的萊夫認為，解除武器禁運還為時過早。

　　聯合國安理會預計會在接下來的幾週內著手處理索馬利亞的這一局勢。

關鍵解析 英文聽力重點看這邊就對了

❶ The news agency says the weapons include IEDs, or improvised explosive devices and machine guns and that the weapons were made in Iran and North Korea.

　　聽到 IEDs 這樣的軍事專業術語時，學習者可能會感覺比較陌生。一般來説，專有名詞縮寫首次出現時，後面接著會出現其全稱，要注意聽。另外，本句中 IEDs 前出現了 weapons include，我們可以據此推測下面談及的是有關武器的詞彙。所以，當聽到一個不熟悉的專業名詞時，應注意上下文是否有解釋該詞或幫助理解詞義的內容。

❷ It's been in effect since 1992. Some other countries are opposed to lifting it or want to see it gradually lifted.

　　第　句中「since + 時間」，表示「自從……起」，句中動詞一般用現在完成式。第一個 it 指代上文提到的 embargo（武器禁運）。be in effect 表示「生效」的意思。第二句中 oppose 表示「反對」的意思，固定搭配 be opposed to doing sth. 意為「反對做某事」。lift 在句中是「撤銷，解除（限制）」的意思。lift 後面的 it 指代的仍是上文提到的 embargo。要注意英文中不喜歡重複，所以常用代詞來指代上文提到過的概念或事物。

題目詳解篇

Unit2 生態環境

NEWS 01 UN Chief Warns of Perils Ahead of Climate Change Conference

氣候變遷大會召開在即，聯合國秘書長警告危機

新聞原文 一知半解？跟著新聞原文，再聽一遍 🎧 *Track 015*

The first decade of this century was the hottest on record, and the vast majority of scientists attribute the changes to greenhouse gases that trap heat in the lower atmosphere. Those gases can be generated naturally or emitted by human activities, such as the burning of fossil fuels.

Extreme weather due to climate change is "the new normal," said U.N. Secretary-General Ban Ki-moon earlier this month.

The existing agreement to reduce emissions is called the "Kyoto Protocol," and its adoption in 1997 set binding targets for industrialized countries. The first commitment period expires at the end of this year, and negotiators will work on an extension at the climate conference in Doha.

The United States is not a party to the agreement, but President Barack Obama says the U.S. has taken steps to reduce emissions. Mr. Obama says the U.S. has doubled the production of clean energy and doubled fuel efficiency standards for cars and trucks in the past four years.

Mr. Obama says the U.S. will not try to curb climate change at the expense of economic growth.

The Kyoto Protocol does not require developing countries to reduce emissions. Some industrialized nations say future agreements to limit emissions should apply to all major economies.

精準翻譯 句句到位，看你是否真的全數聽懂 🔊

本世紀頭十年是史上最熱的十年，絕大多數科學家都把這一變化歸因於溫室氣體將熱量阻隔在了低層大氣中。那些溫室氣體可以自然產生或透過人類活動，如燃燒礦物燃料、排放而產生。

聯合國秘書長潘基文本月早些時候稱，氣候變化導致的極端天氣成為了

「新常態」。

現存的減排協議稱為《京都議定書》，於 1997 年通過。它為工業化國家設定了限排目標。第一承諾期將於今年年底終止，談判代表們將要在杜哈氣候變遷大會上爭取就第二承諾期達成共識。

美國沒有加入這一協議，但其總統巴拉克‧歐巴馬聲稱美國也已經採取了一些減排措施。他說在過去四年時間裡，美國的清潔能源生產已經翻倍，汽車、卡車燃油效率標準也提高了一倍。

但歐巴馬表示，美國不會以損害經濟增長為代價來遏制氣候變遷。

《京都議定書》沒有規定發展中國家的減排任務。一些工業化國家表示，未來的限排協議應該適用於所有主要經濟體。

關鍵解析 **英文聽力重點看這邊就對了**

❶ The first decade of this century was the hottest on record, and the vast majority of scientists attribute the changes to greenhouse gases that trap heat in the lower atmosphere.

attribute...to... 意為「把……歸因於……」。類似的這種引出原因的英文表達還有 as a result of, owing to, due to, thanks to, resulting from 等。greenhouse gas 表示「溫室氣體」，它後面的關係子句說明了溫室氣體是如何導致氣溫升高的。

❷ The existing agreement to reduce emissions is called the "Kyoto Protocol," and its adoption in 1997 set binding targets for industrialized countries.

本句中 agreement 表示「協議」，protocol 意為「議定書」。類似的詞還有 convention（公約）、treaty（條約）等。後半句中 its adoption 指的是《京都議定書》的通過和實行。binding 表示「具有約束力的」，比如 a binding agreement or a binding contract（具有約束力的協議或合同）。industrialized countries 指「工業化國家」。其他相關表達還有 developed nations（已開發國家）、developing nations（發展中國家）、emerging economy（新興經濟體）等。

Asian Water Summit Focuses on Security, Disaster
亞太水資源峰會聚焦水安全與水災害

新聞原文 一知半解？跟著新聞原文，再聽一遍 🎧 *Track 016*

There was no sign of a water shortage here in northern Thailand as delegates gathered for the Asia-Pacific Water Summit. But inside, there was talk about an impending crisis facing Asia.

For the region's biggest users — India and China, there is a heavy price to pay for development, says U.N. Habitat advisor Dr. Kulwant Singh.

"Most of the industries that are driving the economic growth of the region require reliable supplies of fresh water for some part of their production cycle. Secondly, the region's expanding urban populations need more water for drinking, for personal hygiene, and for the industry, institutions and urban agriculture."

Studies say that water demand in India will double in the next 20 years to 1.5 trillion cubic meters, with China's needs rising by 32 percent.

The delegates also focused on preventing water disasters, such as the massive floods in 2011 that claimed 800 lives in Thailand.

Improve technology is one possible solution, says Supajak Waree of Thailand's disaster warning center.

With the supply of clean and plentiful water seemingly imperiled, the effort to manage Asia's thirst for the precious liquid will continue.

精準翻譯 句句到位，看你是否真的全數聽懂 🔊

　　當代表們齊聚泰國北部參加此次亞太水資源高峰會時，這裡並未出現任何水資源短缺的跡象，但在大會上，代表們談論的卻是亞洲即將面臨的水資源危機。

　　聯合國人居署顧問卡爾萬特・辛格博士說，印度和中國是亞太地區水資源消耗量最大的兩個國家，為發展所要付出的代價是相當沈重的。

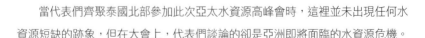

「首先，該地區大多數推動經濟增長的工業，在生產周期的某些環節都需要有穩定的淡水資源供應。其次，該地區不斷增加的城市人口也需要更多的飲用水和個人衛生用水，同時，工業、機構和城市農業也需要更多的水。」

有研究稱，在未來 20 年時間裡，印度的需水量將會翻倍達到 1.5 萬億立方米，中國的需水量也將會增加 32%。

此外，代表們也集中討論了水災害的預防，其中就提到了 2011 年奪去 800 條生命的泰國特大洪災。

泰國災害預警中心的素巴賈克‧瓦雷表示，不斷改進監測技術是一個可能的解決方案。

由於清潔、充足的水資源供應似乎正面臨危險，管理和監測亞洲對寶貴水資源需求的工作將會持續下去。

- -

關鍵解析　英文聽力重點看這邊就對了

❶ But inside, there was talk about an impending crisis facing Asia.

句中的 but 表示語義的轉折，學習者據此可以預測其後面所表達的意思發生了轉折。inside 指的是「會場內」。impending 表示「即將發生」的意思，多修飾不愉快的事件。

❷ Secondly, the region's expanding urban populations need more water for drinking, for personal hygiene, and for the industry, institutions and urban agriculture.

本句中 secondly 表示「其次」的意思。表示先後順序的常用詞有 firstly（首先），secondly（其次），thirdly（再次），lastly（最後）等。句中的 for 表示用途。

NEWS 03　US Coast Guard Monitors Receding Mississippi River Levels

美國海岸警衛隊持續監測不斷下降的密西西比河水位

新聞原文　一知半解？跟著新聞原文，再聽一遍　 *Track 017*

Crew members on board the U.S. Coast Guard Cutter Gasconade are struggling to keep traffic flowing on the Mississippi River.

As the water level beneath them continues to drop, the green and red buoys they deploy to mark the shallow spots are all that stand between successful navigation of the river and disaster.

The Coast Guard's goal is to prevent that from happening, a job Chief Ryan Christensen admits is becoming more difficult as the Mississippi recedes.

Barges that make their way up and down the Mississippi River carry more than $100 billion worth of goods every year. Any disruption has significant consequences for the U.S. economy.

But releasing more of that flow off the Missouri River is a politically and environmentally sensitive decision. Releasing more water upstream might be a quick fix to solve some problems downstream on the Mississippi, but it could impact future water levels throughout the system, particularly without a significant amount of precipitation in the coming weeks.

In the meantime, the U.S. Coast Guard continues to plot a course ahead, showing barges how to make their way along the troubled river, all the while hoping for rain, or snow.

精準翻譯　句句到位，看你是否真的全數聽懂 🔊

　　美國海岸警衛隊「吹牛號」快艇上的隊員們正在力保密西西比河上的航運通暢。

　　腳下的水位在持續下降，他們在河道中布設的紅綠浮標成了救命標線，它們標示出淺水區域，指引船隻成功通航，避免災難的發生。

　　海岸警衛隊的目標就是要避免災難的發生。警衛隊隊長瑞安‧克里斯坦森坦承，隨著密西西比河水位的不斷下降，這一工作正變得越來越艱難。

　　密西西比河上來來往往的駁船每年運載的貨物總價值超過 1,000 億美元，航運的任何中斷都會給美國經濟帶來重大影響。

　　但是，從密蘇里河釋放更多的流量到密西西比河卻是一個不論在經濟或環境保護上都非常敏感的決定。上游地區釋放更多流量也許是一個快速解決下游密西西比河流域一些問題的辦法，但它會影響未來整個系統的水位，尤其是在未來數週仍沒有明顯降水的情況下。

　　與此同時，美國海岸警衛隊仍在繼續向前標示航道，指引駁船順利通過危險水域，同時他們也希望老天爺能儘早下點雨或雪。

- -

關鍵解析　英文聽力重點看這邊就對了

❶ The Coast Guard's goal is to prevent that from happening, a job Chief Ryan Christensen admits is becoming more difficult as the Mississippi recedes.

　　本句中 that 指的是上一段最後提到的「災難」。a job 是前面整個句子的同位語，即指「防止災難的發生」，它後面跟了一個省略了 that 的關係子句，也就是說：Chief Ryan Christensen admits the job is becoming more difficult. 最後面 as 引導的子句表示原因。

❷ In the meantime, the U.S. Coast Guard continues to plot a course ahead, showing barges how to make their way along the troubled river, all the while hoping for rain, or snow.

　　in the meantime 意為「與此同時」。整句話比較長，聽者要注意分析句子結構，才能更加理解句子的意思。all the while 表示「一直，始終」之意。showing 和 hoping 的主詞都是 the U.S. Coast Guard，兩者之間是主動關係，因此使用現在分詞修飾。值得注意的是，句中 troubled 是過去分詞作形容詞的用法，表示「充滿危險和麻煩」的意思。

Agriculture and Forestry: Key to Mitigating Climate Change
農林業：減緩氣候變遷的關鍵

新聞原文　一知半解？跟著新聞原文，再聽一遍　🎧 *Track 018*

While historically both agriculture and forestry have kept a low profile at climate change talks, the 2012 climate convention in Doha saw some attention being paid to the important role forests play in landscaping, biodiversity and food security.

Peter Holmgren, CIFOR director general, is already looking ahead to the planned 2015 climate agreement. In his view of the Doha talks, he said it is time to rethink approaches in agriculture and forestry so that the two green sectors play a more prominent role in future climate talks.

Holmgren observed that while no decisive action was taken regarding conservation of forestry and agriculture at the talks, he is optimistic that the two sectors will play a bigger role in climate change talks in the future.

Scientists say this means that both agriculture and forest must be examined together in terms of the vital role both play in providing sustainable development and food security for billions of people.

Scientists agree that the research should also include biodiversity and socio-economic research, not just the monitoring of forests.

Holmgren added that the key to green growth in Africa and other areas of the world is to focus on agriculture and forestry because they are a very large portion of the economy.

精準翻譯　句句到位，看你是否真的全數聽懂 🔊

　　儘管從歷史上看，農林業在氣候變遷談判中一直未受到重視，但是在 2012 年的杜哈氣候大會上，森林在環境美化、保護生物多樣性和保障食品安全方面所發揮的重要作用已經受到了一定程度的關注。

　　國際林業研究中心（CIFOR）總幹事彼得‧霍姆格倫已經著手計劃將於 2015

年簽署的氣候協議。談到杜哈氣候談判，他説現在應該重新思考對待農業和林業的態度，以便這兩個綠色領域在未來的氣候談判中能扮演更加重要的角色。

霍姆格倫注意到儘管此次談判中並沒有就保護農林業採取重要行動，但是他對這兩個領域將在未來的氣候變遷談判中發揮更大作用還是持樂觀態度的。

科學家稱，這意味著必須把農業和林業放在一起，綜合審視它們在支持永續發展和保障數十億人的食品安全方面所發揮的重要作用。

另外，他們認為應該也把生物多樣性和社會經濟研究包括在內，而不是只注重對森林的監測。

霍姆格倫還補充道，非洲和世界其他地區達到綠色增長的關鍵是要把注意力放在農業和林業上，因為它們在經濟中占有很大的份量。

關鍵解析　英文聽力重點看這邊就對了

❶ While historically both agriculture and forestry have kept a low profile at climate change talks, the 2012 climate convention in Doha saw some attention being paid to the important role forests play in landscaping, biodiversity and food security.

本句中 keep a low profile 表示「不引人注意，不受到關注和重視」的意思。當 the 2012 climate convention 為主語時，see 意為「是……發生的時間或者地點」。這裡可理解為「在 2012 年杜哈氣候大會上」。pay attention to 在句中用了被動形式。最後，句中活用了 play an important role in sth. 這一搭配，其意為「在……方面發揮著重要的作用」。

❷ ...both agriculture and forests must be examined together in terms of the vital role both play in providing sustainable development and food security for billions of people.

examine sth. in terms of... 意為「從……角度審視某事物」，句中使用了被動形式。the vital role 後面跟了一個限制性關係子句，子句中 both 是代詞，代指前面的 agriculture and forests。該子句的意思是「農業和林業在支持永續發展和保障數十億人的食品安全方面所發揮的重要作用」，這是理解上較困難的部分。

05 Scientists Say Climate Change, Dams Threaten Mekong Livelihoods

科學家稱，氣候變化和大壩建設會威脅湄公河流域民眾生計

新聞原文　一知半解？跟著新聞原文，再聽一遍　 Track 019

An estimated 60 million fishermen and farmers depend on the Mekong River for its rich nutrients and abundant fish.

A new study by a group of scientists says by 2050 climate change could raise temperatures in parts of the Mekong basin twice as fast as the global average.

"That would intensify extreme weather events, such as flooding, and reduce fish and crop production," says study leader Jeremy Carew-Reid.

While some species will benefit from hotter climates, important crops such as coffee in Vietnam and rice in Thailand could be forced to move.

But fish in the Mekong system, the largest inland fishery in the world, cannot relocate so easily and fish farming has already reached its environmentally sustainable capacity.

Some 30,000 man-made barriers, such as hydropower dams, compound the effects of climate change, says Carew-Reid.

Scientists at the study's release in Bangkok said dams and other barriers constitute the single largest threat to fish diversity and production.

Laos, controversially, is set to build the first of several hydropower dams on the mainstream of the Mekong.

But just as economics are driving dam construction, scientists say poverty will make it harder for people to adapt to rising temperatures.

精準翻譯　句句到位，看你是否真的全數聽懂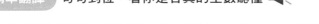

湄公河物產豐富，漁業資源充足。據估計，大約有 6,000 萬漁民和農民依靠它維持生計。

一組科學家的一項新研究稱，到 2050 年，氣候變遷將可能導致湄公河流域部分地區氣溫顯著升高，升溫速度可能會是全球平均速度的兩倍。

　　該項研究的領導者傑里米・卡魯－里德說：「那將會加劇像洪水這樣的極端氣候事件的發生，導致漁業和農作物減產。」

　　儘管一些物種會從暖化的氣候中受益，但諸如越南的咖啡和泰國的大米等重要農作物有可能會被迫轉移到其他地方種植。

　　然而湄公河流域這一世界最大內陸漁場的漁業資源並不是那麼容易就能遷移的，況且當地的漁業養殖也已經達到了環境永續承載能力的上限。

　　卡魯－里德說，河上像水力發電廠大壩這樣的人為阻流建築物約有30,000 個，這會進一步加劇氣候變遷帶來的影響。

　　科學家們在曼谷發表這項研究結果，他們稱大壩和其他阻流建築物對魚類多樣性和漁業生產構成了最大威脅。

　　而在爭議浪潮中，寮國卻決心要在湄公河主流上著手建造第一座計畫中的水力發電廠大壩。

　　但是，就像當前經濟的發展會推動大壩建設一樣，科學家們稱，貧困也使得人們更難以應對氣候暖化的問題。

關鍵解析 **英文聽力重點看這邊就對了**

❶ A new study by a group of scientists says by 2050 climate change could raise temperatures in parts of the Mekong basin twice as fast as the global average.

　　本句的主要部分為：A new study says by 2050 climate change could raise...。句中第一個 by 引出研究的執行者，而第二個「by + 時間點」表示「到……之時或者不遲於……」。twice as fast as 意為「前者的速度為後者的兩倍」。「倍數 + as + adj./adv. + as」這一結構經常用來表達倍數關係。

❷ But fish in the Mekong system, the largest inland fishery in the world, cannot relocate so easily and fish farming has already reached its environmentally sustainable capacity.

　　句中 the largest inland fishery in the world 是 the Mekong system 的同位語，對其做進一步說明。fish farming 指「漁業養殖」。reach its environmentally sustainable capacity 表示「達到環境永續承載能力的上限」。

Report: Widespread Trafficking of Great Apes
報告：野生人猿的非法交易日趨普遍

新聞原文 一知半解？跟著新聞原文，再聽一遍 🎧 *Track 020*

It's estimated at least 3,000 great apes are illegally seized and sold every year. For every ape that is captured alive, many others are slaughtered. A new report says law enforcement is undermanned and too poorly equipped to stop it.

Doug Cress is coordinator of the Great Apes Survival Partnership, or GRASP. He says the report is, what's called, a rapid response assessment.

The report says that over the past decade great apes have become a very lucrative commodity. For example, an illegally seized chimpanzee is worth about $25,000 in China.

The days of individual poachers are over. Cress says poaching of great apes is mostly done by sophisticated organized crime.

Traffickers often transport the apes from country to country in Africa before getting them off the continent. Cress says it's usually inhumane.

The report, "Stolen Apes" says it's not enough to crackdown in countries where poaching occurs. The demand for great apes in Asia, the Middle East and elsewhere must be stopped. It recommends poachers be arrested and prosecuted and given long prison terms if convicted.

It also recommends countries confiscate trafficked great apes and return them to their home countries within eight weeks. Home can be determined by DNA tests. Once returned, they can be brought to sanctuaries and rehabilitation centers.

Cress says trafficking in great apes is morally wrong. But he also says it's bad for the environment. For example, he says when chimpanzees disappear from a forest, the health of the forest declines.

精準翻譯 句句到位，看你是否真的全數聽懂 🔊

　　據估計，每年遭非法捕獲和販賣的野生類人猿至少有 3,000 隻。每活捉一隻猿，就有其他許多隻猿會遭到屠殺。一份新報告中指出，執法部門人手嚴重不足，裝備太落後，根本無法阻止這種非法行為的發生。

類人猿救生協會協調員道格‧克雷斯説，該報告是一份快速反應評估的報告。

裡頭指出，在過去十年，類人猿已成為利潤非常豐厚的商品，一隻非法捕獲的黑猩猩在中國能值大約 25,000 美元。

如今，個體偷獵者的時代已經過去。克雷斯説，類人猿的偷獵大多數都是精心策劃的組織犯罪活動。

販賣者在把這些猿類運離非洲大陸之前，經常先把它們從一個國家運到另一個國家。克雷斯表示，這個過程通常很殘忍。

報告《被偷走的猿》稱，只在偷獵發生的國家打擊犯罪行動是遠遠不夠的。必須制止亞洲、中東及世界其他地方對類人猿的需求。報告建議逮捕和起訴那些偷獵者，一旦罪名成立就判處他們長期監禁。

除此之外，報告還建議各國沒收那些遭非法交易的類人猿，並將它們在八周之內返還其來源國。如果無法確定這些動物的來源地，可以通過基因鑑定來確定。這些猿類被送還回國後，可以放到保護區或康復中心。

克雷斯説，類人猿非法交易不僅在道德上是錯誤的也不利於環境保護。例如，如果黑猩猩從一片森林中消失了，那麼這片森林的健康狀況就會下降。

- -

關鍵解析 英文聽力重點看這邊就對了

❶ A new report says law enforcement is undermanned and too poorly equipped to stop it.

　　本句中 law enforcement 指「執法部門」。undermanned 表示「人手不夠的」，同義詞為 understaffed, 反義詞為 overmanned。under- 是一個常見的字首，意為「不足，未」，比如 undercooked（未熟的），underdeveloped（未發達的）。

❷ It recommends poachers be arrested and prosecuted and given long prison terms if convicted.

　　recommend 表示「建議，推薦」。與之意思相近的動詞還有 advise, suggest 等。它們後面接建議的內容時，子句需要用「should + 動詞原形」，其中 should 常會省略。

Poachers Kill Elephant Family in Kenya
偷獵者在肯亞獵殺了一個大象家族

新聞原文 一知半解？跟著新聞原文，再聽一遍 🎧 *Track 021*

A manhunt has been underway since the weekend in Kenya for a gang of poachers that killed a family of elephants. The Wildlife Service says 12 of the animals were slaughtered. Poaching is on the rise across Africa as demand grows in Asia for ivory and rhino horns.

Kenya Wildlife Service spokesman Paul Mbugua says at least 10 poachers entered the northern side of Tsavo East National Park. It's a remote area with little infrastructure. He says the elephants were killed Saturday.

Mbugua says poaching used to occur only in certain corners of Kenya. Now it's happening across the country.

He says anti-poaching operations should be increased; and parliament needs to pass proposed legislation handing down tough penalties for poaching. Currently, wildlife crime, he says, is treated as a misdemeanor with small fines.

Ivory and rhino horns sell for very high prices in Asia. They're used in traditional medicines and potions.

The Kenya Wildlife Service is calling on China, Vietnam and other Asian countries to do more to end the poaching trade. It says raising awareness would help — telling people that for every piece of ivory they buy an elephant has died.

The World Wildlife Fund estimates that in 2011, more than 23 metric tons of ivory were seized by authorities. That figure, it says, represents 2,500 dead elephants.

精準翻譯 句句到位，看你是否真的全數聽懂 🔊

　　一群偷獵者獵殺了一個大象家族，本週末已在肯亞境內展開了對他們的追捕。肯亞野生動物保護局稱，總共有 12 頭大象慘遭殺害。隨著亞洲市場對象牙和犀牛角的需求不斷上漲，非洲地區的偷獵行為變得越來越猖獗。

　　該保護局發言人保羅‧姆布古阿說，至少有 10 名偷獵者進入了東帝汶國

家公園的北部地區，那裡地處偏遠，幾乎沒有任何基礎設施。他說那些大象是在週六被獵殺的。

姆布古阿說，偷獵行為過去只是在肯亞某些偏遠地區發生，如今卻已蔓延至全國。

他認為應該進一步加強對偷獵的取締；議會需要通過相關立法提案，對偷獵行為實施嚴厲懲罰。他說，現今野生動物犯罪只被當作一種輕罪來處罰，罰款數額也很小。象牙和犀牛角在亞洲售價很高，他們被用來製作傳統藥物和藥劑。目前，肯亞野生動物保護局正呼籲中國、越南和其他亞洲國家更努力地來制止偷獵貿易。該組織表示，提高人們保護野生動物的意識——告訴人們每買一顆象牙，就意味著有一頭大象死去——將會產生一定作用。

世界野生動物基金會估計，2011 年，相關部門共沒收了超過 23 公噸象牙，這意味著共有 2,500 頭大象遭殺害。

- -

關鍵解析 **英文聽力重點看這邊就對了**

❶ A manhunt has been underway since the weekend in Kenya for a gang of poachers that killed a family of elephants.

本句的主句是 A manhunt for a gang of poachers has been underway...，其中的「for + 名詞片語」因有關係子句作修飾而移到了後面。句中 be underway 表示「正在進行中」。以「since + 時間點」作修飾的句子中，動詞用完成式。

❷ The World Wildlife Fund estimates that in 2011, more than 23 metric tons of ivory were seized by authorities. That figure, it says, represents 2,500 dead elephants.

本句中 the World Wildlife Fund 是一個國際組織的名稱，要注意與前面提到的 Kenya Wildlife Service 區分開。學習者平時進行聽力訓練的時候，要多累積一些常用的國際組織名稱及其縮寫，拓展自己的背景知識。句中 metric tons 表示「公噸」。英文中的計量單位在聽力中也是一個難點。在聽到帶有單位的數字時，學習者一方面要記錄下數字，另一方面也要注意理解數字後面計量單位的含義。

Natural Disasters Displace 32 Million in 2012

2012 年，自然災害迫使 3,200 萬人流離失所

新聞原文　一知半解？跟著新聞原文，再聽一遍 Track 022

A new report says more than 32 million people were forced to flee their homes in 2012 due to natural disasters. Most of the displacement occurred in developing countries, but even rich nations, like the United States, were not spared.

Nature had a lot of people on the run last year.

Clare Spurrell is the chief spokesperson for the Internal Displacement Monitoring Center. "In 2012, we saw twice as many people being displaced by natural disasters as compared to the year before. So that was 32.4 million who were newly displaced in 2012. And this is by rapid-onset disasters, such as floods, storms, wildfires and earthquakes."

And these extreme events are becoming much more frequent in many countries.

Also in the last five years, more than 80 percent of global displacement occurred in Asia. India is often the worst affected.

Africa saw a record number of newly displaced people last year — eight-point-two million.

Rich nations also saw displacement as a result of natural disasters. For example, in the U.S., 900 thousand people were forced to flee their homes last year, mostly due to Hurricane Sandy. In 2011, many people were displaced by Japan's triple disaster of a major earthquake, tsunami and the resulting nuclear plant emergency.

精準翻譯　句句到位，看你是否真的全數聽懂 ◀≶

　　一項新的報告顯示，2012 年共有超過 3,200 萬人因自然災害不得不逃離家園，儘管絕大多數案例都發生在發展中國家，但即使像美國這樣的富裕國家也沒能完全倖免。

　　去年一年，自然災害使得很多人都不得不奔波逃亡。國際顯示製成前瞻技

術研討會首席發言人克萊爾‧斯珀雷爾說：「2012 年因自然災害而流離失所的人數是 2011 年的兩倍，具體而言，2012 年新增的流離失所人數為 3,240 萬人。這些都是由突發性自然災害造成的，比如洪水、暴雨、森林大火和地震。」

而且，在許多國家裡，這些極端天氣事件正變得越來越頻繁。過去五年時間裡，全球因自然災害而導致的流離失所情形超過 80% 都發生在亞洲，而印度常常是受影響最為嚴重的地區。

去年，非洲流離失所人數也達到了創紀錄的 820 萬人。甚至在富裕國家中，也發生了自然災害導致居民流離失所的情況。比如在美國，去年一年就有 90 萬人被迫逃離家園，其中多數是由颶風「桑迪」造成的。2011 年，許多日本人在大地震、海嘯和隨之產生的核洩漏危機三重災難的打擊下，也不得不背井離鄉。

- -

關鍵解析　英文聽力重點看這邊就對了

❶ In 2012, we saw twice as many people being displaced by natural disasters as compared to the year before.

本句中出現了倍數的表達，twice as many people as 表示「人數是……的兩倍之多」。compared to 意為「與……相比較」。displace 表示「迫使（某人）離開家園」，句中使用了被動語態。

❷ Rich nations also saw displacement as a result of natural disasters.

本句中 as a result of 表示「由於……的原因」。英文常習慣先說結果，再表明原因。句中的 saw 是 see 的過去式，在這裡並不是常見的「看，看見」之意，而是「經歷，目睹」之意。整個句子意思是說「富裕的國家也發生了自然災害導致民眾流離失所的情形」。

❸ In 2011, many people were displaced by Japan's triple disaster of a major earthquake, tsunami and the resulting nuclear plant emergency.

triple 表示「三重」的意思。聽者據此可以預測下文中會講到三個導致日本民眾流離失所的原因，而後面也隨即出現了三個並列的原因：大地震、海嘯和由此產生的核洩漏。聽者即使不熟悉 tsunami（海嘯）這個單詞的意思，也可以根據上下文推測出它是一種自然災難。學會根據語意來預測不熟悉單詞的大概意思可以幫助學習者減少聽力理解障礙。

NEWS 09 Minister: Zambia Losing Too Many Lions and Leopards
旅遊部長：尚比亞失去了太多獅子和花豹

新聞原文 一知半解？跟著新聞原文，再聽一遍 *Track 023*

Zambia's tourism minister has announced a partial ban on the hunting of lions and leopards. She warns their numbers may be too low to allow safari hunting to continue for now. What's more, there'll be a study of the lucrative industry following reports of corruption and lack of compensation for the government and local communities.

Tourism Minister Sylvia Masebo says the government is breaking from the past and is "putting conservation at the core" of its management policies. She says that Zambia has not fully benefitted from allowing safari hunting to take place. Masebo says Zambia needs to conserve and control its wildlife resources.

Estimates of the number of lions in Zambia's national parks have ranged from about 2,500 to more than 4,600.

The hunting ban covers those 19 areas where leases were just about to be put out to bid. There are other areas where hunting continues because the leases have not expired. Masebo says hunting is also permitted on private game ranches that have valid permits and are fenced in.

The tourism minister says Zambian law requires local communities be consulted about hunting operations. This is done, she says, through community resource boards.

Masebo says breaking from the past is not easy. Without naming names, she says the hunting industry has been controlled by — what she describes as — big cartels.

精準翻譯 句句到位，看你是否真的全數聽懂

尚比亞旅遊部部長正式宣布將部分禁止對獅子和花豹的捕獵行為。她警告，目前獅子和花豹的數量可能已經少到無法支撐遊獵項目再持續下去了。另外，在一些有關腐敗以及政府和當地民眾未獲相應補償的報導出現後，尚比亞將會對這一利潤豐厚的產業展開調查。

　　旅遊部部長西爾維亞‧馬塞博稱，政府如今正在摒棄過去那些不好的做法，把保護作為其管理政策的核心。她表示，尚比亞並沒有從批准遊獵活動中充分獲益。馬塞博說，尚比亞現在需要保護和控制其野生動物資源。

　　據不同的估計，現在尚比亞國家公園中的獅子數量大約在2,500隻到4,600隻之間。該項禁捕令涉及 19 個租約即將到期、又要重新競標的地區。但是，在其他租約尚未到期的地區，捕獵仍在進行。馬塞博說，在那些擁有合法許可證並設有圍場的私人狩獵場裡，是允許進行捕獵的。

　　這位旅遊部部長還指出，尚比亞法律要求狩獵活動的進行需要先徵詢當地社區的意見，而這主要是通過社區資源委員會進行的。

　　馬塞博表示，徹底地改變並不是那麼容易。在她看來，狩獵產業一直被大聯合企業控制著，但是她並沒有具體說明企業的名稱。

關鍵解析 **英文聽力重點看這邊就對了**

❶ She warns their numbers may be too low to allow safari hunting to continue for now.

　　本句中 their numbers 指的是上文提到的 lions and leopards 的數量。too...to... 表示「太……以至於不能……」。allow sb./sth. to do sth. 表示「允許或准許……做某事」。在聽的過程中學習者要注意上下文的指代關係以及一些固定的搭配。

❷ Tourism Minister Sylvia Masebo says the government is breaking from the past and is "putting conservation at the core" of its management policies.

　　本句中的 minister 指的是「政府部門的部長」。政府首腦或一個機構的最高管理者也可以用 head 或 governor 表示。聽力材料中出現人名時，要注意其身份和頭銜。break from 表示「與……分離，摒棄」的意思；而 put sth. at the core 表示「將……置於核心位置」。

NEWS
10 Final Vote Nears on Conserving Sharks
保護鯊魚的最終投票將近

新聞原文 一知半解？跟著新聞原文，再聽一遍 🎧 *Track 024*

Shark fin soup is a delicacy in Asia. But its popularity is helping to decimate shark populations. However, governments voted Monday (today) to protect five species of the predators. Preliminary approval came at a U.N. meeting on wildlife trade in Bangkok, Thailand.

Conservationists have been trying for years to protect sharks. Success finally came at this year's meeting of CITES — the Convention on International Trade in Endangered Species of Wild Fauna and Flora. Governments also voted to protect two species of manta rays, as well. Final approval is expected Thursday, the last day of the meeting.

Conservationists say many times when sharks are caught, they have their fins cut off and are then thrown back into the sea to die. The manta rays are prized for their gills, which are also used as a food delicacy. Proposals to protect sharks were first introduced at a 1994 CITES meeting in the U.S.

If final approval is given, the sharks and rays would be included under Appendix II of CITES. It is not a total ban. Appendix II does allow commercial trade. But countries involved in such trade must do two things. They have to prove that the sharks and rays were, one, legally caught and, two, sustainably caught.

精準翻譯 句句到位，看你是否真的全數聽懂

在亞洲，魚翅羹是一道美味佳餚。但這道廣受歡迎的菜也部分地導致了鯊魚數量的銳減。不過，各國政府本週一（今天）進行了投票表決，決定保護其中的五種食肉性鯊魚。初步的批准是在泰國曼谷所召開有關野生動植物貿易的聯合國會議上作出的。

多年來，生態環保人士一直為保護鯊魚努力不懈。最終，他們在今年的瀕危野生動植物國際貿易公約（CITES）大會上獲得了成功。另外，各國政府也

表決支持將兩種魟魚納入保護範圍。預計在本週四，也就是這次會議的最後一天，將會作出最終批准。

生態環保人士說，很多時候鯊魚被捕獲後，就被割掉魚鰭，然後再被扔回大海中慢慢死去。而魟魚非常珍貴的鰓也常常被人們當做一種美味的食物。保護鯊魚的提議是在 1994 年於美國召開的 CITES 大會上首次提出的。

如果最終獲得批准，鯊魚和魟魚將被納入 CITES 附錄二中，但這並不是全面禁止。附錄二是允許商業貿易的，但那些從事這類貿易的國家必須做到兩點。首先，必須證明鯊魚和蝠魟魚是合法捕撈的；其次，還要證明這樣的捕撈是永續的。

關鍵解析 英文聽力重點看這邊就對了

❶ Conservationists say many times when sharks are caught, they have their fins cut off and are then thrown back into the sea to die.

-ist是英文中的一個常見字尾，通常表示「某類人」。這裡的 conservationist 指的是「自然資源保護者」，與之意思相近的詞還有 environmentalist（環境保護主義者）。平時多總結歸納常見字根和字尾的意思和用法，可以幫助聽者猜測不熟悉詞彙的詞意。

❷ The manta rays are prized for their gills, which are also used as a food delicacy.

本句中 prize 作為動詞，表示「珍視，高度重視」的意思。固定搭配 prize sth. for sth. 多以被動形式出現，比如本句中 The manta rays are prized for their gills（魟魚因鰓而貴）。which 引導的子句是個非限定關係子句。非限定關係子句與被修飾對象之間用逗號隔開，用以補充說明，即使去掉該子句，也不會破壞主句意思的完整性。

❸ They have to prove that the sharks and rays were, one, legally caught and, two, sustainably caught.

本句中聽到的 one, two 在這裡表示序數的概念，即第一，第二，用以說明兩個條件。另外，表示次序的詞語還有 firstly, secondly, thirdly, lastly 等。

NEWS 11 Despite Pollution Worries, China Experiments with Carbon Trading
汙染困擾下的中國碳交易試驗仍在持續

新聞原文　一知半解？跟著新聞原文，再聽一遍　🎧 *Track 025*

Beijing's smoggy days are literally off the charts, with small airborne particles that reduce visibility and threaten health.

It has been a persistent concern in recent years, but spiking pollution levels in January are sparking a public outcry.

Emissions from coal-fired electricity plants and busy factories are part of the problem that officials hope to reign in through carbon trading platforms.

Seven cities are expected to open carbon markets later this year.

China wants to launch a national carbon trading program by 2016. If it is successful, analysts say, the program would be one of the largest in the world and help the country meet its target of cutting carbon dioxide emissions by 45 percent, within seven years.

The platforms allow companies to earn credits for lowering greenhouse gas emissions, which can then be traded. If it works, it would encourage for-profit businesses to invest in green technology.

Although carbon trading in the country's booming economy could be a windfall for the still-struggling global emissions markets, critics say government intervention, state ownership of companies and lack of transparency pose big hurdles to its success.

精準翻譯　句句到位，看你是否真的全數聽懂

毫不誇張地說，北京的霧霾天數已經破紀錄了，空氣中懸浮著微小的顆粒物，降低了能見度的同時，也威脅著人們的身體健康。

近年來，北京的天氣一直備受關注，但是一月份居高不下的汙染指數還是引起了公眾的強烈反應。燃煤發電廠和忙碌的工廠排放的汙染物是造成這一問題的部分原因，政府官員希望能通過碳交易平臺使這一問題得到控制。

　　預計今年下半年，將會有七個城市開放碳交易市場。中國希望在 2016 年啟動一個全國性的碳交易市場。分析人士稱，如果能取得成功，它將會成為當今世界上最大的碳交易市場之一，並且將會幫助中國實現七年內二氧化碳減排 45% 的目標。

　　有了碳交易平臺，那些成功降低了溫室氣體排放量的公司就能夠獲得可在平臺上進行交易的碳信用額度。如果這一措施能行得通，它將會鼓勵營利性企業投資綠色科技。

　　儘管這個經濟蓬勃發展的國家推出的碳交易對於仍在苦苦掙扎的全球碳排放交易市場而言可能會是個意外之喜，但評論人士也指出，政府干預、企業的國有性質和缺少透明度都為它的成功設置了不小的障礙。

- -

關鍵解析 **英文聽力重點看這邊就對了**

❶ Beijing's smoggy days are literally off the charts, with small airborne particles that reduce visibility and threaten health.

　　形容詞 smoggy（煙霧彌漫的）來自 smog 一詞，而 smog 是由 smoke + fog 混合而成，意為「煙與霧的混合物，霾」。off the charts 表示「爆表，打破紀錄」的意思。句子中 with 表示伴隨。airborne 表示「空氣傳播的」，-borne 表示「由……攜帶或傳播的」，類似的詞還有 windborne（風傳播的）。

❷ It has been a persistent concern in recent years, but spiking pollution levels in January are sparking a public outcry.

　　本句中 in recent years 是個多用於現在完成時態的時間副詞。spike 表示「遽增，達到頂峰」的意思，這裡用現在分詞形式 spiking 作形容詞來修飾汙染的程度。spark 表示「引發，觸發」的意思。

❸ The platforms allow companies to earn credits for lowering greenhouse gas emissions, which can then be traded.

　　本句中 credit 表示「信用，信譽」的意思。credit 還有「貸款，稱讚，學分」等意思。在聽到熟悉的詞語，尤其是有多種意思的詞語時，聽者需要結合上下文意來確定其具體意思。

題目詳解篇

Unit 3 衛生健康

Findings Could Help Slash Child Malnutrition
減少兒童營養不良問題的新發現

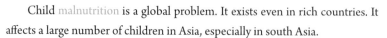

新聞原文 一知半解？跟著新聞原文，再聽一遍 🎧 Track 026

Child malnutrition is a global problem. It exists even in rich countries. It affects a large number of children in Asia, especially in south Asia.

In parts of the world, like sub-Saharan Africa, it threatens child survival.

Dr. Peter Salama represents UNICEF, the United Nations children's agency, in Ethiopia.

"Almost every country in Africa today has rates of severe acute malnutrition. The question is how high it goes."

New studies published in the *Lancet* medical journal show that malnutrition causes 45 percent of all deaths in children under the age of five. Other children suffer stunting, meaning their body and brain fail to develop properly.

The researchers say if countries take some simple measures, they can save the lives of one million children a year.

The proposals include giving pregnant women folic acid and calcium supplements, promoting breast feeding, and giving young children vitamin A and zinc supplements.

The *Lancet* reports that cutting child malnutrition by 20 percent would cost nine billion dollars.

精準翻譯 句句到位，看你是否真的全數聽懂 🔊

兒童營養不良是一個全球性的問題，即使是富裕國家也存在這一問題。在亞洲，尤其是南亞地區，有大量營養不良的兒童。

在其他地方，比如撒哈拉以南的非洲地區，營養不良甚至威脅到兒童的生存。聯合國兒童基金會（UNICEF）駐衣索比亞代表彼得‧薩拉瑪醫生說：「如今，幾乎所有非洲國家都有嚴重急性營養不良發病率記錄，問題只是發病率高低不同。」

最近發表在醫學雜誌《刺絡針》上的新研究顯示，45% 的五歲以下兒童死亡是由營養不良導致的。其他營養不良的兒童則發育遲緩，他們的身體和大腦未能正常發育。

研究人員稱，相關國家如果能採取一些簡單的措施，那它們每年將可以挽救 100 萬兒童的生命。

他們建議的措施包括給懷孕婦女服用葉酸，補充鈣片，提倡母乳餵養，給幼兒補充維生素 A 和鋅。另外，該醫學雜誌的報告還稱，要達成將兒童營養不良發病率降低 20% 的目標，需要花費約 90 億美元。

關鍵解析 英文聽力重點看這邊就對了

❶ Child malnutrition is a global problem.

這是開頭主旨句。學習者可以據此預測下文出現的內容可能是兒童營養不良的具體表現、應對措施等。學會在聽的過程中預測下文，可以幫助聽者更好地理解整篇新聞的內容。

❷ Other children suffer stunting, meaning their body and brain fail to develop properly.

本句中出現了一個令人比較費解的詞 stunting。它的動詞形式 stunt 意為「阻礙……生長（或發育）」，後半句對其意思進行了解釋。在聽力中遇到陌生的概念或單詞時，不要著急，耐心地聽下去，很有可能下文會有進一步的解釋。

❸ The proposals include giving pregnant women folic acid and calcium supplements, promoting breast feeding, and giving young children vitamin A and zinc supplements.

本句的主句部分就是 The proposals include...，後面是所建議措施的具體內容。其中出現了一些營養學的專業術語：folic acid（葉酸），calcium supplements（鈣補充劑），breast feeding（母乳餵養），vitamin A（維生素 A），zinc supplements（鋅補充劑）。學習者平時要注意累積不同領域常用的專業術語。

NEWS
02

Kerry Praises Genetically Modified Crops
克里推崇基因改造作物

新聞原文 一知半解？跟著新聞原文，再聽一遍 🎧 *Track 027*

U.S. Secretary of State John Kerry said Wednesday the United States supports the use of biotechnology to develop so-called "smart" crops that can withstand droughts and floods and require less fertilization.

"So we save money and we save the environment and we save lives. It is a virtuous circle. And through innovation, we believe we can help alleviate the level of hunger and malnutrition today, but more than that, we can, hopefully, live up to our responsibilities for the future."

The United States is the world's biggest producer and consumer of genetically modified food, and U.S.-based Monsanto company is the world's largest developer of genetically altered crops. The company has engineered crops that thrive in some of the world's worst climates and can protect themselves from diseases and pests. The United States has promoted these crops as part of a solution to alleviate the world hunger. But many countries avoid genetically engineered plants fearing harmful long-term effects.

Last month, environmentalists and food safety groups organized a global protest against genetically modified food. Protesters in the city of Knoxville, in southern US state of Tennessee demanded labeling of genetically modified food products.

精準翻譯 句句到位，看你是否真的全數聽懂 🔊

美國國務卿約翰‧凱瑞本週三說，美國政府支持利用生物技術培育能夠抵禦乾旱和洪水災害，並且需要更少肥料的「智能」作物。

「這樣一來，我們節省了資金，保護了環境，同時也養活了更多生命。這是一個良性循環。我們相信，通過不斷創新，我們能幫助緩解當今社會面臨的饑餓和營養不良問題，而更重要的是，我們希望能擔當起對未來的責任。」

　　美國是世界上最大的基因改造食品生產者和消費者，總部位於美國的孟山都公司是當今世界最大的基因改造作物研發商。該公司所培育的基因改造作物能在世界上一些氣候條件最惡劣的地區茁壯生長，並且自身還能抵禦病蟲害的侵襲。如今，美國已在大力推廣這些作物來作為緩解世界饑荒的一項措施。但是，當前仍有許多國家因為擔心會有長遠的不利影響，而避免種植基因改造作物。

　　上個月，一些環保主義者和食品安全組織發起了一場反對基因改造食品的全球性抗議。例如，美國南部田納西州諾克斯維爾市的抗議者就要求基因改造食品必須用專門的標籤加以標註。

- -

關鍵解析 **英文聽力重點看這邊就對了**

❶ U.S. Secretary of State John Kerry said Wednesday the United States supports the use of biotechnology to develop so-called "smart" crops that can withstand droughts and floods and require less fertilization.

　　本句中 U.S. Secretary of State 是「美國國務卿」的意思。聽者平時要多累積時事知識，包括重要國家的領袖、政府機構和官員頭銜的表達。句末 that 引導的關係子句修飾「smart」crops，對「智能」作物的概念進行了詳細的解釋。

❷ And through innovation, we believe we can help alleviate the level of hunger and malnutrition today, but more than that, we can, hopefully, live up to our responsibilities for the future.

　　but 一般表示語義的轉折，而在本句中後面加上了 more than that，表示了意思的遞進，that 指代的是 helping alleviate the level of hunger and malnutrition。片語 live up to sth. 表示「符合，不辜負（他人的期望）」的意思。

❸ The company has engineered crops that thrive in some of the world's worst climates and can protect themselves from diseases and pests.

　　本句中動詞 engineer 的意思是 to modify... by changing its genetic material，即「改良……的基因」。在聽力理解中即使遇到熟悉的詞語，學習者也要結合上下文語意來理解意思，警惕熟詞生義現象。

NEWS
03 Tools to Fight Infectious Diseases Rely on Public Health Programs
戰勝傳染性疾病需仰賴公共衛生計畫

新聞原文 一知半解？跟著新聞原文，再聽一遍 🎧 *Track 028*

A simple bite from a mosquito can end someone's life or change it forever. A sneeze, a handshake or even sharing of a desk can do the same thing. That's how H1N1 — or swine flu — spread around the world a few years ago. Infectious diseases such as malaria, HIV/AIDS and tuberculosis are among the leading causes of death globally.

At a Washington symposium, leading health experts discussed the challenge of confronting persistent and newly-emerging infectious diseases. Dr. Anthony Fauci, with the National Institutes of Health, said most of these diseases result from the fact that as human populations grow, people come into closer contact with animals.

New infectious diseases also emerge when bacteria or viruses mutate and no longer respond to drugs that once killed them. An example is drug-resistant tuberculosis. Other factors include climate change or the expanded habitat of an infectious agent.

While these threats are great, we now have better tools to fight these diseases. According to Dr. Thomas Frieden, head of the U.S. Centers for Disease Control and Prevention, "We've got new technology, we've got better communication, we've got better lab work, more people who are trained."

This means less time elapses between the discovery of a new disease, identifying its genetic makeup and developing drugs or a vaccine to protect against it.

精準翻譯 句句到位，看你是否真的全數聽懂 🔊

　　一次小小的蚊子叮咬就有可能致命或者永遠改變一個人的生活。一個噴嚏、一次握手，甚或是共用一張桌子也可能帶來相同的後果。這就是幾年前 A 型 H1N1 流感病毒——俗稱豬流感——在世界範圍內的傳播方式。在全球各地，像瘧疾、愛滋病（病毒）和肺結核這樣的傳染性疾病是導致死亡的重要原因。

在華盛頓舉行的一次專題研討會上，知名健康問題專家共聚一堂，討論如何應對頑強的和新近出現的傳染性疾病的挑戰。來自美國國立衛生研究院的安東尼‧福西博士稱，這些傳染性疾病大多數都是伴隨著人口增長，人類與動物的接觸更加密切而造成的。

當細菌或病毒發生變異而那些曾經能夠消滅它們的藥物不再起作用時，新的傳染性疾病也會產生。耐藥性肺結核病就是其中的一個例子。其他因素還包括氣候變化或者傳染源寄生範圍的擴大。

雖然面臨的威脅是巨大的，但是現在我們有了更好的手段來對抗這些疾病。美國疾病控制和預防中心主任托馬斯‧弗里登博士說：「我們有新的技術，我們有更良好的溝通，我們有更好的實驗研究和更多受過專業培訓的人員。」

這就意味著我們從發現一種新疾病，到確定它的基因結構，再到研發藥物或疫苗來防治這種疾病，整個過程所需的時間更少了。

- -

關鍵解析　英文聽力重點看這邊就對了

❶ Infectious diseases such as malaria, HIV/AIDS and tuberculosis are among the leading causes of death globally.

　　本句中出現了幾種疾病名稱：malaria（瘧疾）, HIV/AIDS（愛滋病病毒/ 愛滋病）和 tuberculosis（肺結核）。前面指出這些疾病都是 infectious（傳染性的）。leading causes 表示「主要原因」。

❷ Dr. Anthony Fauci, with the National Institutes of Health, said most of these diseases result from the fact that as human populations grow, people come into closer contact with animals.

　　本句中出現了一個人名 Dr. Anthony Fauci，後面用 with 引出其工作機構或者所屬機構。result from 表示「由……導致」。the fact 後面 that 引導的是一個同位語子句，說明 the fact 的具體內容。

❸ New infectious diseases also emerge when bacteria or viruses mutate and no longer respond to drugs that once killed them.

　　本句中 when 引導的子句表示一種條件，即新傳染性疾病產生的條件：mutate 和 no longer respond to drugs... 二者必須兼備。

NEWS 04　World AIDS Day 2012: More Hopeful Than in Past
充滿更多希望的 2012 世界愛滋病日

新聞原文 一知半解？跟著新聞原文，再聽一遍 🎧 *Track 029*

According to the United Nations, about 34 million people worldwide are living with HIV, and 2.5 million were infected last year alone. In the United States, the Centers for Disease Control says there is an alarming rise in the spread of HIV among teenagers and young adults, with 1,000 new infections each month. Yet public officials and health care workers say the world is nearing a turning point on AIDS, the disease caused by the HIV virus.

Dr. Anthony Fauci, who heads AIDS research at the U.S. National Institutes of Health, says medical advances have made the difference.

One of the tools involves treating people early in their infection, before they get sick. This allows those with HIV to lead productive lives. And studies show it dramatically reduces the odds that they will infect a sexual partner.

But experts say that testing and education are also crucial. The CDC recommends routine testing for everyone.

As for the steep rise in HIV infections among young people in the United States, the CDC says doctors, teachers and parents need to ensure that young people receive information about HIV and AIDS, and that they get tested and treated if they have the disease.

精準翻譯　句句到位，看你是否真的全數聽懂 🔊

　　根據聯合國公布的數據，全球約有 3,400 萬愛滋病病毒攜帶者，僅去年一年，感染人數就達 250 萬。在美國，疾病控制中心稱愛滋病病毒在青少年中的傳染率正呈現出驚人的增長，每個月的新感染人數高達 1,000 人。儘管如此，政府官員和醫護人員還是表示，就愛滋病而言，整個世界很快將面臨一個轉折點。

　　安東尼・福西博士——美國國立衛生研究院愛滋病研究項目的負責人——表示，是醫學進步帶來了這一改變。

　　其中一種方法就是在感染愛滋病病毒的早期階段、在發病之前進行治療。這能讓那些感染愛滋病病毒的人生活得更有價值。研究顯示，這一方法大大降低了他們將愛滋病病毒傳染給性伴侶的幾率。

　　不過專家稱，對愛滋病的檢測和教育同樣非常重要。疾控中心就建議對所有人進行定期檢測。對於美國年輕人中感染愛滋病病毒人數急劇上升這一情況，疾控中心認為，醫生、老師和家長需要確保年輕人能充分了解有關愛滋病病毒和愛滋病的知識，確保他們接受檢測，並且如果已經感染的話，要確保他們能得到治療。

關鍵解析　英文聽力重點看這邊就對了

❶ In the United States, the Centers for Disease Control says there is an alarming rise in the spread of HIV among teenagers and young adults, with 1,000 new infections each month.

　　本句最後的 with 表示「伴隨」，引出前面 alarming rise（驚人增長）的具體表現。注意 there be 句型中，be 動詞的單複數取決於後面緊跟的名詞是單數還是複數。

❷ And studies show it dramatically reduces the odds that they will infect a sexual partner.

　　本句中 dramatically 表示「顯著地，引人注目地」，修飾降低的程度。其他常見的程度副詞還有 significantly（明顯地），markedly（明顯地），slightly（輕微地）等。it 代指的是上文提到的方法，即「在感染愛滋病病毒的早期、在病毒發之前進行治療」。the odds 表示「概率，可能性」，其後的 that 引導的是同位語子句而非關係子句，因為 that 子句的內容是對前面 odds 的具體說明。同位語子句的關聯詞在子句中不充當任何成分。

NEWS

05 World Health Day Raises Awareness of Deadliest Condition

世界衛生日：提高對高血壓致命性的意識

新聞原文 一知半解？跟著新聞原文，再聽一遍 🎧 *Track 030*

It's evening at Dakar beach in Senegal, and the sands are packed with people exercising.

But a recent World Health Organization report indicates one out of eight Senegalese women aged over 20 are obese — and suffer from related diseases like high blood pressure.

The World Health Organization says more than one in three adults worldwide has high blood pressure. In some African countries it is as high as 40 percent.

Professor Majid Ezzati chairs the Department of Global Environmental Health at Imperial College London.

Ezzati says high blood pressure puts a huge burden on people and societies.

"It is the leading risk factor for mortality and for disease burden worldwide. It is associated obviously with cardiovascular diseases, large effects on the stroke which is very common throughout the Asia, on heart disease and other cardiovascular diseases."

In remote areas, doctors say a biggest problem is access to healthcare. So a team of medics has developed a solar-powered blood pressure monitor that they hope will transform diagnosis and treatment. Andrew Shennan, Professor of Obstetrics at Kings College London is among the designers.

The monitors are inexpensive. "Although this is a very cheap devise, which we plan to sell for under 20 euros, it is as accurate as a 10,000 pounds machine that I use on the intensive care unit."

The World Health Organization hopes to get more people talking about one of the world's biggest killers.

精準翻譯 句句到位，看你是否真的全數聽懂

到了晚上，塞內加爾的達喀爾海灘上就會擠滿前來鍛煉的人。但是，世界衛生組織最近發布的一項報告卻顯示，每八名 20 歲以上的塞內加爾婦女中就有一位過度肥胖，並且患有高血壓之類的相關疾病。

世界衛生組織表示，世界上每三個成年人中就至少有一人患有高血壓。在一些非洲國家，高血壓患病率甚至高達 40%。

馬吉德·伊紮提教授是倫敦帝國理工學院全球環境健康研究系的主任，他說高血壓給民眾和社會都帶來了巨大負擔。「它是世界各地造成死亡和疾病負擔的重要危險因素。它與心血管疾病有明顯的關聯，對亞洲地區很常見的中風有較大影響，對心臟病以及其他心血管疾病也有較大影響。」

醫生們說，在一些偏遠地區，一個最大的問題就是民眾很難享受到醫療保健服務。為此，一個醫生團隊已經研發出了一種太陽能血壓計，希望能夠改善當地的高血壓診斷和治療情況。倫敦劍橋國王學院的婦產科教授安德魯·申南就是該項發明的設計者之一。

這些血壓計並不貴。「血壓計的計劃售價在 20 歐元以內，儘管很便宜，但是它的準確度跟我在加護病房使用的一萬英鎊的機器一樣。」世界衛生組織希望能有更多的人來談論和關注高血壓——這個世界上最大的健康殺手之一。

- -

關鍵解析 英文聽力重點看這邊就對了

❶ It's evening at Dakar beach in Senegal, and the sands are packed with people exercising.

本句描述的場景是在西非塞內加爾的海灘上，**beach** 和 **the sands** 都表示「海灘」的意思。**be packed with** 意為「擠滿，塞滿」。句末的 **exercising** 是現在分詞作後位修飾。

❷ So a team of medics has developed a solar powered blood pressure monitor that they hope will transform diagnosis and treatment.

句中的 **medic** 是一個非正式用詞，指的是「醫生」。**solar-powered** 是一個複合詞，意思是「太陽能驅動的」。本句句末 **that** 引導的關係子句修飾 **monitor**，說明了這款血壓計的用途。

NEWS 06 Discovery Could Lead to New Drugs to Block Deadly Viruses
新發現促使新藥物研發，有望阻斷致命病毒複製

新聞原文 一知半解？跟著新聞原文，再聽一遍 *Track 031*

Viruses are strange things. Though they are not alive, they have a basic genetic structure that allows them to be biologically active. But they don't have the built-in reproductive capacity of bacteria.

John Connor, a virologist at Boston University in Massachusetts, explains that in order for viruses to reproduce and become a disease threat, they must first hijack the genetic machinery of a living cell.

Connor and his colleagues screen thousands of chemical compounds, looking for ones that show strong antiviral activity.

They identify several small molecules that interfere with the replication of a class of pathogens known as NNS viruses, which cause the deadly Marburg and Ebola infections, as well as measles and mumps.

The most effective compounds discovered by the Boston researchers shut down that replication process — at least in cell-culture experiments —by limiting the viruses' RNA production.

The compounds do not thwart all viruses — they have no effect, for example, on HIV, the virus that causes AIDS — because of differences in the way viral pathogens enter and commandeer cells.

Just as antibiotics are effective against many bacterial illnesses, Connor says he hopes this discovery leads to the development of broad-spectrum antiviral drugs to treat a variety of currently incurable viral infections.

精準翻譯 句句到位，看你是否真的全數聽懂

病毒是一種奇怪的東西。儘管沒有生命，但是它們擁有一種基本的基因結構，這讓它們具有了生物活性。不過，它們並沒有像細菌那樣天生的繁殖能力。

麻薩諸塞州波士頓大學的病毒學家約翰・康納解釋說，病毒要想進行複製，成為一種疾病威脅，首先必須劫持某一活細胞的遺傳機制。

　　康納和他的同事們對數千種化合物進行了分析篩選，以尋找那些擁有強抗病毒活性的化合物。

　　他們發現了幾種小分子，這些小分子會干擾一類被稱為 NNS 病毒的病原體的複製過程，而 NNS 病毒能夠引起麻疹、腮腺炎以及致命的馬堡病毒和伊波拉病毒感染。

　　波士頓大學的研究者發現的最有效化合物是通過限制病毒的 RNA 複製，從而阻斷病毒的複製過程，至少在細胞培養實驗中是這樣的。

　　但是，由於病毒病原體侵入和控制細胞的方式不同，這些化合物並不能阻止所有的病毒——比如，它們對愛滋病病毒就沒有任何作用。

　　康納說，就像抗生素能夠有效治療許多細菌性疾病一樣，他希望這一發現能夠幫助普及抗病毒藥物的研發，從而幫助治療當前無法治愈的多種病毒性感染。

- -

關鍵解析　英文聽力重點看這邊就對了

❶ Though they are not alive, they have a basic genetic structure that allows them to be biologically active.

　　though 表示「雖然」之意，表明句意有轉折。後半句表達的意思是重點。其中 that 引導的是關係子句，修飾先行詞 a basic genetic structure。

❷ They identify several small molecules that interfere with the replication of a class of pathogens known as NNS viruses, which cause the deadly Marburg and Ebola infections, as well as measles and mumps.

　　本句較長，句型結構較複雜，出現了關係子句套關係子句的情況。其中 that 引導的關係子句修飾 small molecules（小分子），which 引導的關係子句修飾 NNS viruses（NNS 病毒）。學習者即使不熟悉 pathogens 的意思，也可以根據下文的 known as NNS viruses 猜測其在該文意下的大概意思。這裡出現了一些比較專業的醫學名詞，如 pathogens（病原體），Marburg（馬堡病毒），Ebola（伊波拉病毒），measles（麻疹）和 mumps（腮腺炎）。學習者要注意在平時的英語閱讀和聽力訓練中，廣泛涉獵，擴大知識面，盡可減少專業詞彙帶來的聽力理解障礙。

FAO Aims to Quickly Measure World Hunger
糧農組織致力於全球饑餓狀況的快速評估

新聞原文　一知半解？跟著新聞原文，再聽一遍 🎧 *Track 032*

　　Measuring the scope of world hunger is a long and complicated process. Often officials and policymakers don't have the most up-to-date information. Now, the U.N. Food and Agriculture Organization, the FAO, hopes to change that with a new project called Voices of the Hungry.

　　The U.N. agency wants to hear from the people themselves and not just evaluate various data, studies and reports. FAO senior statistician Carlo Cafiero says the current system of measuring food supplies and hunger, while important, is subject to long delays.

　　Food consumption surveys are generally conducted every five years.

　　The new Voices of the Hungry project is described as fast and more precise. It will use surveys of individuals to gather information on the extent and severity of hunger. The surveys will be done annually in collaboration with the survey giant Gallup.

　　The FAO statistician says the survey is not subjective and the information will be evaluated by experts. It takes only three months from the time a survey is taken to the time FAO officials receive the information.

　　Voices of the Hungry surveys will eventually be expanded to 160,000 respondents in 150 countries. The five-year project will lead to a new FAO standard for food security.

精準翻譯　句句到位，看你是否真的全數聽懂

　　全球饑餓範圍的評估是一個漫長而複雜的過程。相關官員和決策者們常常無法掌握最新的信息。現在，聯合國糧農組織（FAO）希望通過一個名為「饑餓之聲」的新項目來改變這一狀況。

　　糧農組織想要聽取民眾自身發出的聲音，而不只是評估各種數據、研究和報告。糧農組織高級統計師卡洛‧卡菲羅認為，當前的食物供應和饑餓監測體系儘管非常重要，但是常常存在長時間滯後的情況。

　　一般來講，每五年才會進行一次食品消耗量調查。

　　據描述，「饑餓之聲」這一新項目在監測上會更加快速，監測結果也更加準確。它將會採用對個人進行調查的方式來收集有關饑餓廣泛程度和嚴重程度的信息。調查每年會進行一次，將與諮詢業巨頭蓋洛普公司合作完成。

　　卡菲羅說，這種調查並不只是主觀性的調查，相關信息將會由專家來進行評估。從調查開始到糧農組織官員收到相關信息，整個過程僅需三個月時間。

　　最終，「饑餓之聲」調查將會擴大到涵蓋 150 個國家的 160,000 名調查對象。這個五年項目將會幫助糧農組織制定出一套新的食品安全標準。

- -

關鍵解析　英文聽力重點看這邊就對了

❶ FAO senior statistician Carlo Cafiero says the current system of measuring food supplies and hunger, while important, is subject to long delays.

　　本句中 while 表示「雖然，儘管」的意思，插入 while important 修飾 the current system。be subject to sth. 表示「易受……的影響」。be subject to long delays 表示「常出現長時間的滯後」。

❷ It takes only three months from the time a survey is taken to the time FAO officials receive the information.

　　It takes some time (to do sth.) 表示「完成某事需要花費一定的時間」。from...to... 表示「從……到……」，這裡的兩個時間點後面都有一個關係子句來修飾限定。

NEWS 08
Horse Meat Scandal Spreads Across Europe
「馬肉風波」席捲歐洲

新聞原文　一知半解？跟著新聞原文，再聽一遍 🎧 *Track 033*

The horse meat scandal started in Ireland and the United Kingdom in January, but has since spread all around the EU. DNA checks on beef have found that some products, including hamburgers, contained as much as 30 percent horse meat. The list of tainted products has since widened to include frozen lasagna, tortellini, and bolognese sauce.

Europol, the EU's police agency, is leading a Europe-wide fraud investigation. So far, three men are under arrest in England and Wales. They are accused of disguising cheap horse meat as frozen beef. The arrests come as French authorities said meat wholesaler Spanghero re-labeled and then sold horse meat from Romanian suppliers. The company denies wrongdoing. By Friday, supermarkets in Germany, Denmark, Hungary, and elsewhere had begun recalling suspect products.

Some food safety experts are blaming supermarkets for pushing down prices and squeezing wholesalers. Others think lax inspections are to blame. As for the supermarkets, they say they have been tricked too, and promise tougher inspections of their own going forward.

精準翻譯　句句到位，看你是否真的全數聽懂 🔊

這場「馬肉風波」1 月份起於愛爾蘭和英國，至今已經蔓延到了整個歐盟地區。對牛肉的 DNA 檢測結果發現，包括漢堡在內的一些牛肉製品中含有高達 30% 的馬肉成分。受馬肉汙染的產品清單也已經擴大到了包括冷凍義大利千層面、義式餃子和番茄肉醬在內的很多產品。

歐洲警察署正在領導一場全歐洲的詐欺調查。目前，已有三名男子在英格

蘭和威爾斯被捕，他們被指控用便宜的馬肉冒充冷凍牛肉出售。法國當局稱肉類批發商斯潘蓋羅把從羅馬尼亞供應商那裡進口的馬肉換上牛肉標籤進行出售。隨之，這幾個人被逮捕。但是該公司否認自己有違法行為。截至週五，德國、丹麥、匈牙利等國的超市已經開始召回可疑產品。

一些食品安全專家指責超市過分壓低價格，過度擠壓批發商的利潤。其他專家則認為問題出在寬鬆懈怠的檢查環節上。超市方面則聲稱它們也是受騙者，並且承諾在未來的經營中會自身進行更加嚴格的檢查。

關鍵解析 英文聽力重點看這邊就對了

❶ The horse meat scandal started in Ireland and the United Kingdom in January, but has since spread all around the EU.

開頭的第一句話就點出了這則新聞所報道的主題，即「馬肉風波」。在進行聽力訓練時，聽者需要特別留意開頭的內容，因為它經常會開宗明義。句中 since 作為副詞，表示「自此以來」，多與現在完成式或者過去完成式連用。spread 在這裡是過去分詞形式，拼寫與原形相同。聽者平時要注意常見不規則動詞過去式和過去分詞的累積和學習。

❷ They are accused of disguising cheap horse meat as frozen beef.

本句中 be accused of 表示「被控告（做某事）」，其主動結構為 accuse sb. of sth.，比如 accuse sb. of theft/murder（控告某人盜竊/謀殺）。disguise A as B 表示「用 A 冒充 B」的意思，文中是「用廉價的馬肉冒充冷凍牛肉」。固定搭配是英語學習者需要掌握的另一個重點。

❸ Some food safety experts are blaming supermarkets for pushing down prices and squeezing wholesalers.

本句中 blame sb./sth. for sth. 表示「把……歸咎於某人/某物」的意思。push down prices 意指「過分壓低價格」。動詞 squeeze 有「擠壓，榨取」的意思，結合上下文語境，此處可譯為「過度擠壓其利潤」。學習者在聽錄音的過程中，要注意結合語意來確定詞的具體含義。

199

Looking Better Helps Cancer Patients Feel Better
好看的容貌有助於癌症病人的恢復

新聞原文　一知半解？跟著新聞原文，再聽一遍 Track 034

Millions of women who undergo chemotherapy around the world face the harsh reality of hair and weight loss and skin damage. But many are turning to "Look Good Feel Better" a program that teaches women simple beauty techniques so they can once again not only look better physically but also feel stronger emotionally.

Created by the Personal Care Products Council and supported by the American Cancer Society, the "Look Good Feel Better" program has been running free beauty classes across the United States since 1989. Here, makeup artists and hair stylists teach cancer survivors how to put on makeup and cover their bald heads in flattering ways.

Participants receive free makeup kits full of brand-name cosmetics.

The program's research indicates that after seeing the visible side effects of cancer treatment, such as hair and weight loss, many women are dissatisfied with their appearance. After taking the beauty class, most women begin to like what they see in the mirror.

The program is now running in 25 countries. So far it has helped more than 1.2 million women look good — and feel better.

精準翻譯　句句到位，看你是否真的全數聽懂

　　全世界數百萬接受化療的女性都不得不面對頭髮脫落、體重驟降和皮膚損傷的殘酷現實。但是現在很多人正參與一個叫做「容貌好，心情好」的項目。該項目會教女性一些簡單的美容技巧，能再次讓她們不僅在外表上看起來更美，而且在精神上也會感覺更加堅強。

　　「容貌好，心情好」這一項目是由個人護理產品協會創辦，並得到了美國癌症協會的支持，自 1989 年開始就一直在美國各地開辦免費的美容課。在美

容課上，化妝師和髮型師會教癌症倖存者們怎樣化妝，以及怎樣遮蓋光禿的頭部使其更好看。

參與者都會得到一個裝有許多名牌化妝品的化妝包。該項目的研究顯示，在看到癌症治療帶來的明顯副作用，比如頭髮脫落和體重驟降之後，許多女性會對她們的外表感到不滿。但是，上了美容課之後，多數女性開始喜歡她們在鏡子中的樣子了。

這一項目如今正在 25 個國家展開，目前已經幫助了 120 多萬名女性，讓她們看上去更美，感覺更好。

- -

關鍵解析 英文聽力重點看這邊就對了

❶ Millions of women who undergo chemotherapy around the world face the harsh reality of hair and weight loss and skin damage.

在聽的過程中學習者需要認真解析本句的結構，找到主句部分：women face the harsh reality。本句中 who 引導的是一個關係子句，修飾先行詞 women。harsh reality 後面的「of + 名詞片語」說明殘酷現實的具體內容，包括「脫髮、體重驟降以及皮膚損傷」。

❷ But many are turning to "Look Good Feel Better" a program that teaches women simple beauty techniques so they can once again not only look better physically but also feel stronger emotionally.

本句結構比較複雜，聽者需要認真分析句子結構，才能更好地理解其意。句中 a program 和「Look Good Feel Better」是同位語關係，後面的同位語對前面提到的這個項目進行解釋和說明。program 後面跟了一個 that 引導的關係子句。固定搭配 not only... but also... 表示「不但……而且……」的意思，這個平行結構需要連接兩個對等的成分。

❸ 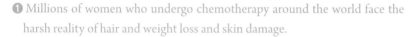 The program's research indicates that after seeing the visible side effects of cancer treatment, such as hair and weight loss, many women are dissatisfied with their appearance.

本句 indicate 後面 that 引導的是一個較長的受詞子句，子句的主語為 many women。be dissatisfied with 表示「對……不滿意」。

NEWS 10　Parasites, Trauma: Causes of Epilepsy
寄生蟲、外傷：癲癇病的誘因

新聞原文　一知半解？跟著新聞原文，再聽一遍 Track 035

A new study says it's possible to substantially reduce the number of epilepsy cases in Africa. The neurological disorder, which is characterized by seizures, is much more common in poor countries and rural areas.

The study is the largest ever done on epilepsy in Sub-Saharan Africa. Nearly 600,000 people were evaluated in five countries: Kenya, South Africa, Uganda, Tanzania and Ghana.

It can cause not only physical suffering, but emotional pain as well.

Newton and his team say the study is the "first to reveal the true extent of the problem and the impact of different risk factors." And it's not just genetics. One big risk factor is parasites. The study found that adults, who had been exposed to a parasitic disease, were up to three times more likely to develop epilepsy.

"In the children under 18 years of age, we found that although the parasitic causes were there they weren't as important as the abnormal pregnancies of their mothers — and particularly events that occurred around their birth. So it looks like that these children are suffering from birth trauma."

The study says parasitic disease control projects can help to greatly reduce the number of epilepsy cases. One example is the success of efforts to control river blindness.

As for birth trauma, better pre-and-ante natal care in developing countries could greatly reduce the risk of epilepsy.

精準翻譯　句句到位，看你是否真的全數聽懂

　　一項新研究稱有可能大幅減少非洲癲癇病例的數量。這種以突然發作為特點的神經性疾病在貧困國家和一些國家的農村地區更為常見。

　　該研究是迄今為止在撒哈拉以南的非洲所進行的規模最大的一次癲癇病研究。來自五個國家——肯亞、南非、烏干達、坦尚尼亞和迦納——的近600,000 人參與了這一研究。

　　癲癇不僅會給患者帶來身體上的痛苦，還會給他們帶來精神上的折磨。

　　牛頓教授和他的研究小組稱，此項研究「首次揭示了問題的真實狀況和不同危險因素所產生的影響」。而它不只是遺傳現象。其中一個很重要的危險因素就是寄生蟲。該研究發現，曾經得過寄生蟲病的成年人，患癲癇的可能性甚至要比普通人高出三倍。

　　「在 18 歲以下兒童中，我們發現感染寄生蟲病雖然是致病原因，但更重要的原因卻是孩童母親在懷孕期間的異常妊娠，特別是發生在生產前後的事件影響更嚴重。這些孩童似乎是遭受了生產創傷。」

　　該研究稱，寄生蟲病控制項目能夠幫助大幅減少癲癇病例的數量。其中，盤尾絲蟲病的成功控制就是一個很好的例子。

　　至於產傷，提高發展中國家的孕期和產前護理水準可以大幅降低癲癇症的發病風險。

關鍵解析 英文聽力重點看這邊就對了

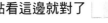

❶ The neurological disorder, which is characterized by seizures, is much more common in poor countries and rural areas.

　　the neurological disorder（這種神經性疾病）指的就是前面提到的 epilepsy（癲癇）。which 引導的是一個非限定關係子句。非限定性關係子句往往與其所修飾的先行詞之間用逗號隔開。be characterized by 表示「以……特點」。

❷ The study found that adults, who had been exposed to a parasitic disease, were up to three times more likely to develop epilepsy.

　　本句中 who 引導的關係子句修飾先行詞 adults。子句使用的是過去完成式的被動語態。過去完成式一般表示過去某一時間或動作以前已經發生或完成的動作，即「過去的過去」。也就是說，已經結束的研究發現，以前得過寄生蟲病的成年人，後來患癲癇病的可能性遠高於其他人。

Report: Superfood for Babies
報告：嬰兒的超級食物

新聞原文　一知半解？跟著新聞原文，再聽一遍　🎧 Track 036

A new report says more than 800,000 babies' lives could be saved every year, if all women began breastfeeding within the first hour of giving birth. Save the Children calls breastfeeding one of the best ways to prevent malnutrition, a major killer of children under age five.

Save the Children CEO Carolyn Miles says it's vital to begin breastfeeding soon after a child is born.

The report describes colostrum as a child's "first immunization." But in some cultures, such as parts of Niger, there's a myth that colostrum is dangerous.

Many mothers believe their babies need to eat something besides breast milk. Miles says water, sugar water and tea are not necessary.

The head of Save the Children says another obstacle to breastfeeding is a shortage of healthcare workers in developing countries.

The report, Superfood for Babies, recommends that every country should ensure minimum maternity leave of at least 14 weeks. And when women do return to work, they should receive support so they can continue to breastfeed.

She says great strides have been made in recent years in efforts to reduce child mortality. She says even more lives could be saved if many more women breastfed their babies.

精準翻譯　句句到位，看你是否真的全數聽懂 🔊

　　一項新的報告稱，如果所有產婦在生完孩子一小時內就開始給嬰兒哺乳，那每年將會挽救超過 800,000 名嬰兒的生命。救助兒童會認為母乳餵養是預防營養不良的最佳方式之一，營養不良是威脅五歲以下兒童生命的一大殺手。

　　救助兒童會總裁卡羅琳·邁爾斯說，在新生兒出生後盡早開始給嬰兒哺乳是非常重要的。該報告認為初乳是給孩子的「初次免疫」。但是在有些文化裡，

比如在尼日的部分地區，就存在「初乳是危險的」這樣的錯誤認識。

許多媽媽都認為她們的寶寶除了母乳之外，還需要吃點別的東西。但是邁爾斯説，沒必要給嬰兒喝水、糖水和茶。

這位救助兒童會負責人還説，在發展中國家，母乳餵養的另一個障礙是衛生保健人員十分短缺。

《嬰兒的超級食物》這一報告建議所有國家都應該確保至少 14 週的最短產假。而且，婦女回到工作崗位上後，她們也應該獲得支持，以便能繼續給寶寶哺乳。

邁爾斯表示，近年來降低兒童死亡率的努力已經取得了重大成效。如果更多的婦女能用母乳餵養寶寶，那麼就將會有更多的生命獲救。

- -

關鍵解析 英文聽力重點看這邊就對了

❶ Save the Children calls breastfeeding one of the best ways to prevent malnutrition, a major killer of children under age five.

本句中 Save the Children 是一個兒童慈善組織的名稱，即救助兒童會。句中 malnutrition 和 a major killer 是同位語關係，它們想要表達的意思即「營養不良是威脅五歲以下兒童生命的一大殺手」。

❷ And when women do return to work, they should receive support so they can continue to breastfeed.

句中的 do 用於加強語氣，表示強調。本句在意思上承接上句，強調「當女性回到工作崗位上後，她們也應獲得支持以便能繼續給孩子餵奶」。

❸ She says even more lives could be saved if many more women breastfed their babies.

本句中使用了虛擬語態，if 引導的了句用的是過去時。虛擬語態多用來表示説話人所説的情況並不是事實，而是一種假設、願望、懷疑或推理。本句話的意思是「如果更多的女性用母乳餵養孩子，那麼更多的生命就可以被挽救」。句中描述的不是現有的事實情況，而是一種願望，因此，she says 後面主句用了 could + 動詞原形，子句用了一般過去式。

NEWS

12 South African Traditional Healers Face Increased Competition

南非傳統治療師面臨日益激烈的競爭

新聞原文 一知半解？跟著新聞原文，再聽一遍 *Track 037*

It is estimated that South Africa has about 200,000 traditional healers and more than 30 million people seek their counsel.

But in modern times, some fringe elements have tarnished their reputation. South African authorities say there have been 300 murders in the last 10 years allegedly for body parts to use in traditional potions — known as muti.

In order to protect their image, sangomas created the Traditional Healer Organization, known as THO. Launched in the 1970s, it does lobbying and also trains and teaches new sangomas on the ethics of the job.

These new recruits are learning about physiology, HIV/AIDs and other sexually transmitted diseases. Program manager Thlakele Shongwe helped create the code of conduct — which she says protects sangomas and their clients.

Recognizing the cultural importance of sangomas, the government created regulatory guidelines in 2003 in the Traditional Health Practitioners Bill to protect both the public and the practice. But it has yet to be fully implemented.

Sangomas also face increasing competition from Western medicine as general health care has been made more accessible to more South Africans in the last 20 years.

More sangomas are no longer able to earn a living from their practice alone.

A recent poll says 70 percent of South Africans still visit sangomas on a regular basis.

精準翻譯 句句到位，看你是否真的全數聽懂

據估計，南非現有約 200,000 名傳統治療師（巫醫），而向他們求醫問診的人數超過 3,000 萬。但是在當今社會，一些邊緣事件的發生卻玷汙了他們的聲譽。南非相關部門稱，過去十年已經發生了 300 起特殊的謀殺案，謀殺者涉嫌摘取受害者身體的某些部位來製造被稱為「靈藥」的傳統藥液。

巫醫們為了保護自己的形象，創立了傳統治療師組織（THO）。自 20 世

紀 70 年代開始，該組織做了大量的遊説工作，還對新巫醫進行了培訓並教授他們相關的職業道德。

這些剛入行者正在學習生理學、愛滋病（病毒）和一些其他性傳播疾病的知識。培訓項目管理人特拉克勒‧雄圭幫助制定了一套執業守則，他説這一守則可以保護巫醫和他們的客戶。

南非政府也認識到巫醫在文化中的重要性，於 2003 年在《傳統衛生從業人員法案》中規定了一些監管方針，以保護公眾和這一傳統行業。但是，目前該法案還未全面付諸實施。另一方面，在過去 20 年時間裡，越來越多的南非人已能夠享受到普通的衛生健保服務，巫醫們也面臨著來自西藥日趨激烈的競爭。很多巫醫無法再僅靠行醫來謀生。儘管如此，最近一項民意測驗顯示，70% 的南非人仍然會定期去找巫醫問診。

- -

關鍵解析 **英文聽力重點看這邊就對了**

❶ It is estimated that South Africa has about 200,000 traditional healers and more than 30 million people seek their counsel.

本句中 It is estimated that... 表示「據估計」的意思，使用的是被動形式。當沒有必要指明動作的執行者時可以採用這樣的句式。類似的結構還有 It is believed that...（據信），It is reported that...（據報道），It is said that...（據説）等。另外，在聽力訓練中，聽者要特別注意出現的數字，不僅要能聽懂，還要能準確地記下來。

❷ South African authorities say there have been 300 murders in the last 10 years allegedly for body parts to use in traditional potions — known as muti.

本句中 in the last 10 years 是現在完成式的典型時間副詞，因此句子中動詞用的是 there have been。聽者可能並不熟悉 muti 的意思，但是根據前面提到的 traditional potions, 可以推測出它是一種藥液。

❸  Sangomas also face increasing competition from Western medicine as general health care has been made more accessible to more South Africans in the last 20 years.

be accessible to sb. 表示「某人可使用……」，文中指的是「越來越多的南非人能享受到普通的衛生健保服務」。

題目詳解篇

Unit 4 政治熱點

"Fiscal Cliff" Deal Highlights Messy US Democracy in Action

「財政懸崖」決議凸顯美國民主制度的混亂

新聞原文　一知半解？跟著新聞原文，再聽一遍 🎧 Track 038

Many visitors to the U.S. Capitol, like David Stark from Maryland, come to admire this monument to democracy but express frustration with the political polarization inside its halls.

While Congress and President Barack Obama were able to reach a deal to avert the "fiscal cliff" deadline — which would have imposed drastic spending cuts and steep tax increases — the process highlighted politicians' inability to work together.

Negotiations between President Obama, a Democrat, and the Republican Speaker of the House of Representatives, John Boehner broke down. Democratic and Republican leaders in the Senate also failed to agree.

In the end, it was the personal relationship between Vice President Joe Biden, a former senator, and Senate Minority Leader Mitch McConnell that overcame the deep divide. And the bill that passed during a special session of Congress on New Year's Day only postponed dealing with the growing federal deficit.

Allan Lichtman, a professor of history at American University, is concerned that future budget battles will overly dominate the new legislative session.

Lichtman says as Congress draws out the budget debate, it is less likely to deal with more important issues like disaster relief and reducing the effects of climate change.

精準翻譯　句句到位，看你是否真的全數聽懂 🔊

　　來自馬里蘭州的大衛・斯塔克，以及很多像他一樣來美國國會大廈參觀的人，在仰慕這座民主紀念碑的同時也對大廈內兩極化的黨派紛爭感到沮喪。

　　儘管美國國會和總統歐巴馬最終成功達成協議，逃過了「財政懸崖」到來的最後期限——若非如此，將會導致大幅的開支削減和稅收增加——但是這個過程卻暴露了一大問題，那就是政治家們無法做到同心協力，共渡難關。

　　現任總統、民主黨代表歐巴馬和眾議院議長、共和黨人約翰‧博納之間進行過反覆協商，但還是以失敗告終。參議院中民主黨和共和黨領導人之間也難以達成一致。

　　最終，副總統、前參議員喬‧拜登憑藉與參議院少數派領袖米奇‧麥康奈爾的私交解決了分歧。新年期間，國會特別會議上通過的提案只不過推遲了不斷增長的聯邦財政赤字問題的解決時間。

　　美國大學歷史教授阿蘭‧利希特曼擔心，新一期的立法會議將會深陷未來的財政預算紛爭中。

　　利希特曼表示，如果在預算問題上難以達成共識，久拖不決，國會將會無暇顧及災難援救以及減少氣候變化影響這樣更重要的事件。

- -

關鍵解析　**英文聽力重點看這邊就對了**

❶ While Congress and President Barack Obama were able to reach a deal to avert the "fiscal cliff" deadline — which would have imposed drastic spending cuts and steep tax increases — the process highlighted politicians' inability to work together.

　　本句破折號之間的關係子句用以說明 fiscal cliff（財政懸崖）的直接影響。句中 drastic 和 steep 都表示「巨大的，大幅度的」之意。

❷ In the end, it was the personal relationship between Vice President Joe Biden, a former senator, and Senate Minority Leader Mitch McConnell that overcame the deep divide.

　　句中的 Vice President Joe Biden 和 a former senator 是同位語關係。整個句子比較長，其主句為 it was the personal relationship... that overcame the deep divide，是一個強調句的句型。句末的 divide 在這裡作名詞，表示「分歧」的意思。

❸ And the bill that passed during a special session of Congress on New Year's Day only postponed dealing with the growing federal deficit.

　　本句的主句是 the bill postponed...，句中 the bill 後面 that 引導的是一個限制性關係子句。postpone doing sth. 意為「推遲做某事」。

US "Patriotic Millionaires": "Tax Us More"

美國「愛國百萬富翁」呼籲：「向我們徵收更多的稅吧！」

新聞原文 一知半解？跟著新聞原文，再聽一遍 🎧 *Track 039*

In Washington — a group calling themselves "Patriotic Millionaires," storming Capitol Hill with their message for the president and Congress: "tax us more, we can take it."

They are in line with President Obama, who has vowed to raise taxes on the wealthiest Americans as part of a budget deal needed to avoid the looming crisis. The so-called "fiscal cliff" would force tax increases and deep budget cuts if there is no deal by December 31st.

But House Speaker John Boehner has made it clear the wealthiest Americans should not see their taxes go up.

Patriotic Millionaires disagree with Speaker Boehner. They take issue with the Republican Party's argument that taxing wealthy job creators will lead to fewer jobs.

The millionaires argue that over-burdening the middle-class with taxes to pay for the U.S. deficit would be far worse for the economy.

Frank Patitucci is CEO of NuCompass Mobility. "It is especially important about the middle class. If you lose the middle class, you are losing customers. So a strong middle class that is helped by a fair tax system leads (to) long-term to a healthy economy."

精準翻譯 句句到位，看你是否真的全數聽懂 🔊

在華盛頓，一群自稱「愛國百萬富翁」的人向總統以及國會發出的訊息激盪國會：「向我們徵收更多的稅吧，我們可以接受。」

他們此舉是響應歐巴馬總統的提議，總統此前已鄭重表示作為預算方案的一部分，要向美國最富有人群徵收更高的稅，來避免迫在眉睫的危機。如果在 12 月 31 號之前無法達成協議，這一「財政懸崖」將會迫使稅收增加，預算開支大幅削減。

但是，眾議院議長約翰・博納已經明確表示反對向美國最富有階層增稅。

「愛國百萬富翁們」不同意博納的觀點。他們不贊同共和黨的論點：提高富有雇傭者的稅收將會導致工作崗位的減少。

百萬富翁們認為，通過向中產階級徵收重稅來解決美國的財政赤字將會對經濟造成更嚴重的負面影響。

弗蘭克・帕蒂圖奇是 NuCompass 移動公司的首席執行官。他說：「中產階級至關重要。失去了中產階級，你就失去了客戶。而一個能得益於公正的稅收系統的強大中產階層將會引領經濟長期健康發展。」

- -

關鍵解析 英文聽力重點看這邊就對了

❶ They are in line with President Obama, who has vowed to raise taxes on the wealthiest Americans as part of a budget deal needed to avoid the looming crisis.

　　本句中 be in line with 表示「與……觀點一致」的意思。who 引導的非限定性關係子句修飾 President Obama。vow to do sth. 表示「鄭重宣布做某事」。needed 是過去分詞作後位修飾前面的 a budget deal。looming crisis 意為「迫在眉睫的危機」。

❷ They take issue with the Republican Party's argument that taxing wealthy job creators will lead to fewer jobs.

　　本句中 take issue with 相當於 disagree with，表示「對……持有異議」。that 引導的是一個同位語子句，說明前面 argument（論點）的具體內容。句中 tax 用作動詞，表示「對……徵稅」。

❸ So a strong middle class that is helped by a fair tax system leads (to) long-term to a healthy economy.

　　本句的主句為 A strong middle class leads to a healthy economy，即「強大的中產階層有助於經濟的健康發展」。句中 that 引導的關係子句修飾 a strong middle class。注意，leads (to) long-term to a healthy economy 疑為 leads to a long-term healthy economy 的口誤說法。

NEWS
03 US Presidential Election Has Global Implications
美國總統大選的全球性影響

新聞原文　一知半解？跟著新聞原文，再聽一遍　 Track 040

If the polls are right, the 2012 election will be decided by a few crucial votes in a handful of hotly contested states. But far from being just a domestic ballot — Bruce Stokes at the Pew research Center says the U.S. election will have global implications.

With a gross domestic product equal to about a quarter of the world's total output, no other country has a larger economic footprint. A common refrain among economists is that when the U.S. sniffles, the rest of the world catches a cold.

On the campaign trail, both candidates agree a healthy U.S. economy is crucial to global stability.

Fighting to win a second term, President Obama says U.S. trade has increased significantly under his leadership.

The key to a strong economy, says Obama, is to bring manufacturing jobs back to the U.S.

A recent survey by the Pew Center shows Western Europe overwhelmingly in favor of a second term for Mr. Obama: 92 percent in France, 89 percent in Germany and 73 percent in Britain.

History suggests the world will adapt to whomever America chooses. What is clear, say experts, is that the outcome will shape economic and geopolitical attitudes around the world for years to come.

精準翻譯　句句到位，看你是否真的全數聽懂 🔊

　　如果民意調查的結果是準確的，那麼 2012 年美國總統大選結果將會由幾張關鍵選票決定，這些選票分布在幾個競爭激烈的州中。而美國調查機構皮尤研究中心的布魯斯・斯托克斯說，美國大選不僅僅是一個國內的選舉，它對全球都會產生影響。

　　美國的國內生產總值約占世界生產總值的四分之一，其經濟影響力令其他國家望塵莫及。經濟學家中間流行這樣一句話：美國打噴嚏，全世界都會感冒。

　　在競選中，兩位候選人都認為健康發展的美國經濟對全球的穩定具有至關重要的作用。

　　想要力爭取得連任的歐巴馬總統指出，在他的領袖下，美國的貿易大幅增長。他認為，要恢復強有力的經濟，關鍵是讓製造業回歸美國本土。

　　皮尤研究中心最近的一次調查顯示，西歐國家非常希望歐巴馬取得連任：法國民眾的支持率為 92%，德國民眾的支持率為 89%，英國民眾的支持率為 73%。

　　歷史證明，無論美國選擇誰來擔任總統，整個世界都會去適應。專家指出，可以確定的是，選舉結果將會影響今後幾年內各國經濟以及地緣政治方面的態度。

關鍵解析 英文聽力重點看這邊就對了

❶ If the polls are right, the 2012 election will be decided by a few crucial votes in a handful of hotly contested states.

　　這句話說明，兩名候選人將在幾個關鍵州的選票上展開激烈爭奪。在這裡，學習者需要了解美國總統選舉的一些背景知識。美國總統是由各州議會選出的選舉人團選舉產生，而不是選民直接選舉產生。各州按人口比例確定選舉人團的票數，絕大多數州實行「勝者全得」制度，即在一州獲得選票多者獲得該州所有的選舉人票。

❷ But far from being just a domestic ballot — Bruce Stokes at the Pew research Center says the U.S. election will have global implications.

　　本句中 far from 表示「不但不，遠非」的意思。far from being just a domestic ballot 是一個獨立結構，其邏輯主語是後面的 the U.S. election。implication 在句中意為「影響」。

❸ With a gross domestic product equal to about a quarter of the world's total output, no other country has a larger economic footprint.

　　gross domestic product 指「國內生產總值」，即 GDP。economic footprint 的直譯是「經濟足跡」，這裡可以理解為「經濟影響力」。

US Public Split Over NSA Surveillance

美國民眾對國安局監聽事件反應不一

The American public is split over whether the National Security Agency, or NSA, should continue phone and email surveillance to stop terrorists.

Three years ago, Americans overwhelmingly supported anti-terrorism actions over civil liberties. Pollster Peter Brown says a slight majority now think those efforts are eroding freedoms.

But other polls show a majority of Americans — 58 percent — support the government's collection of telephone and Internet data. The basic questions are these — is the surveillance relevant to a terrorist investigation? And, does the government monitor actual conversations and emails, or just look at who's involved?

The Foreign Intelligence Surveillance Court meets inside this federal building in Washington. The NSA must first make its argument in this court before listening to phone calls of an American.

But the Electronic Privacy Information Center (EPIC) says the court should not have made the Verizon Communications company provide its phone records on all Americans. EPIC filed an emergency petition to the U.S. Supreme Court to stop the NSA's surveillance.

It's not known if the Supreme Court will take up the case. In the meantime, Americans will continue to debate whether the NSA surveillance goes too far.

精準翻譯　句句到位，看你是否真的全數聽懂 🔈

對國家安全局（NSA）是否應該繼續監控民眾電話和電子郵件以防止恐怖襲擊一事，美國民眾態度不一。

三年前，絕大多數美國民眾都支持反恐行動比起公民自由權更重要，如今，民意調查員彼得‧布朗稱，半數稍多的民眾認為國安局的那些舉動正在侵犯民眾的自由權。

但是，其他一些民意測驗顯示，超過半數的美國人（58%）還是支持政府

收集電話和網路數據的。這其中的一些基本疑問是：監聽是否與調查恐怖份子有關？政府到底是在監控通話和電子郵件的實際內容，還是只調查那些涉嫌恐怖襲擊的人？

外國情報監視法庭人員就在華盛頓的這座聯邦大廈內辦公。國安局在監聽美國民眾的電話通話前必須首先向該法庭陳述理由。

但美國電子隱私信息中心（EPIC）稱，該法庭不應該讓威瑞森通信公司向國安局提供所有美國民眾的通話記錄。該中心已向美國最高法院遞交了一份緊急申請，請求立即停止國安局的這種監聽行為。

現在，最高法院是否會受理這一案件還無從得知。與此同時，美國民眾也會繼續就國安局的監聽行為是否做得太過分爭論下去。

關鍵解析 英文聽力重點看這邊就對了

❶ The American public is split over whether the National Security Agency, or NSA, should continue phone and email surveillance to stop terrorists.

本句中 be split over 表示「在……上存在分歧」。聽力材料中首次出現機構或者組織時，常會給出全稱和簡稱，聽者要有意識地識記，因為它在下文可能還會出現，並且通常以縮寫的形式出現。比如本句中的 the National Security Agency, or NSA 即指「美國國家安全局」。

❷ Pollster Peter Brown says a slight majority now think those efforts are eroding freedoms.

本句中的 those efforts 指上文提到的國家安全局的監控行為。動詞 erode 原指物理或化學上「腐蝕，侵蝕」，在本句中可引申為「侵害」的意思。

❸ The Electronic Privacy Information Center (EPIC) says the court should not have made the Verizon Communications company provide its phone records on all Americans.

本句的主語是一個組織機構，即 EPIC（電子隱私訊息中心）。should not have done 結構表示「本不該做某事，卻做了某事」。而 should have done 表示「本該做某事，卻沒有做」。這樣的表達體現了說話者的立場和態度，聽者要注意體會。

Italian Political Gridlock Threatens Euro
義大利陷入政治僵局威脅歐元區

Italians surprised the world, and perhaps themselves — splitting their vote among disgraced former Prime Minister Silvio Berlusconi, a center-left coalition and a protest movement led by a former comedian. The current prime minister, an economist praised by the international community, got only 10 percent of the vote.

Retired couple Gabriella Magini and Mario Pezzella were as surprised as anyone. They worry about their finances, and even more about their grandchildren.

And there is good reason for concern. Unemployment is nearly 12 percent. Italy has had virtually no economic growth for more than 10 years. It struggles to pay the interest on its huge debt and it needs extensive reforms to make it competitive again. And now, the parliament is deadlocked.

Economics professor Nicola Borri says even if a government is formed it will not have the power to take the necessary steps to revive the Italian economy and end talk of a collapse of the 17-nation euro system.

European leaders are determined not to let that happen. And at least one longtime Italian analyst, Andrea Margelletti, believes his country will get through this economic, and now also political, crisis.

But that is more difficult than ever now, with a paralyzed parliament. No one expects much progress at least until after new elections, which could come before the end of the year.

精準翻譯　句句到位，看你是否真的全數聽懂 🔊

　　義大利人震驚了全世界，或許他們自己也感到吃驚。他們的選票結果一分為三，分散投給了前總理西爾維奧‧貝盧斯科尼、一個中左翼聯盟和一個由前喜劇演員帶領的抗議運動政黨。而現任總理，一位深受國際社會讚譽的經

濟學家，只得到了 10%的選票。

退休夫婦加布里埃拉‧馬吉尼和馬里奧‧佩澤拉也跟其他人一樣，深感震驚。他們擔心自己的財務狀況，更擔心自己的孫輩們。

而這種擔憂並非多餘。義大利現在的失業率接近 12%，十多年間經濟幾乎沒有增長。義大利在艱難地支付巨額債務的利息，目前急需全面改革來恢復自身的競爭力。然而現在，議會又陷入了僵局。

經濟學教授尼古拉‧博里認為，即使新政府能夠成功組建，它也沒有足夠的權力來採取必要措施重振義大利經濟並終結十七國歐元體系崩潰的傳言。

歐洲各國領袖態度堅決，他們不想讓此種局面出現。至少義大利資深分析家安德烈亞‧馬爾傑萊蒂相信，他的國家能夠度過這次經濟及政治危機。

但由於議會陷入癱瘓，目前的情況比以往任何時候都要困難，至少在年底可能舉行的新選舉到來之前，沒人會期待有太多進展。

- -

關鍵解析 英文聽力重點看這邊就對了

❶ Italians surprised the world, and perhaps themselves — splitting their vote among disgraced former Prime Minister Silvio Berlusconi, a center-left coalition and a protest movement led by a former comedian.

本句中 themselves 是反身代詞，指「義大利人自己」。split 表示「使分裂，使分開」的意思，因為與其邏輯主語 Italians 是主動關係，所以句中用現在分詞形式。among 通常表示「在三者或更多者之間」。

❷ And there is good reason for concern.

there is good reason for sth./to do sth. 表示「有充足的理由去……」。這句話在原文中可以起到提示下文內容的作用。聽者可以預測，下面會提到擔憂的原因。

❸ But that is more difficult than ever now, with a paralyzed parliament.

句中 with 結構用來表明「比以往任何時候都更困難」的原因。paralyzed 是過去分詞作形容詞，修飾 parliament，表示「陷入癱瘓的議會」。

06 John Kerry: First White, Male Secretary of State in 16 Years

約翰・克里：美國 16 年來首位白人男性國務卿

新聞原文 一知半解？跟著新聞原文，再聽一遍 🎧 *Track 043*

For the first time in almost a decade, members of the Senate Foreign Relations Committee were using the term, "mister," to address a prospective Secretary of State.

And at least online, it's been causing a buzz.

Jezebel.com — a website aimed at women — recently posted a piece asking satirically, "Is America Ready for a White, Male Secretary of State?"

After all, the last time a white male had the job was 1997. The Secretary of State, Warren Christopher.

Years of diplomatic leadership from Madeleine Albright ... Colin Powell ... Condoleezza Rice ... and Hillary Clinton have left a mark.

None of that seemed to be on the minds of senators at Thursday's confirmation hearing — like long-time Kerry friend John McCain, who praised Kerry's personal qualities, "which I think are well suited to the position."

So, does it matter what the top U.S. diplomat looks like? Whether it's a man or a woman? Whether he wears pants or she wears a skirt? Maybe not.

In the end, it comes down to being tough. Something that — in U.S. diplomatic circles — no longer appears to be relegated to white males.

精準翻譯 句句到位，看你是否真的全數聽懂 🔊

近十年來，美國參議院外交委員會的委員們首次使用「先生」這一稱謂來稱呼未來的國務卿。這件事至少在網上引起了一片熱議。

一個針對女性的網站 Jezebel.com 最近不無諷刺地發文詢問：「美國準備好接受一位白人男性國務卿了嗎？」畢竟上一位白人男性任美國國務卿已是 1997 年的事了。當時的國務卿名為沃倫・克里斯托弗。

這些年來，從馬德琳‧奧爾布賴特到科林‧鮑威爾，從康朵麗莎‧萊斯到希拉蕊‧科林頓，這些外交領導人都在國務卿的位置上留下了自己的印記。

但是，週四參加國務卿提名人審議聽證會的參議員們卻似乎沒有考慮這些。比如，克里多年的朋友約翰‧麥凱恩就稱讚克里擁有優秀的個人品質，「非常適合這個職位」。

所以，美國最高外交官長什麼樣子重要嗎？此人是男性還是女性重要嗎？他／她是穿褲子還是穿裙子重要嗎？也許並不重要。

說到底，最重要的是他／她要強硬。而這一特質，在美國外交圈，似乎不再是白人男性的長項。

關鍵解析　英文聽力重點看這邊就對了

❶ For the first time in almost a decade, members of the Senate Foreign Relations Committee were using the term, "mister," to address a prospective Secretary of State.

學習者應該對美國政體有所了解。美國國會（Congress）分為兩院：眾議院（House of Representatives）和參議院（the Senate）。其中參議院裡有多個常設委員會來處理具體事務，如司法委員會、外交委員會等。在這裡，參議院外交委員會正在審議總統提名的國務卿人選。本句中 address 作為動詞，表示「稱呼」的意思。

❷ Jezebel.com — a website aimed at women — recently posted a piece asking satirically, "Is America Ready for a White, Male Secretary of State?"

本句中 Jezebel.com 和 a website 是同位語關係。aimed at women 是過去分詞作後置形容詞，修飾 a website。satirically 表示「諷刺地」之意。學習者可以透過這個單詞的提示了解下面一句話的諷刺意味。

❸ None of that seemed to be on the minds of senators at Thursday's confirmation hearing — like long-time Kerry friend John McCain...

句中 confirmation hearing 指「針對國務卿提名人選的審議聽證會」。

NEWS 07 Kenyatta Follows Father to Win Kenya's Top Job
肯雅塔子承父業，當選肯亞總統

新聞原文 一知半解？跟著新聞原文，再聽一遍 🎧 *Track 044*

After days of vote counting, Kenya's electoral commission announced Uhuru Kenyatta has been elected the country's fourth president.

Mr. Kenyatta came out on top with a razor-thin margin of victory.

He beat out his nearest rival, Prime Minister Raila Odinga, with 50.07 percent of the vote — just enough to avoid a run-off.

Mr. Kenyatta was born into a life of politics, as the son of Kenya's first president Jomo Kenyatta. He was educated in the Untied States, and has served as Deputy Prime Minister in the coalition government since 2008.

Mr. Kenyatta's political career has been largely overshadowed by his trial at the International Criminal Court.

He and his running mate, William Ruto, are both facing charges at The Hague for their alleged roles organizing the post-election violence that followed the last disputed election in 2007.

Western nations have suggested the charges against the new president could complicate relations with Kenya.

The charges have actually helped to unite Mr. Kenyatta's supporters against the same western powers, who they accuse of meddling in Kenyan affairs.

The president-elected is to be inaugurated in next fourteen days or so, but the constitution does allow room for legal challenges.

精準翻譯 句句到位，看你是否真的全數聽懂

經過幾天的選票統計後，肯亞選舉委員會宣布烏胡魯・肯雅塔當選為該國的第四任總統。

肯雅塔得票數位居首位，以些微優勢勝出。

他以 50.07％的得票率擊敗競選勁敵拉伊拉・奧廷加總理，贏得選舉。這一得票率剛好能夠避免再進行一次決勝選舉。

肯雅塔出生於政治世家，是肯亞開國總統喬莫・肯雅塔之子。他在美國接受教育，自 2008 年起在聯合政府中擔任副總理一職。

肯雅塔在國際刑事法院受到審訊一事對他的政治生涯影響較大。

他和競選搭檔威廉・魯托，因被懷疑參與組織 2007 年極具爭議的大選之後的暴力事件，都面臨海牙國際刑事法院的起訴。

西方國家指出，對於新一屆總統的指控可能會使得西方國家與肯亞的關係複雜化。這些指控實際上幫助將肯雅塔的支持者聯合了起來，共同對抗西方勢力。他們指控西方國家干涉肯亞內政。

當選總統的就職典禮約在兩周後舉行，但是憲法會為司法質疑保留一定的時間。

關鍵解析 英文聽力重點看這邊就對了

❶ Kenyatta came out on top with a razor-thin margin of victory.

　　本句中 come out on top 表示「勝出，出人頭地」的意思。razor-thin 表示「極其微弱的」之意。margin 表示「超出或不足的數量」的意思。

❷ He and his running mate, William Ruto, are both facing charges at The Hague for their alleged roles organizing the post-election violence that followed the last disputed election in 2007.

　　本句中 his running mate（他的競選夥伴）和 William Ruto 是同位語關係。charges 表示「指控」的意思，後面的 for 指出他們受到指控的原因。The Hague 是荷蘭的海牙，上文提到的「國際刑事法院」總部設在海牙。最後 that 引導的關係子句修飾 the post-election violence。disputed 是過去分詞作形容詞，意為「頗具爭議的」，修飾 election。

❸ The president elected is to be inaugurated in next fourteen days or so, but the constitution does allow room for legal challenges.

　　句中的 president-elected 指「已當選但尚未正式就職的總統」。be to do sth. 表示「按既定計劃將要……」的意思。allow room for 表示「為……留出餘地」。

NEWS 08 Obama Hopes Charm Offensive Will Lead to Grand Bargain

歐巴馬寄希望於魅力攻勢

新聞原文 　一知半解？跟著新聞原文，再聽一遍　🎧 *Track 045*

If you've come to Washington for a tour of the White House, you're out of luck. Because President Obama and Republicans in Congress could not agree on legislation to prevent automatic government spending cuts, White House tours are canceled for now, and many other government operations are on hold.

So Mr. Obama is trying a new approach, which the media are calling a "charm offensive."

He has made several trips to Capitol Hill to meet with Republican and Democratic lawmakers, and has even treated a group of Senate Republicans to dinner.

So far, the response from Republicans, including House Speaker John Boehner, has been cautiously positive.

Former legislative adviser Steve Bell, now at Washington's Bipartisan Policy Council, thinks the president's shift in tactics is a good move.

President Obama's approval ratings in public opinion polls have slipped lately, and Bell says he now understands that he must work with Congress.

While many in Washington are pessimistic about the chances for a deal in the coming months, Steve Bell predicts the Democratic-led Senate may reach agreements on a number of issues, which he says would prod House Republicans to do the same.

And if that happens, the White House doors will open again.

精準翻譯 　句句到位，看你是否真的全數聽懂

　　如果你現在來華盛頓參觀白宮，那你實在是不走運。因為歐巴馬總統和國會的共和黨人在避免自動減支的立法上難以達成一致，白宮的參觀活動被暫時取消，其他不少政府活動也暫被擱置。

　　為此，歐巴馬總統正在嘗試一種新方法，媒體稱之為「魅力攻勢」。他數次造訪國會大廈，會見共和黨以及民主黨的立法者，甚至還設宴款待一群共

和黨的參議員。

到目前為止，共和黨人作出了謹慎積極的反應，包括眾議院議長約翰‧博納。

現任職於華盛頓兩黨政策委員會的前立法顧問史蒂夫‧貝爾認為，總統在策略上的轉變是一個明智的舉措。貝爾表示，歐巴馬總統最近在民意調查中的支持率有所下滑，他現在意識到自己必須要與國會合作。

儘管華盛頓的很多人對兩黨在未來幾個月中達成一致的前景表示悲觀，但史蒂夫‧貝爾預測民主黨領袖的參議院或許能就數項議題達成一致意見，而這將會促使眾議院的共和黨人作出同樣的決定。

如果這一切能夠如願，白宮的大門將會再次向公眾開放。

關鍵解析 英文聽力重點看這邊就對了

❶ If you've come to Washington for a tour of the White House, you're out of luck.

這句話是全文的一個引子。out of luck 表示「不走運」的意思。在此可以大膽預測：白宮肯定是發生了什麼事才使得遊客無法參觀。

❷ Because President Obama and Republicans in Congress could not agree on legislation to prevent automatic government spending cuts, White House tours are canceled for now, and many other government operations are on hold.

動詞片語 agree on sth. 表示「就……達成一致意見」。而 agree to do sth. 表示「同意做某事」。agree with sb. 表示「同意某人的觀點或想法」。句中的 operations 指「活動，事務」。on hold 表示「被擱置」的意思，如果聽者不知道這個片語的具體含義，可以聯繫與之相關的動詞片語 hold on（等一等，停一下）來猜測其大概意思。

❸ Former legislative adviser Steve Bell, now at Washington's Bipartisan Policy Council, thinks the president's shift in tactics is a good move.

本句中 Bipartisan Policy Council 指「兩黨政策委員會」。句中的 shift 是名詞，表示「轉變，改變」的意思。

題目詳解篇

Unit 5 教育科技

BlackBerry Unveils Two New Smartphones
黑莓機發布兩款新智慧型手機

新聞原文　一知半解？跟著新聞原文，再聽一遍　🎧 Track 046

Two brand new devices and perhaps a fresh start for a company that has seen its global market share plummet from 20 percent three years ago to just over three percent today.

For BlackBerry CEO Thorsten Heins, it's another chance to remake a faded brand.

The company promises the same high level of network security the BlackBerry is known for — along with a fast new browser, a more intuitive operating system, and a revamped library featuring more than 70,000 apps. The Z10 looks much like the touchscreen phones popularized by its rivals, but the Q10 maintains the "qwerty" keyboard that has become BlackBerry's trademark.

Shareholders will be watching if customers adopt the new devices. The company's stock has dropped as much as 90 percent in the last four years as it lost ground to competitors. But company shares have doubled in the last four months as anticipation grew for the new models.

Analysts say the new devices could make or break a company that many credit for starting the technological revolution in smartphones.

精準翻譯　句句到位，看你是否真的全數聽懂 🔊

對於一個眼看自己的全球市場份額從三年前的 20% 驟降到如今的 3% 的公司來說，這兩款新產品也許意味著一個新的開始。

而對於黑莓機首席執行長托爾斯滕・海因斯來說，這也是一個重塑已逐漸沒落的品牌的機會。

該公司承諾，新產品仍會保證黑莓機一貫的高網路安全性，同時配備了更加快捷的新瀏覽器、更加直觀的操作系統和一個全新的、包含 70,000 多款應

用軟體的應用商店。儘管黑莓機 Z10 看起來很像競爭對手們推出的大受歡迎的觸控手機，但是 Q10 卻保留了已經成為黑莓機標誌的 QWERTY 全鍵盤設計傳統。

股東們正在翹首觀望，看消費者是否會接受這兩款新產品。在過去四年裡，隨著競爭的不斷失利，黑莓機公司的股價已經跌去了 90%。但是最近四個月，隨著人們對新產品的預期看漲，公司的股價已經開始翻倍。

分析人士稱，對於這樣一家被認為開啟了智慧型手機技術革命的公司來說，成敗在此一舉。

- -

關鍵解析　英文聽力重點看這邊就對了

❶ Two brand new devices and perhaps a fresh start for a company that has seen its global market share plummet from 20 percent three years ago to just over three percent today.

　　本句並不是一個完整的句子，這裡缺少動詞，或者也可以理解為開頭省略了 These are。a company 後面跟了一個由 that 引導的很長的關係子句。其中，plummet 表示「垂直下降」的意思。

❷ The company promises the same high level of network security the BlackBerry is known for — along with a fast new browser, a more intuitive operating system, and a revamped library featuring more than 70,000 apps.

　　be known for 表示「以……而著稱」。後面的 along with 表示伴隨，緊跟三個並列成分。動詞 feature sth. 表示「以……為特色」，句中用其現在分詞形式作後位修飾 library。

❸ Analysts say the new devices could make or break a company that many credit for starting the technological revolution in smartphones.

　　句中 make or break a company 意為「成就或毀掉一個公司」。修飾 a company 的 that 子句是本句的理解難點，其中 many 是代詞，表示「許多人」；credit 在這裡用作動詞，credit (the company) for... 意為「把……的功勞或榮譽歸於（該公司）」。該子句的意思就是「許多人認為是這個公司開啟了智慧型手機的技術革命」。

NEWS 02 Giant Airship Could Move Huge Amounts of Cargo
能夠運載大量貨物的巨型飛艇

The prototype unveiled in this immense World War II hangar near Los Angeles is just half the size of the final working model. But the prototype is massive, at 75-meters-long.

The craft was built with $35 million in funding from the Pentagon and the U.S. space agency, NASA. The final version will double the length and carry up to 60 metric tons in cargo. The craft needs no ground support, says the company's Shenny Yao.

The airship has a rigid structure made of carbon fiber and aluminum, with rotating propellers for takeoff and landing, and a new ballast system that compresses helium to control the lift. Sometimes the aerocraft is heavier than air, and sometimes lighter.

With advanced computer controls, the ship can reach out-of-the-way places, bringing turbines to wind farms and moving other kinds of cargo thousands of kilometers, says Shenny Yao.

The prototype has been tested inside the hangar, rising and descending under its own power. If it works as planned, and potential customers show interest, a commercial version could be in production in two to three years.

在洛杉磯附近這個二戰時期的大型飛機庫中，這艘飛艇原型機揭開了神秘面紗。儘管它的體積只是最終成品機的一半，但還是很巨大，長度達到了 75 公尺。

為建造該飛艇，美國五角大樓和國家航空航天局（NASA）共出資 3,500 萬美元。飛艇製造公司的姚盛雪稱，其最終版將會有現在的兩倍長，載貨量

可達 60 公噸，且不需要地面支持。

該飛艇擁有堅固的碳纖維和鋁合金結構，利用螺旋槳推進器起飛和著陸，依靠全新氦氣壓縮系統來控制升力。此飛艇有時候比空氣重，有時候比空氣輕。

姚盛雪還指出，該飛艇配備先進的電腦控制系統，能夠到達比較偏僻的地區。它可以將渦輪機運往風力發電站或將其他貨物運到數千公尺以外的地方。

該飛艇原型機已經在飛機庫中進行過測試，完全可依靠自身動力進行起降。如果該飛行器能夠像計劃的那樣運轉良好，而且潛在客戶也有購買興趣的話，那麼兩三年後公司即可生產出一款商用機型。

- -

關鍵解析　英文聽力重點看這邊就對了

❶ The prototype unveiled in this immense World War II hangar near Los Angeles is just half the size of the final working model.

本句的主句是 The prototype is just half the size of the final working model. 句中 unveil 表示「揭開面紗，展示」的意思，這裡用過去分詞形式，表示被動，修飾 the prototype（原型機）。

❷ The final version will double the length and carry up to 60 metric tons in cargo. The craft needs no ground support, says the company's Shenny Yao.

本句中 double the length 表示 be twice as long (as...) 意為「長度是……的兩倍」。up to 表示「高達，多達（某一數量）」。

❸ With advanced computer controls, the ship can reach out-of-the-way places, bringing turbines to wind farms and moving other kinds of cargo thousands of kilometers, says Shenny Yao.

句中「with + 名詞 / 名詞片語」的結構表示擁有或伴隨。out-of-the-way 是形容詞，意思是「偏遠的」。bringing 和 moving 作為修飾，與邏輯主語 the ship 是主動關係，因此用現在分詞形式。

NEWS

03 Holiday Season Features Latest, Hottest Electronic Gadgets

節慶日：新款、熱門電子產品的銷售旺季

新聞原文　一知半解？跟著新聞原文，再聽一遍 Track 048

When it comes to electronic devices, there are more choices today than ever before, which can be daunting for some consumers.

Brian Tong is Senior Editor of CNET.com, a website that reports tech news and trends and reviews the latest electronic products. He says tablet computers are one of the hottest items this year.

Another hot gadget: smart cameras. They connect to the Internet through Wi-Fi so consumers can email or upload photos to a social networking site directly from the camera, says Elman Chacon of the electronics store, Best Buy.

Streaming media boxes also connect to the Internet and allow people to view web content, such as movies and YouTube videos, on their televisions.

Another gadget: wireless speakers, which work with any device that has Bluetooth technology, including smart phones, laptops and tablets.

With the increasing popularity of Internet shopping, many consumers are first coming to a retail store to look at the actual product, and then go online to find it at a lower price and buy that item on the Internet.

Retail stores like Best Buy understand that and are trying to stay competitive.

With so many options in prices and products, it is up to consumers to do their homework before making a purchase.

精準翻譯　句句到位，看你是否真的全數聽懂

提到電子產品，如今的選擇比以往任何時候都要多。有些消費者面對這麼多的選擇甚至會心生畏懼。

CNET.com 是一家專門報道科技新聞和發展趨勢，並對最新電子產品進行評論的網站。網站的資深編輯布賴恩・唐說，平板電腦是今年最熱門的電子產品之一。

另一款熱門設備是智能相機,電子產品商店百思買公司的埃爾曼‧查康說,這種相機可以通過 Wi-Fi 連接到網路上,讓消費者能直接把相機裡的照片用郵件進行發送或者上傳到社交網站上去。

串流媒體盒也可以與網路相連接,人們通過它們可以在電視機上瀏覽網上內容,比如電影和 YouTube 上的影片。

另外一個小設備是無線擴音器,它可以用於任何有藍牙技術的設備,比如智慧型手機、筆記型電腦和平板電腦。

隨著網路購物變得越來越流行,許多消費者會先到零售店裡去看實際產品,然後再去網路上搜尋並以更低的價格購買這款產品。而像百思買這樣的零售商店也理解消費者的這種做法,它們正在努力保持自己的競爭力。

面對這麼多可供選擇的價格和商品,消費者常需要在購買前做一番功課。

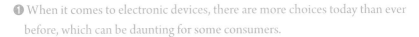

關鍵解析 英文聽力重點看這邊就對了

❶ When it comes to electronic devices, there are more choices today than ever before, which can be daunting for some consumers.

　　when it comes to sth./to doing sth. 表示「說到某事物或做某事」。後面的 which 與前面的先行詞之間有逗號隔開,引導的是非限定性關係子句。which 在這裡代指前面的整個句子。

❷ Another gadget: wireless speakers, which work with any device that has Bluetooth technology, including smart phones, laptops and tablets.

　　本句中出現了兩個關係子句嵌套的情況,聽者要注意釐清句子結構。句末出現了幾種常見數碼產品的英文表達,分別為 smart phones(智能手機)、laptops(筆記型電腦)和 tablets(平板電腦)。

❸ With so many options in prices and products, it is up to consumers to do their homework before making a purchase.

　　be up to sb. to do sth. 表示「由某人來做某事」。句中的 do their homework 並不是指學生做家庭作業,而是「做準備工作」的意思,因此,即使聽到熟悉的詞語時也不能想當然,要結合上下文語意來判斷具體意思。

iPhone Becomes Low Cost Microscope
iPhone：價格低廉的顯微鏡

新聞原文　一知半解？跟著新聞原文，再聽一遍 Track 049

The Apple iPhone can be used for a lot of things—make calls, send pictures, video and text, and play games. But scientists say it also can be converted into a low-cost microscope that can detect worm infections in children.

Microscopes are an important tool when diagnosing disease. But they are not always readily available, especially in places like rural Tanzania. Now for a few dollars and a little ingenuity, the iPhone can become a medical diagnostic tool. It can probably work on other smart phones, too. Dr. Issac Bogoch is an infectious disease specialist at Toronto General Hospital. Bogoch is the lead author of a new study on the iPhone-turned microscope.

Bogoch and his colleagues from Massachusetts General Hospital and the Swiss Tropical and Public Health Institute tested their idea on Pemba Island in Tanzania.

The make-shift microscope could detect parasitic infections to varying degrees. The best results came in detecting moderate to heavy infections. Results were not as good for mild infections. However, Bogoch thinks that will change when the technology improves.

Bogoch says the next step is to improve the image quality. He says the smartphone microscope could greatly enhance disease control in poor, rural areas. He says treatment for many intestinal parasites is generally widely available and very well tolerated.

精準翻譯　句句到位，看你是否真的全數聽懂 🔊

蘋果公司的 iPhone 手機可以用來做很多事情：打電話，發送照片、影片和文本，以及打遊戲。但是科學家稱，它還可以變身為一種價格低廉的顯微鏡，用來檢測兒童是否感染了蟯蟲。

顯微鏡是診斷疾病的一種重要工具。但是它們並不總是那麼現成，尤其是在像坦尚尼亞農村這樣的地區。而現在，只需花上幾美元，再加上那麼一點點創造力，iPhone 手機就可以變成一種醫學診斷工具。當然，其他智慧型手機可能也行。多倫多綜合醫院的伊薩克‧博高什醫生是一位傳染病專家，他是 iPhone 變顯微鏡這一新研究的主要領導者。

他和來自麻薩諸塞州綜合醫院和瑞士熱帶與公共衛生研究所的同事們在坦尚尼亞的奔巴島測試了他們的想法。

結果顯示，這種簡易的顯微鏡對各種寄生蟲感染情況的檢出程度不盡相同。它在檢測中度和重度感染方面的效果最好，而對輕微感染的檢測效果則不是那麼理想。但是博高什醫生認為，隨著技術的改進，這一狀況也會發生改變。

他說，下一步要做的是提高圖像質量。這種由智慧型手機轉換而成的顯微鏡將會大大增強貧困農村地區的疾病控制能力。許多腸道寄生蟲病基本都是可以得到醫治的，並且很多人也願意接受治療。

關鍵解析 英文聽力重點看這邊就對了

❶ Now for a few dollars and a little ingenuity, the iPhone can become a medical diagnostic tool. It can probably work on other smart phones, too.

第一句句中介詞 for 表示一種條件，可譯為「只需要……，只要花上……（就能……）」。第二句中的 it 代指的是前一句所說的情況。動詞 work 在這裡表示「可行，行得通」。綜合起來，上文的意思就是「只需幾美元和一點創造性，iPhone 手機就能變成醫學診斷工具，而這一點在其他智慧型手機上可能也能實現。」

❷ He says treatment for many intestinal parasites is generally widely available and very well tolerated.

學習者如果對小句中 intestinal parasites（腸道寄生蟲）的意思不太熟悉，可以根據 treatment（治療）推斷這是一種疾病。available 表示「可以獲得的，現成的」。be tolerated 是被動形式，表示「被容忍，被接受」，其邏輯主語是前面的 treatment。

NEWS
05
New Generation of Laptops Unveiled
新一代筆記型電腦

新聞原文　　一知半解？跟著新聞原文，再聽一遍　🎧 Track 050

For over three decades Intel has been providing semi-conductor chips for computer hardware makers around the world. Intel's chips have been running many computers for years — both Macs and PCs. But, since tablet computers hit the market — the trend has shifted towards the small, mobile devices while sales of desktop computers drop.

Earlier this year, Intel introduced a new genre of laptops called "Ultrabook™ convertible laptops." Intel Marketing Associate Mike Fard explains, "What that means is you have a standard laptop that converts into a tablet and we have multiple designs that feature this capability of going from a tablet to a laptop."

Intel has adopted a technology called "Ivy Bridge" on its new line of chips which reduces power consumption dramatically. At this year's Consumer Electronics Show, the company surprised everyone with its announcement that it is ahead of schedule in reducing the power requirements for one group of its processors.

This newest generation of laptops is sure to be a hit with consumers, with lower prices than before. Earlier thin laptops were in the $1,000 price range. The Ultrabook™ convertible however, is expected to sell for around $600 — making them more competitive against regular tablet PCs.

精準翻譯　　句句到位，看你是否真的全數聽懂 🔊

　　三十多年來，英特爾一直在給全世界的電腦硬體製造商們提供半導體芯片。英特爾的芯片已經在許多電腦中運行了多年，既包括蘋果公司的 Mac 電腦，也包括普通的個人電腦。但是，自從平板電腦面市以來，桌上型電腦的銷量不斷下降，整個行業的發展趨勢已經開始轉向體積更小的移動設備。

　　今年初，英特爾推出了一種名為「超極本 TM」的新型兩用筆記型電腦。

英特爾公司負責營銷的邁克‧法爾德解釋說：「這意味著你擁有了一臺可以轉變成平板電腦的標準筆記型電腦，我們的很多設計都圍繞平板電腦變為筆記型電腦的性能而展開。」

英特爾在它的新芯片生產線上採用了一種名為 Ivy Bridge 的技術，從而大大降低了筆記型電腦的耗電量。在今年的消費電子展上，英特爾公司宣布它的一批處理器已經提前實現了降低功耗的目標，這一消息讓所有人都感到吃驚。

加上價格比之前更低廉，這種最新一代的筆記型電腦定會大受消費者的歡迎。比如，早前的輕薄筆記型電腦價格都在 1,000 美元左右，而「超極本TM」兩用筆記型電腦的定價預計只有 600 美元左右，因而與普通平板電腦相比，更具競爭力。

關鍵解析 英文聽力重點看這邊就對了

❶ For over three decades Intel has been providing semi-conductor chips for computer hardware makers around the world.

本句中使用的是現在完成進行式，其結構為「主語 + have/has + been + 動詞的現在分詞」，表示從過去的某個時間開始的動作，到現在還在繼續進行，強調動作的未完成性。semi-conductor chips 是「半導體芯片」的意思。

❷ But, since tablet computers hit the market — the trend has shifted towards the small, mobile devices while sales of desktop computers drop.

句中 since 引導一個時間副詞子句，表示「自從……以來」。一般來說，since 引導的子句中用一般過去時態，而主句用現在完成時態。while 在本句中表示一種伴隨狀況。

❸ What that means is you have a standard laptop that converts into a tablet and we have multiple designs that feature this capability of going from a tablet to a laptop.

本句中第一個 that 指的是 Ultrabook™ convertible laptops，即「超極本TM」兩用筆記型電腦。後面解釋這種筆記本因為可轉變成 tablet（平板電腦）而實現「兩用」功能，其中的許多設計也是圍繞此轉換功能而作的。

NEWS 06　Online Universities Offer Free Classes to Millions
網路大學為數百萬人提供免費課程

一知半解？跟著新聞原文，再聽一遍　🎧 *Track 051*

　　This engineering class at Stanford University is also being recorded as an online course. The university is offering 30 to 40 free courses online, and more than 1.5 million students have enrolled. There are regular schedules, homework and tests but those enrolled do not earn credit towards a university degree. John Mitchell, the Vice Provost for Online Learning at Stanford, says the university offers these courses as a public service.

　　These free courses are also meant to entice students to apply to Stanford or enroll in other online classes that are not free. While online education is expanding the reach of major universities, Mitchell says they will not replace the on-campus experience.

　　While the number of universities offering online classes is growing, some classes are free and others are not. The Khan Academy is a non-profit free website that contains over 3,500 video classes in a variety of languages and is utilized by six million people each month.

　　Critics say there are flaws with online education, citing studies that show a higher dropout rate for online students. But proponents say the evolving technology is coming together to open up new educational opportunities as never before to millions around the world.

句句到位，看你是否真的全數聽懂 🔊

　　史丹佛大學的這堂工程課也正被錄製下來作為網路課程。目前，該大學已經在網上開設了三四十門免費課程，註冊學生人數超過 150 萬。這些網路課程有固定的上課時間表、家庭作業和測試，只是註冊學生不會獲得大學學位所需要的學分。史丹佛大學網路學習處副教務長約翰・米切爾說，學校開設這些課程是在提供一種公共服務。

這些免費課程也旨在吸引學生們去申請史丹佛大學或者註冊其他收費的網路課程。米切爾説，儘管網路教育擴大了一些重點大學的覆蓋範圍，但是它們無法取代校園裡的求學體驗。

雖然提供網路課程的大學數量越來越多，但是並非所有的課程都是免費的。可汗學院是一家非營利的免費網站，網站上提供了 3,500 多節各種語言的影像課程，每個月大約有 600 萬人會使用這些資源進行學習。

批評人士指出網路教育有其弊端，他們援引一些研究的結果稱，網路學習者的輟學率較高。但網路教育的支持者們卻表示，不斷進步的技術正在合力為世界上數以百萬計的人創造前所未有的新教育機會。

- -

關鍵解析 **英文聽力重點看這邊就對了**

❶ John Mitchell, the Vice Provost for Online Learning at Stanford, says the university offers these courses as a public service.

句中 the Vice Provost 是 John Mitchell 的同位語，對此人身份作進一步的説明。provost 在英國表示某些大學的學院院長，在美國表示某些大學的教務長。

❷ These free courses are also meant to entice students to apply to Stanford or enroll in other online classes that are not free.

本句中 be meant to do sth. 相 于 be supposed to do sth.，表示「意在，旨在」。entice 表示「吸引，誘惑」的意思。apply to sth. 表示「向……申請」。要表示「申請某物」用 apply for，如 apply for a job/a passport 等。

❸ Critics say there are flaws with online education, citing studies that show a higher dropout rate for online students.

本句中 citing 作伴隨，與前面的主詞 critics 是主動關係，因此用現在分詞形式。Studies 後面 that 引導的是一個關係子句。dropout rate 表示「輟學率」的意思。

NEWS 07 Turkey Provides Schools for Syrian Refugee Children
土耳其為敘利亞難民子弟設立學校

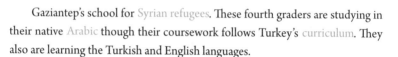

新聞原文 一知半解？跟著新聞原文，再聽一遍 🎧 *Track 052*

Gaziantep's school for Syrian refugees. These fourth graders are studying in their native Arabic though their coursework follows Turkey's curriculum. They also are learning the Turkish and English languages.

The school was opened in October when it became clear that they would not be going home anytime soon.

Nearly 600 Syrian children study in the eight classrooms here, the younger ones in the morning, the older ones in the afternoon. At night more than 300 parents come to learn Turkish.

Like most children, these kids love to draw. Many drawings show disturbing scenes. Director Orhan Buyukaslan says art helps them deal with trauma.

The Gaziantep city government funds the school and pays student expenses. Mayor Asim Guzelbey says the presence of so many foreigners can cause tensions. But he says local people remember Turkey's suffering following the First World War.

Guzelbey is disturbed by the humanitarian suffering and the destruction in Syria, which shows no sign of ending soon.

As classes end, the Syrian children are dismissed, leaving Gaziantep officials to worry about how to possibly handle thousands more waiting to escape the violence engulfing their country.

精準翻譯 句句到位，看你是否真的全數聽懂 🔊

這是土耳其加濟安泰普市為敘利亞難民設立的學校。這些四年級的孩子們正在用他們的母語阿拉伯語進行學習，而課程是按照土耳其的課程表開設的。另外，他們也在學習土耳其語和英語。

這所學校是在 10 月份設立的，因為當時的情況很明顯，這些孩子不會很快回到他們的家園。

在這裡，近 600 名敘利亞兒童在 8 個教室中學習，年齡較小的孩子上午上課，年齡較大的則下午上課。到了晚上，300 多名家長會來學習土耳其語。

和大多數孩子一樣，這些孩子也喜歡畫畫。但許多畫中描繪的卻是讓人感到不安的場景。奧爾汗‧布尤卡斯蘭校長說，藝術能夠幫助他們撫平創傷。

加濟安泰普市政府給這所學校提供資金，並且支付學生們的費用。市長阿西姆‧居澤爾貝伊說，這麼多外國人的到來可能會引發緊張局勢。但是他說當地人民依然清晰地記得土耳其在一戰後所經歷的傷痛。

居澤爾貝伊對敘利亞的人道主義災難和破壞表示擔憂，尤其是沒有跡象顯示這一切將會很快結束。

課上完了，這些敘利亞孩子都散去了。加濟安泰普的官員們仍在擔心如何安置更多的難民，因為還有數以千計的人正等著逃離戰火彌漫的家園。

- -

關鍵解析 英文聽力重點看這邊就對了

❶ The school was opened in October when it became clear that they would not be going home anytime soon.

when 引導的副詞子句中，it 是虛主詞，真正的主語是後面的 that 從句。

❷ Guzelbey is disturbed by the humanitarian suffering and the destruction in Syria, which shows no sign of ending soon.

be disturbed by 表示「為……感到擔心」。本句中 which 引導的是非限定關係子句，進一步說明 humanitarian suffering（人道主義災難）和 destruction（破壞）的情況。

❸ As classes end, the Syrian children are dismissed, leaving Gaziantep officials to worry about how to possibly handle thousands more waiting to escape the violence engulfing their country.

本句中 leaving 表示一種伴隨狀況，意思是「使……處於某種狀態」。句中 thousands more 後面省略了 refugees。engulf 表示「包圍，吞沒」的意思，其邏輯主語為 the violence。

TVs: Bigger, Better at Las Vegas CES
拉斯維加斯消費電子展上更大、更好的電視

新聞原文 一知半解？跟著新聞原文，再聽一遍 🎧 *Track 053*

Technology enthusiasts gathered by the thousands for CES 2013. And what they got was eye-opening. Bigger TVs. 3-D TVs. TV screens that are curved.

Tablet computers are also getting bigger, like this one from Lenovo, which can replace the traditional family board game.

Other video screens are designed to look and feel more like paper. Products are getting tougher, too.

Because in the end, says LG's Katie Krauss, technology is becoming all about the convenience of being constantly connected.

Even in the kitchen, where your new refrigerator can send a shopping list to your phone, get discounts, plan the meal and tell the stove to start cooking... Of course, you might be tempted to eat too much, so there's Hapi Fork, which can tell your smartphone if you are eating too much, too fast.

And if you worry the kids are too addicted to technology, there's iBitz, which connects to your smartphone, to get them moving.

How is all this interconnected technology supposed to make you feel? There's technology for that, too.

精準翻譯 句句到位，看你是否真的全數聽懂

　　數以千計的科技迷齊聚 2013 年國際消費電子展，在這裡，更大的電視、3D 電視和曲面螢幕讓他們大開眼界。

　　另外，平板電腦也變得越來越大，比如聯想的這款平板就可以取代傳統的家庭桌上遊戲。其他一些影像螢幕的設計則在外觀和感覺上輕薄如紙，產品也更加堅固耐用。

LG 公司的凱蒂‧克勞斯説，因為説到底，技術其實就是要為人們與世界的持續互動提供便利。

即使在廚房裡，你的新式冰箱也可以把一份購物清單發送到你的手機上，可以尋找打折訊息，準備飯菜，以及通知爐灶什麼時候開始做飯。當然，你可能會經不住誘惑而吃得太多，因此就有了 Hapi Fork 這款智能叉子，它可以告訴你的智慧型手機，你是否吃得太多，吃得太快。

如果你擔心孩子們太過沈迷於技術，這裡還有可以與智慧型手機相連的 iBitz 智能兒童活動追蹤器，它可以告訴孩子們該活動活動了。所有這些智能互動的技術會給你什麼樣的感受呢？不要擔心，也有這樣的技術。

關鍵解析　英文聽力重點看這邊就對了

❶ Tablet computers are also getting bigger, like this one from Lenovo, which can replace the traditional family board game.

本句中 which 引導的是非限定性定語從句，修飾先行詞 this one from Lenovo，one 指代前面提到的 tablet computer（平板電腦）。board game 意為「棋盤遊戲，桌上遊戲」，可泛指棋類、牌類、益智遊戲等。

❷ Of course, you might be tempted to eat too much, so there's Hapi Fork, which can tell your smartphone if you are eating too much, too fast.

be tempted to do sth. 表示「受誘惑去做某事」。學習者初聽到 Hapi Fork 時，可能無法確定它到底是人名、地名還是事物的名稱，而緊跟著的 which 引導的非限定關係子句暗示這應該是能跟智慧型手機實現連接的某種叉子。所以聽到一個新的概念時，要耐心，因為下文常會有進一步的説明。

❸ And if you worry the kids are too addicted to technology, there's iBitz, which connects to your smartphone, to get them moving.

be addicted to 表示「對……十分著迷」。後半句的主句為 there's iBitz to get them moving，其中 them 代指上文提到的 kids。

題目詳解篇

Unit 6 財經商貿

Banks in Cyprus Remain Closed after Bailout
財務紓困之後，賽普勒斯多家銀行仍在歇業

新聞原文　一知半解？跟著新聞原文，再聽一遍　🎧 Track 054

On March 15 banks in Cyprus closed their doors, and they haven't re-opened. The trickling cash flow has already taken its toll.

Small businesses say they are doing very little, some say they've already had to lay off employees.

But the worst may be yet to come. The deal struck with international lenders aims to shrink the Cypriot banking sector, which is about eight times the size of the economy.

The country's biggest lender, the Bank of Cyprus, will be radically restructured and Laiki Bank, the second largest, is set to close. A massive blow. It employs 8,000 people in a country of less than 1 million.

This EU/IMF deal differs from other euro zone bailouts because, instead of taxpayers footing the bill, depositors with large balances are to bear the costs.

On Monday the head of the Eurogroup, Jeroen Dijsselbloem, suggested the rescue program for Cyprus could be a new template for Europe.

For now, most Cypriots are powerless and are trying to deal with the immediate impact of their banking fiasco.

精準翻譯　句句到位，看你是否真的全數聽懂 🔊

3 月 15 日賽普勒斯的多家銀行歇業後，至今仍未正常開張。少量的現金流造成的影響已經開始顯現。

很多小公司表示他們的業務量很少，有些稱他們已不得不開始解雇員工。

但是更糟的局面可能還在後面。因為與國際債權人所達成的協議目的是要壓縮賽普勒斯的銀行業，其銀行業規模目前是其經濟規模的八倍。

賽普勒斯最大的債權人賽普勒斯銀行將會徹底重組，而第二大銀行大眾銀行將會被關閉。該銀行現有 8,000 名員工，對於一個人口不到 100 萬的小國家來說，這是一個重大的打擊。

這份與歐盟／國際貨幣基金組織達成的協議與其他歐元區紓困計劃不同，因為這次不是納稅人來買單，而是由那些帳面上有大額存款的存款人來買單。

周一，歐元集團主席傑倫·迪塞爾布洛姆表示，對賽普勒斯的救援計劃可以作為歐洲解決銀行業危機的一個新榜樣。

目前，大部分的賽普勒斯人對此都無能為力，只能竭力去應對銀行業大災難所帶來的直接後果。

關鍵解析　英文聽力重點看這邊就對了

❶ But the worst may be yet to come. The deal struck with international lenders aims to shrink the Cypriot banking sector, which is about eight times the size of the economy.

　　本句中 struck 的動詞原形為 strike, strike a deal/bargain 是「達成協議」的意思。此處用 strike 的過去分詞形式作 the deal 的後位修飾。句末 which 引導的非限定關係子句修飾的是 the Cypriot banking sector。注意，子句中出現了倍數的一個常用表達方式。

❷ The country's biggest lender, the Bank of Cyprus, will be radically restructured and Laiki Bank, the second largest, is set to close.

　　本句中兩次使用了同位語。the country's biggest lender 和 the Bank of Cyprus，以及 Laiki Bank 和 the second largest 都是同位語關係。

❸ This EU/IMF deal differs from other euro zone bailouts because, instead of taxpayers footing the bill, depositors with large balances are to bear the costs.

　　本句中 EU 是「歐盟」的縮寫，IMF 是「國際貨幣基金組織」的縮寫。bailout是「緊急財政援助」的意思。foot the bill 和 bear the costs同義，都指「負擔或承擔費用」。英文不喜歡重複，常會用不同的詞語來表達相同的含義。

Despite Slow Start, Starbucks Expands in India
星巴克在印度：起步緩慢擴張有序

新聞原文 一知半解？跟著新聞原文，再聽一遍 Track 055

This Starbucks outlet in New Delhi's Connaught Place has been open for more than a month and still draws long lines and interest from young people like Vikram Maour, who until now had only seen the coffee chain on television.

Starbucks opened its first store in India in October of 2012, through a joint venture with India's Tata Global Beverages. The U.S.-based coffee chain had planned to open 50 outlets in the country by the end of last year, but so far has a total of nine stores in the cities of Mumbai and New Delhi.

Starbucks officials say despite the delay, the coffee giant wants to eventually make India one of its top five global markets.

Tata Starbucks CEO Avani Davda says India is a complex market for foreign investors, both socially and economically, but that it carries tremendous potential.

That potential can be seen in India's 300 million-strong rising middle class and a younger population that is increasingly espousing Western tastes. Starbucks has deliberately kept prices lower compared to its pricing in neighboring China, in an effort to make the brand more accessible.

With India's coffee consumption increasing 80 percent in the last decade and India's coffee market expected to top $500 million in the next few years, Starbucks officials say they are confident the company's investment will pay off.

精準翻譯 句句到位，看你是否真的全數聽懂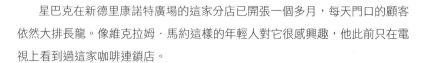

　　星巴克在新德里康諾特廣場的這家分店已開張一個多月，每天門口的顧客依然大排長龍。像維克拉姆·馬約這樣的年輕人對它很感興趣，他此前只在電視上看到過這家咖啡連鎖店。

　　透過與印度的塔塔全球飲料公司成立合資公司，星巴克在印度的第一家分店於 2012 年 10 月開張。這家總部位於美國的咖啡連鎖店原計劃到去年年底

在印度開設 50 家分店，但迄今為止只在孟買和新德里開設了 9 家分店。

　　根據星巴克相關人員的說法，儘管有所延遲，但是這家咖啡連鎖巨頭希望最終能將印度發展成為其全球前五大市場之一。

　　塔塔星巴克首席執行官阿瓦尼・達夫達說，對於國外投資者而言，印度無論從社會角度還是經濟角度來說都是一個複雜的市場，但它蘊含著巨大的潛力。

　　巨大的潛力存在於印度不斷崛起的 3 億中產階級人口中，也存在於口味越來越偏向西方化的一代年輕人身上。與在中國的定價相比，星巴克在印度的定價有意偏低，意圖提高品牌的接受度。

　　印度的咖啡消費在過去的十年裡增加了 80%，其咖啡市場預計在未來的幾年內將達到 5 億美元。星巴克相關人員稱他們很有信心，公司在印度的投資一定會獲得回報。

關鍵解析 英文聽力重點看這邊就對了

❶ This Starbucks outlet in New Delhi's Connaught Place has been open for more than a month and still draws long lines and interest from young people like Vikram Maour, who until now had only seen the coffee chain on television.

　　本句中 draw 後面跟了兩個受詞，draw long lines 表示「引來很多人排隊」；draw interest 表示「引起某人的興趣」。句末 who 引導的非限定關係子句，修飾的是前面的 Vikram Maour。由於關係子句中的動作發生在星巴克分店開張之前，是過去的過去，因此此子句用了過去完成式。

❷ That potential can be seen in India's 300 million-strong rising middle class and a younger population that is increasingly espousing Western tastes.

　　本句中 300 million-strong 中 strong 用於數字後，表示「多達……的」。rising 是現在分詞修飾 middle class, 表示「崛起的中產階級」。 espouse 是表示「支持，擁護，偏好」的意思。

NEWS 03　E-Commerce Challenges Traditional Stores
電子商務與傳統商店之爭

新聞原文　一知半解？跟著新聞原文，再聽一遍　🎧 Track 056

Lynne Shaner used the Internet to buy everything she needed for her wedding and holiday gifts for her husband and step daughter.

Other than food, 90 percent of her purchases are made on the computer in her Washington apartment.

Shaner has lots of company. Analysts say U.S. online shopping has hit records in November and December. Fifty-seven percent of Americans have made at least one online purchase.

Traditional merchants worry that growing e-commerce will shrink their share of the market.

Cornell University Marketing Professor Ed McLaughlin says they have reason for concern.

McLaughlin says traditional stores can keep their customers by offering goods like clothing, which customers may want to see and try on before purchasing — as well as items that are difficult to ship. He says some "bricks and mortar" stores are also pleasing customers with services that set up or repair computers and electronics. Traditional stores also offer a social experience that some shoppers enjoy.

Experts say as more and more people have Internet access and smart phones, online commerce is likely to continue its growth here in the United States and in other countries.

精準翻譯　句句到位，看你是否真的全數聽懂 🔊

　　琳內・沙納從網路上購置了自己婚禮所需的一切物品，還在網路上為丈夫和繼女購買了節日禮物。

　　除了食品的購買，沙納 90% 的購物活動都是在她華盛頓的公寓裡透過電腦完成的。

同沙納一樣的消費者大有人在。分析人士稱，美國 11 月和 12 月份的網購已創了新紀錄。57% 的美國人至少在網路上購物過一次。

傳統商人們擔心不斷壯大的電子商務會壓縮他們的市場。

康奈爾大學市場營銷學教授艾德‧麥克勞克林稱，他們的擔憂確實不無道理。

麥克勞克林說，想要留住消費者，傳統商店可以銷售諸如衣服之類的商品，這些商品消費者在購買之前可能想要親眼看到並且試穿。它們還可以銷售不容易運輸的貨品。一些實體商店還為顧客提供安裝以及修理電腦或其他電子產品的服務，以此來取悅消費者。傳統商店還能夠提供一種社交體驗，一些消費者對此頗為青睞。

專家稱，隨著越來越多的人擁有網路和智慧型手機，電子商務在美國以及其他國家都很可能會持續增長下去。

關鍵解析 英文聽力重點看這邊就對了

❶ McLaughlin says traditional stores can keep their customers by offering goods like clothing, which customers may want to see and try on before purchasing — as well as items that are difficult to ship.

本句中 by 表示手段或方式，後面跟的是「留住顧客」的具體方法。as well as 連接兩個並列成分：clothing 和 items（商品）。which 引導的非限定關係子句修飾 clothing, 而 that 引導的限定關係子句修飾 items。

❷ He says some "bricks and mortar" stores are also pleasing customers with services that set up or repair computers and electronics.

本句中「bricks and mortar」 stores 是「實體店」的意思，其中 bricks and mortar 字面意思為「磚塊和砂漿」。與實體店相對應的虛擬店稱作 virtual store。please sb. with sth. 表示「用……取悅某人」。句末 that 引導的關係子句修飾的是 services。

NEWS 04 EU Confronts Youth Unemployment Crisis
歐盟正視青年失業危機

新聞原文　一知半解？跟著新聞原文，再聽一遍　🎧 Track 057

In Spain and in Greece, unemployment among under-25 year-olds is running at over 50 percent.

In Portugal, there are lines every day outside the Angolan and Brazilian consulates, as job-seekers look for better fortunes in the country's former colonies.

Meeting in Brussels Friday, EU leaders agree to spend $7.8 billion over the next two years to tackle youth unemployment. Herman Van Rompuy is president of the European Council.

"We know that reforms take time and results won't be immediate. So we're also concentrating on launching actions with direct impact, fighting youth unemployment and helping SMEs access to credit."

European commissioners have described this week as a good one for the EU — after a deal was clinched on a $1.25 trillion seven-year budget for the bloc, ending months of argument between member states.

Croatia joins the European Union on July 1, while EU leaders agreed Friday to begin accession talks with Serbia no later than January next year. President of European Commission Jose Manuel Barroso hailed the agreement.

Meanwhile, Latvia gained formal approval Friday to join the euro zone on January 1, 2014 — becoming the 18th country to use the currency.

精準翻譯　句句到位，看你是否真的全數聽懂

在西班牙和希臘，25 歲以下青年人的失業率已經超過 50%。

在葡萄牙，找工作的人幾乎每天都在安哥拉和巴西領事館外面大排長龍，希望能去葡萄牙的前殖民地國家尋找更好的機會。

週五，歐盟各國領袖齊聚布魯塞爾，共同商定在接下來的兩年時間內投入 78 億美元來解決青年失業問題。

歐洲理事會主席赫爾曼‧範龍佩說：「我們知道改革需要時間，而且改革的成效不可能即刻顯現。因此，我們也在努力採取一些能即刻見到成效的措施，應對青年失業問題，幫助中小企業獲得貸款。」

歐盟委員會的委員們認為，本週對歐盟而言是不錯的一週，因為歐盟各成員國終於結束了數月以來的爭論，敲定了一項七年期、總額為 1.25 萬億美元的歐盟財政預算法案。

克羅埃西亞於 7 月 1 日加入歐盟，此外，歐盟領導人周五也已經同意在明年一月份之前同塞爾維亞展開入盟談判。歐盟委員會主席若澤‧曼努埃爾‧巴羅佐對這一決定表示歡迎。

與此同時，拉脫維亞週五也獲得了正式批準，將於 2014 年 1 月 1 日加入歐元區，成為第 18 個使用這一貨幣的國家。

關鍵解析 英文聽力重點看這邊就對了

❶ European commissioners have described this week as a good one for the EU — after a deal was clinched on a $1.25 trillion seven-year budget for the bloc, ending months of argument between member states.

句中動詞 clinch 表示「敲定，達成」的意思，常與 a deal 搭配。trillion 是「萬億」的概念。對於 thousand（千），million（百萬），billion（十億）和 trillion（萬億）這些表示數量的詞，學習者一定要熟悉其讀法和意思，聽到時才能快速準確地記憶、理解和換算。the bloc 本意為「多個國家或政黨組成的集團」，這裡指的是歐盟。

❷ Meanwhile, Latvia gained formal approval Friday to join the euro zone on January 1, 2014 — becoming the 18th country to use the currency.

Latvia（拉脫維亞）是歐洲東北部的一個國家。the euro zone 指「歐元區」，是歐盟成員中使用歐盟統一貨幣歐元的國家區域，之前已有 17 個國家。

05 EU Solar Panel Ruling Sparks Fears of Trade War with China
歐盟太陽能板裁決引發中歐貿易戰擔憂

新聞原文　一知半解？跟著新聞原文，再聽一遍　🎧 Track 058

New estimates show Chinese-made solar panels account for about 80 percent of the world's market share. But European manufacturers say that's because Chinese manufacturers are not playing fair — selling their products far below cost — and driving the competition out of business.

On Wednesday, the European Union said it was moving forward with plans to impose sharply higher duties on Chinese solar panels. But facing resistance from some European member states, EU trade commissioner Karel de Gucht offered to phase in the higher tariffs.

"As of the 6th of June, a tariff of 11.8 percent will be imposed on all Chinese solar panel imports. Two months later, as of the 6th of August, the average tariff will be 47.6 percent. Overall, the duties will range from 37.2 to 67.9 percent at that stage."

It didn't take long for a response from Beijing — which said it is investigating EU subsidies for European wines.

Chinese Foreign Ministry spokesman Hong Lei said he hopes the Europeans will reconsider.

Some European countries fear higher Chinese tariffs on European wines could affect other industries — at a time when Europe desperately needs growth.

精準翻譯　句句到位，看你是否真的全數聽懂 🔊

最新估計顯示，中國生產的太陽能板大約占據了世界市場份額的 80%。但是歐洲製造商卻稱，那是因為中國太陽能板製造商實行不公平競爭，以遠低於成本的價格出售自己的產品，從而將其他競爭對手擊垮。

本週三，歐盟稱其目前正在計劃大幅提高對中國生產的太陽能板所徵收的

關稅。但是面對歐盟一些成員國的反對，歐盟貿易專員卡雷爾‧德古特提議逐步提高關稅。

他說：「從6月6號開始，歐盟將對從中國進口的太陽能板徵收11.8%的關稅。兩個月之後，即從8月6號開始，平均關稅率將達到47.6%。綜合來說，第二階段的稅率將會在37.2%到67.9%之間浮動。」

對此，中國方面很快就作出了回應，稱其正在對原產於歐盟國家的進口葡萄酒展開反補貼調查。

中國外交部發言人洪磊表示希望歐盟能重新考慮其決定。

一些歐洲國家擔心，在歐洲迫切需要經濟增長之時，中國對從歐洲進口的葡萄酒徵收更高的關稅可能會影響到其他工業的發展。

關鍵解析 英文聽力重點看這邊就對了

❶ But European manufacturers say that's because Chinese manufacturers are not playing fair — selling their products far below cost — and driving the competition out of business.

　　play fair 原指「在比賽中光明正大地進行較量」，這裡指「在市場上進行公平競爭」。句中破折號引出的內容進一步說明「進行不公平競爭」的具體表現。

❷ But facing resistance from some European member states, EU trade commissioner Karel de Gucht offered to phase in the higher tariffs.

　　本句中 facing 是現在分詞作伴隨狀語可譯為「由於面臨……」。動詞片語 phase in sth. 表示「逐步引入，分階段實施」的意思。tariff 意為「關稅」，與文中的 duty 意思相同。

❸ As of the 6th of June, a tariff of 11.8 percent will be imposed on all Chinese solar panel imports.

　　as of the 6th of June 意為「從 6 月 6 日起」，as of 或 as from 常用於表示某事或某規定正式開始的日期。impose (a tariff) on 表示「對……徵收（關稅）」。

NEWS 06 OECD Says Global Economy Rebounds, but Not in Europe
經合組織稱，全球經濟回升，但歐洲步伐滯後

新聞原文　一知半解？跟著新聞原文，再聽一遍　🎧 *Track 059*

New government data shows the U.S. economy expanded at a faster clip last year than earlier estimates. And it's likely to perform better in 2013.

The OECD says the world's largest economy will post annualized growth of about three and a half percent in the first three months of 2013 — slowing to about 2 percent from April to June.

Japan follows closely behind — with 3.2 percent between January to March — and then 2.2 percent in the second quarter.

OECD Chief economist Pier Carlo Padoan released the group's latest forecast.

"It is an outlook which points at an improvement of the global economy, especially in the United States and Japan, a bit less so in the euro area."

Although Europe has successfully addressed a number of imbalances caused by the region's debt crisis, Padoan says the outlook for the 17-nations that make up the euro zone remains mixed.

A separate report by the Paris-based organization paints a more optimistic picture for China and emerging market economies. Despite a number of potential financial and environmental challenges in the coming years, the OECD expects China to grow between 8 and 9 percent this year.

精準翻譯　句句到位，看你是否真的全數聽懂 🔊

新的政府數據顯示，美國去年的經濟增長速度高於之前的預測。其在 2013 年的表現可能會更好。

經合組織（OECD）稱，2013 年第一季度，世界最大經濟體的年增長率將會達到 3.5% 左右，4 月份到 6 月份會有所下滑，降到 2% 左右。

日本緊隨其後，1 月份至 3 月份的增長率約為 3.2%，第二季度為 2.2%。

經合組織首席經濟學家皮爾‧卡洛‧帕多安發布了該組織最新的預測。

帕多安說：「總體趨勢顯示全球經濟開始回升，尤其是在美國和日本，歐洲地區稍滯後。」

雖然歐洲已成功解決了由地區債務危機引發的數個失衡問題，帕多安稱歐元區 17 國的經濟前景仍是喜憂參半。

這個總部位於巴黎的組織發布的另一份報告則對中國以及其他新興經濟體的情況做了更為樂觀的描繪。儘管在今後幾年內，中國會面臨許多潛在的金融和環境挑戰，但是經合組織預計中國今年的增長率會達到 8% 到 9%。

關鍵解析 英文聽力重點看這邊就對了

❶ The OECD says the world's largest economy will post annualized growth of about three and a half percent in the first three months of 2013 — slowing to about 2 percent from April to June.

句中 OECD 為首字母縮寫詞，其全稱為 Organization for Economic Co-operation and Development（經濟合作與發展組織，簡稱「經合組織」）。the world's largest economy （世界最大的經濟體）指的是美國，這屬於常識知識。學習者如果不了解，從上下文應該也能推測出來。

❷ It is an outlook which points at an improvement of the global economy, especially in the United States and Japan, a bit less so in the euro area.

本句中 which 引導的關係子句對 an outlook（前景）做進一步說明。point at 表示「指向」的意思。a bit less so 中的 so 指的是前面提到的「經濟前景向好」。

Nigerian Gold Miners Seek the Right to Mine
奈及利亞黃金礦工尋求採礦權

新聞原文 一知半解？跟著新聞原文，再聽一遍 🎧 *Track 060*

Gold mining in this part of northern Nigeria is not glamorous. But these men say it's more dignified than extreme poverty, which used to be the norm around here.

Sani Bila heads a local mining association. As he perches on a pile of rocks laced with gold, he says nowadays business is booming.

Other miners say success is coupled with fear, as the government continues to call their operations illegal.

At a news conference in the capital, Abuja, State Minister of Health Muhammad Ali Pate says a lot of small-scale mining is illegal because it is dangerous. He blames the small operations for the lead poisoning outbreak that has crippled the Zamfara region and killed hundreds of children.

Pate says the lead poisoning is caused by dust emitted as gold is processed. But activists say the threat of mining bans only aggravates the crisis.

These men say they fear neither bans nor licensing laws and they will continue to work in peace. But before they would allow a camera on site they insisted that their exact location be kept a secret.

精準翻譯 句句到位，看你是否真的全數聽懂

在奈及利亞北部這片地區的金礦開採工作並非那麼令人嚮往，但是這裡的人說，與以前的極端貧窮相比，採礦能讓人覺得更有點尊嚴。

賽尼‧畢拉是當地一個採礦協會的工頭。正坐在一堆金礦石上的他說，現在生意很火紅。

其他一些採礦者表示採礦雖然賺錢了，但也要擔驚受怕，因為政府不斷指稱他們的採礦作業是違法的。

在首都阿布賈召開的一次新聞發布會上，奈及利亞衛生部部長穆罕默德・阿里・帕特說，很多小型金礦開採作業之所以違法是因為它們很危險。他指責小型採礦作業造成了嚴重鉛汙染事故，致使柰姆法拉地區很多人殘疾，數百名兒童死亡。

帕特指出，鉛汙染是金礦石加工過程中產生的粉塵造成的。但是一些支持者認為禁止採礦只會進一步加劇危機。

當地人說他們不怕禁令也不怕許可經營的法律，他們會繼續安穩地作業。但是他們不允許我們將相機帶入採礦場，除非我們能對他們開採的確切地點進行保密。

關鍵解析 英文聽力重點看這邊就對了

❶ But these men say it's more dignified than extreme poverty, which used to be the norm around here.

本句中 it 代指的是上文提到的 gold mining（金礦開採）。used to be 表示「過去曾是」，used to be the norm around here 意為「過去曾是這裡的常態」。

❷ He blames the small operations for the lead poisoning outbreak that has crippled the Zamfara region and killed hundreds of children.

blame sb./sth. for sth. 表示「把……歸咎於（某人或某事）」。前面主句的意思為「他指責小型採礦作業造成了鉛汙染事故」。that 引導的關係子句修飾前面的 the lead poisoning outbreak。cripple 表示「使傷殘，嚴重損壞」的意思。關係子句中 has crippled 和 killed 是並列關係，該子句的意思是「鉛汙染導致該地區很多人殘疾，數百名兒童喪生」。

❸ But before they would allow a camera on site they insisted that their exact location be kept a secret.

此句中的 insist 表示「堅持要求」的意思，後面的受詞子句使用了虛擬語氣，句子結構為「insist that sb./sth. +（should +）動詞原形」，句中 be kept a secret 前面省略了 should。

Burger Makers Fight to Repeal Biofuel Law
漢堡製造商要求廢止生物燃料法

新聞原文 一知半解？跟著新聞原文，再聽一遍 🎧 *Track 061*

When you drive up to Wendy's or other fast-food chains in the U.S., you are consuming corn in at least two ways.

The chicken or hamburger in your meal comes from an animal raised on corn. And the fuel in your car is 10 percent ethanol, which is made from corn. The two are competing for the same grain, says University of Missouri economist Pat Westhoff.

"Well, Ethanol diverts a significant share of the US corn crop each year. So by doing so, it makes corn prices higher than they otherwise would be."

Higher corn prices mean higher meat prices.

Ethanol has consumed a growing share of the corn market since a 2005 law required it be added to U.S. gasoline.

Now, the restaurant industry wants the law repealed.

At a recent news conference, franchise owner Ed Anderson said that the mandate costs each of his four Wendy's restaurants up to $30,000 per year.

But ethanol's backers disagree that the law is driving up food prices.

Ethanol is typically cheaper than petroleum. Fuel makers now add it to gasoline regardless of the law. So waiving the mandate would not matter much for now.

Current policy calls for increased use of ethanol. Westhoff says that will require even more corn and put more pressure on food prices.

Until alternatives to corn ethanol materialize, the tension between burgers and biofuels will continue.

精準翻譯 句句到位，看你是否真的全數聽懂 🔊

當你開車到溫蒂漢堡或美國其他快餐連鎖店用餐時，你至少在以兩種方式消耗玉米。

你所吃的雞肉或牛肉漢堡裡使用的肉，都來自用玉米餵養的動物。而你的

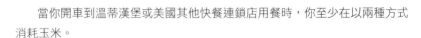

汽車使用的燃料中含有 10% 的乙醇，它也來源於玉米。密蘇里大學經濟學家帕特‧維斯特霍夫表示，兩者在玉米的使用上展開了競爭。

他說：「乙醇的生產每年都會消耗美國玉米總產量的相當大一部分，這樣一來，玉米價格就比原先提高了很多。」

而玉米價格的升高使得肉類價格也隨之提高了。

自 2005 年美國通過的一項法案規定美國汽油中要加入乙醇之後，製造乙醇所消耗的玉米數量就在不斷增加。

現在，餐飲業希望廢止這項法律。

在最近的一次新聞發布會上，特許經營店店主埃德‧安德森說，因為這一命令，他的四家溫蒂漢堡餐廳，每一家每年要多花費 3 萬美元。

但是，乙醇的支持者們卻對該法律致使食物價格上漲的說法不以為然。

乙醇的價格明顯低於石油，不管有沒有這條法律，現在的燃料生產商都會把乙醇添加到汽油裡。所以，眼下取消這項命令的意義不大。

當前的政策號召多使用乙醇。維斯特霍夫表示，那將會需要更多的玉米，也會給食品價格帶來更大的壓力。

但在玉米乙醇的替代產品出現之前，漢堡和生物燃料之間的緊張關係仍將持續。

- -

關鍵解析 英文聽力重點看這邊就對了

❶ And the fuel in your car is 10 percent ethanol, which is made from corn. The two are competing for the same grain.

動詞片語 be made from 表示「由……製造而成」。the two 指的是上面提到的「漢堡」和「乙醇」這兩種消耗玉米的事物。compete for 指「為……展開競爭」。

❷ Until alternatives to corn ethanol materialize, the tension between burgers and biofuels will continue.

until 意為「到……為止，在……之前」，表示一種條件。alternative 在句中用作名詞，常與介詞 to 搭配，表示「……的替代品」。materialize 意為「實現，成為現實」。

NEWS 09 Fed Chief Warns of Economic Headwinds from Budget Stalemate
美聯準會主席警告預算僵局將導致經濟下滑

新聞原文　一知半解？跟著新聞原文，再聽一遍　 Track 062

With no progress in Washington to avoid looming spending cuts, Federal Reserve Chairman Ben Bernanke warned lawmakers that inaction would sharply slow U.S. economic growth.

Despite the high stakes, the only action from Washington has been mostly — finger pointing.

Republican House Speaker John Boehner says it's time for the president and the Democratically controlled Senate to take the lead.

The automatic spending cuts, roughly three percent of the federal budget, would slash defense spending and affect government services from border security to meat inspections.

The White House wants a more balanced approach that includes cuts and higher taxes.

But as it stands, President Barack Obama calls the sequester arbitrary and irresponsible.

Republicans say the president is grandstanding.

But economist William Gale says Republicans' insistence on across-the-board spending cuts ignores economic reality.

Reports suggest Republicans may be willing to modify the sequester to give the administration discretion in deciding which programs to cut. Analysts say such a move would give Republicans political cover but place responsibility for the economic impact squarely on the president.

精準翻譯　句句到位，看你是否真的全數聽懂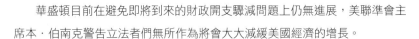

華盛頓目前在避免即將到來的財政開支驟減問題上仍無進展，美聯準會主席本‧伯南克警告立法者們無所作為將會大大減緩美國經濟的增長。

儘管面臨這樣巨大的危機，華盛頓各方卻依舊互相指責。

　　共和黨眾議院議長約翰‧博納稱，現在到了需要總統以及民主黨主導下的參議院帶頭行動的時候了。

　　約占聯邦預算 3% 左右的自動減支計劃會大幅削減國防開支，政府的多項職能和服務——從邊境安全到肉類檢驗——都會受影響。

　　白宮希望採取一種更加平衡的方式，其中包括削減開支和提高稅收。

　　但是從現在的情況來看，歐巴馬總統認為自動減赤計劃過於武斷和不負責任。

　　共和黨卻稱總統只是在嘩眾取寵。

　　但是經濟學家威廉‧蓋爾指出，共和黨堅持全面削減開支是忽略經濟現狀。

　　報告建議共和黨可以調整減赤措施，由政府來酌情決定削減哪些項目。分析人士指出此舉能夠給予共和黨政治保護，並將經濟受影響的責任直接歸到總統身上。

關鍵解析　英文聽力重點看這邊就對了

❶ With no progress in Washington to avoid looming spending cuts, Federal Reserve Chairman Ben Bernanke warned lawmakers that inaction would sharply slow U.S. economic growth.

　　句首的「with + 名詞 + 介詞片語」結構作修飾，表明發出警告的原因。Federal Reserve Chairman 是「美聯準會主席」的意思。學習者平時聽經濟類的英文教材時，要多留心經濟術語和金融機構的英文表達。

❷ Despite the high stakes, the only action from Washington has been mostly — finger pointing.

　　句中 the high stakes 表示「很大的風險」，具體就是指上面提到的「美國經濟受到嚴重影響的可能性很大」。finger pointing 表示「互相指責」的意思。

❸ Reports suggest Republicans may be willing to modify the sequester to give the administration discretion in deciding which programs to cut.

　　本句中的 Republicans 指共和黨人。美國實行兩黨制，一是共和黨，另一黨是民主黨（Democratic Party）。give sb./sth. discretion in doing sth. 表示「給予某人 / 某組織處理某事的決斷權」。

IMF Lowers Its Global Economic Prospects
國際貨幣基金組織下調全球經濟增長預期

新聞原文　一知半解？跟著新聞原文，再聽一遍　🎧 Track 063

The world's economy is not growing as fast as many had hoped. The IMF revised its global growth forecast in 2013 to just a little over 3 percent — down from earlier projections of 3.3 percent.

IMF chief economist Olivier Blanchard says the revisions are based on several factors.

Global demand for goods and services has declined — especially in Europe, where a debt crisis and tough austerity measures have produced the longest economic slump in the 17-nation euro zone's history.

It's a vicious circle. Reduced demand has slowed growth in faster-growing economies, particularly in the so-called BRIC countries — Brazil, Russia, India, and China.

Blanchard says that has repercussions for advanced economies.

"If, for example, growth in BRICS was to go down by two percent relative to what we predict, then the effect on the U.S., for example, would be half a percent. So it matters."

The IMF has lowered expectations for U.S. growth, even though recent housing and employment data suggest slow but steady progress.

The IMF sees improving global economic conditions in 2014, but only if the world's major economies continue to promote policies that foster near-term growth, while cutting long-term debt.

精準翻譯　句句到位，看你是否真的全數聽懂 🔊

世界經濟的增長速度並不像許多人預想的那樣快。國際貨幣基金組織修正了其對 2013 年全球經濟增長的預測，從早前預測的 3.3% 下調至僅 3% 多一點。

國際貨幣基金組織首席經濟學家奧利維耶・布朗夏爾稱此次修正是基於幾個方面。

全球的貨物和服務需求在下降，這在歐洲尤其明顯。一場債務危機和隨之採取的嚴厲緊縮措施令歐元區 17 國陷入了有史以來持續時間最長的一次經濟蕭條。

這是一種惡性循環。需求下降也使經濟增長較快的經濟體，尤其是所謂的金磚國家——巴西、俄羅斯、印度和中國——放慢了增長腳步。

布朗夏爾說這又反過來進一步影響發達經濟體。他說：「例如，如果金磚國家的增長率較預期下降 2%，那麼它給美國帶來的影響將會是 0.5% 的降幅。因此，影響還是不小的。」

此外，儘管最近的房地產銷售和就業數據顯示美國經濟正在緩慢而穩定地增長，但國際貨幣基金組織還是下調了其對美國經濟增長的預期。

國際貨幣基金組織預計全球經濟在 2014 年將會有所好轉，但前提是世界主要經濟體繼續採取措施促進短期經濟增長，同時削減長期債務。

- -

關鍵解析 英文聽力重點看這邊就對了

❶ The world's economy is not growing as fast as many had hoped.

本句是篇章開頭句，開宗明義，點明主旨，即「世界經濟增速不如預想的快」。在聽力訓練過程中，學習者尤其要注意聽開頭部分，因為這部分很可能會概括地提出新聞最主要、最明顯的事實，後面的內容會圍繞它而展開。

❷ Global demand for goods and services has declined — especially in Europe, where a debt crisis and tough austerity measures have produced the longest economic slump in the 17-nation euro zone's history.

本句的主詞是 global demand，因此後面的動詞 has declined 用的是單數。tough austerity measures 意為「嚴厲的緊縮措施」。economic slump 在此表示「經濟蕭條或衰退」的意思。

❸ The IMF sees improving global economic conditions in 2014, but only if the world's major economies continue to promote policies that foster near-term growth, while cutting long-term debt.

本句中 see 與 foresee，predict 意思相同，表示「預見，預計」的意思。only if 條件子句用於說明事情發生的條件，可譯為「只有……（才），除非」等。

Robots Help US Manufacturers Compete with China
機器人助美國製造業與中國抗衡

新聞原文 一知半解？跟著新聞原文，再聽一遍 Track 064

In what may be the beginning of a new trend in American manufacturing, Sunit Saxena recently moved his production operation from China to the United States.

Saxena is the CEO of Altierre Digital Retail in San Jose, California. The company makes digital price displays and signs for retail stores that can be updated from a computer.

Altierre now employs between 50 and 60 workers, fewer than it used to in China, and pays them about $10.00 an hour. Using new electronic testing stations, Saxena says the company has doubled productivity — making it cost-competitive with China.

Up to now, automation technology has been used mostly on tasks that require identical and repetitive motion. But technology developers like Troy Straszheim are building robots with new capabilities.

Using cameras and sensors, Straszheim is developing machines that can recognize and select specific shapes — creating robots that, in this case, could be used at loading docks and shipyards.

These technological innovations are helping U.S. manufacturing expand for the first time in a decade. And industry officials say automation will lead to more high skilled jobs and higher pay for workers over time as companies expand their operations in America.

精準翻譯 句句到位，看你是否真的全數聽懂

在美國，製造業似乎正開始呈現出一種新的趨勢，蘇尼特・薩克塞納最近就將其生產線從中國轉移到了美國。

薩克塞納是位於加州聖荷西的阿爾蒂埃爾數碼零售公司的首席執行長。公司為零售商店生產數字價格標籤和標牌，所展示的價格可以通過電腦更新。

公司現在雇用了 50 到 60 名工人，比之前在中國時的員工要少，所付的報酬為每小時 10 美元。薩克塞納説，通過使用新的電子測試臺，公司的生產力提高了一倍，與中國的公司相比具有了成本競爭力。

迄今為止，自動化技術主要用於重複性工作。但是像特洛伊·斯特拉斯海姆這樣的技術開發商正在開發具有新功能的機器人。

通過使用照相機和傳感器，其所研發的機器能夠識別以及篩選特定形狀，這樣的機器人可用於碼頭和船塢的裝運。

有了這些技術創新，美國製造業十年來首次實現了擴張。工業部官員稱，隨著各公司在美國製造業務的進一步擴展，自動化技術的應用將會催生更多技術含量更高的工作，工人收入也會增加。

- -

關鍵解析 英文聽力重點看這邊就對了

❶ The company makes digital price displays and signs for retail stores that can be updated from a computer.

注意，本句最後 that 引導的關係子句修飾先行詞 digital price displays and signs，其意為「可以通過電腦來更新的數字價格標籤和標牌」。

❷ Using new electronic testing stations, Saxena says the company has doubled productivity — making it cost-competitive with China.

本句中 using 作動名詞片語，其邏輯主語是 the company。句子的後半部分，現在分詞 making 作補充。句中的 it 代指的是 the company。double 作動詞，表示「翻倍，提高了一倍」的意思。cost-competitive 是一個複合詞，表示「在成本上有競爭力的」。在練習聽力中遇到複合詞時，聽者可以根據各構成部分的意思大致猜測整個詞的意思。

❸ But technology developers like Troy Straszheim are building robots with new capabilities.

本句句首出現了表示轉折的連詞 but，聽者需要重點關注轉折詞後面所要表達的意思。雖然 Troy Straszheim 聽上去比較陌生，但是根據前面提到的 technology developers，學習者應該能明白這是一家技術開發商的名字。

NEWS

12

Russia Re-Industrializes as Energy Boom Fades
能源熱消退後，俄羅斯開始再工業化進程

新聞原文　一知半解？跟著新聞原文，再聽一遍　🎧 *Track 065*

Post-Soviet Russia is often seen as an industrial rust belt. But here, outside St. Petersburg, American car maker GM is investing to triple its production capacity.

Romuald Rytwinski, GM's Manufacturing Manager for Russia, says the quality is world class.

With these new cars, Russia is expected this year to top the peak car production of the Soviet Union — 2.2 million in 1985.

The rebirth of car making may signal the start of Russia's re-industrialization.

Anders Aslund, a Swedish economist, says Europe's most populous nation may be headed in a new direction.

"The oil price now seems to be leveling out, and you would expect it to go down a bit rather soon. And then the crowding out of other sectors by energy would diminish and at that time we would see a substantial revival of Russian manufacturing."

As gas and oil production increases around the world, Russia's energy boom is slowing.

With the end of easy money in sight, foreign investors believe Russia will embark on industrialization.

Russia is growing by forecast 3.5 percent this year while Europe struggles with recession.

With lower energy price on the horizon, the word from the Kremlin to local authorities is encourage investment in manufacturing.

So while Russia depends today on oil and gas prices, its future maybe manufacturing.

精準翻譯　句句到位，看你是否真的全數聽懂 🔊

　　蘇聯解體後的俄羅斯常被視為一個工業鐵鏽地帶。但就在這聖彼得堡的郊外，美國汽車製造商通用汽車公司卻增加投資，將生產力擴大三倍。

羅穆亞爾德・呂特溫斯基是通用汽車俄羅斯分公司的製造經理。他表示，這裡製造的汽車品質是世界一流的。

隨著這些新車的出廠，俄羅斯今年的汽車產量預計將超過蘇聯時期的巔峰產量——1985 年的 220 萬輛。

汽車製造業的新生或許代表著俄羅斯再工業化過程的開始。

瑞典經濟學家安德斯・阿斯倫德說，這個歐洲人口最多的國家可能正在朝一個新的方向前進。

目前，油價似乎已趨於平穩，預計很快會出現小幅下跌。能源對其他行業的擠出效應會減弱，屆時俄羅斯的製造業將會顯著復甦。

隨著世界各地天然氣、石油產量的不斷增加，俄羅斯的能源繁榮發展局面正在放緩。

鑒於這個依靠能源輕鬆獲利的時代不久將結束，外國投資者認為俄羅斯將會開啟一個工業化的新時代。

俄羅斯今年的經濟增長率預計為 3.5%，而歐洲其他國家正在艱難地應對經濟衰退。

考慮到能源價格不久可能會走低，克里姆林宮指示地方當局要鼓勵在製造業領域的投資。

所以，雖然俄羅斯目前依賴石油和天然氣價格，但將來可能要靠製造業。

關鍵解析 英文聽力重點看這邊就對了

❶ Post-Soviet Russia is often seen as an industrial rust belt.

post-Soviet 指「蘇聯解體後的」。1991 年底，蘇聯解體，俄羅斯正式成為獨立國家。rust belt 意為「鐵鏽地帶」，是指從前工業繁盛如今已衰落的地區。

❷ With the end of easy money in sight, foreign investors believe Russia will embark on industrialization.

easy money 指上面提到的「靠能源輕鬆賺錢」。in sight 是「臨近，即將發生」的意思。embark on sth. 表示「開始（做）某事」。

❸ With lower energy price on the horizon, the word from the Kremlin to local authorities is encourage investment in manufacturing.

句中 on the horizon 表示「即將發生」的意思。the word 在此表示「指示，命令」。句中用 the Kremlin（克里姆林宮）來指代俄羅斯中央政府。

269

US Budget Impasse Could Affect Air Travel
美國預算僵局可能影響航空旅行

新聞原文　一知半解？跟著新聞原文，再聽一遍 Track 066

Flying in and out of U.S. airports could become a challenge, with delays on the ground and in the air.

The disruptions could begin when automatic government spending cuts hit the nation's aviation sector in April.

The budget cuts mean there will be fewer workers and longer wait times for travelers clearing security and customs checkpoints, officials say.

With fewer air traffic controllers to guide pilots, officials predict delays of up to 90 minutes at big airports.

Marion Blakey is the president of the Aerospace Industries Association in Washington. She says the cuts will also harm the U.S. aerospace defense industry.

"Anything that disrupts air travel is disruptive of the economy," Virginia Senator Tim Kane and other members of Congress are calling for an end to the spending cuts.

Maryland Congressman John Sarbanes worries that reduced traffic at Baltimore's BWI Airport could mean a loss of 94,000 jobs.

Still — transportation officials say, budget cuts to civil aviation will not compromise safety on the ground or in the air.

精準翻譯　句句到位，看你是否真的全數聽懂

由於地面以及空中的延誤，飛機進出美國機場將可能會成為一個艱巨的任務。

自動削減政府開支方案將在 4 月份影響到航空產業，屆時有可能會出現上述的混亂情形。

　　有關官員指出，預算削減意味著工作人員數量減少，乘客在安檢以及海關檢查處需要等待更長時間。

　　有關官員預測，隨著引導飛行員的空中交通管理員人數的減少，大型機場的航班延誤可能會長達 90 分鐘。

　　瑪麗昂‧布萊基是位於華盛頓的美國航空工業協會的主席。她表示，開支削減也會影響美國航空和國防工業。

　　維吉尼亞州參議員蒂姆‧凱恩以及國會的其他成員也呼籲停止支出削減。他們說：「任何擾亂航空旅行的舉動都會對經濟造成影響。」

　　馬里蘭州的國會議員約翰‧薩班斯擔心，巴爾的摩華盛頓國際機場航空運輸量的減少將會導致 94,000 人失去工作。

　　不過，交通部官員稱，民用航空領域預算的削減將不會累及地面或空中的安全。

關鍵解析 **英文聽力重點看這邊就對了**

❶ The disruptions could begin when automatic government spending cuts hit the nation's aviation sector in April.

　　本句中 the disruptions 指上文提到的「美國機場地面與空中的延誤」。automatic government spending cuts 是指「自動生效的一系列聯邦政府支出削減措施」。因在最後截止日期到來時美國兩黨未能就替代方案達成一致，所以「自動減支方案」生效，它影響到政府的眾多部門，進而影響到美國經濟的多個領域。

❷ Still — transportation officials say, budget cuts to civil aviation will not compromise safety on the ground or in the air.

　　句中出現的動詞 compromise，聽者平時比較熟悉的意思是「妥協，讓步」，在這裡引申為「使陷入危險，連累，損害」的意思，在這裡交通部官員所要表達的意思是「不會讓民航預算削減影響到空中和地面的交通安全」。

War in Syria Hurts Lebanese Tourism Sector
敘利亞戰爭影響黎巴嫩旅遊業

新聞原文 一知半解？跟著新聞原文，再聽一遍 🎧 *Track 067*

The nickname of this Lebanese mountain town Aley is 'Arous el Masayif' — 'the bride of touristic places.' But the picturesque village outside Beirut that once attracted many Saudis and other Gulf nationals for its quaint atmosphere and cool evening breezes, looks abandoned these days.

Many restaurants are empty. Some have closed down for good.

With its beautiful mountains, stunning beaches, Roman ruins and Ottoman architecture, Lebanon's economy has long leaned on tourism, which accounts for more than a quarter of its gross domestic product. Visitor numbers are down nearly 38 percent from 2010.

The war in neighboring Syria is just one of the factors.

Lebanon's Minister of Tourism Fady Abboud: "We don't have a road link with the rest of the world because, you know, we don't have a link with Israel, the only link is through Syria and you know, probably I lost about a quarter of a million tourists coming by road to Lebanon, mainly Jordanians, Iranians and certainly from the Gulf."

To entice tourists, the ministry recently offered a promotion of 50 days for 50 percent off. Discounts were offered on airline tickets, hotels and restaurants.

So Lebanon is trying to diversify its pool of tourists by reaching out to new audiences from Russia, Latin America and Africa, among other regions.

精準翻譯 句句到位，看你是否真的全數聽懂 🔊

　　黎巴嫩山城阿萊的暱稱是 Arous el Masayif，意思是「旅遊勝地的新娘」。貝魯特市外的這個小鎮風景如畫，古樸典雅，晚風習習，許多沙烏地阿拉伯以及海灣國家的遊客慕名而來，但是現在，這裡看上去卻是一片荒涼景象。

　　許多餐館裡面空無一人，有些已經永久關門了。

黎巴嫩擁有秀麗的山川、迷人的沙灘、眾多古羅馬遺跡以及鄂圖曼帝國時期的建築，經濟長期以來依賴旅遊業，其旅遊業收入占國內生產總值的 1/4 以上。但現在的遊客數量與 2010 年相比減少了約 38%。

而鄰國敘利亞的戰爭正是造成此種情況的原因之一。

黎巴嫩旅遊部部長法迪·阿布德説：「我們與世界其他地區沒有道路相連通。我們當然沒有道路與以色列相連，我們與外界連通的途徑只有通過敘利亞。我們流失了約 25 萬通過陸路來黎巴嫩的遊客，他們主要是約旦人、伊朗人，當然還有海灣國家的遊客。」

為了吸引遊客，黎巴嫩旅遊部最近推出了為期 50 天的五折優惠活動，優惠涵蓋機票、酒店以及飯店。

看來，黎巴嫩正在努力推動遊客客源的多樣性，力爭從俄羅斯、拉丁美洲、非洲以及其他國家和地區吸引更多新遊客。

關鍵解析　**英文聽力重點看這邊就對了**

❶ The nickname of this Lebanese mountain town Aley is 'Arous el Masayif' — 'the bride of touristic places.'

本句的主句是：The nickname is...。我們在聽新聞過程中常會遇到像 Arous el Masayif 這樣的非英文發音、意思也無從知曉的單詞或表達。聽者不要著急，耐心聽下去，就會發現下文常會對其意思進行解釋。

❷ But the picturesque village outside Beirut that once attracted many Saudis and other Gulf nationals for its quaint atmosphere and cool evening breezes, looks abandoned these days.

這個句子比較複雜，其主句為：the village looks abandoned. that 引導的關係子句修飾的是 village。picturesque 表示「風景如畫」，quaint 是「古樸典雅」的意思。在聽的過程中，要注意理清句子結構，以免造成理解偏差。

❸ With its beautiful mountains, stunning beaches, Roman ruins and Ottoman architecture, Lebanon's economy has long leaned on tourism, which accounts for more than a quarter of its gross domestic product.

lean on 相當於 depend on 或 rely on, 表示「依靠，依賴」的意思。gross domestic product 是「國內生產總值」的意思，其縮寫為 GDP。

題目詳解篇

Unit 7 社會百態

NEWS 01
Africa's First Ladies Promote Women's, Children's Health
非洲五國第一夫人聯合推廣婦女兒童健康

The risk of death from childbirth is still very real for women in countries throughout Africa. Whether their children will reach adulthood is another worry.

The first ladies of Guinea, Mali, Mozambique, Niger and Namibia — and many more African officials — are voicing their concerns for the health and welfare of the women and children in their countries. They are meeting at the second African First Ladies Health Summit to talk about issues including infant and maternal mortality, the transfer of HIV/AIDS from mother to child and problems with sanitation.

Emilienne Raoul, the Republic of Congo's Social Affairs Minister says poverty is the main cause of many problems in Africa.

"Many people do not have access to health and education, but together we can attend to it, that is to say, with international solidarity, with private partners, we can eliminate those problems."

They are not only exchanging ideas at this health summit, but also seeking partnerships from private and non-profit organizations. Some of these ladies say they hope there will be a way to measure progress in improving the lives of women and children in Africa so that the next time they meet, they will know what works and what needs improvement.

精準翻譯　句句到位，看你是否真的全數聽懂 🔊

在許多非洲國家裡，女性死於分娩的危險仍然是真切存在的。而出生後的孩子能否長大成人又是另一個擔憂。

幾內亞、馬利、莫三比克、尼日、納米比亞五國的第一夫人以及其他許多非洲政要都表達了他們對本國婦女和兒童健康以及福利狀況的關注。他們集體

出席第二屆非洲第一夫人健康高峰會，共同探討如何降低嬰兒和產婦死亡率，如何防止愛滋病（病毒）在母嬰之間的傳染以及如何解決公共衛生等問題。

剛果共和國社會事務部部長埃米利安娜‧拉烏爾指出，貧窮是造成非洲許多問題的主要原因。

她說：「因為貧窮，很多人得不到醫療救治以及受教育的機會，但是透過共同努力，我們應該能夠解決這一問題，也就是說，有了國際社會的團結和私人組織的合作，我們就能夠消除那些問題。」

在這次健康高峰會上，她們不僅是交流觀點和思想，同時也在積極尋求同一些私人和非營利組織合作。與會的一些第一夫人表示，她們希望能有某種方法來監測非洲婦女和兒童生活的改善狀況。這樣到下一次會議時，她們就能夠了解哪些措施有效，哪些仍需提高。

關鍵解析 英文聽力重點看這邊就對了

❶ They are meeting at the second African First Ladies Health Summit to talk about issues including infant and maternal mortality, the transfer of HIV/AIDS from mother to child and problems with sanitation.

本句中 they 指上文提到的非洲第一夫人們和其他許多非洲政要。句子後半部分列出了他們討論的議題，包括「嬰兒和產婦死亡率、愛滋病（病毒）的母嬰傳染以及公共衛生問題」。

❷ Many people do not have access to health and education, but together we can attend to it, that is to say, with international solidarity, with private partners, we can eliminate those problems.

do not have access to 表示「沒有使用或享用……的機會或權利」，在這裡表示「得不到（醫治和受教育）的機會」。attend to sth. 表示「處理，解決（問題）」的意思。that is to say 是一個插入語，意思是「也就是說」。

NEWS 02 Around the World, 2012 Holiday Shopping is Subdued
2012 全球節日購物熱潮受抑

新聞原文 一知半解？跟著新聞原文，再聽一遍 🎧 Track 069

At U.S. shopping centers, parking lots were full — as thousands of last-minute shoppers descended into crowded malls.

But the big crowds mask larger concerns. Consumer confidence has fallen to a 6-month low, and retailers say shoppers don't seem to be spending as much.

But if flagging consumer confidence worries retailers, shoppers say they have other things on their minds.

In Greece, despite the festive decorations — the issue is not confidence but economic reality. After six years of recession, Greeks expect even tougher austerity measures in the New Year. So while shoppers in Athens look at the brightly decorated shop windows, few carry shopping bags.

In Spain, where unemployment is 26 percent, shop owners are dropping food prices to tempt consumers. But Emilio Perez, a butcher, says customers have less money to spend.

But American retailers who enjoyed a brisk start to the holiday shopping season last month — are not ready to give up.

Worldwide, the bigger concern is whether American lawmakers are willing to drive the U.S. economy back into a recession. Despite the threat of economic shock from higher taxes and automatic spending cuts, neither political party appears willing to bend on a year end deadline for a budget deal.

精準翻譯 句句到位，看你是否真的全數聽懂

在美國的購物中心，停車場裡停滿了車，成千上百選在最後一刻出手的購物者湧進了擁擠的購物商場。

但是大量的人群背後隱藏著更大的擔憂。消費者信心已跌至 6 個月以來的最低點，而且零售商們說，購物者花錢也不像以往那麼多了。

　　一方面，消費信心萎靡令零售商擔憂，另一方面，購物者則說他們心頭還有其他的擔憂。

　　在希臘，儘管節日的裝點隨處可見，但這裡的問題不在於消費信心而在於經濟現實。經過了六年的經濟蕭條，希臘在新一年預計將實行更大力度的緊縮措施。所以在雅典，很多購物者只是欣賞裝飾一新的櫥窗，很少有人提著購物袋購物。

　　在西班牙，失業率達到 26%，商店老闆正降低食品價格來吸引消費者，但肉店老闆埃米利奧‧佩雷斯說，顧客手裡沒有那麼多錢來消費。

　　但美國零售商在上個月經歷了節日購物季不錯的開端之後，並不打算輕易放棄。

　　全世界各地，大家更為關注的是美國的國會議員們是否會讓美國經濟再次陷入蕭條。儘管增加稅收以及自動削減開支可能會讓美國經濟深受打擊，但是兩黨似乎都不願意在年底最終期限到來前就預算協議作出讓步。

關鍵解析　**英文聽力重點看這邊就對了**

❶ But the big crowds mask larger concerns. Consumer confidence has fallen to a 6-month low, and retailers say shoppers don't seem to be spending as much.

　　本句中 mask 作動詞，表示「掩藏，掩飾」的意思。聽的過程中要注意前後的邏輯關係。第一句中 larger concerns 的具體內容，在第二句中作了說明。

❷ But if flagging consumer confidence worries retailers, shoppers say they have other things on their minds.

　　本句中 if 可理解為「如果說」，表示對比。修飾 consumer confidence（消費者信心）的形容詞 flagging 意為「疲弱的，萎靡的」。

❸ But American retailers who enjoyed a brisk start to the holiday shopping season last month — are not ready to give up.

　　學習者在聽本句話的時候，要把握住句子主幹，即 American retailers are not ready to give up。句中 who 引導的關係子句修飾 American retailers。brisk 表示「繁忙，火紅」的意思。聽錄音過程中，還要注意句子所用的時態，關係子句中 enjoyed 表示過去「享受到」，而主句用一般現在時 are not ready to do sth.，表示現在的情形或狀況。

NEWS

03 Civil Rights Pioneer Rosa Parks Honored with Capitol Statue

民權先驅羅莎・帕克斯榮獲國會大廈雕像

新聞原文　一知半解？跟著新聞原文，再聽一遍 *Track 070*

It's a lasting tribute to Rosa Parks — known as "the mother of the U.S. civil rights movement."

Dignitaries gathered to unveil a nearly three-meter-tall bronze sculpture of Parks in the U.S. Capitol's Statuary Hall. It honors the African-American woman who changed American history in 1955 when she refused to move to the back of a segregated bus.

It's the first full-size statue of an African-American woman in the Capitol. It recognizes Parks' signature achievement, her rejection of racial segregation in the south in the 1950s.

Parks made history in Montgomery, Alabama, in December 1955 when she refused to move to the back of the bus and give her seat to a white passenger. She was jailed, charged and fined. At the time, laws in the south required racial separation in buses, restaurants and public accommodations. Her action inspired a citywide bus boycott by blacks, and it spawned nationwide efforts to end segregation.

Parks' minister, Dr. Martin Luther King, joined her cause and helped organize the bus boycott which lasted a year until the Supreme Court struck down segregation.

The Parks statue was authorized by an act of Congress in 2005 after she died.

Now, this recognition at the U.S. Capitol ensures that her life and legacy will live on.

精準翻譯　句句到位，看你是否真的全數聽懂 ◀┊

這是對被譽為「美國人權運動之母」的羅莎・帕克斯的一個永久紀念。

各界名人齊聚美國國會大廈雕像大廳，為近三公尺高的帕克斯銅像揭幕。銅像所紀念的這位非洲女性曾在 1955 年登上一輛實行種族隔離的公交車後，拒絕坐到後面黑人區的座位上，她因此而改變了美國歷史。

這座雕像是國會大廈中首座為美國黑人女性而建的全身像。帕克斯在 20 世紀 50 年代堅決反對南方實行的種族隔離制度，這座雕像表彰了她所做出的非凡貢獻。

1955 年 12 月，帕克斯在阿拉巴馬州的蒙哥馬利創造了歷史。在公車上的她拒絕把座位換到車後部，拒絕為一位白人乘客讓座，她因此被監禁、起訴和罰款。當時，南方的法律規定在公車、餐廳及其他公共場所實行種族隔離。她的行為激起了全市範圍內黑人對公交的抵制，進而引發了全國各地的廢除種族隔離的運動。

帕克斯的牧師，馬丁‧路德‧金博士，也加入了她的事業，幫助組織巴士抵制運動。這場運動持續了一年，最終最高法院宣布廢除種族隔離。

2005 年帕克斯去世之後，國會通過一項法案，批准為帕克斯立一座雕像。

現在，有了美國國會大廈對她的這種褒揚和肯定，她的精神和遺產將會不斷流傳下去。

關鍵解析 英文聽力重點看這邊就對了

❶ It's a lasting tribute to Rosa Parks — known as "the mother of the U.S. civil rights movement."

本句開頭的 it 指的是新落成的雕像，它可以「表達對帕克斯的一種永久悼念」。如果學習者不熟悉 Rosa Parks，破折號後面提供的信息就非常重要。

❷ It honors the African-American woman who changed American history in 1955 when she refused to move to the back of a segregated bus.

本句中 who 引導的這個長關係子句修飾 the African-American woman。segregated 表示「實行種族隔離的」，這是理解本句意思的一個關鍵詞。1955 年，實行種族隔離政策的公車裡，白人坐在車的前半部分，黑人只能坐在後面。

❸ It recognizes Park's signature achievement, her rejection of racial segregation in the south in the 1950s.

本句中的 signature 不是我們通常所熟悉的「簽名」之意，而是表示「明顯特徵，鮮明特色」，在這裡與 achievement 搭配，表示「非凡的成就」。

NEWS 04 Families Still Rebuilding 5 Years After Massive China Quake
汶川大地震五年後家庭仍在重建

新聞原文　一知半解？跟著新聞原文，再聽一遍　🎧 *Track 071*

Ma Tang was just 12 years old when the Wenchuan earthquake robbed him of his father. He is 17 now, his mother has remarried and his young step-sister keeps him busy.

Four years ago, VOA met Ma Tang's step-father Yao Yunbing. At the time, Yao was still struggling to cope with the tremendous loss of his wife and 17-year-old daughter. Both died during the quake.

Yao's daughter was one of the thousands of students who died when their schools collapsed on them.

In late 2009, Yao and Ma Tang's mother married.

The Yao family's home was rebuilt using steel and cement, but they are struggling to pay off their loan.

Yao works eight hours away and comes home once a week. Ma Tang's mother would like to work too, but says opportunities are few as she never finished elementary school.

Keenly aware of his family's challenges, Ma Tang says that when he wants to buy something he thinks first of his young step-sister.

He says he loves sports and wants to play soccer in high school. Ma Tang says he hopes some day he might even get a chance to play on the national team.

精準翻譯　句句到位，看你是否真的全數聽懂

馬塘年僅 12 歲時，汶川地震就奪去了他父親的生命。現在，他已經 17 歲，母親已改嫁，他正忙著照顧自己同母異父的小妹妹。

4 年前，美國之音記者見到了他的繼父姚雲兵。姚雲兵的妻子和 17 歲的女兒都在汶川地震中喪生，那時的他仍沒有從巨大的創傷中走出來。

姚雲兵的女兒和其他數千名學生一樣，是在地震中倒塌的學校建築中喪生的。

2009 年下半年，姚雲兵和馬塘的媽媽結了婚。

他們的新家是用鋼筋和水泥重新建成的，但是現在他們仍在努力地償還貸款。

姚雲兵打工的地方離家有八個小時的車程，他一周回一次家。馬塘的媽媽也想找份工作，但是她說因為自己連小學都沒念完，所以適合她的工作機會寥寥無幾。

馬塘很清楚自己家裡的困難，他說自己想買東西時，總是會首先想到同母異父的小妹妹。

馬塘說他熱愛運動，想在中學裡踢足球，他甚至希望某一天能為國家隊效力。

關鍵解析　**英文聽力重點看這邊就對了**

❶ Ma Tang was just 12 years old when the Wenchuan earthquake robbed him of his father.

rob sb. of sb./sth. 表示「奪去某人的……」的意思，在文中指「地震奪去了他父親的生命」。

❷ Yao works eight hours away and comes home once a week.

注意，句中 Yao works eight hours away 表示「姚工作的地方離家有 8 小時的車程」。類似的例子還有：The best casino is only a couple hours away from Palm Beach。（最好的娛樂場距離棕櫚海灘只有幾小時的車程。）而如果是 Yao works eight hours every day，則表示「姚每天工作 8 小時」。

❸ Keenly aware of his family's challenges, Ma Tang says that when he wants to buy something he thinks first of his young step-sister.

keenly 表示「深切地，敏銳地」之意。Ma Tang says 後面的主從複合句中，動詞用的是一般現在式形式，強調了這是他的一種習慣性、規律性的做法，即只要一想買東西，就會先想到他的同母異父的小妹妹。

NEWS 05 Fiscal Cliff Could Have Greatest Impact on Poor, Unemployed

窮人和失業者可能成為財政懸崖的最大受害者

新聞原文 一知半解？跟著新聞原文，再聽一遍 🎧 *Track 072*

At this Los Angeles center, Catholic charities provides food and other assistance to the poor, unemployed, and homeless. Recipient, John Wood says he doesn't know the details of the talks in Washington, but he says that an eventual agreement is important.

"It will directly affect the economy if they don't do it. Many people will lose jobs and that will be more of a downturn for the economy."

Yolanda Barber, who volunteers at the charity, hopes that President Obama and Congress will put politics aside in the interests of the country.

"OK, this is Democratic and this is Republican. It's not about that. It's about doing the right thing for people, period. And it's very troubling where the economy is right now. If the issue is not resolved, then what will happen?"

Cuts in federal funding for health and welfare programs as well as to unemployment benefits would hurt the poor more than others, but Chris Sanchez, who is looking for a job, says he was certain the nation's leaders will avoid the fiscal cliff.

Political analysts say although Congress did not meet its midnight deadline, lawmakers and the president can soften the impact of going over the fiscal cliff by taking quick action to limit the damage. These Los Angeles residents say they're waiting for good news from Washington.

精準翻譯 句句到位，看你是否真的全數聽懂 🔊

　　在洛杉磯這個救助中心，天主教慈善組織為窮人、失業人員以及無家可歸者提供食物以及其他幫助。接受救助的約翰‧伍德說他雖然不了解華盛頓會談的細節，但是他認為最終達成協議十分重要。

　　他說：「如果不能達成協議，它將直接影響到經濟。許多人會失業，經濟會進一步下行。」

　　約蘭達‧巴伯是在該慈善組織裡工作的一名志工，她希望總統歐巴馬和國會能為了整個國家的利益將政治分歧放到一邊。

　　「好嘛，這是民主黨，這是共和黨。其實這都不重要，重要的是要心懷民眾，正確決斷。就這麼簡單。我們目前的經濟形勢很令人擔憂。如果財政懸崖的問題不解決，那麼將會出現什麼後果？」

　　削減聯邦政府在衛生醫療、福利項目及失業救濟方面的支出，受傷害最大的就是窮人。但是正在找工作的克里斯‧桑切斯相信，總統一定會避免財政懸崖的到來。

　　政治分析人士表示，雖然國會在最後期限到來前未取得進展，但國會議員和總統可以盡快採取措施來減輕跌下「財政懸崖」所帶來的影響。這些洛杉磯民眾說，他們正在等待從華盛頓傳來好消息。

- -

關鍵解析　英文聽力重點看這邊就對了

❶ At this Los Angeles center, Catholic charities provides food and other assistance to the poor, unemployed, and homeless.

　　英語中常用「the ＋ 形容詞」表示一類人。本文中出現的 the poor, unemployed, and homeless 表示「窮人、失業者和無家可歸的人」。

❷ Cuts in federal funding for health and welfare programs as well as to unemployment benefits would hurt the poor more than others, but Chris Sanchez, who is looking for a job, says he was certain the nation's leaders will avoid the fiscal cliff.

　　在聽前半句時學習者要抓住句子的主幹，即 Cuts would hurt the poor …。在聽後半句的時候，要留心轉折連詞 but。一般說來，but 後面的內容是講話者要強調的部分，是關鍵訊息。

❸ Political analysts say although Congress did not meet its midnight deadline, lawmakers and the president can soften the impact of going over the fiscal cliff by taking quick action to limit the damage.

　　要完整地理解這句話的意思，就需要對美國政治中的「財政懸崖」（即自動削減財政赤字機制引發的聯邦政府財政支出銳減）以及美國兩黨在此問題上的博弈有所了解。

Gay NBA Player Breaks Athletic Barrier
美職籃同性戀球員打破運動員心理障礙

新聞原文　一知半解？跟著新聞原文，再聽一遍　🎧 Track 073

Jason Collins has spent 12 years in the NBA. But his playing career has never drawn as much public attention as his recent revelation. In an interview with ABC News, Collins said his decision to go public with his sexual orientation was difficult.

Collins said he first thought about revealing his sexuality last year, after years of what he called "living a lie." But he said the recent Boston Marathon bombing finally convinced him to come out.

Several male athletes in major U.S. pro sports have revealed they were gay after they retired, but Collins is the first to do so while planning to continue playing. Sports writer Christine Brennan says he should be a role model for other professional athletes.

Since his story appeared in *Sports Illustrated*, Collins has received an outpouring of support from across the nation, including President Obama.

Reaction to Collins' announcement from NBA league officials and fellow players was also positive.

"If he plays another year, that is going to be a defining moment in the NBA or in professional sports, because now you are going to have an openly gay man in a male dominated locker room."

Collins is now a free agent, and he is looking for a new contract to play in the NBA next season.

精準翻譯　句句到位，看你是否真的全數聽懂 🔊

　　雖然賈森‧科林斯已經為美職籃效力 12 年，但是他的職業生涯從未像他最近的公開出櫃那樣引人關注。在一次接受美國廣播公司（ABC）新聞記者採訪時，科林斯說公開自己的性取向對他而言是一個艱難的決定。

　　科林斯說，「在謊言中生活」多年之後，自己第一次萌生公開性取向的想

法是在去年，但最近發生的波士頓馬拉松爆炸事件讓他最終決定出櫃。

此前，已經有幾位曾在美國幾大職業聯賽中效力的男運動員在退役後宣布自己是同性戀，但是科林斯卻是第一個現役運動員中公開這麼做的。在體育記者克里斯蒂娜‧布倫南看來，他應該成為其他職業運動員的榜樣。

自從科林斯的故事出現在《體育畫報》上以後，他就得到了全國各地人士源源不斷的支持，這其中就包括美國總統歐巴馬。

美職籃的官員和其他球員對科林斯的這份聲明也紛紛表示支持。

「如果他能再打一年，那將是美職籃甚至職業體育歷史上一個具有決定意義的時刻，因為你會看到一位公開承認自己是同性戀的球員出現在被認為是男性天下的更衣室中。」

科林斯現在是一名自由球員，他正在為下一個賽季繼續效力美職籃尋求一份新合約。

關鍵解析　英文聽力重點看這邊就對了

❶ But his playing career has never drawn as much public attention as his recent revelation.

revelation 原指「真相揭秘」，從下文中我們就會明白，這裡指的是「公開自己的性取向」。學習者在聽到像這樣意思或所指不確定的詞時，要耐心聽下去，下文一般會有進一步的說明。

❷ Several male athletes in major U.S. pro sports have revealed they were gay after they retired, but Collins is the first to do so while planning to continue playing.

本句中 major U.S. pro sports 指的是美國的幾大職業體育運動，如職業籃球、職業棒球、職業橄欖球運動等。pro 是 professional（職業的）之縮寫。

❸ If he plays another year, that is going to be a defining moment in the NBA or in professional sports, because you are going to have an openly gay man in a male dominated locker room.

本句中 that 代指前面子句所表達的意思，即「他再打一年」。defining moment 表示「意義重大的時刻」。句尾的 male dominated 表示「男性占主導的，男性天下的」。locker room 指的是「球員的更衣室」。

NEWS 07 Nigerians Demand Return of Ancient Art
奈及利亞要求返還其古代藝術品

新聞原文 一知半解？跟著新聞原文，再聽一遍 🎧 *Track 074*

What was once the ancient Kingdom of Benin is now the heart of the Nigerian art world, with statues adorning the streets and an art museum in the Benin City town square. But locals say the displayed art is only part of Benin's collection. They say British colonials stole nearly 4,000 pieces more than a century ago.

Umogbai Theophilus is the curator for Nigeria's National Museum in Benin City.

Theophilus says after decades of negotiations, some Benin art has been sent back to Nigeria.

The art was taken at the end of the 19th century when the British launched a "punitive expedition" in retaliation for what they said was Benin aggression, sacking the city and deposing the king or "Oba."

Local artist Williams Edosowan says art in Benin is more than just decoration. It is how they record their history.

Collectors argue that the history of Benin Kingdom is kept alive by the art as it travels the world. Critics also say repatriating the art requires more commitment from Nigerian officials. Artists in Benin City say every piece lost is a lost piece of their history.

精準翻譯 句句到位，看你是否真的全數聽懂 🔊

這裡曾經是古代的貝寧王國所在地，現在成了奈及利亞藝術世界的中心：雕塑裝點著街道，而一座藝術博物館就位於貝寧城的廣場上。但是據當地人說，展出的這些藝術品只是貝寧所收藏藝術品的一部分。一百多年前英國殖民者從這裡竊走了近 4,000 件藝術品。

　　奈及利亞國家博物館位於貝寧市，烏莫格拜·西奧菲勒斯是那裡的館長。他說，經過幾十年的協商，一部分貝寧藝術品已經被歸還給了奈及利亞。

　　19 世紀末，英國打著所謂「報復貝寧侵略」的旗號，發動了一場對貝寧的「討伐」，洗劫了這座城市，廢黜了當時的國王，很多藝術品就在那時被掠走。

　　當地藝術家威廉斯·埃多索旺說，貝寧的藝術品不僅僅是裝飾品，它們記錄了貝寧的歷史。

　　一些藝術品收藏家卻認為，正是這些藝術品在世界各地的流散，使得貝寧王國的歷史得以流傳。評論家也表示，藝術品的追回需要奈及利亞官方付出更多努力。貝寧城的藝術家說，每件丟失的藝術品都是他們失落的一段歷史。

關鍵解析　英文聽力重點看這邊就對了

❶ What was once the ancient Kingdom of Benin is now the heart of the Nigerian art world, with statues adorning the streets and an art museum in the Benin City town square.

　　本句句首 what 引導的是一個主要子句。在句子的後半部分裡，with 引導了兩個獨立主格結構，分別是：「with + 名詞 + 動詞 -ing」和「with + 名詞 + 介詞片語」。

❷ The art was taken at the end of the 19th century when the British launched a "punitive expedition" in retaliation for what they said was Benin aggression, sacking the city and deposing the king or "Oba."

　　動詞 launch 表示「發起，發動（尤指有組織的活動）」。in retaliation for sth 表示「對……進行報復」，what they said was Benin aggression 意為「他們所謂的貝寧入侵」，綜合起來就是說「他們打著報復貝寧入侵的幌子」。動詞 sack 表示「（在攻陷的城市中）掠奪」的意思，depose 意為「罷免，廢黜」。Oba（奧巴）指古代貝寧王國的統治者，與 the king 同義。

NEWS 08 Obama Calls for Action on Gun Violence
歐巴馬呼籲采取行動遏制槍支暴力

新聞原文 一知半解？跟著新聞原文，再聽一遍 *Track 075*

Gunfire erupted on December 14 at Sandy Hook Elementary School, where a heavily armed young man shot and killed 20 children and several school administrators. The entire nation recoiled in grief and horror.

Days later, President Barack Obama issued a call to action.

As victims were laid to rest and the country continued to mourn, Mr. Obama appointed Vice President Joe Biden to head a task force on preventing gun violence.

Biden has met with a broad spectrum of interested parties in the gun-control debate, including gun rights advocates. Far from restricting access to firearms, the National Rifle Association urges a greater armed presence in America's schools.

Others say steps can be taken to keep the most lethal weapons out of the hands of evildoers without strangling Americans' constitutional right to bear arms.

Possible recommendations from Vice President Biden include banning assault weapons as well as high-capacity ammunition clips, strengthening regulation of gun sales, and improving U.S. mental health services.

The Sandy Hook shootings stunned a nation long accustomed to gun violence. Vice President Biden's recommendations come at a time of continued universal outrage over the incident. But congressional consideration of his proposals will likely occur later in the year, when the immediacy of Sandy Hook may have faded.

精準翻譯 句句到位，看你是否真的全數聽懂 🔊

12 月 14 日，美國桑迪胡克小學發生惡性槍擊事件。一名全副武裝的年輕男子射殺了 20 名兒童和數名學校行政人員。整個國家陷入悲痛和恐懼之中。

幾天後，歐巴馬總統發出了行動呼籲。

遇難者已安息，全國仍沈浸在悲痛中。歐巴馬總統任命副總統喬‧拜登來領導一個預防槍擊暴力的特別行動組。

拜登在槍支控制辯論會上會見了眾多的相關利益團體，包括持槍權的擁護支持者。非但不提倡限制擁有武器，全國步槍協會甚至極力主張在美國的學校中加強持槍保衛。

其他一些人表示，也可以在不侵害美國憲法賦予民眾的槍支持有權的情況下，採取措施確保那些致命性武器不流入壞人之手。

副總統拜登給出的可行性提議包括：禁止持有攻擊性武器以及高容量彈夾，加強槍支銷售管理以及提高美國的精神健康服務水準。

桑迪胡克小學槍擊事件震驚了美國這個已習慣於槍擊暴力的國家。在全國民眾都還在為此感到憤怒時，副總統拜登提出了這些建議。但國會可能要到今年下半年才會考慮他的提議，而到那時，桑迪胡克槍擊事件的急迫性可能就已經減弱了。

- -

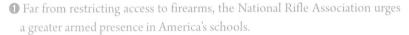

關鍵解析 英文聽力重點看這邊就對了

❶ Far from restricting access to firearms, the National Rifle Association urges a greater armed presence in America's schools.

　　far from doing sth. 表示「遠未做，不但不做」的意思。access to sth. 指「有權使用，接觸」的意思。the National Rifle Association 指「美國的全國步槍協會」。armed presence 指「持槍的警力」。

❷ Others say steps can be taken to keep the most lethal weapons out of the hands of evildoers without strangling Americans' constitutional right to bear arms.

　　keep sth. out of hands of sb. 表示「使……遠離某人，使……不落入某人手中」。strangle 原是「掐死，扼殺」的意思，在這裡意為「限制，妨礙」。

❸ But congressional consideration of his proposals will likely occur later in the year, when the immediacy of Sandy Hook may have faded.

　　本句跟它前面的一句話在意思上形成對比。前面講全國民眾仍義憤難平時副總統提出了那些提案，而本句的意思：但國會還要過一段時間才會審議這些提案，到那時可能事過境遷，事件就不顯得那麼刻不容緩了。句中 immediacy 表示「急迫性，刻不容緩」之意，fade 表示「消退，變弱」的意思。

Report: Up to Half of World Food Production is Wasted

09

報告稱，全世界多達半數的糧食遭浪費

新聞原文　一知半解？跟著新聞原文，再聽一遍 　　🎧 *Track 076*

Every year the world produces around four billion tons of food. And between a third and half of it goes to waste, according to the report from the British Institution of Mechanical Engineers.

Much of this can be traced to how it is harvested, stored and transported, says report co-author Colin Brown.

In developed economies such as in Europe and the United States, the report says more efficient farming practices ensure that more of the food produced reaches consumers. But it claims millions of tons of food is thrown away because it's past its sell-by date, or sometimes because it doesn't reach the supermarket shelves at all.

Many aid agencies and charities welcomed the report for highlighting the huge amount of waste at a time when millions of people suffer from malnutrition.

The aid agency Save the Children says there is enough food in the world to feed every child — but still 2.3 million children die as a result of hunger every year.

Brendan Cox is Director of Policy.

"The families are having to choose between feeding themselves and feeding their children and nobody should have to make that choice."

Large amounts of land, energy, fertilizers and water are also lost in the process, according to the report authors.

And with the global population predicted to peak at 9.5 billion people by 2075, the report concludes that reducing wastage must be part of the plan to meet that demand.

精準翻譯　句句到位，看你是否真的全數聽懂

根據英國機械工程師學會的報告，全球每年約生產 40 億噸糧食，其中有三分之一到一半都被浪費掉了。

　　報告的作者之一科林‧布朗説，很大一部分浪費出現在收割、儲存以及運輸過程中。

　　該報告稱，在歐洲以及美國這樣的發達經濟體中，較為高效的農業生產方式保證了更多的食物能到達消費者手中。但是報告指出，仍有千百萬噸的食物因為過期或者有時沒能在超市上架而被丟棄。

　　許多援助機構以及慈善組織對報告高度關注糧食的大量浪費表示歡迎，因為現在仍有許多的人正處於營養不良的狀態中。

　　慈善機構救助兒童會表示，全球生產的糧食其實足以養活所有孩子，但每年仍有 230 萬兒童死於饑餓。

　　其政策主管布倫登‧考克斯説：「許多家庭不得不在養活大人和養活孩子之間進行選擇，他們本可以不必做這種選擇。」

　　報告的作者同時指出，大量的土地、能源、化肥和水在糧食生產過程中也被浪費了。

　　到 2075 年，世界總人口預計將達到 95 億的高峰。報告最後總結説，為了滿足那麼多人口的需求，減少浪費是必不可少的舉措之一。

- -

關鍵解析　英文聽力重點看這邊就對了

❶ And between a third and half of it goes to waste, according to the report from the British Institution of Mechanical Engineers.

　　本句中 a third 表示「三分之一」，half 表示「二分之一，一半」。學習者要熟悉英文中分數的表達。通常説來，英文中一個分數的分子用基數詞表示，分母用序數詞表示。當分子大於 1 時，分母用複數形式，例如，三分之二可以説 two thirds。比較特殊的分數，如四分之一，可以説 a quarter。go to waste 表示「被浪費掉」。

❷ And with the global population predicted to peak at 9.5 billion people by 2075, the report concludes that reducing wastage must be part of the plan to meet that demand.

　　本句句首的 with 結構表示原因，因為其中的名詞 global population 和動詞 predict（預測）是被動關係，所以這裡用了過去分詞 predicted。peak 在句中用作動詞，表示「達到高峰，達到最大值」的意思，後跟介詞 at 引出具體數值。

NEWS 10 Supporters of Gay Marriage Await US Court Rulings
美國同性婚姻支持者等待最高法院裁決

新聞原文 一知半解？跟著新聞原文，再聽一遍 🎧 Track 077

Supporters of same-sex marriage rallied this week in Los Angeles and other American cities, urging the Supreme Court to overturn California's 2008 gay marriage ban, called Proposition 8, and the Defense of Marriage Act, a 1996 federal law that defines marriage as a union of one man and one woman.

18,000 same-sex couples were married in California in a five-month period in 2008, before the state supreme court ruled that Proposition 8 prevents more gay marriages.

The women face restrictions not faced by heterosexual couples, says Marita Forney.

"Our love is the same, our needs, you know, it's all the same, and I think the idea that we're somehow so different is what… It's so important for people to understand we're not."

At the recent Los Angeles rally, supporters of same-sex marriage said they are optimistic. Alejandro Escoto, a minister and his partner Ramiro Vasquez hope a favorable ruling will allow them to get married.

"Because we have a life together for 15 years, and for the state or for someone not to tell us that's not right, that's not OK."

Nine U.S. states permit gay marriage. Thirty-nine states ban it. The court could rule narrowly on the California law, or more broadly on the issue nationwide.

精準翻譯 句句到位，看你是否真的全數聽懂 🔊

同性婚姻支持者本周在美國洛杉磯以及其他城市集會，呼籲最高法院推翻加利福尼亞州在 2008 年通過的禁止同性婚姻的「8 號提案」，並宣布 1996 年頒布的聯邦法律《婚姻保護法》無效。在該法律中，婚姻被界定為一名男性與一名女性的合法結合。

2008 年，在州最高法院宣布「8 號提案」正式生效之前的 5 個月內，加利福尼亞州約有 18,000 對同性伴侶登記結婚。提案的生效阻止了更多的同性婚姻。

瑪麗塔‧福尼說，與異性夫婦相比，同性夫婦面臨著諸多限制。

「我們的愛情是一樣的，我們的需求等等，都是一樣的。我覺得那些認為我們太另類的想法是，是⋯⋯讓人們了解我們沒那麼不同很重要。」

在最近的洛杉磯集會中，同性婚姻支持者說他們對結果持樂觀態度。亞歷杭德羅‧埃斯科托是一位牧師，他和自己的伴侶拉米羅‧瓦斯凱蒂希望法院能作出支持同性婚姻的判決，能讓他們合法結婚。

「我們一起生活 15 年了，不希望我們的州或是誰告訴我們這是不對的，這是不好的。」

美國有 9 個州允許同性婚姻，39 個州禁止同性婚姻。最高法院可以僅僅針對加州法律進行裁決，也可以在全國範圍內對此進行裁決。

關鍵解析 英文聽力重點看這邊就對了

❶ Supporters of same-sex marriage rallied this week in Los Angeles and other American cities, urging the Supreme Court to overturn California's 2008 gay marriage ban, called Proposition 8, and the Defense of Marriage Act, a 1996 federal law that defines marriage as a union of one man and one woman.

句中 overturn 的受詞有兩個：一是 California's 2008 gay marriage ban，即 Proposition 8，二是 the Defense of Marriage Act，後面的 a 1996 federal law 是其同位語成分，對其做進一步說明。define sth. as sth. 表示「將⋯⋯定義為⋯⋯」。

❷ The court could rule narrowly on the California law, or more broadly on the issue nationwide.

rule on 意為「就⋯⋯做出裁決」。裁決是僅針對加利福尼亞州的「8 號提案」，還是針對全國範圍內的同性婚姻，決定了裁決適用的範圍是 narrowly 還是 broadly。

NEWS 11 Abused Chinese Women Push for Domestic Violence Law

遭遇家暴的中國女性將推動相關法律的制定

新聞原文 一知半解？跟著新聞原文，再聽一遍 🎧 *Track 078*

This woman, Kim Lee put a face on the otherwise anonymous stories of domestic violence in China, when she posted photos of her bruises online. They reveal what she says were chronic beatings by her then-husband, the celebrity English teacher Li Yang.

China's official women protection agency estimates that one quarter of women are abused by their spouses, but the actual figure is likely to be higher. Many episodes likely go unreported because authorities seldom take action.

Lee won her divorce case on the grounds of domestic violence, a result that legal workers hailed as a landmark decision.

But, without a national law defining domestic violence, police, social workers and the courts are not equipped to handle such cases.

Women rights' organizations had urged the government to pass a domestic violence law during this year's annual National People's Congress. A draft was discussed during the meetings but was not passed. Activists expect such a law will be adopted — eventually — in the coming months or years.

精準翻譯 句句到位，看你是否真的全數聽懂 🔊

　　李金，著名瘋狂英語創始人李陽的妻子，將自己身上帶有多處淤青的照片放到了網路上，揭露她當時的丈夫李陽長期對她施暴。與中國很多無名的家庭暴力事件不同的是，這位女性選擇了公開面對這個問題。

　　據中國婦女權益保護組織估計，有四分之一的女性遭到過配偶的虐待，而

實際的數字可能比這還要高。許多家庭暴力事件可能沒有被報告，因為相關部門很少採取措施。

這樁因家庭暴力而起的離婚案最終以李金勝訴收場，法律工作者視此案的判決結果為一個里程碑。

但是，由於沒有明確界定家庭暴力的全國性法律，警方、社會工作者及法庭都缺乏處理類似案件的有力武器。

婦女權利保護組織此前已呼籲政府在今年的全國人大會議上通過反家庭暴力的法案。會議討論了相關的草案，但草案未獲通過。活動人士期望在未來幾個月或幾年間，相關法律最終能夠制定完成。

關鍵解析　英文聽力重點看這邊就對了

❶ They reveal what she says were chronic beatings by her then-husband, the celebrity English teacher Li Yang.

本句中 they 指上文提到的 photos of her bruises online（李陽妻子顯示瘀傷的網路照片）。her then-husband 和 the celebrity English teacher Li Yang（著名的瘋狂英語創始人李陽）是同位語關係，then-husband 指「當時的丈夫」，從下文中可以得知現在二人已經離婚。

❷ Lee won her divorce case on the grounds of domestic violence, a result that legal workers hailed as a landmark decision.

本句中 on the grounds of 表示「以……為由」，「因為……」的意思。比 如，His former employee is claiming unfair dismissal on the grounds of age discrimination.（他的前雇員聲稱因為年齡歧視，自己遭到了不公平的解雇。）a result 指的是前面整個句子的內容，即「李金家暴離婚官司的勝訴」這個結果。hail 在本句中表示「歡迎，讚揚」的意思，常與介詞 as 搭配使用。要更理解後半句的內容，我們可以將其還原成：legal workers hailed this result as a landmark decision.

US Adds 171K Jobs; Unemployment Rate Rises to 7.9%
美國增加 171,000 個職缺，失業率反升至 7.9%

新聞原文　一知半解？跟著新聞原文，再聽一遍　🎧 *Track 079*

　　The last major economic report before Americans head to the polls shows hiring accelerated in October. That's welcome news for more than 12 million unemployed Americans, and for a president fighting to keep his job. President Barack Obama told supporters in Ohio that since July the private sector has added more than 170,000 jobs each month.

　　But the improving outlook is just one aspect of the government report. Despite upward revisions to job numbers in August and September, the nation's unemployment rate inched higher to 7.9 percent as more people started looking for work.

　　Since World War II, no U.S. president has ever won re-election with unemployment above 7.4 percent. But the White House says the new report is further evidence that the economy is healing from the worst downturn in decades. Still, the latest job numbers are unlikely to sway voters.

　　Despite the better-than-expected job numbers, lingering signs of economic weakness remain. Average hourly pay declined in October, and paychecks have not kept pace with inflation.

　　After an initial bounce on Wall Street, stock futures fell more than one percent, as investors worried about a deepening recession in Europe and a looming budget crisis in the U.S.

精準翻譯　句句到位，看你是否真的全數聽懂 🔊

　　在美國民眾前去投票之前，最新的一份大型經濟報告顯示，10 月份美國的雇用人數進一步增加。這對於 1,200 萬失業的美國人來說是好消息，對正在奮力爭取連任的總統來說也是好消息。現任總統巴拉克‧歐巴馬對俄亥俄州的支持者表示，自 7 月份以來，私營產業每月增加 170,000 多個工作職缺。

　　但是前景稍有起色只是這份政府報告的一個方面。儘管 8 月和 9 月份工作職缺數量開始掉頭回升，但隨著更多的人開始出來找工作，全國的失業率仍進一步攀升至 7.9%。

　　自二戰以來，還沒有哪位美國總統在失業率高於 7.4% 的情況下成功獲得連任。但白宮方面稱，這份最新報告進一步證明了美國經濟正從近幾十年來遭遇的最低谷緩慢復甦。只是，最近的就業數據不太可能動搖選民的決心。

　　儘管就業職缺數據好於預期，但經濟疲軟跡象仍然存在。10 月份的平均時薪下降，工資也沒能與通貨膨脹程度保持同步。

　　由於投資者擔心歐洲經濟衰退會進一步加劇以及美國預算危機日益臨近，華爾街的股票期貨經歷了最初短暫的反彈後，下跌超過了 1%。

關鍵解析　**英文聽力重點看這邊就對了**

❶ Despite upward revisions to job numbers in August and September, the nation's unemployment rate inched higher to 7.9 percent as more people started looking for work.

　　句首的 despite（儘管）表示轉折之意，後半句所要表達的意思才是重點。revision 原是「修改，修正」的意思，而結合文意，「工作職缺的數量被修正」，而且趨勢是 upward（上升的，向上的），這裡所表達的意思就是：「工作職缺的數量開始掉頭回升」。句中 inch 作動詞，表示「（朝某方向）緩慢地移動」，unemployment rate inched higher to 表示「失業率緩慢攀升至……」。

❷ Despite the better-than-expected job numbers, lingering signs of economic weakness remain.

　　句中 better-than-expected 是合成詞，其節奏感很強，意思是「比預期要好的」。lingering 作形容詞修飾 signs，意為「逗留不去的，殘存的」。

❸ After an initial bounce on Wall Street, stock futures fell more than one percent, as investors worried about a deepening recession in Europe and a looming budget crisis in the U.S.

　　本句中 as 引導的子句表明原因。英語和漢語的表達習慣不同，本句「先結果後原因」的表達順序在英語中是很常見的，而漢語表達習慣則相反，一般先原因後結果。學習者對此要有所了解並逐步適應。

題目詳解篇

Unit8 體育娛樂

Gay Documentary Makes Inroads in Turkey
同性戀紀錄片成功進入土耳其

The Gala Night in Istanbul of the documentary *My Child* drew a packed audience. The film tells the story of Listag, a parent's support group of lesbian, gay, bisexual and transgender children, or LGBT. It follows the group, helping fellow parents come to terms with their children's sexuality as well as challenging prejudice in society.

Director Can Candan hopes the film will help challenge traditional attitudes towards LGBT people.

A leading newspaper made the film front-page news, reporting positively on the parents' work. The Turkish media are more accustomed to reporting about attacks and even murders by parents or family.

But the society appears to be changing. Last year Istanbul hosted its 20th Gay Pride Day, drawing a record attendance of thousands. In June two women from the group were invited by the main opposition party to address a parliamentary commission.

The documentary is being shown across Turkey and in a special screening that was shown in neighboring Armenia and in the Palestinian territory city of Ramallah. The hope of the filmmaker and the parents is that barriers will continue to be broken down not only in Turkey but eventually across the region.

精準翻譯　句句到位，看你是否真的全數聽懂 🔊

　　紀錄片《我的孩子》在伊斯坦堡的放映之夜觀眾爆滿。影片講述了一個名為 Listag 的組織的故事。該組織主要為女同性戀、男同性戀、雙性戀和變性兒童的父母提供支持。影片記錄了這個組織幫助家長們接受孩子的性取向以及挑戰社會偏見的過程。

　　導演詹·詹丹希望這部影片能幫助改變人們對女同性戀、男同性戀、雙性戀和變性人群的傳統態度。

一份很有影響力的報紙在頭版報導了有關這部紀錄片的消息，對影片中父母所做的努力給予了積極正面的評價。通常，土耳其媒體更傾向於報導同性戀者遭到父母或家人攻擊甚至謀殺的新聞。

但是，這個社會似乎正在轉變，去年伊斯坦堡爾舉辦了第 20 屆「同志驕傲日」大遊行。出席人數達到了創紀錄的數千人。6 月份，該組織的兩位女士受主要反對黨之邀，向一個議會特別委員會發表演說。

這部紀錄片正在土耳其全國上映，並在鄰國亞美尼亞和巴勒斯坦領地拉姆安拉市進行了特別放映。製片人以及這些父母們希望不僅是在土耳其，最終在整個地區，這些群體所面臨的障礙能被不斷破除。

關鍵解析 **英文聽力重點看這邊就對了**

❶ It follows the group, helping fellow parents come to terms with their children's sexuality as well as challenging prejudice in society.

come to terms with sth. 表示「妥協順從，接受（令人不快的事情）」。本句的主幹部分是 It follows the group，it 指的是「影片（的拍攝人員）」。後面的 helping 和 challenging 是並列關係，用 as well as（和，以及）連接，二者的邏輯主語應該是 the group。

❷ A leading newspaper made the film front-page news, reporting positively on the parents' work.

make sb./sth. sth 這種「make + 雙受詞」的結構表示「使某人 / 某物成為……」。made the film front-page news 意為「把這部電影做為頭版新聞」。而 reporting 是現在分詞作修飾的用法。

❸ The hope of the filmmaker and the parents is that barriers will continue to be broken down not only in Turkey but also eventually across the region.

在聽到本句時，要明確句子的主幹是 The hope is that...，後面的 that 從句說明希望的具體內容。break down barriers 表示「破除障礙」，本句中使用的是其被動形式。

Hollywood Celebrates Holidays with Great Films
好萊塢用精彩影片歡慶節日的到來

新聞原文　一知半解？跟著新聞原文，再聽一遍　🎧 *Track 081*

Joe Wright's *Anna Karenina*, based on the Tolstoy novel, is a quintessential holiday production. It offers rich costumes, and enchanting music, and stellar actors.

In his film, Joe Wright emphasizes the pretense of 19th century Russian aristocracy. He stages Anna Karenina's world in a controlled space that is lavish, but claustrophobic.

Life of Pi, about survival and faith, is more upbeat. It's also adapted from a book, and it requires a willing suspension of disbelief. Oscar winning director Ang Lee enchants us with his other-worldly cinematography. For the shots in the boat, the production team created a digital tiger.

The Hobbit, also coming out this holiday season, is a fantasy epic. With this prequel, director Peter Jackson promises a spectacle for the millions of fans of *the Lord of the Rings* trilogy and J. R. R. Tolkien's novel.

The holiday films will be capped by the musical *Les Miserables*, directed by Oscar winner Tom Hooper. Unlike *Anna Karenina*, Hooper's adaptation of Victor Hugo's 19th century classic is traditional and sticks close to the book.

These movies — and more — not only have the ingredients for a lucrative season at the box office. They're also raising the curtain on January's Academy Award nominations.

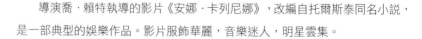

精準翻譯　句句到位，看你是否真的全數聽懂 🔊

導演喬・賴特執導的影片《安娜・卡列尼娜》，改編自托爾斯泰同名小說，是一部典型的娛樂作品。影片服飾華麗，音樂迷人，明星雲集。

喬・賴特在影片中突出表現了 19 世紀俄國貴族階層的虛偽和浮華。他在一個奢華、幽閉的有限空間裡展現了安娜・卡列尼娜的世界。

《少年 Pi 的奇幻漂流》是一部關於生存與信仰的電影，內容樂觀向上。影片同樣改編自一本小說，它讓觀看者在觀看過程中收起質疑之心。奧斯卡獲獎導演李安用他超凡脫俗的電影導演技術征服了我們。為了拍攝船上的畫面，製作組用電腦數位合成了一頭老虎。

《霍比特人》也在這個假期推出，這是一部奇幻史詩電影。導演彼得‧傑克遜對《魔戒》三部曲和托爾金小說的粉絲們承諾這部前傳會非常壯觀。

音樂劇《悲慘世界》將會給娛樂電影錦上添花，該片由奧斯卡獲獎導演湯姆‧胡珀執導。與《安娜‧卡列尼娜》不同，胡珀對維克托‧雨果這部 19 世紀經典作品的改編非常傳統且忠實於原著。

這些以及其他更多的電影，不僅擁有賺取豐厚票房回報的元素，同時也拉開了競逐一月份奧斯卡獎提名的序幕。

- -

關鍵解析 英文聽力重點看這邊就對了

❶ He stages Anna Karenina's world in a controlled space that is lavish, but claustrophobic.

　　本句中 stage 用作動詞，表示「上演，在舞臺上展現」的意思。後面 that 引導的關係子句中出現了兩個比較難的形容詞。lavish 表示「奢華的，豐富的」，而 claustrophobic 指「地方或空間引起幽閉恐怖的」。學習者在聽錄音過程中難免會遇到生詞，這時不要因為生詞而卡住，而要藉由文意，對生詞做大致猜測，比如可以判斷一個形容詞是正面評價還是負面評價。

❷ It's also adapted from a book, and it requires a willing suspension of disbelief.

　　adapt 表示「改編，改寫」的意思。a willing suspension of disbelief 的意思是「在觀看過程中自願地暫停質疑或懷疑」，其中 suspension 表示「暫停，中止」的意思。

N. Korean Film Screened at S. Korean Festival
北韓電影於南韓電影節上映

The Busan International Film Festival is Asia's largest and features movies from across the continent and beyond. This year that included a film from North Korea.

Comrade Kim Goes Flying is a romantic comedy about a young coal miner who dreams of joining the circus as an acrobat. With her strong determination and support from her co-workers, Comrade Kim gets a spot on the trapeze team and wins over her love interest. Unlike many other North Korean films, there is very little political ideology in the screenplay.

That might have something to do with the influence of European co-directors Anja Daelemans of Belgium and Britain's Nicholas Bonner. They, along with North Korean filmmaker Kim Gwang Hun, directed the entirely North Korean cast of *Comrade Kim*.

Bonner says the movie's humor was not lost on the audience who came to see the film in Busan.

Organizers at the Busan International Film Festival say North Korean films have a place at this annual event.

The producers of *Comrade Kim Goes Flying* hope the film will get picked up for more screenings on both sides of the Korean Peninsula.

精準翻譯 句句到位，看你是否真的全數聽懂 🔈

釜山國際電影節是亞洲最大的電影節，主要展映亞洲及其他一些地區的電影。今年，一部北韓電影也被列入其中。

《飛吧，金同志！》是一部浪漫輕喜劇，講述了一個年輕的礦工夢想加入馬戲團成為一名雜技演員的故事。憑著堅強的意志和礦友的支持鼓勵，金同志最終在空中飛人表演隊覓得一席之地並贏得了她的所愛。與其他很多北韓電影

不同，這部電影中政治意識形態成分很少。

這可能與參與聯合執導的兩位歐洲導演的影響有關。他們一位是來自比利時的安雅・戴爾曼斯，另一位是來自英國的尼古拉斯・邦納。兩人與北韓電影製作人金光遜合作，共同執導了這部完全由北韓演員出演的影片。

邦納説，釜山電影節的觀眾感受到了影片中散發出的幽默感。

釜山國際電影節的組織者稱，北韓電影在這個一年一度的盛事中占有一席之地。

電影製片方希望《飛吧，金同志！》在朝鮮半島的南北兩邊都能有更多的放映機會。

關鍵解析 英文聽力重點看這邊就對了

❶ The Busan International Film Festival is Asia's largest and features movies from across the continent and beyond.

釜山國際電影節（BIFF）每年在韓國的港口城市釜山舉行，是亞洲最大的電影節之一。句中 feature 並非學習者熟悉的表示「特點，特徵」的名詞用法，而是作動詞，意為「以……為特色」。

❷ With her strong determination and support from her co-workers, Comrade Kim gets a spot on the trapeze team and wins over her love interest.

本句中的 her 指的就是 Comrade Kim。句中 spot 意為 a position in a competition，即「一席之地」。請注意，trapeze 的重音落在第二個音節上，指「馬戲團演員使用的高空鞦韆」。這個詞與上一句的 acrobat （雜技演員）相照應，聽者即使不熟悉其具體意思，也可猜測出它是一種雜技形式。win over 表示「贏得」。her love interest 意為「所愛的人，愛人」。

❸ That might have something to do with the influence of European co-directors Anja Daelemans of Belgium and Britain's Nicholas Bonner.

本句中 have something to do with 表示「與……有關」。co-director（聯合導演）中，字首 co- 表示「聯合，共同」的意思，又如 coexist（共存），co-produce（共同生產）等。

Russia's Winter Olympics to Break Spending Records
索契冬季奧運會將破冬季奧運會開支記錄

新聞原文 一知半解？跟著新聞原文，再聽一遍 🎧 *Track 083*

It is the largest construction site in Europe: 100,000 men and 500 companies are working around the clock.

They are building hotels, skating rinks and ski jumps for next year's Winter Olympics in Sochi, on Russia's Black Sea coast.

After Russian President Vladimir Putin declared that construction would meet the deadlines for the February Olympics, fireworks greeted the president's progress report.

But there is a price to pay. At $51 billion, the Sochi Olympics will be the most expensive in the history of the Games. They are running five times over the budget of six years ago and will cost almost six times as much as the last Winter Olympics, in Vancouver.

Vladimir Kimaev is an environmentalist. He says the Kremlin is wasting money on a prestige project that will last two weeks.

But with the one-year countdown now under way, the Kremlin is hoping that hoopla and excitement will carry the day in February, when Russia hosts its first Winter Olympic games.

精準翻譯 句句到位，看你是否真的全數聽懂

這裡如今是歐洲最大的建築工地：500 家公司的 10 萬人正在這裡夜以繼日地工作著。

他們正在俄羅斯的黑海沿岸，為明年的索契冬季奧運會建設酒店、滑冰場和滑雪跳臺。

俄羅斯總統佛拉迪米爾‧普丁宣布，將於 2 月份舉行的冬季奧運會各項設施的建設會在規定期限內完成。聽到此消息後，人們以煙火慶祝了總統的進度

報告。

　　但這其中是要付出代價的。索契冬季奧運會預計會耗資 510 億美元，將成為奧運會歷史上最昂貴的一屆。如今的花費已達到了 6 年前預算的 5 倍，幾乎是上屆溫哥華冬季奧運會支出的 6 倍。

　　佛拉迪米爾・基馬埃夫是一名環保人士。他說克里姆林宮是在浪費錢財，大搞只持續兩周的面子工程。

　　但隨著倒數一周年活動的進行，俄羅斯中央政府希望能在喧鬧和興奮中迎來明年 2 月俄羅斯首次主辦的冬季奧運會。

關鍵解析　**英文聽力重點看這邊就對了**

❶ But there is a price to pay.

　　本句中的 price 不是指「價錢」，而是指「代價」。

❷ They are running five times over the budget of six years ago and will cost almost six times as much as the last Winter Olympics, in Vancouver.

　　句中 they 代指 the Sochi Olympics, 而 Olympics 即 Olympic Games，是複數形式，所以用 they 來指代。run 表示「達到或進入（某個水平）」，例如：Inflation is running at 11 percent. 另外，學習者在此還需要留心倍數的表達。我們一般用 twice 表示兩倍的概念，而用 ... times 表示三倍或三倍以上的倍數，six times as much as 即「六倍」的意思。

❸ But with the one-year countdown now under way, the Kremlin is hoping that hoopla and excitement will carry the day in February, when Russia hosts its first Winter Olympic games.

　　本句中 under way 表示「已經開始，在進行中」的意思。在聽力訓練中，學習者如果碰到片語，切記不可望文生義，比如本句中的 carry the day，其意思是「（某人、某事或是某種意見）占據上風」。而結合文意，「hoopla（喧鬧）和 excitement（興奮）占據上風」，也就是「屆時將充滿喧鬧和興奮的情緒」。

Taylor Swift's "Red" Among 2012's Best Sellers

泰勒絲的專輯《紅》名列 2012 最暢銷專輯

新聞原文　一知半解？跟著新聞原文，再聽一遍　🎧 *Track 084*

Taylor Swift is used to breaking sales records and she continues that trend with her new album *Red*. The album sold more than 1.2 million copies in its first week of release, which makes Taylor the only female artist in Sound Scan history to have two consecutive albums sell more than one million copies in an opening week.

Red leans more towards pop-rock than Swift's previous three albums. Most music critics agree that the 16 songs reflect a more mature and confident artist.

Swift explains why she titled the album *Red*. "I think red is a really daring adventurous color and I think it really kind of symbolizes what I wanted to do musically with this record which was make something new and bold and it's definitely that."

"We Are Never Ever Getting Back Together" was the first single from *Red*. Swift is known for writing songs that deal with her personal relationships. Although she never reveals her subject, many listeners believe that song is about Taylor's ex-boyfriend, actor Jake Gyllenhaal.

As confident as Taylor comes across in her songwriting and live shows, she admits she has many fears. During a question-and-answer session at a recent college performance in California, Taylor told the audience that one of her concerns is "people getting tired of me." For now, her millions of fans around the world remain loyal.

精準翻譯　句句到位，看你是否真的全數聽懂 🔊

　　對於泰勒絲來說，打破銷量紀錄已成家常便飯，而她的新專輯《紅》無疑延續了這一氣勢。該專輯發行首周銷量就超過了 120 萬張，泰勒絲也因此成為音樂排行榜歷史上唯一一位連續兩張專輯在發行首周內銷量過百萬的女歌手。

　　與她的前三張專輯相比，專輯《紅》當中的流行搖滾元素更多一些。大多數樂評人都認為其中的 16 首歌曲展示了一種更為成熟自信的音樂人風格。

　　對於她的專輯為什麼取名叫《紅》，泰勒絲解釋說：「我覺得紅色是一種勇敢大膽、充滿冒險精神的顏色，它能代表我在這張專輯中想要進行全新而大膽的音樂探索與嘗試，這張專輯正是這樣。」

　　《我們再也回不到過去》是這張專輯的第一主打單曲。泰勒絲擅長融合個人的情感經歷來創作歌曲。儘管她從未透露歌詞所指的對象，但是許多聽眾都認為這首歌是關於她的前男友，演員傑克‧葛倫霍。

　　儘管在歌曲創作和現場演出時，泰勒絲給人的感覺是自信十足，但她也承認自己有許多的擔憂。近期，在加利福尼亞一所大學獻唱時的問答環節中，泰勒絲告訴觀眾，她的憂慮之一便是「人們會對我感到厭倦」。不過，到目前為止，她在世界各地的數百萬歌迷都十分忠實於她。

關鍵解析　英文聽力重點看這邊就對了

❶ Taylor Swift is used to breaking sales records and she continues that trend with her new album *Red*.

　　本句中 be used to doing sth. 表示「習慣於做某事」，學習者要注意將它與另一個片語 used to do sth.（過去曾做某事）區分開來。break records 表示「打破紀錄」的意思。需要注意的是，英文中有些詞雖然動詞和名詞同形，但是發音卻有所不同。例如，record 作名詞時，意為「紀錄；記錄；唱片」，其重音在第一個音節 [ˈrekɔːd]；而 record 作動詞時，表示「記錄，錄製」的意思，其重音在第二個音節 [rlˈkɔːd]。

❷ As confident as Taylor Swift comes across in her songwriting and live shows, she admits she has many fears.

　　句首的 a...as 引導子句，表示「儘管」之意，comes across as 表示「看（或聽）上去是，給人的印象是，表現得……」，該從句的意思即「儘管泰勒在歌曲創作和現場演出時表現得很自信」。

China-Hollywood Connection Changes Movie Business

中國與好萊塢聯合，改變電影產業

新聞原文 一知半解？跟著新聞原文，再聽一遍 🎧 *Track 085*

The upcoming *Iron Man 3* was partly filmed in China, and its script was subject to scrutiny by Chinese officials. And Chinese sensibilities influence the disaster epic *2012*, says Stanley Rosen at the University of Southern California. He studies China's film industry.

"Even if you're not shooting in China, a film like *2012* will be very careful to include positive references to China. Negative references will simply kill the market."

Chinese audiences love big movies with special effects. Hollywood films account for half of the receipts from Chinese theaters.

China's expanding middle class has given a boost to the country's own film industry. Last year's comedy *Lost in Thailand* from director Xu Zheng was a huge box office success, coming in second in all-time Chinese film revenues, after Hollywood *Avatar*.

Hollywood studios are finding Chinese partners for co-productions, and Disney and DreamWorks Animation are investing in tourist attractions in Shanghai, says Stanley Rosen.

And China is coming to Hollywood. The Chinese company TCL has purchased the naming right to the historic Grauman's Chinese Theatre on Hollywood Boulevard. And the Chinese conglomerate Dalian Wanda Group has bought a major American theater chain, AMC. The ties between China and Hollywood are expected to grow in the future.

精準翻譯 句句到位，看你是否真的全數聽懂 🔊

即將上映的《鋼鐵人 3》的部分拍攝是在中國進行的，其劇本接受了中國官方的審查。南加州大學的斯坦利・羅森說，中國人的感受也影響到了災難大片《2012 世界末日》。

　　「即使不在中國拍攝，像《2012 世界末日》這樣的影片也需要特別謹慎，提到中國時應是正面積極的，負面的指涉直接會扼殺市場。」

　　中國觀眾愛看特效大片。好萊塢電影占到了中國電影票房收入的半數。

　　中國不斷壯大的中產階級有力地推動了國內電影業的發展。去年由徐崢執導的喜劇《人在囧途之泰囧》創下中國電影市場票房歷史第二高的成績，僅次於好萊塢大片《阿凡達》。

　　斯坦利‧羅森説，一些好萊塢電影公司正在尋找中國合夥人共同製作電影。迪士尼和夢工廠動畫公司也在上海投資建設旅遊景點。

　　同時，中國也正在進軍好萊塢。中國的 TCL 集團股份有限公司已購買了好萊塢大道上歷史悠久的格勞曼中國大劇院的更名權。而中國企業集團大連萬達也收購了美國的一家主要連鎖電影院 AMC。今後，中國和好萊塢的聯繫預計會更緊密。

關鍵解析　英文聽力重點看這邊就對了

❶ The upcoming *Iron Man 3* was partly filmed in China, and its script was subject to scrutiny by Chinese officials.

　　upcoming 意為「即將出現的」，這裡指「即將上映的」。be subject to scrutiny 表示「需要接受審查，須經審查」的意思。

❷ Last year's comedy *Lost in Thailand* from director Xu Zheng was a huge box office success, coming in second in all-time Chinese film revenues, after Hollywood *Avatar*.

　　come in second 表示「獲得第二名」的意思。後面的 after 表示「位列……之後」，也就是説《阿凡達》足「票房第一」。all-time 表示「創紀錄的，空前的」。句中提到的《泰囧》創造了中國電影市場票房歷史第二高的紀錄，僅次於《阿凡達》。

題目詳解篇

Unit 9 文化博覽

Christmas Celebrations Underway Around the World
世界各地歡慶聖誕節

新聞原文　一知半解？跟著新聞原文，再聽一遍　🎧 Track 086

It is an annual tradition in Thailand — elephants dressed as Santa Claus on parade, handing out toys to school children.

Halfway across the world in Mexico, Santa takes a human form, going for a swim with the fishes, delighting children at a zoo in Guadalajara.

In frozen Moscow it is cold…but not too cold for Grandfather Frost to make an appearance by bus and even call on a bit of holiday magic.

In Germany, families warm up before heading into the forest to cut down their own Christmas trees…and lug them back home.

Wherever you go there is plenty of shopping to do. These American shoppers are packing into stores hoping to find last-minute gifts and deals.

In Lagos, Nigeria, decorations are up…But many last-minute shoppers worry the celebrations will be dampened by frequent power outages.

There are also more traditional celebrations — like this one in Bethlehem, where bands play in Manger Square as crowds gather to celebrate Midnight Mass.

Even in war-ravaged Syria, there are signs of Christmas, though one Christian woman says this year the holiday is more about hope than joy.

The Syrian choir is finding reasons to sing as many in Syria and across the world pray for a safer and happier new year.

精準翻譯　句句到位，看你是否真的全數聽懂 🔊

這是泰國一年一度的傳統活動——大象裝扮成聖誕老人在街頭遊行，給學齡兒童們發放玩具。

而遠在地球的另一端，在墨西哥，聖誕老人化身人形，在瓜達拉哈拉的一座動物園裡，與魚群嬉戲，逗孩子們開心。

　　在冰天雪地的莫斯科，寒冷並沒有阻止冰雪爺爺在公車上現身並表演一段節日魔法。

　　在德國，許多家庭熱身後進入森林，砍倒聖誕樹並拖回家為節日做準備。

　　不管你到哪裡，總是有一大堆東西要買。這些美國購物者正擠進商店，希望買到在最後一刻大促銷的商品和禮物。

　　在奈及利亞的拉各斯市，聖誕裝飾隨處可見。但許多參加最後時刻搶購的人們擔心不時的停電可能會減弱人們的慶祝熱情。

　　還有很多傳統的慶典活動也在進行中。例如在伯利恆，幾個樂隊正在馬槽廣場上表演，越來越多的人聚攏過來參加子夜彌撒慶祝。

　　即使是在飽受戰爭蹂躪的敘利亞，也有些許的聖誕氣氛。只是一位女基督徒表示，今年的聖誕節，希望大過快樂。

　　與許多敘利亞人和世界其他地方的人們一樣，敘利亞的一個唱詩班正在用歌聲祈禱一個更安全、更快樂的新年。

關鍵解析 **英文聽力重點看這邊就對了**

❶ It is an annual tradition in Thailand — elephants dressed as Santa Claus on parade, handing out toys to school children.

　　本句中 annual 表示「一年一度」的意思；dress as 表示「裝扮成，打扮成」的意思。句中 handing out 是現在分詞做修飾，因為與其邏輯主語 elephants 是主動關係，因此用現在分詞形式。

❷ There are also more traditional celebrations — like this one in Bethlehem, where bands play in Manger Square as crowds gather to celebrate Midnight Mass.

　　本句中 one 代指 traditional celebration。聽錄音過程中碰到人名、地名時，學習者需要學會容忍和適應一定程度的語意模糊。比如本句中的地名 Bethlehem（伯利恆）和廣場名 Manger square（馬槽廣場）。熟悉聖經文化的學習者可能會了解，在《聖經》中記載了耶穌基督降生於伯利恆的一個馬槽。不過，即使不知道地名的翻譯，不了解這一背景也沒太大關係。Midnight Mass 指的是「子夜彌撒」。

NEWS 02 Despite Paralysis, Hawking's Mind Soars
癱瘓的身體，活躍的大腦——霍金

新聞原文 一知半解？跟著新聞原文，再聽一遍 Track 087

Universe equation

Hawking, born in Oxford, England in 1942, studied at both Oxford and Cambridge Universities. He became a math professor at Cambridge and held that post for more than 30 years. In 2009, he left to head the Cambridge University Center for Theoretical Physics.

The big push at Cambridge is to reduce the universe to one equation that encompasses everything.

Bridging the gap

Hawking's work has focused on bridging the gap between Albert Einstein's theory of relativity — which explains how the pull of gravity controls the motion of large objects like planets — and the theory of quantum physics, which deals with the behavior of particles on the subatomic scale.

Overcoming the odds

Since 1970, Hawking has been almost completely paralyzed by ALS, an incurable, degenerative condition. He has been confined to a wheelchair, and uses an advanced computer synthesizer to speak.

Despite his disabilities, he continues to work, write and travel.

New era

Speaking at a 2008 ceremony marking the 50th anniversary of the U.S. space agency, NASA, Hawking called for a new era in human space exploration, comparable, he said, to the European voyages to the New World more than 500 years ago.

精準翻譯 句句到位，看你是否真的全數聽懂

宇宙方程式

霍金 1942 年生於英格蘭的牛津郡，曾就讀於牛津和劍橋大學。畢業後的 30 多年裡，霍金一直在劍橋大學擔任數學教授。2009 年，他被調到了劍橋大學理論物理研究中心當主任。

他在劍橋最大的成就是提出宇宙方程式，將宇宙濃縮為一個包含萬物的方程式。

彌合鴻溝

霍金的研究旨在彌合愛因斯坦的相對論和量子物理理論之間的鴻溝。愛因斯坦的相對論解釋了重力如何控制像行星這樣的大型物體的運動。而量子物理研究的是次原子級別的微粒的運動。

與病魔抗爭

由於患有肌萎縮側索硬化症（ALS）這種無法治癒的神經系統退行性疾病，1970 年之後，霍金幾乎全身癱瘓。他被長期禁錮在輪椅上，只能借助一種先進的電腦合成器來說話。

儘管身體癱瘓，霍金仍然堅持工作、堅持寫作並外出講學。

新紀元

在 2008 年美國航空航天局成立 50 周年的一個紀念會上，霍金呼籲人類的太空探索應該邁入一個新紀元，新的探索將可以和 500 多年前歐洲人發現新大陸相媲美。

關鍵解析 **英文聽力重點看這邊就對了**

❶ The big push at Cambridge is to reduce the universe to one equation that encompasses everything.

本句中 push 用作名詞，可以引申為「推動，努力」的意思，在此可以理解為「貢獻，成就」。reduce...to 表示「把……歸納（或濃縮）為」。

❷ Hawking's work has focused on bridging the gap between Albert Einstein's theory of relativity — which explains how the pull of gravity controls the motion of large objects like planets — and the theory of quantum physics, which deals with the behavior of particles on the subatomic scale.

focus on 表示「專注於，集中於（某事）」。而 bridge the gap between...and...，表示「縮短……的差距」，「彌合……之間的鴻溝」的意思。theory of relativity 指「相對論」，theory of quantum physics 指「量子物理理論」。兩個理論後面各有一個關係子句分別對理論作了簡單的解釋。

Interfaith Worshipers Celebrate Sea, Surf
不同宗教信仰者共同表達對大海和沖浪的熱愛

新聞原文　一知半解？跟著新聞原文，再聽一遍　🎧 **Track 088**

Each morning at Huntington Beach, which calls itself Surf City, the surfers are out early to catch the waves.

It is a passion and a lifestyle, says a veteran surfer, who invented a modified surfboard called the boogie board.

Surfers say their goal is to catch a wave and ride it. Once a year, an interfaith service called the "Blessing of the Waves" draws surfers and others to talk about their love of the ocean.

A Muslim leads an Islamic prayer. A synagogue member blows the Jewish ram's horn called the shofar.

A choir of immigrants from the island nation of Tonga provides music.

Two Roman Catholic priests also preside over the service. Both are avid surfers who are at home on this beachfront. After the service, both went in for a swim.

There is much to be thankful for, says Dean Torrence, who was half of the 1960s pop duo Jan and Dean. They helped to popularize surf music with songs like "Surf City."

"The sand, the ocean, the blue sky, the weather. I mean, what could be better? I am very, very, very blessed to be here in a place that we call Surf City."

Those who gathered here say for those of any faith, this beachfront setting is inspirational.

精準翻譯　句句到位，看你是否真的全數聽懂 🔊

每天早晨，在被稱為「沖浪之都」的杭亭頓海灘，衝浪者們早起迎接海浪。

一位衝浪高手說，衝浪是一種激情，是一種生活方式。他甚至還發明了一種叫做「布吉」的改良型衝浪板。

　　衝浪者們說他們的目標就是衝上一個浪頭然後隨浪騰躍。一年一度的跨宗教衝浪盛會名曰「海浪的祝福」，吸引了大批衝浪愛好者和其他遊客來此慶祝，表達他們對海洋的熱愛。

　　一位穆斯林在領誦伊斯蘭教祈禱辭，而一位猶太教教徒在吹他們的羊角號。

　　來自島國東加的一個移民唱詩班在提供音樂。

　　兩位天主教牧師也主持了他們的宗教儀式，兩人都是狂熱的衝浪愛好者，對這片海灘非常熟悉。儀式結束後，他們都下海去遊泳了。

　　迪恩‧托倫斯說，有很多值得感激的事。他是 1960 年代流行二人組合 Jan & Dean 的成員之一。這個樂隊曾以《衝浪之都》等歌曲幫助大力推廣衝浪音樂。

　　托倫斯說：「沙灘、大海、藍天、晴空。你說，還有比這更美好的嗎？能來這個我們稱作『衝浪之都』的地方，我感到非常、非常幸福。」

　　來這裡的人說，不論你信仰什麼宗教，這片海灘都能給予你靈感和啟發。

關鍵解析　**英文聽力重點看這邊就對了**

❶ It is a passion and a lifestyle, says a veteran surfer, who invented a modified surfboard called the boogie board.

　　本句中 it 指上文提到的 surfing（衝浪）。veteran 相當於 experienced，意為「經驗豐富的」。who 引導的是一個非限定關係子句，進一步補充說明這位衝浪者的訊息。

❷ There is much to be thankful for, says Dean Torrence, who was half of the 1960s pop duo Jan and Dean.

　　本句中 be thankful for 表示「對……表示感激」的意思。1960s pop duo Jan and Dean 意為「1960 年代流行二人組合 Jan & Dean」，此樂隊是用兩名成員的名字來命名的。其中 duo 在這裡表示「二人組合」。

NEWS **04**

Seattle, 'City of Clocks' Keeps on Ticking
西雅圖——鐘錶之城

新聞原文　一知半解？跟著新聞原文，再聽一遍　🎧 *Track 089*

If you've been to Seattle, Washington — or even just heard about it — you'd probably guess that its nickname is something like "The Space Needle City."

That 184-meter-high tower, with an observation deck and restaurant, was built for the 1962 world's fair there, and has become the city's most famous landmark.

Or maybe Seattle is "The City Where It's Always Raining."

Seattle gets long, drizzly showers off the Pacific Ocean, sometimes with days of cloudy skies before and afterward.

But the city's nickname comes from none of these sources, and when you hear it, you'll want an explanation.

Seattle is the "City of Clocks."

Not alarm clocks or huge clock towers but street clocks. "Post clocks," they're sometimes called.

Most of these clocks served as ticking advertising testimonials for the jewelry shops that maintained them.

So many were dark green that there's even a color called "street clock green." Others were red, in the faint hope that truckers would see and avoid them.

Whenever there's a story about the old post clocks, Seattle's newspapers just can't seem to resist a play on words.

"Time Will Tell," a headline will read.

Or, when one gets restored, "It's About Time."

One Seattle historian mused that the old public timepieces had wonderful stories to tell, "if only they could tock."

As in … tick … tock.

精準翻譯　句句到位，看你是否真的全數聽懂

　　如果你曾到過華盛頓州的西雅圖，或只聽聞過這座城市，那麼你可能會猜測它的暱稱是「太空針塔之城」之類的。

　　那座 184 公尺高的塔形建築，上有觀景臺和豪華餐廳，是為 1962 年在此舉辦的世界博覽會而建，現在已成為西雅圖最著名的地標性建築。

　　或者你可能會猜西雅圖是「雨城」。來自太平洋的水氣使得西雅圖常常連續多日細雨濛濛，陰雲蔽日。

　　但這個城市的暱稱跟上面提到的這些都沒關係，你聽到之後肯定想要個解釋。

　　西雅圖其實是「鐘錶之城」。

　　不是鬧鐘，也不是大塔鐘，而是街鐘，有時也被稱作「郵鐘」。

　　這些鐘大多都被用作珠寶店的廣告招牌，並由這些珠寶店負責維護。

　　因為很多鐘都是深綠色的，以至於有一種顏色就被叫做「街鐘綠」。其他鐘則是紅色的，暗暗希望卡車司機能看見並避免撞到它們。

　　每次報導這些老鐘時，西雅圖的報紙總會禁不住玩一下文字遊戲。

　　比如某個標題會寫：「時間會證明一切。」

　　或者，當一個街鐘被修好後，報紙會寫「這次事關時間／是時候了」。

　　西雅圖一位歷史學家若有所思地說道，這些古老的鐘錶有許多有趣的故事要訴說，「要是它們能滴答說話就好了」。

　　就像這滴……答……聲。

關鍵解析　英文聽力重點看這邊就對了

❶ Most of these clocks served as ticking advertising testimonials for the jewelry shops that maintained them.

　　本句中 serve as 表示「充當……用」。testimonial 表示「證明」的意思，ticking advertising testimonials 在這裡可以理解為表示一種「滴答走著的廣告招牌」。

❷ One Seattle historian mused that the old public timepieces had wonderful stories to tell, "if only they could tock." As in... tick... tock.

　　本句中 muse 表示「沈思，若有所思」的意思。「if only they could tock」中 tock 表示「鐘錶走動」，就如 tick-tock 表示「鐘錶走動的滴答聲」。另外，因為本句前面提到「講述有趣的故事」，這裡的 tock 可以視為 talk 的諧音，這句話可以理解為「要是它們能滴答說話就好了」。

Afghan Youth Orchestra Prepares to Play US Venues
阿富汗青年管弦樂團赴美演出

新聞原文　一知半解？跟著新聞原文，再聽一遍　🎧 *Track 090*

The Afghanistan Youth Orchestra performed for the Afghan community in Alexandria, Virginia. The venue was intimate, the audience small.

But within days, these Afghan musicians will play in two of the famous concert halls in the world: the Kennedy Center in Washington and Carnegie Hall in New York.

Ahmad Sarmast, who founded the orchestra, says his group is ready to play on the world's biggest stages.

The group traveled from Afghanistan to the United States on a tour funded largely by the U.S. embassy in Kabul.

When the Taliban took power in 1996, it banned music entirely.

But since 2010, Sarmast has kept the small National Institute of Music in Kabul running. The orchestra grew out of that school.

The musicians are between the ages of 10 and 22. Most are orphans or street children. The ensemble includes girls, who under the Taliban were not allowed to be educated after the age of eight.

Now, the musicians are rehearsing for their big debut at the Kennedy Center. Then it's on to New York and Carnegie Hall, before returning to Kabul and a life full of music.

精準翻譯　句句到位，看你是否真的全數聽懂 🔊

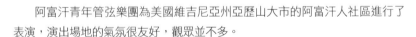

　　阿富汗青年管弦樂團為美國維吉尼亞州亞歷山大市的阿富汗人社區進行了表演，演出場地的氣氛很友好，觀眾並不多。

　　但是，幾天後，這些阿富汗音樂家們將在華盛頓特區的甘迺迪藝術中心和紐約的卡內基音樂廳這兩座世界著名的音樂廳內進行演奏。

　　樂團的創立者艾哈默德‧薩爾馬斯特表示，他的樂團已準備好在世界最大的舞臺上演奏。

　　他們此次從阿富汗前往美國的表演之行，基本上是由美國駐喀布爾大使館資助的。

　　塔利班 1996 年掌權之後，音樂活動就被完全禁止了。

　　但自 2010 年以來，薩爾馬斯特一直在努力維持著小小的國家音樂學院在喀布爾的運行。這個樂團的成員都是由這所學校培養的。

　　這些音樂家們的年齡在 10 至 22 歲之間，其中大多數為孤兒和流浪兒。樂團中還有一些女孩子，之前在塔利班的統治下，女孩在 8 歲後就不允許再接受教育了。

　　現在，這些音樂家們正在為他們在甘迺迪藝術中心的首場演奏加緊排練。隨後，他們會前往紐約卡內基音樂廳進行表演。之後，他們將返回喀布爾，繼續他們有音樂相伴的人生。

- -

關鍵解析　**英文聽力重點看這邊就對了**

❶ Afghan Youth Orchestra Prepares to Play US Venues

　　這是本篇新聞的標題。其中，play US venues 不是很好理解，而它對於理解本篇新聞的內容卻很關鍵。在這裡，play 相當於 perform at，venue 表示「演出場地，演出地點」，綜合起來就是「在美國的演出場館表演」的意思。再舉一例：The group planned to record an EP as well as play local venues in the future.（樂隊未來計劃錄制一張單曲並在當地進行演出。）

❷ The ensemble includes girls, who under the Taliban were not allowed to be educated after the age of eight.

　　學習者如果不熟悉 the ensemble 的意思，可以根據上下文推測出它指的是前面提到的「樂團」。它與 orchestra，group 同義，是為了避免重複而使用的同義詞。在聽錄音過程中結合文意來推測詞義是一項重要的聽力技能，學習者要有意識地進行訓練。

❸ Then it's on to New York and Carnegie Hall, before returning to Kabul and a life full of music.

　　句中的 it 指的是 the orchestra 或 the ensemble（樂團）。returning to Kabul and a life full of music 中 return to 後面跟了一實一虛兩個受詞，一個是地點 Kabul，一個是 a life full of music，可分別理解為「返回喀布爾」和「回到充滿音樂的生活中去」。

Chinese Pursue Volunteer Opportunities in Africa
中國人爭取擔任援非志工

新聞原文　一知半解？跟著新聞原文，再聽一遍　🎧 Track 091

At a recent training session in Beijing, doctors, information technology specialists, business professionals and others prepare for a one-to-two-year stint in Africa with international development charity VSO, Voluntary Services Overseas.

When professionals in China volunteer, many do not know if they will get their old jobs back when they return.

But they say the opportunities abroad make it worth the risk.

China has been sending medical volunteers to Africa for decades. They are now in 45 countries on the continent. China's youth volunteer corps, an effort similar to the United States' Peace Corps, is a path that some choose.

But Liu Haifang, deputy director of Peking University's Africa Research Center, says students are increasingly turning to other organizations for overseas volunteer work.

"My impression is that young volunteers are finding their own ways to go abroad. They are not inclined to say that they represent China. They are not interested in saying who they represent. They represent themselves. They have ambitions and dreams that they want to realize."

Liu says the trend highlights the changes in how China and its citizens are reaching out to the rest of the world.

精準翻譯　句句到位，看你是否真的全數聽懂 🔊

最近在北京舉辦的一期培訓課上，一些醫生、資訊技術專家、商務人士等正在為去非洲做一至兩年的志工服務進行準備，這次活動是由國際發展慈善組織海外志工服務社組織的。

這些中國的專業人士參加這次志工活動時，許多人都不知道當他們結束志

工活動回國後還能否重新回到原來的工作崗位上。

但是他們覺得能有這次海外服務的機會，即使冒險也值得。

中國向非洲派遣醫療志工已持續幾十年了。他們的足跡遍布非洲大陸的 45 個國家。中國的青年志工服務隊是一個與美國的和平工作團相類似的志工組織，許多人選擇參與其中。

不過，北京大學非洲研究中心劉海方副主任表示，越來越多的學生也在透過其他組織尋求海外志工服務工作。

「年輕人開始以他們個人的方式去追求走向外界，他們不再有意地説我們其實是代表中國，他們不是有意地去説我們代表誰，我們其實就是我們自己……我們有自己的夢想，我們要去追逐，要去實現。」

劉海方説，這個趨勢突出反映了中國和中國人民與外界接觸方式上的變化。

關鍵解析 英文聽力重點看這邊就對了

❶ When professionals in China volunteer, many do not know if they will get their old jobs back when they return.

本句中 many 作代詞，相當於 many of the professionals。後面的 if 不是「如果，假設」的意思，而是「是否」的意思，相當於 whether。

❷ But Liu Haifang, deputy director of Peking University's Africa Research Center, says students are increasingly turning to other organizations for overseas volunteer work.

本句中 deputy director 是 Liu Haifang 的同位語，對其作進一步的介紹説明。deputy director 指的是「副主任」，而副校長常用 vice-chancellor, vice-president，學習者平時要多留意不同頭銜、職位的表達方式。Peking University 指「北京大學」。

❸ Liu says the trend highlights the changes in how China and its citizens are reaching out to the rest of the world.

本句中 the trend 指的是「越來越多學生透過其他組織尋求海外志工工作」。學習者在聽的過程中要注意上下文的銜接，在上下文的文意中理解句意。highlight 表示「強調，突出」的意思。reach out to 在句中表示「接觸，聯繫」之意，該片語另外還有「向……伸出援助之手」的意思。

First Lady's New Hairstyle Creates Buzz
就職典禮上，第一夫人的新髮型引起轟動

新聞原文　一知半解？跟著新聞原文，再聽一遍　Track 092

　　When President Barack Obama took the official oath of office Sunday, the gray in his hair was noticeable. But it was First Lady, Michelle Obama's hair creating all the buzz — with her new haircut featuring "bangs."

　　People magazine described it as "a youthful new hairstyle: a straight, shoulder-skimming cut with bangs." And the prestigious *Wall Street Journal* called it "a bold move at a high profile time."

　　It's likely no accident of timing. Stylist Lauren Rothman says Michelle Obama used her style-sense to make a statement with her dress from four years ago.

　　And right from the start, it seemed Mr. Obama enjoyed having the first lady steal some of the spotlight.

　　For Sunday's ceremony, Michelle Obama also drew notice for her royal blue dress and cardigan by American designer Reed Krakoff.

　　"They want to be wearing an outfit that says that, that says, 'We're proud to be here and thank you for re-electing us.'" (said Rothman.)

　　But even the president knows, it all comes back to the hair.

　　"I love Michelle Obama. And to address the most significant event of this weekend, I love her bangs."

精準翻譯　句句到位，看你是否真的全數聽懂

　　周日，當歐巴馬總統正式宣誓就職時，他髮絲中的白髮引人注目。然而，真正引起轟動的卻是第一夫人蜜雪兒·歐巴馬的頭髮——她的齊瀏海新髮型。

　　《人物》雜誌評價稱，「齊肩直髮加上齊瀏海：這是一個年輕而有活力的新髮型。」《華爾街日報》則稱新髮型是「在這令人矚目時刻的一個大膽舉動」。

　　這絕不是偶然為之。設計師勞倫‧羅斯曼說，四年前，蜜雪兒‧歐巴馬就以她獨特的衣著品味來表達自己的個性和態度。

　　而從一開始，歐巴馬總統似乎也樂意看第一夫人搶走他的一些風頭。

　　周日的典禮上，蜜雪兒‧歐巴馬身穿海軍藍禮服和開襟毛衫，這套由美國設計師里德‧克拉科夫設計的禮服同樣引起了人們的關注。

　　（羅斯曼說：）「他們希望所穿的服裝能表達他們內心的感受：能夠站在這裡，我們感到很自豪，感謝你們再次選擇了我們。」

　　但是，即便是總統也知道，一切最終還是要回到頭髮上：

　　「我愛蜜雪兒，而說到這個周末最重要的事件，我愛她的瀏海。」

- -

關鍵解析　英文聽力重點看這邊就對了

❶ When President Barack Obama took the official oath of office Sunday, the gray in his hair was noticeable. But it was First Lady, Michelle Obama's hair creating all the buzz — with her new haircut featuring "bangs."

　　開頭第一句話中 take the official oath of office 表示「正式宣誓就職」。office 在這裡表示「職位」的意思，比如片語 come into office 意為「就職，走馬上任」。這裡涉及美國的一個文化常識，即美國總統在正式就職時，需要舉起右手，左手按在《聖經》上進行宣誓。第二句話中談到了美國第一夫人的頭髮。聽到表示轉折的連接詞 but 後，學習者可以預測，相對於前面所講的，之後所要表達的意思才是重點。create all the buzz 表示「引起轟動」。feature 在此用作動詞，表示「以……為特色」的意思。

❷ And the prestigious *Wall Street Journal* called it "a bold move at a high profile time."

　　the Wall Street Journal 是美國的《華爾街日報》。美國的主流報紙期刊還有 the New York Times（《紐約時報》），Time（《時代》周刊）等。句中的 it 指的是美國第一夫人的新潮髮型。move 在新聞英語中作名詞時，多指「某一舉動，行動」。high profile 意為「引人注目的，高調的」意思。

NEWS 08 German Theater Company Helps Minorities Tell Their Stories

德國劇院幫助弱勢族群講述自己的故事

新聞原文　一知半解？跟著新聞原文，再聽一遍 🎧 *Track 093*

It's not every day that you see Turkish-German school kids filming in the German parliament. These kids are interviewing the head of Germany's Roma community as part of a new program at a theater company in Berlin called Ballhaus Naunynstrasse.

The program pairs youths with mentors who work in TV and film. The end product is an hour-long film discussing what it feels like to be a minority in Germany.

The Ballhaus' previous films have made headlines nationwide. The last film dealt with racism and hate crimes against black people, Turks and others in German cities.

The program's aim is to introduce young minorities to the arts, says program director Veronika Gerhard.

The latest film project is about what it means to be black in Germany.

The young people are being led by Michael Goetting, a journalist and by filmmaker Janine Jembere.

Jembere says she wants to help young people have a voice in the debate about the lack of diversity in public life.

The film will be screened at the theater on April 15, and hopefully serve as a bridge between Germans of all backgrounds.

精準翻譯　句句到位，看你是否真的全數聽懂 🔊

不是每天你都可以看到土耳其裔德國學生在德國國會大廈進行拍攝。這些學生正在採訪德國的羅姆人社區的首領，它是柏林的巴爾豪斯·瑙寧施特拉塞劇院籌劃的一個新項目的一部分。

該項目給學生們分配了導師，他們都是電視或電影工作者。最終的成品是

一部長達一小時的電影，講述在德國身為弱勢族群的人們是何感受。

該劇院此前的一些影片也曾上過全國新聞的頭條。其上一部電影關注的是針對德國城市中的黑人、土耳其人及其他有色人種的種族歧視和仇恨犯罪。

該項目的導演薇羅妮卡‧格哈德說，這個電影項目旨在引導弱勢族群的年輕人走近藝術。

最近的一個電影項目探討的是：在德國，身為黑人意味著什麼。

這些年輕人在記者邁克爾‧格廷和電影製作人雅尼娜‧金貝雷的帶領下進行拍攝。

金貝雷說，她想幫助年輕人在關於公共生活的多樣性缺失之辯中發出自己的聲音。

所拍攝的影片將在 4 月 15 日上映，希望它能為不同背景的德國人之間加深了解並架起一座橋梁。

- -

關鍵解析　英文聽力重點看這邊就對了

❶ These kids are interviewing the head of Germany's Roma community as part of a new program at a theater company in Berlin called Ballhaus Naunynstrasse.

本句句型結構並不十分複雜，但是在聽力理解過程中遇到這麼長的句子，尤其是還包含一些陌生的組織、機構名稱時，理解其意往往會比較困難。學習者需要把握句子的主幹，即 These kids are interviewing the head...。初聽到 Roma community 時，學習者可能並不理解其確切所指，但結合後面所聽到的，可以猜測出它是一個弱勢族群社區，具體來說就是「羅姆人社區」。Rom 指「羅姆人」，有時也稱為「吉普賽人」。Roma 是 Rom 的複數形式。劇院的名稱比較複雜，聽者即使記不住它的準確發音也不要緊，它並不影響我們對整句話意思的理解。

❷ The program pairs youths with mentors who work in TV and film.

本句中 pair 用作動詞，表示「將……配對」的意思，在聽力訓練過程中，學習者要根據具體文意來判斷詞的用法，弄清其到底是作名詞還是作動詞。

UN Spearheads Drive to Protect Journalists After Deadly 2012

致命 2012 年過後：聯合國帶頭展開記者保護行動

新聞原文 一知半解？跟著新聞原文，再聽一遍 🎧 *Track 094*

When shells fall on the Syrian city of Homs in February 2012, a building used by foreign media takes a direct hit — killing renowned *Sunday Times* correspondent Marie Colvin, along with French journalist Remi Ochlik. Their colleague *Sunday Times's* photographer Paul Conroy is injured.

The incident was among the most high profile of 2012. But there were many more fatal attacks on members of the news media.

Exact figures vary, but the United Nations says more than 100 journalists were killed while doing their jobs in 2012, many of them victims of targeted attacks. Late last year at a conference in Vienna, the UN launched what it calls its Action Plan on the Safety of Journalists and Combating Impunity.

At an October symposium at the BBC College of Journalism, members of the world's media gathered to discuss attacks on journalists.

Nearly 20 Somali journalists were killed in 2012 alone. Pakistani media are also under threat for their coverage of schoolgirl activist Malala Yousafzai — now discharged from a British hospital after being shot in the head by the Taliban.

American freelance reporter James Foley has not been seen since he was kidnapped by unidentified gunmen in November. It is another reminder of the dangers of the job — dangers that appear to be getting worse.

精準翻譯 句句到位，看你是否真的全數聽懂 🔊

2012 年 2 月，炮彈從敘利亞城市霍姆斯空中落下，直接擊中了一座外國媒體所在的建築，《星期日泰晤士報》著名記者瑪麗·科爾文以及法國記者雷米·奧克里克不幸遇難。他們的同事、《星期日泰晤士報》攝影師保羅·康羅伊也身受重傷。

這次暴力事件是 2012 年所有事件中最引人關注的一起。但是針對媒體從業人士還有很多更嚴重的致命襲擊。

雖然目前具體的數字各方說法不一，但是據聯合國統計，2012 年共有 100 多名記者在工作中遇難。很多人是因為他們的報導而遭到了專門的攻擊。

去年年底，在維也納召開的一次會議上，聯合國發起了一場保護新聞記者在戰爭中不受傷害的安全行動計劃。

10 月份，英國廣播公司新聞學院召開了一個研討會，全世界的媒體代表齊聚一堂來探討針對記者發動的襲擊。

僅 2012 年一年，就有近 20 名索馬利亞記者遇難。巴基斯坦的媒體也因為報導馬拉拉的故事受到威脅。這名積極爭取權利的女學生曾被塔利班武裝射中頭部而受傷，現在已從英國一家醫院出院。

美國自由職業記者詹姆斯‧福利自 11 月份在敘利亞被不明身份的武裝人員綁架後就一直未再露面。這起事件再次提醒人們記者這個職業所面臨的危險，而且危險似乎在不斷加劇。

- -

關鍵解析 英文聽力重點看這邊就對了

❶ The incident was among the most high profile of 2012.

incident 表示「嚴重事件，暴力事件」之意，這裡指的是上文提到的「兩名記者遇難事件」。the most high profile 意為「最引人注目的事件」。

❷ Exact figures vary, but the United Nations says more than 100 journalists were killed while doing their jobs in 2012.

本句中 figures 表示「數字，數據」。英文中表示數據的詞彙還有 statistics, data 等。句中 doing their jobs 這一動作的邏輯主語是 100 journalists，用現在分詞形式表示狀態，意思是「在工作時，在新聞報導過程中」。

❸ American freelance reporter James Foley has not been seen since he was kidnapped by unidentified gunmen in November.

子句為 since 引導的時間副詞子句時，主句一般用完成時態。unidentified 是過去分詞作形容詞，修飾 gunmen，指「不明身份的武裝人員」。

10 Protesters Block Dismantling Part of Berlin Wall
拆毀柏林圍牆遺跡引發抗議

新聞原文 一知半解？跟著新聞原文，再聽一遍 🎧 **Track 095**

The Berlin Wall was once of the starkest reminders of the Cold War. It was put up by communist East Germany in 1961, to stop its citizens from fleeing to West Berlin. But today, the wall that once snaked around the whole German capital is almost entirely gone.

Except for here at the East Side Gallery. Today, the one-mile-long stretch of the wall contains murals by artists from around the world.

But on Friday, construction workers began removing a 22-meter chunk of the wall, the first step in a project that aims to build a luxury apartment tower on the site.

And that caused a stir — 200 people turned out to protest, and three were arrested.

The mayor of Berlin declined to comment for this story. But Volker Thoms, a spokesman for the builder, Living Bauhaus, told VOA that his company intends to reconstruct the pieces of the wall elsewhere on its property. Thoms also noted something that even local papers and some Berliners have pointed out — that this valuable land had been sitting disused for years.

The protesters vow to continue their fight next week in court. But whether they'll be ultimately successful in protecting and keep intact a piece of Cold War history remains to be seen.

精準翻譯 句句到位，看你是否真的全數聽懂 🔊

　　柏林圍牆曾是冷戰最明顯的標誌物，最能勾起人們關於冷戰的回憶。1961年，當時的東德為阻止民眾流往西柏林而建起了這堵牆。但是如今，柏林圍牆所剩無幾，已不再有蜿蜒穿越整個德國首都的那種氣勢了。

留下來的其中就有「東邊畫廊」。如今，這段一英里長的柏林圍牆上有來自世界各國的藝術家們所畫的壁畫。

但是在周五，建築工人開始拆除一段 22 公尺長的柏林牆牆體，這裡要建一座豪華公寓，拆牆是第一步。

這一動作引起了不小的騷動——200 人走上街頭抗議遊行，有 3 人被捕。

柏林市長拒絕對此作出評論。不過，負責該項目的建築商家居包豪斯的一位發言人福爾克爾・湯姆斯告訴美國之音記者説，他們公司計劃在別處重建這部分柏林圍牆遺跡。另外，他還談到了當地報紙和一些柏林人都已指出的一個問題，那就是，這塊寶地已經閒置多年了。

抗議者發誓要在法庭上繼續他們的抗議，但他們最終能否成功保存下這件冷戰歷史紀念物，我們將拭目以待。

- -

關鍵解析　英文聽力重點看這邊就對了

❶ But today, the wall that once snaked around the whole German capital is almost entirely gone.

　　本句中 that 引導的關係子句修飾 the wall。關係子句中的 snake 作為動詞，學習者根據它作名詞的意思，可以推斷出其動詞表示像蛇一樣的動作，即「蜿蜒穿越」的意思。最後的形容詞 gone 表示「消失的，不再存在的」。

❷ But on Friday, construction workers began removing a 22-meter chunk of the wall, the first step in a project that aims to build a luxury apartment tower on the site.

　　這個句子比較長，學習者要注意理清句子結構。本句的主句是 workers began removing...，而 the first step 指的就是 removing a 22-meter chunk of the wall（拆除一段 22 公尺長的柏林牆），這是該建築項目進行的第一步。aim to do sth. 表示「旨在做某事」的意思。

❸ Thoms also noted something that even local papers and some Berliners have pointed out — that this valuable land had been sitting disused for years.

　　這句話關鍵要注意破折號後面 that 子句的理解，實際上它是一個受詞補語，是動詞 note 的受詞，説明談到的具體內容，即 He also noted that this valuable land had been sitting disused for years.

英語學習 *012*

新聞英語聽力完整攻略
聽《美國之音》新聞英語，提升英聽真實力！

從 VOA 美國之音訓練聽力，掌握最即時、最真實的新聞英語

作　　　者	楊熹允
顧　　　問	曾文旭
社　　　長	王毓芳
編輯統籌	耿文國、黃璽宇
主　　　編	吳靜宜、姜怡安
美術編輯	王桂芳、張嘉容
執行主編	李念茨
封面設計	阿作
法律顧問	北辰著作權事務所　蕭雄淋律師、幸秋妙律師

初　　　版	2020 年 03 月
出　　　版	捷徑文化出版事業有限公司——資料夾文化出版
電　　　話	（02）2752-5618
傳　　　真	（02）2752-5619
地　　　址	106 台北市大安區忠孝東路四段 250 號 11 樓 -1

定　　　價	新台幣 350 元／港幣 117 元
產品內容	1 書＋ MP3

總 經 銷	知遠文化事業有限公司
地　　　址	222 新北市深坑區北深路 3 段 155 巷 25 號 5 樓
電　　　話	（02）2664-8800
傳　　　真	（02）2664-8801

港澳地區總經銷	和平圖書有限公司
地　　　址	香港柴灣嘉業街 12 號百樂門大廈 17 樓
電　　　話	（852）2804-6687
傳　　　真	（852）2804-6409

本書部分圖片由 Shutterstock 提供

捷徑 Book站

本書如有缺頁、破損或倒裝，
請寄回捷徑文化出版社更換。
106 台北市大安區忠孝東路四段 250 號 11 樓之 1
編輯部收

【版權所有　翻印必究】

國家圖書館出版品預行編目資料

新聞英語聽力完整攻略：聽《美國之音》新聞英語，提升英聽真實力！／楊熹允 著．
-- 初版 .-- 臺北市：資料夾文化，2020.03
　　面；　公分（英語學習：012）
ISBN 978-986-5507-13-8 (平裝)

1. 英語　2. 讀本

805.18　　　　　　　　　　108022196